Lady Robyn

R. GARCIA Y ROBERTSON

A TOM DOHERTY ASSOCIATES BOOK
NEW YORK

LADY ROBYN

Copyright © 2003 by R. Garcia y Robertson

This book is printed on acid-free paper.

A Forge Book
Published by Tom Doherty Associates, LLC
175 Fifth Avenue
New York, NY 10010

www.tor.com

Forge® is a registered trademark of Tom Doherty Associates, LLC.

Library of Congress Cataloging-in-Publication Data

Garcia y Robertson, Rodrigo, 1949–
    Lady Robyn / R. Garcia y Robertson.—1st ed.
       p. cm.
    "A Forge book"—T.p. verso.
    ISBN 0-312-86995-9
    1. Great Britain—History—Wars of the Roses, 1455–1485—Fiction. 2. Americans—England—Fiction. 3. Time travel—Fiction. I. Title.

PS3557.A71125 L33 2003
813'.54—dc21

                                                        2002032527

First Edition: February 2003

Printed in the United States of America

0 9 8 7 6 5 4 3 2 1

Withdrawn

Lady Robyn

For Darci and Matt

PART 1

High Summer

Now is the winter of our discontent
Made glorious summer by this sun of York.
—Shakespeare, *Richard III*

1

⊸⊸⊸ Tournament Day ⊸⊸⊸

Saturday, 26 July 1460, Saint Anne's Day, Baynards Castle, London

Morning, just before prime. Up and dressed ahead of the dawn, I hear cock crows from the city. Way too nervous to sleep. Tournament today in the Smithfield mud, the Middle Ages at its messiest. Collin will ride, maybe Edward. Scary when you think about, so I try not to. I must be the only woman in medieval England who craves a mocha in the morning. Happily, I still have some instant . . .

*R*obyn *stopped typing* into her journal, tearing open a foil packet lifted from a restaurant table on her last day in twenty-first-century London. Pouring dark crystals into a china cup, she added boiling water from a kettle, enjoying the warm feel of hand-beaten silver on a cold July morning, making modern magic on her medieval oak table. Coffee aroma filled the chill air of her tower bedroom, covering over the dank musty morning-in-a-castle smell while her toes dug for warmth in a carpet that came by caravan over the Roof of the World. This stormy summer of 1460 was the coldest and rainiest the locals could remember—as they said in Southwark, "Wetter than a bathhouse wedding."

When witchcraft first brought her to medieval England—much against her will—Robyn would wake up wondering where she was, thinking she was back in modern Britain. Maybe some weird part of Wales. Or at home in California, waking in a strange bed after a wild Hollywood party. (Where am I? And whose bed am I in?) By now she was no longer shocked to awake in 1460—half a millennium before her birth—but having her own bedroom was a pleasant novelty. Most medievals slept two or more to a bed. But not Lady Robyn Stafford of Holy Wood, the barefoot contessa from Roundup, Montana—she wiggled her toes in triumph.

Lady Robyn had a room of her own, with a wood beam floor, *Arabian Nights* carpets, a cozy fireplace, and three tall narrow views of medieval London, all in an honest-to-god castle, Baynards Castle:

the white-towered keep set in the southwest corner of the city walls, London headquarters for the House of York. Edward had offered her any room in the family castle, and she picked this one for its fireplace and semiprivacy—it had been a tower guardroom, but now it was all hers, complete with handwoven tapestries and a tall wooden bathtub. Unbelievable—magical, really—especially when her last address had a West Hollywood ZIP code. Three months in the Middle Ages, and she practically owned the place.

So what use was worrying? She tried not to think about the tournament—while planning her Saturday around it. Actually, Saint Anne's Saturday.

Happily, she had a head start on her morning, being up and looking like Lady Robyn, sitting at her carved oak table in a long red-gold gown with tight scarlet sleeves buttoned by gold wire studs tied in Stafford knots. Very medieval. Right now Robyn was only nominally a lady, and some had harsher names for her, since not everyone liked her having the most popular boyfriend in London. But one day she would be a countess, and eventually a duchess. "Robyn Plantagenet, Duchess of York," had a heady ring, even for a former Miss Rodeo Montana. Like a witch condemned to the water test, she was thrown into this wet summer of 1460 to sink or swim; three months later, she was doing quite well, thank you. Half a pound of gold went into her gown, and she had warm fresh milk for her coffee, brought to the castle gate that morning by a man with a cow.

Saying a silent prayer to Aurora, goddess of dawn, and to Saint Anne, whose day it was, she took a first hot grateful sip. "Here's to tournament day, and hoping no one gets hurt. May Mary's mother save them from their foolishness."

Her first dry Saturday in who knows how long, and she would spend it in the mud at Smithfield, seeing horsemen crash headlong into each other. All because of Edward, who claimed to love her. Men will make you crazy, if you let them, especially medieval men—but by now she had survived worse, way worse. On her fourth morning in the Middle Ages she had to watch a trial by combat, with herself as the prize. Two men in steel armor fought on horseback and afoot beneath the spreading oaks of Sudeley park, deciding if she should be freed or burned at the stake for witchcraft. Freed or fried, all on the swing of a broadsword, something so incredibly frightening it brought shivers to her in the chill safety of her castle bedroom. How could a Saturday joust in the Smithfield mud hope to compare?

Hearing someone stirring on her big white canopy bed, Robyn called out in Gaelic, "Good morning."

Deirdre, her Welsh-Irish maid, raised her head from amid the bed linen, the girl's sleepy smiling face shining in a halo of red hair. "More witches' brew, m'lady?"

"Want some?" she raised the cup to entice her maid out of bed. At sixteen—"or thereabouts"—Deirdre liked to sleep in. And last night's supper had ended in an impromptu Saint Anne's Eve ball, where grooms, serving girls, young lords, and spirited ladies danced to live music under the stars, a Welsh harp, several drunk fiddlers, and tiny cymbals on the women's fingers sending music out onto the dark streets of London. Half the castle had to be sleeping late this Saint Anne's Day.

"Oh, please yes, m'lady." Green eyes went wide with anticipation. Introduced to caffeine only a week ago, Deirdre was already an addict.

"If you come get it," Robyn coaxed her sleepy maid, holding out the cup. When they were alone, or feared being overheard, she used her maid's language. Before coming here, Robyn barely knew Gaelic existed; now she spoke it with Deirdre's Wexford accent as easily as she spoke Latin. Or medieval French. Or Walloon. The spell that brought her here from modern England displaced her "in body and soul, to breathe the air, drink the water, and speak the speech." Whatever anyone said made immediate sense, and she answered back, be it in Greek or Gaelic. A handy knack, in fact her most useful magical talent. The spell had not brought her here to harm her or strand her among uncomprehending strangers, so it could not have worked otherwise. Witchcraft was like that—intent mattered as much as technique. In fact, the spell was not even meant for her, per se, having been aimed at Edward; making her a fairly innocent bystander.

Deirdre wormed her way down to the foot of the tall canopied bed, still wrapped in Robyn's down comforter. Without getting out of the covers, the teenager leaned over and kissed her mistress good morning; then she took the coffee, sipping greedily. Castles were cold in the morning, even July mornings, and Deirdre slept mother-naked in summer.

"Ummm!" Deirdre murmured, "What makes it so sweet?"

"Chocolate," she explained, wishing she had brought back more. "Comes from the seeds of the cocoa tree in America."

"America must be amazing, if this is what grows on trees."

"Most amazing," Robyn agreed, watching her redheaded bed worm drink—knowing Deirdre lumped all her America stories together, imagining the pre-Columbian United States inhabited by Indians cruising the Internet in SUVs, eating chocolate out of trees. Picked up during Robyn's one-day stay in Ireland, Deirdre was a cheerful Welsh-Irish bastard, determined to get as far as guts and talent could take her. Quick with languages, the girl was alternatively talkative and dreamy, her head full of teenage lust and fairy tales, believing in true love, pixies, leprechauns, and birds born from barnacles. Happily doing chores for pennies a day and a chance to sleep out of the rain, Deirdre was fairly useless as a lady's maid, but a godsend nonetheless. Despite their vast differences in rank, age, and nationality—not to mention coming from different millennia— Robyn and her maid were soul mates, exiles forced to live by other people's rules. Deirdre saw it at once, going straight from serving girl to lady's companion and sometime partner in crime, the first member of Lady Robyn Stafford's household-to-be.

It said much about the Middle Ages that her Welsh-Irish maid got more use out of the big feather bed than she did—in part because Robyn was newly betrothed to a teenage sex maniac—but mostly because the Middle Ages was one grand game of musical beds. Deirdre normally slept on the floor, moving up to the bed when her mistress slept in the master bedroom or went visiting. Noble households could be incredibly nomadic. Since coming here, Robyn had slept in palaces on silk sheets, in open fields and rain-soaked tents, in churches and nunneries, in shepherds' rests and dungeon cells—a great succession of beds, not all as clean as they could be—sharing them with everyone from an imprisoned witch-child to an amorous young earl.

Prime bells sounded, calling Baynards Castle to chapel. Deirdre surrendered the coffee, smiling mischievously. "Today is tournament day. Will Lord Edward ride?"

"Mayhap." She did not like to think of Edward hurling himself at another heavily armored horseman, not even in fun. Fortunately, her true love was impetuous but not foolhardy. Most days at least.

Deirdre grinned at her, warm and snug, happy to be "far and away" sharing her magical adventure on this fairy isle with its feather beds and dark, sweet potions. "Mayhap my Lord Edward of March has ridden himself full out already this morning?"

Grabbing a big feather pillow from the bed, Robyn swatted her maid, saying, "No wonder Saxons hang the wild Irish out of hand."

"The wild *godless* Irish," Deirdre giggled from beneath the pillow. Last time Robyn roomed with a teenager was in college—but in some ways the Dark Ages were like one long sleepover, sans CDs or VCRs, with no privacy and nothing to do but play dress-up and gossip about each other's sex lives, while prepping for pop quizzes in medieval history. Deirdre stuck her red head out from under the bedding, begging for details. "Well, has he, then?"

"No! My Lord Edward of March has not 'ridden' this morning. I left him fast asleep, another young lie-abed like you." Edward thoroughly enjoyed last night's dancing, and would sleep past morning Mass—too bad he would not sleep through the tournament too. She swatted her maid again. Born and brought up in a family bed—listening to her parents making more siblings—Deirdre was a shameless bastard child, demanding in on everything. "Come! Up with you!" Robyn commanded, ordering her "household" out of bed. "Get your naked heathen body up and dressed for chapel—or I shall surely have the Saxons hang you."

"More witches' brew first," Deirdre insisted, showing why the Irish made such hopeless servants. Deirdre knew her mistress from the far future was an uncommonly soft touch, with no heart to turn her out, or even to see her beaten. Having stumbled onto an amazingly good thing, Deirdre made the most of it, mixing willful disobedience and deathless devotion. Robyn handed up the cup, keeping her maid occupied while she typed in her journal.

> Make that the only woman out of her teens who craves chocolate and caffeine. Deirdre is definitely hooked. Prime already, have to run. More later . . .

She hit SAVE. Closing her electronic journal, she tucked it in an inner pocket in her flowing red-gold gown. Medieval women had a hundred places to hide things on their person, a huge advance over tight jeans and a halter top. Aside from her digital watch, her journal was the only bit of consumer electronics she'd brought with her—all that remained of the high-tech third millennium. That plus a thermos flask, some small lighters and flashlights, and her precious stock of pain pills, antibiotics, tampons, batteries, chocolate, and toilet paper. Real medieval musts, doled out sparingly, like her supply of coffee—four more foil packets and five pounds of drip grind. That was almost all she brought with her from the twenty-first century, unless you counted things like her VISA card—which got her out of Berkeley Castle by lifting the dungeon door latch from inside but was otherwise fairly useless. Slipping on her crimson slippers, she dressed Deirdre in red-gold Stafford livery, then led her maid down to the castle's ornate chapel to pray—still worried for Edward, sleeping away on his white-and-gold canopy bed.

Today was Saint Anne's Day. Mary's mother. Jesus' grandmother. Going down on her knees, Robyn begged Mary's mother for her blessing and guidance on this, her day, and in the days to come. She beseeched Saint Anne to keep the contestants safe in the coming tourney and to specifically keep Edward, earl of March, out of the lists completely. Amen.

Her prayers were utterly heartfelt. Morning prayer was compulsory, but that was no reason to waste it. Three months in the Middle Ages had made a believer out of her. Religion was everywhere here: in people's hearts, thoughts, and daily deeds, in the songs she sang, in the air she breathed. Before coming here, she had not so much as heard of Saint Anne. Now she absolutely believed in Saint Anne and in the miracles Saint Anne could do. She had *seen* the miracles. Sounds crazy? You literally had to be here.

For Saint Anne was also Hecate, the witch goddess. God's grandmother, the pagan death crone. The Mother's mother. Goddess of death and rebirth. Which was why Saint Anne's symbol was a witch's broom. Whether you called her Saint Anne, or Hecate, or Lilith, her power had brought Robyn to the Middle Ages—to stubbornly deny that miracle would do her no good.

Crossing herself, she took Communion; not for the first time in the Middle Ages breaking her fast with the body of Christ. Another medieval miracle.

Then off to Smithfield. Putting herb tea and burnt toast on top of the Blessed Sacrament, she ordered her white mare saddled, along with Deirdre's chestnut gelding. Her bullion-trimmed gown was hopeless on horseback, but she had a gold riding dress and a tight sleeveless crimson jacket given to her the day she arrived in medieval England—Sir Collingwood Grey would see what good use she got of them. She added pearls at her throat and a horned headdress with silk streamers trailing almost to the ground; being a lady in London meant looking the part. Little silver bells rang on her saddle bow as she rode out of Baynards Castle with Deirdre in tow. Hidden beneath her dress folds was a heavy double-edged saxe knife, tucked in a leather sheath sewn to her saddle—this was, after all, the Middle Ages.

Beggars waited by the castle gate, baring their stumps and sores, crying, "Have pity, m'lady. Please have pity."

How could she not? She had silver pennies ready in her purse, and she leaned in the saddle to pass them out, along with words of good cheer, getting beggars' blessings in return. Expecting to see hordes of beggars in the Middle Ages, Robyn was surprised to find most medievals had jobs, or plots of land to work, leaving little time to go begging. Those who did so took the task seriously—going straight to the gates of the wealthy or the steps of cathedrals. Prime spots were like handicap parking spaces, and gate tolls for the rich to pay. She gladly gave out the pennies, paying her debt to poverty with an open heart, thanking Heaven to have escaped such suffering. Three months ago she arrived here alone and friendless, and she could have ended up a penniless cripple or worse, instead of a countess-to-be. She was luckier than they, infinitely luckier, and every morning she gave thanks, sharing a little of her luck.

Blind and maimed faces smiled back at her, enthusiastically calling out gap-toothed blessings, not blaming her in the least for being healthy and pretty and for riding a beautiful white mare. None of which was her doing anyway—health and good looks were God's fault, and Lily was a gift from Edward, given to her when they were in Calais. So was Deirdre's chestnut gelding, Ainlee—named for a line in the sagas:

Tall Ainlee bearing a load on his back . . .

Most medievals did not blame her for her good fortune, believing that Heaven's mercy must be arbitrary and undeserved, or else it would be justice—not mercy.

Thanking the beggars for their blessings, she straightened in the saddle, trotting on into the city. Baynards Castle stood beside the river on Upper Thames Street—between Blackfriars and Saint Paul's Wharf. Emerging from the castle gatehouse, she saw the river docks jammed by horse drays and cursing stevedores while huge cranes swung casks of Spanish wine out of a caravel blown by the wind from Cádiz to her castle door. Men called out, "Wage! Wage!" and "Go we hence!" to boatmen plying the slack tide above London Bridge, while a nearby cog unloaded dirt from the Holy Land, used for church foundations and for filling graves. She loved how the city hit you, a wall of sights and sounds, beggars with their hands out, boatmen doing business amid barges reeking of offal and spices, making her feel like Queen Alice riding through the looking-glass world "of shoes—and ships—and sealing wax— / of cabbages—and kings."

Sailors waved, shouting ribald greetings that Lady Robyn did not return. Veering away from the traffic jam on Thames Street, she urged Lily up Ludgate Hill, with Deirdre close behind her, headed for the massive pile of Saint Paul's, which towered above the city walls, its gold-tipped steeple thrust fifty stories into the sky, a stone spear aimed straight at God. In the churchyard beneath, lawyers consulted with cutpurses while visiting clerics ranted against the sinful city and Cock Lane whores loitered patiently, ready to give sinners something to confess. Lacking TV and newspapers, medievals made do with reality, living life on display, a perpetual live-action pageant-cum-morality play with faith, toil, pomp, and poverty all playing parts in the daily drama. Priests proclaimed God's word at Saint Paul's Cross, competing with street musicians and bakers' touts. Criminals sat pelted in the stocks or begged alms from cell windows. Artisans worked before their customers. Love offered herself brazenly for sale. Shakespeare would not be born for a hundred years, but this was the world his metaphors came from: "All the world's a stage, / And all the men and women merely players. . . ."

Back home in Hollywood, Robyn had ached for a starring role, and now she had one, in this real-time theater in the round—Lady Robyn Stafford, countess-to-be and friend of the king—she could hardly complain at the casting.

She paused to admire the huge cruciform cathedral—having become a connoisseur of churches—the Middle Ages being pretty much made for them. In Manhattan, even cathedrals could look small, squatting beneath skyscrapers, but Old Saint Paul's reared over packed rooftops the way a cathedral should, braced by flying buttresses and studded with crosses, a huge hymn to Heaven sculpted out of glass and stone. And Robyn was the only person from her time to see it—Old Saint Paul's would burn in the Great Fire of 1666, two hundred years in "the future."

Ignoring cook's boys crying, "Kidney pie!" or "Hot sheeps' feet! Cheap!" she checked her watch—10:12:17 A.M.—deciding to dawdle. Tournament time was not until noon; nor was she in a rush to get there. Instead of going straight out Ludgate to Smithfield, she set off the long way around, down Watling Street to Newgate, drawing greetings from the doorways to drapers' shops. Serving women stopped work to wave and smile, leaning out of upper-story windows to get a look at her gown—which cheered her immensely. She returned the greetings merrily, to show that seeing into the future and sleeping with an earl did not make her snooty. Lord Edward's witchy lady was genuinely popular in London, almost from the moment the city opened her gates to the rebel earls and she rode in behind Edward. Three weeks ago on the fourth of July, diehard lords holding the Tower of London threw wildfire onto East Cheap, setting fires and sowing terror. Riding into Cheapside to return a missing child, she promised Edward would bring King Henry back to London and retake the Tower. Her offhand prophecy came true—partly by her doing—sealing her reputation as a seeress, a white witch with London's good at heart. She heard an apprentice boy shout, "Look, 'tis Lord Edward's lovely strumpet. Gawd, I would I were him."

British boys did not lack ambition. And she loved dirty old London back, despite the appalling sights and smells. This was the Middle Ages at its most magical, when one could personally right wrongs and see justice done, then get grateful thanks. She risked her life to return the king to London, free the Tower, and bring down Lord Scales—suffering mightily to do it. For which she deserved a single tower room, a white mare, a few outrageous outfits, a dreamy teenage maid, and a rich boyfriend. At least most Londoners thought so, and who was she to argue?

Deirdre bought a branch of cherries from a fruiterer, offering her some. "Cherries, m'lady?" Seeing they were unwashed, Robyn ate a couple, figuring cherries off the branch were safer than the tainted water used to wash them—and she never need worry about industrial pollutants or insecticides.

"More, m'lady?" Her maid hopefully held out another handful. One of Deirdre's duties was to force doubtful food on her picky mistress—notorious for demanding boiled water and thorough cooking.

"Too tart." She shook her head. "With all this rain, they have not sweetened." Green cherries for sale were a bad sign; maybe all they would see of this summer's crop. Deirdre finished off the branch, enjoying a teenager's appetite, eating like a plow horse but never looking worse than "shapely."

Turning at Bow Lane, she passed the parish church of Saint Mary le Bow—one of her favorites. The Bow Bell sounded the nine-o'clock curfew, and the hours of the night along with Saint Bride's, Saint Giles without Cripplegate, and All Hallows Barking. When she was a girl growing up in Montana, her father read her the story of Dick Whittington, who traded his cat for a fortune and won the hand of his true love—it was the Bow Bell that called Dick back to London when he despaired, promising to make him lord mayor. Like London Bridge, this little Cheapside church was a place out of a fairy tale that had come alive for her.

And like Joan of Arc, Mary le Bow was a secret reference to Diana, the witch goddess with the moon bow. Robyn's coven name was Diana, and one of Mary le Bow's parishioners, Beth Lambert, the ten-year-old daughter of a Cheapside alderman, was her sister-initiate. As she passed, she said a silent prayer to her secret namesake, Hecate's granddaughter, the virgin huntress, protector of women and children.

Hearing low piping, she urged Lily forward, saying, "Let's see what's happening." Medievals used music when they wanted to make noise—using trumpets for loudspeakers, and pipes and bells for sirens—a most pleasant practice. She emerged on West Cheap, London's great market street running from Newgate to the center of town. Called Cheapside—or simply the Street—West Cheap was the medieval Rodeo Drive, reputedly the richest thoroughfare in Christendom, lined with gold- and silversmiths, clothiers and tapestry dealers. Venetians confessed that all the cities in Italy could not match the array of handwrought silver found along Cheapside. Absolutely the perfect spot for a slow Saturday morning ride, taking her mind off the coming tournament.

Her happy mood evaporated as soon as she saw the source of the music. Robyn halted, instantly sorry she went this way, wishing she had gone straight out Ludgate to Smithfield. Down the street marched a dismal parade led by pipers, constables, an undersheriff, and a herald in city colors—escorting a wretched prisoner to punishment. Behind them walked a teenage waif with short ragged hair, sad brown eyes, and dirty bare feet, her neck in a rope halter, her small hands tied behind her. Her homespun tunic had the striped hood of a prostitute. Seeing the poor bound girl led past the Cheapside goldsmith shops by gaily dressed men in padded doublets summed up just about all Robyn's misgivings about the Middle Ages.

Her heart went out to this child hauled along by a hard-faced pack of men. Many medieval women were little, but this one was tiny, looking barely old enough to have sex, much less wear a whore's hood. Excited boys followed her, aiming to see her punished, maybe hoping to lend a hand. At least no one was jeering. Medieval justice could be ugly; a month ago in Sandwich, Robyn saw a thief nailed to a post by his ear. Given a knife to cut himself free, the felon stood nerving himself for the deed as she rode past—medieval jurisprudence at its most picturesque. Deirdre drew rein beside her, asking blandly, "Which way, m'lady?"

Which way, indeed? All hope of a thoughtless shopping spree vanished. Sunny Saint Anne's Day had suddenly darkened. Just up the street was Saint Paul's churchyard, and across from it London's chief sanctuary, Saint Martin-le-Grand—a haven for thieves, murderers, and political refugees. Farther along lay Newgate and the city walls, and beyond that Smithfield. This unhappy procession was headed the other way, down Cheapside toward the stock and poultry markets, deeper into the city.

And she had to follow. She had not hung around to see that thief in Sandwich cut his ear off, but this girl was different, with her child's eyes and tearstained cheeks. Robyn could not just leave her to whatever these men devised. She told Deirdre, "This way," turning to join the sad parade down Cheapside.

Deirdre understood at once, deftly steering her gelding to follow her gold-and-scarlet lady down the street. Her maid might sleep in, and have to be dressed most mornings, but Deirdre was smart, brave, and incredibly loyal, trusting no one but her mistress amid all these mad Saxons. Warily she switched to Gaelic, asking, "What will they do to her?"

"I do not know," Robyn admitted. Aside from twitchy subjects like heresy, witchcraft, and treason, laws here and now were not much worse than at home. Torture and animal testimony were frowned on, and women had surprisingly many rights—even though the laws were made and administered by men. Laws on whoring were better than most. Instead of criminalizing harlots, London tried to keep them out of the city, in Cock Lane in Smithfield, or across the river in Southwark, where the kindhearted Bishop Waynflete saw that his "Winchester Geese" were not confined to baths and brothels but had their own homes—keeping men from living off the earnings or prostituting their wives. "I do not think they will hurt her," she told Deirdre. "They probably mean to humiliate her, then march her to Cock Lane."

Her maid looked dubious, pointing out, "Cock Lane is in the other direction."

Which it was, back behind them, beyond the city walls, between Newgate and Smithfield. Robyn sighed, admitting, "They may want to pillory her too."

Deirdre did not reply, having a healthy Irish dread of English justice. Both maid and mistress felt instant sympathy for any woman abused over sex, knowing their own personal lives and pedigrees could not stand much critical scrutiny. Robyn herself rode a fine white mare and wore a gold dress, gifts from an earl and a knight, both of whom she had made love to—only luck, poetic license, and a lot of romantic derring-do separated Lady Robyn from this girl being led along on a rope.

Green odors came from the grocers' shops on Bucklersbury Lane, mixed with the smell of soap and spices. Robyn saw the bound bedraggled girl gaze longingly toward the Great Conduit, where spring water was piped in from Paddington, looking back as the rope pulled her past. Plainly the child was thirsty. Luckily Robyn never left the castle without clean bottled water in her saddlebag; her problem was getting it to the prisoner. She had more silver pennies in her purse, as well, and five gold nobles each worth a week's wages, not much for a bribe, but it might pay a fine. Her current popularity also counted for something—medieval London was still a fairly small town, with small-town notions of justice. Who you were, and who you knew, mattered a lot. But she never planned putting her popularity on the line for some unknown teenage prostitute. Up to now she had just been enjoying her celebrity.

Silver bells rang softly on her saddle as she entered the dark heart of the city, which was poorer, dirtier, and packed with ordinary folks. Cheapside became the Poultry, cutting though the Stocks Market, a mass of open-air stalls for poulters, butchers, fishmongers, and secondhand dealers—the narrow crowded gut of London, where hen-wives came to sell their eggs and burglars unloaded their loot. Ahead lay Cornhill, the city's bread basket. Glad to see no one gathering offal and spoiled eggs from the stalls, Robyn tried to judge the mood of the crowd. When she first arrived, she feared the medievals would be stupid and cruel—and some exceeded her expectations wonderfully—but most were incredibly friendly, cheerfully enduring appalling hardships, happily sharing their pittance with her. Yet these same pious, friendly folks gladly took the law in their hands, and not just to fling filth at some wretch in the stocks. When Edward and Warwick gave the lord constable a safe conduct in exchange for surrendering the Tower, London boatmen beat his lordship to death for daring to throw fire on East Cheap. Happily the mood today seemed more somber; no one looked to hurt this girl—the law would see to that.

Seeing a woman walking ahead of her in a flowing green velvet gown along with a lady's maid in matching livery, Robyn urged Lily forward, catching up as they climbed Cornhill. Introducing herself to the startled matron, she discovered this was Dame Agnes Forster, wife of a wealthy fishmonger and former mayor. White haired, with that prematurely aged look much in vogue here and now, Dame Agnes turned out to be another medieval surprise, a prison reformer, busy building an addition to Ludgate prison "for the better sort of felons, debtors, and shopkeepers taken with stolen goods—well embattled, but with large fair walks where prisoners may take their ease." Dame Agnes pleaded with her, "Will you help this girl? I did talk with her in Newgate, and believe her to be both godly and innocent."

Robyn promised to do what she could. "I have money to pay a fine, but I feared they would put her in the pillory."

"Fine? Pillory?" Dame Agnes looked quizzically up at her, clutching her rosary beads; like everyone else hereabouts, Dame Agnes was a Catholic. "This girl is to be burned."

"Burned?" Shock washed over Robyn like ice water, freezing her in the saddle. "What do you mean?"

"Burned alive at the stake," Dame Agnes explained patiently, as if Lady Robyn might be somehow unacquainted with the custom. "At Tyburn within the hour."

"What in Heaven for?" Her first thought was witchcraft, but she did not say so aloud. Being a future sorceress herself, she hated getting people thinking in that direction, especially when the law was at hand, with women already in custody.

"Murder," replied Dame Agnes as simply as if it made sense.

"Murder?" The girl was not big enough to assault a mouse.

"That is what the law called it, and no one spoke for her. Is it true you know the king?" asked Dame Agnes, who clearly knew her reputation.

Robyn nodded silently. She had indeed eaten off the royal plate and spent an uncomfortable half hour in King Henry's tent, waiting to see who won the battle of Northampton. Poor Mad King Henry liked her, and he was another notorious soft touch who hated seeing harm done or women abused. But Henry was in Westminster—by the time she got there and back this girl would be burnt.

"And my lord, the earl of March?" Dame Agnes added hopefully, hinting that Robyn's noble paramour might help.

She nodded again. Edward was a far better bet than King Henry: more attentive, decisive, and eager to act—but even harder to find. He was meeting that morning with the Nevilles, then would be headed for Westminster himself, planning to be back at Smithfield by noon. At the moment Edward could be anywhere between Warwick Street and Westminster. His crisp way of getting things done made him nearly impossible to catch, as Edward's enemies learned to their cost.

"Surely Lord Edward would listen if you begged to spare this girl," Dame Agnes suggested, seemingly well acquainted with Lady Robyn's love life. Lacking paparazzi and tabloid TV, Londoners had to observe romance among the rich and famous firsthand. Nor did pious Dame Agnes balk at using sin to save a soul. British practicality easily triumphed over Church dogma.

"He would," Robyn agreed, tightening her headdress before going into action. "If we could but find him in time." Seeing Dame Agnes looking downcast, nervously telling her beads, she advised the old woman, "Have courage, and pray to Saint Anne. This is her day, and she will not see it sullied." And Hecate's day, as well. Privately Robyn begged the goddess of death not to take the child. No rich, powerful, good-intentioned man was going to save this girl—that would be up to her and Deirdre. And Hecate. And Dame Agnes, if the former Mrs. Mayor was game for it.

Parade's end came at Cornhill, London's grain market, where citizens bought big, carted-in country loaves and drew water piped from Tyburn through "The Tun Upon Cornhill." Atop the Tun sat a cage full of drunks and nightwalkers snared by the city watch; nearby stocks held an egg-spattered apothecary, his crooked weights hanging around his neck. Medieval justice was relentlessly public—going beyond courtroom TV to audience participation. Crime must hide, but law was there for all to see, and even take part in. Far from being bashful about burning this girl, they piped her through the heart of the city to proclaim her guilt right at the bread counter of this huge open-air shopping mall.

Sellers and buyers stopped to stare at the small scared convict brought for sentencing. Bright solid colors made a London mob look like a walking tarot deck, ready to reveal this girl's fate. Women in the crowd clumped around Robyn and Dame Agnes, drawn by a lady's presence, taking this chance to stand near one of the new stars in the noble soap opera that passed for national politics. Robyn's own gaze stayed on the girl. On Saturday, "foreign" butchers from the countryside set up their blocks in Cornhill before stalls full of livestock, letting customers select animals for slaughter. It was heartbreaking to see the barefoot girl standing with her hands bound behind her, unself-consciously studying the doomed pigs. Every so often her brown eyes turned toward the Tun, and her pink tongue licked at parched lips.

Burning this child was one thing, but making her stand near a fountain, aching to drink, was needlessly cruel. Reaching into her saddlebag, Robyn found the squeeze bottle of boiled water; then with a silent nod to Deirdre, she rode out from amid the knot of women, bells jiggling softly on her saddle. Parting the men with her horse, she reined in right before the thirsty girl. Guards looked question-ingly at their betters. Sitting up in the saddle, she spoke loudly to the undersheriff: "Please to God, let me give her water. Worse criminals than her walk free—and we all have unpunished sins on our conscience."

Searching the silent crowd for friends, she recognized only one man, Matt Davye, no longer wearing Duke Holland's livery—but his bluff alert features were unmistakable. Ironically he was one of the guards who held her and Joanna Grey prisoner in the Tower, and someone for whom her words should have real meaning. Matt Davye had felt pity for his prisoners, bringing them food, blankets, and words of hope—this good deed kept Matt Davye from standing trial before Earl Warwick in the Guildhall when the rest of Duke Holland's men were condemned. But did Matt Davye know his mercy had saved him? And what difference would it make to him if he did?

Ashamed, the undersheriff signaled for his sergeants to step back. Unscrewing the plastic squirt cap, Robyn gave the girl a drink straight from the bottle. Gulping greedily, head tilted back, eyes closed, and hands tied behind her, the prisoner let cool clean water flow down her slim throat. Finally, the girl paused to breathe, looking up at her and saying softly, "Thank you, m'lady."

She nodded, holding the bottle level with the girl's lips, knowing the child would want more, asking, "What is your name?"

"Mary, m'lady," the girl replied, doing a polite bobbing curtsy without taking her gaze off the bottle.

Named for the Virgin; that made it perfect. She gave Mary more water, making sure the girl drank her fill. When the girl was done, Robyn asked, "How old are you?"

Mary wiped her lips on her shoulder and thought for a moment. "Fifteen—or so."

Medievals were often unsure of their age, and they were not bashful about trying teenagers as adults. Edward, her betrothed, was condemned to death for treason at seventeen—a sentence still not officially lifted. And Joan of Arc was burned at nineteen. But both Joan and Edward had asked for it, putting on armor and leading rebellions against Mad King Henry. Robyn could not believe this girl's offenses were anywhere near that grave, asking, "Did you kill anyone?"

"No, m'lady." Mary said it easily, without hesitation, as though politely answering an adult's question that had little to do with her predicament.

Robyn screwed the plastic cap back on and slipped the squeeze bottle into her saddlebag, unsure of what to do next. Send Deirdre to find Edward? No way—not enough time, and far too chancy. Do that, and she was sure to end up wishing Deirdre were with her. Plead Mary's case to these men? Another waste of time. Without the power to pardon her, all they could do was stubbornly haul Mary to Tyburn and carry out the sentence. Medievals could be sticklers for doing the right thing—especially when it was all wrong. Nor would they relent just because her boyfriend was the earl of March. Gripped with a sick feeling, Robyn somehow had to stop this. Seeing men burn this grave, serious girl would surely drive her mad.

Mary made a soft sound to get her attention, asking shyly, "If it pleases m'lady, could I but beg a favor?"

Robyn nodded slowly, saying, "If I can, I will." She hated to sound grudging, but she had to be careful of what she promised. As a known seeress and not too secret witch, she had to be wary of flat-out defying the law.

Leaning closer, balancing on her bare toes, Mary whispered her request. "Please have them hang me, m'lady. For I sorely fear the fire."

Who did not? But the matter-of-fact way Mary put it tore at Robyn's heart. She had been near to where this girl stood, accused of treason and witchcraft, waiting beneath the oaks of Sudeley park to see if she would be saved or burned—but there at least she'd had a champion, and a fighting chance. Mary had neither, making simple hanging seem a blessing. She searched the men's faces for someone to listen to her pleas, to be Mary's champion, and still saw no one she knew but Matt Davye, who'd only lately escaped the gallows himself. Where were are all those handsome knights-errant when you needed them? Some of the best would be breaking lances at Smithfield this afternoon, but Mary would be ashes by then. She forced herself to smile for the girl, saying gently, "I will see what I can do."

"Thank you, m'lady." The girl smiled back up at her. "I would have twelve hangings before one burning." Medievals well knew a person could be hanged more than once; public executions were sometimes taken on the road, with repeat performances in various cities. Mary did another bobbing hands-bound curtsy, buoyed by the hope of being hanged.

Unrolling his scroll, the herald in city colors turned his face to one side, opening his mouth like a trumpet, blasting out words that reached the back of the crowd. Robyn stayed with the girl while sentence was read, hearing Mary called a harlot and murderer, guilty of fornication, incest, and manslaughter—leading a brief life so steeped in sin it could be cleansed only by fire. Medievals would be apalled by the secretive hospital-cum-assembly-line executions held at home, believing punishment must be brutal and public. Secret executions were the tool of tyrants afraid to do their deeds in daylight. Also a terrible waste—what was learned from a tragedy no one saw? Rejecting modern one-size-fits-all justice, medievals had degrees of capital punishment, and Mary's most heinous crime was domestic treason—according to the herald, the man she killed was both her stepfather and her husband. Burning was saved for hardened rebels against nature, like heretics who denied God—and wives who murdered their husbands.

Smooth and smug as the jack of hearts, the herald finished off by begging God's mercy and declaring the sentence to be carried out this day at Tyburn. Guards moved to separate the girl from Robyn, and Mary started to look scared, tears welling in her eyes, saying, "Please do not leave, m'lady. Tell them I must hang."

Reaching down from the saddle, Robyn laid her hand on the girl's small shoulder, feeling fine bones through the thin fabric. Mary calmed immediately, murmuring thanks and kissing "m'lady's" fingers. For a long moment Robyn sat there saying a secret prayer to Hecate and Saint Anne, letting the girl draw courage from her presence. Then reluctantly she removed her hand, turning the girl over to the priest-confessor, saying, "Do not fear, I will go with you. Heaven will protect you."

Heaven had better hurry, because these men meant to burn her. Holding down a hollow ache, Robyn turned to rejoin Deirdre and saw that the formerly silent crowd was weeping. Men's eyes were wet, and women sobbed quietly. Medievals saw suffering aplenty—even the rich and beautiful must kneel to a tortured Christ and pass beggars at the castle gate—but who could not be moved by Mary's plight? At absolute worst Mary killed a man who married his teenage stepdaughter in order to abuse and pimp her—more cause for a medal than for burning. Small wonder taking her to Tyburn was put on an undersheriff and some sergeants. No one felt good about this. No one but the law—which had a killing and a "murderess," and meant to make the most of it. Law had not changed a lot in five-hundred-odd years, except to get less squeamish. Instead of hiding its mistakes in clogged courts and lengthy appeals, medieval law would march Mary back up Cheapside and out Newgate, to Tyburn, where the wood and stake were waiting, playing sad music all the way.

Which left justice pretty much up to Lady Robyn. How horribly unfair. She got up this morning, not meaning to help anyone except Edward—stopping him from riding in his silly tournament. Had she resisted the urge to shop and put things off, she could be in Smithfield right now, having a so-so morning preparing for the joust. When she finally heard about Mary's fate, she would have been perfectly horrified, saying a prayer for the poor sinner and then going on with her day. Only it was not her day—obviously—it was Saint Anne's.

Turning about, the sad procession headed back down Cornhill through the stock markets. Medieval law took the "last mile" literally. Riding a couple of horse lengths behind the condemned, Robyn felt her stomach tighten. Thankfully, she had nothing in her but burned toast, a pair of green cherries, and the Communion wafer. She felt totally pure. Which was good—since Mary plainly needed a miracle, and needed it now. Three months in the Middle Ages had taught Robyn that miracles never happened on their own. Heaven always had a helping hand. Feeling under her gold dress folds, she checked her saxe knife, sliding off the leather loop holding it in the saddle sheath. Given to her by a Welsh witch, the big knife was razor sharp and ready.

Defying the law could cost her everything: position, comfort, her proposed marriage, her promised duchy, even her life. But she asked Saint Anne to show her the way, and here was Heaven's answer, "Make yourself useful." Living in a castle, being betrothed to a handsome boy on the Royal Council, having a fine white mare to ride— it all came at a cost. At home in West Hollywood, horrible things happened to teenage prostitutes, but there she did nothing aside from feeling sorry and afraid. Here she lacked that luxury. She was Lady Robyn Stafford, beloved of an earl and friend to the king; if she could do nothing for this child, who could? Letting Mary be dragged off and burned made a mockery of noblesse oblige—not to mention the rebel claim to be building a better England. Having accepted the rewards of running the country, Robyn had to take the risks, as well.

Drawing her heavy knife, she signed to Deirdre, and her maid was alongside her at once. Handing Deirdre the saxe knife, she made sure their hands touched, drawing strength from the warm contact, whispering in Gaelic, "Be ready."

Deirdre understood, deftly palming the big knife. Never pretending to trust Saxon justice, Deirdre had her skirts tucked and her palfrey ready. For somone so excitable, her maid could be amazingly cool in a crisis, anticipating trouble and awaiting her moment. No matter how bad things got, a Wexford girl had seen worse. Much worse.

The Poultry turned back into Cheapside, with its drapers' shops and silversmiths. Ahead she could see Saint Paul's and the sanctuary of Saint Martin-le-Grand, and beyond them Newgate, and the road to Tyburn. Finish line in sight, she summoned up her courage, clutching sweat-soaked reins, her legs gripping her saddle leather. The former Miss Rodeo Montana, her heart in her throat, was ready to ride. At Mary's age, she had ridden before roaring crowds at breakneck speeds, becoming a blue-ribbon barrel racer, before she fell and broke her leg. Beyond the sanctuary of Saint Martin-le-Grand, she saw the barred windows of Newgate, where Mary's day had begun. Prisoners would be watching the procession, some undoubtedly awaiting their own trip to Tyburn.

Time to give the shut-ins a show. She leaned forward in the saddle, saying a silent prayer to Hecate and Saint Anne, then calling to Deirdre in Gaelic, "Cut the rope."

Deirdre bolted past her, blade in hand, riding like an Irish Comanche, legs tucked, head down, red hair streaming behind her. Bowling aside surprised sergeants, the serving girl drew rein, seizing the long dangling rope tying Mary to the undersheriff ahead. Looping it around the double-edged blade, Deirdre jerked hard, slicing the loop.

Spurring Lily, Robyn shot after her maid, pounding down the path Deirdre cleared, leaning low in the saddle, silk flapping on her headdress. As the line parted, Robyn scooped up the bound girl, then did a barrel-racing turn, and headed for the gateway of Saint Martin-le-Grand with Mary tucked across her lap. Dodging startled spectators, she made for the open gate, bells ringing madly on her saddle, showing surprised Londoners how Miss Rodeo Montana could ride. Mary stared up at her, wide-eyed in wonder, her striped hood badly askew, astonished at finding herself on horseback with the cut halter rope still dangling from her neck.

Suddenly an armored sergeant appeared in the gateway, bellowing threats and waving a brown bill—a huge ugly pole arm, half-ax and half-pruning hook. She could not go around him—no room. His hideous weapon went up to block her, gleaming in the sunlight, able to take off her head or Lily's leg. But if she reined in, hands would seize her from behind, pulling her back out of the saddle—like Joan of Arc's capture at Compiègne.

Without warning, the sergeant pitched suddenly forward, hit behind the knees by a perfect flying block. Seeing him go down, Robyn urged Lily to leap, holding tight to the girl in her lap. Hoofbeats ceased, giving way to a tinkling of saddle bells as they flew through the air. Looking down, she saw the sergeant and his assailant grappling beneath her in the gateway. Matt Davye had his knee in the sergeant's armored midriff—delivering a timely goal-line block.

Courtyard cobblestones rushed up to greet her. She tightened her grip on Mary as Lily came crashing to earth like a white avalanche. Iron hooves rang sparks on the stones, drawing cheers from the cutthroats and gallows' bait inhabiting the sanctuary of Saint Martin-le-Grand, accompanied by cries of, "Well ridden, m'lady. Welcome to Saint Martin's."

Doing a skidding dismount, Robyn slid out of the saddle and onto the stones, hoisted Mary to her shoulders, and staggered up the broad steps of Saint Martin's, tripping on her skirts, her headdress askew. The assembled outlaws cried delightedly, "Mind the gown, m'lady!" And, "Spare your haste, Mass is on the morrow."

Ignoring the gibes, she lurched through the open church door with Mary on her shoulders and stumbled into the tall stone nave bathed in colored sunlight that fell from stained glass. Astonished monks rushed to meet her as she tottered toward them like Quasimodo in a gold gown, crying, "Sanctuary! Sanctuary!"

Eager monks reached out to catch her as she collapsed in the nave. They helped untangle Mary, who was half-strangled by the cord around her neck. Robyn realized she'd come alarmingly close to hanging the girl, as requested. The monks could hardly hide their glee at having two such interesting fugitives come crashing into sanc-

tuary—far better than the usual run of cutpurses and failed politi-
cians. Sanctuaries were judged by their clientele, and Westminster
got all the glamorous sinners, lords on the lam, and great ladies in
distress, while Saint Martin's made do with the ne'er-do-wells of
London.

As monks unwound the rope halter, an amazed Mary gasped her
thanks. "Oh, my God—m'lady, you have saved me."

Kneeling, Robyn untied the girl's small hands, finding them red
and torn from the ropes. "Saint Martin saved you." She nodded at
the cavernous church. "I just got you here." Saint Martin-le-Grand
was the primary sanctuary within the walls of London, and even a
murderess with blood on her hands was safe as soon as she crossed
the threshold—or better yet threw herself on the altar. God's forgiveness stood above human law. People in the third millennium
might *say* that, but medievals truly believed it, building a huge free
base for convicts and escapees just down the street from Newgate
prison, right on the execution route. God's forgiveness was always
there—sometimes just steps away, if sinners would but take them.

Robyn dropped the bloody rope, smiling at Mary, "I said Heaven
would hear you." Small arms went immediately around Lady
Robyn's neck, astonishingly strong for someone so slight. Mary
pulled them together, holding tight. After hearing her death sentence
read minutes ago without batting an eyelash, Mary suddenly let go,
burying her head in a gold shoulder and sobbing like a faucet now
that she was safe.

Reaching around to comfort her, Robyn pushed back the whore's
hood, stroking the girl's short brown hair, telling Mary she was free
to cry; meanwhile robed monks stood watching a lady in a gold
riding dress and a girl in a burning smock kneeling together on the
big stone church floor. Ignoring the men of God—and the mayhem
she'd made of Saint Anne's Day—Robyn took a moment to thank
Heaven while holding on to the crying teenager, feeling Mary's fine
bones and frail shoulders, overwhelmed by the humanness of the girl
she had saved—not caring what came next. Whatever happened
now, this was a rare moment of victory, and it needed to be savored
and blessed.

By stages the girl's shaking and sobbing subsided; Robyn could
feel the thin ribs returning to a normal breathing rhythm. But when
Robyn tried to separate herself a bit, Mary clung tighter, clutching

the gold fabric, whispering, "Please do not leave me, m'lady. Stay with me, for I have been sore alone."

She could well imagine—having been in a Tower cell herself, alone and expecting to die—finding it pretty damn awful. But Robyn had at least known Edward was outside, trying to break in, and it had given her a sliver of hope. This girl had been truly alone, in body and soul, with only Heaven to call on. And Saint Anne had answered. Gently Robyn reminded the girl, "You are no longer alone." Far from it—this was a fairly crowded sanctuary. She nodded to the monks around them. "And these men of God will see you safe."

Mary looked at the men around them, then back at Robyn, not at all liking the trade. "Must m'lady leave?"

"M'lady must." She nodded sadly, having left a mess outside she needed to face. Deirdre was in Saxon hands, which made Robyn especially anxious; otherwise, she could have sat for some time in the cool of the church, holding this girl and hearing her story. "But I will see you are well cared for, I swear."

Looking even more worried, Mary asked, "Will they not be wroth with you for freeing me?"

"Mayhap," she admitted. "Definitely an angry undersheriff awaits without."

"Then stay here with me, m'lady," Mary begged, hugging her tighter, "that we may both be safe."

She smiled at the girl's concern. "Do not fear—you are but the least of my sins." Heretics, witches, and traitors had no right to sanctuary—and Robyn was all three. If her enemies meant to take her, no Church could save her. But Mary, a mere murderer, should be tolerably safe in Saint Martin's. Robyn told the girl, "I am a worse sinner than you can ever hope to be, and must face the folks outside."

"But you will come back." Mary said it like an unquestioned fact.

"I will come back," she assured the girl. How could she not? She had saved this teenager's life, and was now responsible for her—the latest addition to her growing circle of dependents.

"When, m'lady?" Mary demanded. Being saved from burning must have made Mary think she could get away with anything.

Robyn knew the feeling. On the night she was freed from the Tower she'd slept with Edward for the first time. Freedom was a heady thing, and the threat of hideous death made one greedy for life. She promised to be back "before the day is out."

"Good." Getting the answer she wanted, Mary laid her head back against Robyn's shoulder, still loath to let go. Offered food, shelter, and safety, all the girl cared about was seeing her savior again. Robyn stroked the girl's short hair, which felt fine and silky beneath her fingers, telling Mary how the monks would care for her—swearing to take her case to the earl of March.

"But you will come back," Mary insisted.

"Before vespers if I can." But first she must leave—slowly she pried herself free of the girl, at the same time pulling off Mary's striped hood, not wanting to give the sanctuary's denizens unsavory ideas. Folding the hood under her arm, she asked the monks to care for the girl, impulsively offering up her purse as a gift to Saint Martin. "Should she need anything, send for me, Robyn Stafford in Baynards Castle with the household of my lord, the earl of March."

They nodded knowingly; even monks in their cloisters knew all about her personal affairs, or imagined they did. Luckily, English clergy could be amazingly tolerant of sin. Lords, knights, and sergeants-at-law had threatened her with burning for witchcraft, treason, and being "the earl of March's whore"—but not a single cleric had been so much as uncivil to her, cheerfully offering her food, shelter, and solace whenever she was in need. Sometimes a little too much solace, but that, too, was an act of love.

Untwining the girl's fingers from her dress, she kissed their tips and then turned Mary over to a young nun summoned by the monks. Reluctantly Mary accepted, letting the nun lead her to a woman's cell in the sanctuary—where she would be safe for at least the forty days allowed by law. And forty days could easily be forever in medieval law; especially when you were supposed to be burned before noon.

Straightening up, Robyn was free for the moment, though still surrounded by thieves and murderers, with an angry undersheriff waiting at the door. So much for not daring to "flat-out defy the law." Sometimes the law left one small choice. Lady Robyn adjusted her headdress, surprised not to have lost it completely; then she walked down the tall nave to kneel before the altar, thanking Saint Martin personally for his mercy. Crossing herself, she rose and went to reclaim her horse, which she left with the killers and cutpurses outside.

At the church door she was greeted by cheers from the assembled outlaws, along with calls of "Welcome to sanctuary!" and "Where did m'lady learn to ride?" Giving them her best Miss Rodeo Montana smile, she strode down the steps with the whore's hood under her arm, getting still more cheers. Sanctuary inmates were shockingly easy to please. Stopping a couple of steps from the bottom, she acknowledged the applause, looking out over ill-shaven faces lit with crooked smiles. Producing a carrot from the folds of her dress, she signed for her horse.

Smiles turned to laughter. Scuffling broke out, but it was swiftly settled, and the winner led Lily over to her. He was a square dark cutthroat, with three days' growth of black stubble on his face and a shifty smile. Heaven knew why he was in sanctuary, but the easy way he upended the opposition and brought Lily out showed he had a deft hand with other people's horses. Going down on one knee, he offered up the reins, saying in broad Northumberland, "Yer mount, m'lady."

As soon as she heard the northern accent, she knew she had already met this felon; he was a border reiver, a Percy moss-trooper brought south to fight for Mad King Henry. She had seen his swarthy face three weeks ago beneath a steel bonnet on the Sunday before the battle of Northampton, when Lord Egremont's harbingers descended on the village of Hardingstone, and they had chatted briefly at a farmwife's door. Now his lord was dead, and he had lost his helmet and chain-mail shirt, but he still wore Percy colors—russet and yellow. Too bad she lacked Edward's knack for names, for she could not remember this fellow's. Taking the reins, she thanked him in his native Northumberland.

His eyes widened with delight, hearing his home speech so far south of the Tyne. "Then you are indeed she? The bonny lass who spoke so fair to us the Sunday before the battle. When I rode with Fingerless Will, Mary's Jock, Sweet-milk Selby, and Bangtail Bell. I hardly recognized you in yer fine headdress, but I well knew this mare."

"Her name is Lily," she told him, stroking the mare's mane as she gave her the carrot. "And you are?"

"Black Dick Nixon," he replied, bowing low. "At yer ladyship's service."

Black Dick Nixon, how could she have forgotten that? "What are you here for?"

He grinned at her, "Bad debts, m'lady."

That she could believe. From the look of him, Black Dick Nixon had left a trail of fines, forfeitures, blackmail, and skipped bail stretching halfway to Scotland. Anyone recruited for loot was bound to have a cavalier attitude toward law and property. "And how long do you have left in sanctuary?"

"Better than a month," Bad Dick Nixon boasted, happy to have most of his forty days ahead of him.

Two weeks ago, Lord Egremont's northern riders went down to defeat in the brief battle of Northampton, leaving them stranded and penniless among southerners they had come to loot, and landing Black Dick Nixon in sanctuary for unspecified crimes. Stuffing the whore's hood into her saddlebag, she let him help her to mount. Then, having given away her purse, she stripped a ring off her finger—a gold band she bought the day before in Cheapside, with a red stone matching her dress. Handing the ring down to Nixon, she told him, "Keep watch over the lass I brought here, and I will see those debts are paid. Her name is Mary, and mine is Robyn Stafford. I am lodged in Baynards Castle with the household of the earl of March; send for me if anything threatens that girl."

"Whatever Yer Ladyship desires," the blackguard promised, deftly kissing her hand. "And I will ask no more than a swift horse and a day's start."

"That you shall have for sure," she assured him. What did Black Dick Nixon care if his creditors never got paid? And whatever crimes Nixon had on his conscience probably did not compare to the charges she faced, particularly when it came to lurid penalties. Leaning forward, she patted Lily, telling her, "Good girl, that was a real leap. But we may need to do it again. Be ready to run, and you get another carrot."

Straightening in the saddle, she saw no sense in putting off the unpleasant. She must see to Deirdre, and Matt Davye, who had come to her aid when she needed it. Twice. Waving good-bye to the assembled inmates, she nudged Lily toward the gate, hearing a chorus of groans from heartbroken desperadoes. "Why so soon, m'lady? You are safer with us in Saint Martin's."

"True, too true," she called back, figuring she might need friends in sanctuary. "But I have business without."

Her heart climbed back in her throat as she headed for the gate.

Rank required you to do right, otherwise you were just a genteel parasite, living off the sweat of others. Dame Agnes, a lowly mayor's wife, spent her days letting air and light into the prisons. So how could a countess-to-be see injustice and not act? Her only real regret was not having Edward here with her; his easygoing good humor and sturdy six-foot frame had a soothing effect on folks. Twice she had seen him talk armed and desperate opponents into surrendering, without so much as touching his sword—both times she had been almighty glad to have him at her side. Saying a quiet prayer to Saint Anne, whose day it was, and to Hecate, who had gotten her in this mess, she rode briskly out the sanctuary gate.

Stunned silence greeted her. She saw Dame Agnes standing between Deirdre and the undersheriff—in a heated discussion seconded by armed sergeants and concerned clerics. Still on horseback, Deirdre was saying nothing, holding hard to her saxe knife and playing dumb for the Saxons, letting Dame Agnes do the talking. Matt Davye had disappeared, but the sergeant he tackled was back on his feet, still holding his hideous pole arm. Cheapside shoppers, clerks from Saint Paul's cloisters, and the crowd from Cornhill looked up in surprise as she emerged, her silk headdress high, soft bells jingling on her saddle.

For a long moment folks stared at her, startled by her sudden return. Then cheering erupted, long and loud, spontaneous applause that turned to cries of, "Hay-hay, Hurray! Hay-hay, Hurray!"—growing into a full-throated roar, a standing ovation easily eclipsing the cheers from the men in sanctuary. Her hollow ache vanished, replaced by waves of giddy relief and mounting excitement. London did love her, even above the law. This Saturday crowd of Cheapside shoppers, market women, Saint Paul's clerics, drapers' boys, and drunken sailors sided with her, glad to see Mary in the hands of Mother Church. She had given a surprise ending to the morning's tragedy, a happy miracle that drove the audience wild.

Pressing closer, people patted Lily and plucked at Robyn's gold hem, touching, squeezing, offering up their hands the way they did when the rebel earls first entered the city. Her own love for London's commons welled up, bringing happy tears to her eyes for the first time in this godawful morning. In a weird way these were her people—maybe she was not a medieval, but beneath her silks and satins she was as common as they. From the day she arrived in the Middle

Ages common people had welcomed her, especially women and girls, but men, as well—not knowing she was from the future, just knowing she looked cute and lost. Armed nobles and king's men had hounded and threatened her, but from Sandwich to North Wales, ordinary Britons had been nothing but nice to her, feeding her and sheltering her, standing up to the law when they had to—asking only to hear tales of far-off places, or life at Court, or what young Lord Edward was like in bed. Women called to her, waving their brooms triumphantly from upper-floor windows in honor of Saint Anne.

Buoyed by the applause, she rode happily forward, blissfully grateful. In Hollywood she had been a production assistant, wishing she were a star; here she was on center stage in the theater of the world, and London loved her act. Any objections from the undersheriff were drowned out by the crowd, and the knowledge that she enjoyed the earl of March's "good lordship." Much as she loved the commons, Robyn was thankful rank had its privileges, especially when they rubbed off on her. Reaching down, she touched people's outstretched hands, guiding Lily with her knees through the cheering throng, glad to be so loved, but also anxious to reclaim her maid and saxe knife from a thankful Dame Agnes. She still had a tournament to go to.

2

✦⇒ Smithfield ⇐✦

By noon she was at Smithfield, the big smelly Stocks Market north of the city, surrounded by the chaos preceding a tournament—part pageant, part rodeo-cum-armored prize fight, with rich and famous contestants. Pretty pavilions were going up, and prettier horses were led splashing past her, draped in livery colors. Upholsterers banged away overhead, tacking down carpets and hanging tapestries, turning covered grandstands into plush apartments. She stood in the shade of Edward's striped pavilion at the west end of the lists, dressed as a squire in harlequin hose and doublet, complete with dagger and codpiece, and long leather riding boots with their tops turned down at the knee—all done in Edward's personal colors, murrey and blue. Murrey was a deep purple the third millennium might call mulberry, and Edward's blue was a most royal blue.

Life in the Middle Ages required frequent costume changes—this being the third outfit she had worn this morning. Fourth, if you counted the witch's smock she wore at midnight. Deirdre wore matching page's livery, and they had charge of a beautiful black warhorse, a strong tall Friesian with long, silky fetlocks called Caesar. He, too, wore murrey and blue over his horse armor. Deirdre had a huge grin, almighty glad to have put one over on the Saxons. "Never did I see a burning end so happily."

We aim to please. Horrified at how close things had come to the unthinkable, Robyn still felt dazed and shaken, amazed the rest of the morning could be so relentlessly matter-of-fact, pretending to be a fancy dress stableboy preparing for mock combat. Her heart went out too easily to people in trouble; somehow she had to get more hardened.

All around her, young women were dressed like squires, laughing and joking, wearing Collin's blue and white. Or Wydville white and red. Some even wore bollock daggers between their legs, the knobbed pommels standing up like steel erections. Just another gay day at Smithfield. It was Joanna Grey's idea to come in drag, dressing as squires and helping with the horses. Even a stay in the Tower for witchcraft had not cowed Jo—out barely a week, and back making trouble. Jo's idea caught on with younger "gentlewomen" too high-spirited to just watch from the stands. Stands were for old ladies and married women. The boldest, most athletic young nobles in the kingdom would be competing in the lists—for the honor of Saint Anne and for their ladies' favor. Without a chance to flirt and pet the horses, jousting was just another male blood sport, more dangerous than most, but not intrinsically more interesting.

Not that Robyn came to flirt. She was here to watch over the man she had; being eighteen and the earl of March sometimes made Edward think he was invincible, as well. Shields of intended combatants hung in a line along one side of the lists, so ladies could inspect them and report any unchivalrous acts. Happily, Edward's white lion shield was not among them.

Londoners in bright summer dresses and wool tunics crowded the double-tiered stands, sweating under an uncommon summer sun, laughing, talking, watching the preparations from behind a line of tall palings. Brits could wait patiently for hours, days even, if they had beer at hand. Peace, plus a free show, put this colorful Saint Anne's Day crowd in a holiday mood. Normally people paid to see tournaments, at pretty stiff prices in the penny-ante medieval economy, but today's tournament was free to all, a thank-you to the city of London, put on by the rebel earls as a show of harmony, saying all was right with the realm—now that they had the king.

She liked that it was free. And for peace. If you must bash yourself silly, best to do it for a good cause. And Miss Rodeo Montana knew how to work a bored crowd. She had Deirdre lead the black stallion back and forth, getting him loose and used to the armor. Deirdre did it right, having a colleen's natural sense of drama, waving and showing off the big Friesian—the way any young squire would—friendly but not trying to upstage the horse, letting Caesar be the star. Folks loved it, especially the men, loudly applauding the girl and the horse.

Cheers perked Robyn up, a stimulant stronger than coffee. London had clearly adopted her—not caring if she came from some fairy-tale future—just so long as she brought the city luck and spoke its language. Londoners were not shy about showing their favor, and they cared little for rank—it was ages since the queen dared show herself in the city. Thanks in part to Lady Robyn, Londoners were at last getting a government to their liking—one that lived within its means and let London do business. Mad King Henry's blockades of Ireland and Calais were lifted, legalizing trade with England's overseas possessions, turning smuggling back into jobs. And Londoners liked seeing her wearing the livery of the youngest and handsomest lord on the Royal Council, hoping she spoke for them, particularly across a pillow, "when young Lord Edward is most like to be listening."

But they also burned witches at Smithfield. Here was where Gilbert FitzHolland meant to burn her, had he won that trial-by-combat beneath Sudeley's spreading oaks. Joan of Arc was burned for wearing pants, foretelling the future, and having a pert attitude—all things Robyn was already guilty of, and it was barely noon, 12:03:16 according to the watch on her wrist.

By half past noon the pavilions were up, topped with knights' pennants. Minstrels announced the arrival of the tournament procession with ladies leading their champions on silver chains. Gentlefolk filed in behind the mayor, aldermen, foreign ambassadors, and tournament judges, parading past the common folks taking their places in upholstered galleries shaded by tapestries and facing away from the sun, furnished with wine and sweetmeats to comfort the well born and well married. Stands for the commons were literally that, plain raised platforms to stand on, with only the fickle English weather overhead—not that anyone seemed to care. Londoners were in a mood to cheer their betters, buoyed by retaking the Tower and the return of the king. Most medievals were too well off for charity, but too poor to pay taxes—so cheap, entertaining government was all they hoped for. Women craned their necks to inspect the court silks and satins, glad the fashion show came first. Ladies wore elaborate butterfly headdresses over dazzling bejeweled gowns, while men had on short-cut tunics, and absurdly pointed shoes. Boys hawked flat home brew at a penny a tankard, making the Saturday crowd even happier.

What Robyn craved was coffee. Luckily, she had broken down and brewed a thermosful before leaving Baynards Castle, guessing it would be that sort of day—her prowess as a seeress could be scary.

Actually it was that sort of week. Last Saturday she was a prisoner in the Tower of London along with Joanna Grey, charged with witchcraft and treason. Since then, she had foiled her captors, seen her tormentors tried and condemned, and become secretly betrothed to an earl—all in less than a week. An alarming turn of fortune, no matter how welcome. Topping that off with a tournament required a second cup. Giving Deirdre charge of Caesar, she unscrewed her silver thermos lid, pouring steaming brown coffee into her china cup.

"What witches' brew is that?" asked a friendly familiar voice. Glancing up, she saw Edward standing beside her, as strong and lovely as when she'd left him at first light—only no longer naked. He wore a purple-gold doublet with fashionably slashed sleeves over particolored hose tucked into tall leather boots turned down at the knee, and his long tawny hair hung free to his shoulders, framing a handsome clean-shaven face. Warm brown eyes smiled at her happy surprise.

Worries and fears melted away. Edward was here, cheerful, relaxed—and not in armor, always a good sign. Radiating casual confidence, Edward made everything seem easy and exciting. He had certainly turned her life around—any man able to keep her in the Middle Ages by choice was capable of anything. Edward was smart, caring, and handsome, and his favorite sport was dancing, making him well-nigh irresistible, even if he was born in 1442—giving a whole new meaning to "age difference." He peered at the brown contents of the cup, asking, "Wing of bat, mayhap?"

"Hot café au lait with honey." She offered up her china cup, forgetting she was supposed to be his squire. "Here, try some." Deirdre stayed in character, managing to bow and doff her cap without letting go of the big black charger.

Edward patted Caesar hello, then took the steaming cup from her, and sipped. Many medievals are small, and Robyn had gone from average height, to being tall, taller than many men—but at six feet something, Edward topped her comfortably. His eyes widened, just as Deirdre's had. "Marvelous sweet potion," he declared. "Wing of bat does brighten up the day."

Another addict. Who would have thought that the fifteenth century wanted a caffeine fix? "It is made from beans," she told him. But beans from where? Arabia maybe—like in Arabian blend? "Arabian beans."

"Magic beans from Araby." Edward arched an eyebrow. "Another future fairy story?" She had trouble making people take her claim to be from twenty-first-century America seriously—especially since America was not yet discovered. Clearly she came from somewhere weird, saying outlandish things in various tongues, but most people put polite spins on her fancies, pretending "Holy Wood" was "up near Coventry." Or that America was an island out beyond "Brasil." Which, in a way, it was. Medievals made up for the appalling lack of privacy with artless denial, accepting whatever you said, or inventing something even more far-fetched. Some just thought her a flat-out witch, not caring if she came from Camelot or California, so long as she was burnt. Edward believed her, but teased her seriousness about the fabulous third millennium, where everything was bigger and better. Nothing he had seen or heard of the future impressed him much, and he liked her being here with him, not in some far off wonderland.

"There is nothing future about it," she replied primly. "Bedouins are probably brewing thick black coffee over their camel dung fires at this very moment—and not all that far off." Her horse Lily was part Arab, and the cup in his hand came all the way from China.

"Camel dung?" Edward looked suspiciously into the pearl white cup. "I liked it better when it was wing of bat."

"Never mind. Venetian merchants will know." Venetians were always delighted to talk to her, brightening up as soon as she spoke Italian—like they could not believe their luck. And the Venetians owed them. Mad King Henry's government had taken to shaking down Italian merchants for ready cash, jailing them, and then letting them make bail with loans to the crown—but Edward and Warwick put an end to all such ingenious forms of financing.

He tried another sip, braving bat wings and camel dung to savor the hot sweet stimulation. Used to plain bread and beer for breakfast, Edward took an immediate liking to café au lait. He handed back the cup, letting their fingers touch, saying, "I missed you."

She bet he did. His warm firm touch felt like a static shock, making her catch her breath and setting her skin to tingling. Last night was the first since their betrothal that they did not make love. Couples betrothed on Mary Magdalen's Day need not wait for marriage, or so Edward claimed—being engaged to a teenager was both exciting and exhausting. But last night was Witches Night, and she came late to bed, then was up at cockcrow having her first nervous coffee without him. She took a sip, admitting, "I missed you, too."

And she had been the one with doubts—much to Edward's astonished dismay. Unbeaten in battle and an earl at eighteen, Edward was unused to disappointment, wanting her at his side and in his bed, not just as his lady, but as his countess. She had not even wanted to be in the Middle Ages—but love overcame reason, and here she was, opening for a Smithfield tourney. For political reasons, she wore Stafford red and gold to chapel and kept their betrothal secret. But here at tournament, she could do as she pleased, wearing his colors, even coming in a codpiece—this was very much a young people's tourney, celebrating peace, summer, and the victory of youth.

"Did you, truly?" Edward looked delighted to be missed.

She nodded, taking another sip. On Cornhill she had nearly cried out aloud for Edward, though it might hurt him to know that what she missed was his noble rank and his prowess at persuasion, and his sense of justice—all of which she counted on to set Mary free. But seeing him standing there, so pleased at having been missed, she could not bring herself to blurt out how she made a royal mess out

of the morning, defying the courts and creating a huge commotion—
on the day the rebel earls had picked to celebrate peace, harmony,
and the rule of law. Robyn had nothing against the rule of law, so
long as those she cared about did not suffer for it. What was the use
of having a boyfriend on the Royal Council if every dreary medieval
statute and outdated custom was enforced on you? Still, it was awkward to ask Edward to blandly side with her against the courts,
especially with thousands of curious Londoners looking on, hoping
for some show of romance between the young earl and his "squire."

"Have you heard of the miracle in Cheapside?" Edward asked,
reaching again for her coffee.

Surprised to have him reading her mind, she guiltily gave up the
cup. "What miracle?"

"Sheriffs were taking some poor girl to Tyburn," he told her, "to
be burned. But when they got to Cheapside, Saint Anne herself
swooped down and saved the murderess, magically parting the rope
and sweeping her straight into Saint Martin-le-Grand. A most amazing miracle, right on the streets of London."

She lifted an eyebrow. "Saint Anne herself?"

"Many there saw her." Edward took an enthusiastic sip.

"Indeed." She knew by his innocent tone he was teasing. Normally
Edward never joked about religion, leading a very moral rebellion—
except when it came to her. "Riding a milk-white mare, I suppose?"

"At a gallop they say. How did you know?"

"I was there," she admitted, but he knew that already.

"Truly?" Edward feigned surprise.

"Her name is Mary," she told him. "And she is too young and
small to hurt anyone, making it a ghastly farce." Just thinking about
it sickened her. "I had to do something. And I would have gladly
called for you if I could. Or talked them out of it if they would have
listened. Luckily I can at least ride—so I saved her. You would have,
too, if you could have seen her." Or so she hoped. Edward could be
ridiculously chivalrous, especially toward women, and was remarkably level-headed for a medieval, with a mind all his own—which
came from being young, successful, and sure of himself.

"So Saint Anne had naught to do with it?" he asked in mock
surprise. "Not even miraculously parting the halter rope?"

She shook her head. "Deirdre cut the rope ahead of me, nearly riding down a pair of billmen." Deirdre did another bow, showing her dimples without breaking character or letting go of Caesar's reins.

"Good for her." Edward happily pictured the havoc Robyn and her maid had wreaked on Cheapside. "Would to God I had seen it, but I was away in Westminster when I heard, and no doubt the tale grew in the telling." Not by much. Edward's sources were usually sound, and his intuition excellent—he listened to others almost as intently as he listened to her.

"When you see her, you will know what I mean," Robyn explained. "Mary is timid and sweet, and I could not let them burn her knowing she was innocent."

"How innocent?" Edward asked, taking a slow sip of coffee.

Sort of innocent. Mary had been a prostitute, barely surviving what must have been the medieval childhood from hell. "She says she did not kill anyone." Despite having excellent cause.

Edward arched an eyebrow. "And you do believe her?"

More than she believed the law. "I do. And you would, too."

"This Mary could not convince a court," Edward noted, truly serious now, no longer teasing, but instead trying to figure out just what she had gotten him into. Being betrothed to a witch from the future must not be easy, even for Edward of March, medieval boy wonder—at the moment she was making him choose between her and the law that he had overturned a kingdom to uphold.

"Who knows what chance she got to tell her story?" Robyn had found medieval courts better than she supposed, honest and unimaginative, unless some lord leaned on them to get the verdict he wanted. But at best they were all-male affairs, full of classical references and learned nonsense, followed by unbelievably harsh sentences. However much they might strive to be fair and honest, it was like being tried for your life by a local Elks Lodge speaking pig latin. "She is small, and young, and not likely to be heard in court—sorely needing a champion."

"And it seems Saint Anne found her one. You have taken her out of the courts," he reminded her, "giving her to Mother Church."

"Who should have had her to begin with." One of the nice surprises of the Middle Ages was how the Church stood up for women, being rightly suspicious of men's baser instincts. "You must see Mary to understand."

"Must I?" Edward smiled at her earnestness.

"Absolument!" What was the use of being engaged to a boy earl if you could not order him about?

He handed her back the coffee. "Then I suppose I must."

She was so pleased, she kissed him right there in front of his pavilion and the open lists—which was what Edward and the Londoners in the stands wanted. He felt strong, tender, and exciting all at the same time, wise for his years, but with a fresh sense of wonder, combining the best elements of man and boy. What had John-Amend-All called him? "England's best hope." It said a lot about the Middle Ages that you could hold the hope of England in your arms.

Cheers erupted from the cheap seats, hearty *hip-hip-hoorays* for the pregame show. Londoners were so happy on this sunny Saturday that anything drew applause: trick riding acts, free tournaments, even a young earl necking with his squire. Robyn would have preferred a more private setting, but every so often you had to give men and the public just what they wanted. Love between lords and commoners linked people to the nobility. Edward might be earl of March, and heir to the duke of York, but she was living proof that he was human, as well. When their lips parted she asked, "Will you be riding?"

He nodded thoughtfully. "Mayhap."

Not what she hoped to hear. Moments ago she had shamelessly enjoyed her influence, but now it seemed that some things were not had for a kiss. This was their tourney, celebrating their victory—Mad King Henry gave royal permission, but the bookish monarch would not attend, leaving them free to run things as they wished. Edward could sit safe on the sidelines for once. Was leading the vanguard at Northampton not enough? "Let someone else break a lance for Saint Anne," she suggested. "Mary's mother will understand." It showed how medieval she had become that she nonchalantly discussed the feelings and opinions of long-dead saints with her fiancé.

"No doubt Saint Anne would," Edward admitted. "Mary's mother is most patient and forgiving." Despite being on a first-name basis with the Holy Family, Edward was remarkably rational for a medieval, and he did not enjoy fighting for its own sake—relying instead on his generous good humor to get him out of trouble.

Trumpets sounded, and she turned to see three steel-clad challengers entering through a covered gate at the east end of the lists, riding armored chargers in livery colors. An electric wave went through the crowd as mounting cheers signaled the main event. Trotting the whole length of the saddle-high tilt barrier, the challengers stopped midway to dip their lances to the ladies and to the tournament judges in their tall tapestried gallery. Three men-at-arms were challenging all comers, dedicating their lances to Saint Anne and the peace of the realm, led by Sir Collingwood Grey, champion of the last Westminster Tournament.

Riding a tall gray charger, Sir Collingwood Grey wore shining plate armor and blue-white livery decorated with silver wyverns, the two-legged flying dragon that was Sir Collin's armorial beast. His sallet visor was tipped back, showing dark alert eyes and a broad forehead adorned by a stray black curl; you had to know Collin's face to imagine the spade beard and confident smile hidden by his bevor. His nose was straight and unbroken—a rarity among veteran jousters. Leading his horse and dressed in his livery was his sister, Joanna Grey, who thought up the idea of coming as squires, vowing to lead the parade, wearing blue-white hose, and hiding her long straight black hair in a boy's velvet cap. Robyn saw that tied around Sir Collin's steel sleeve was his lady's favor, a kiwi green Minnie Mouse scarf from Euro Disneyland.

Hers, of course. Collin was Robyn's champion, having fought Gilbert FitzHolland for her freedom under the oaks of Sudeley park, winning the right to stand for her. Though she and Collin were both engaged to others—she to Edward and he to Bryn—in a chivalric sense Collin was her champion, ready to defend her with his body, making him a very handy man to have around. Collin and Jo tied her to the Greys, who stood for her at her betrothal, acting as her surrogate medieval family.

Behind Collin came Sir Anthony Wydville on a beautiful bay draped in Wydville white-and-red. He, too, had his visor tipped back, showing a clean-shaven face with heavy-lidded, sleepy-looking eyes. Sir Anthony was a knight troubadour, pious, athletic, and scholarly, equally skilled with lance and lute. His squire was his sister Anne, fair and unmarried, her golden hair barely contained by her boy's cap. Two more smiling blond Wydville women stood by Sir Anthony's pavilion, his younger sister Margaret and teenage Jacquetta, both dressed as squires in white-and-red hose and both casting sly sidelong glances at Edward, who in two weeks had gone from being their young and handsome enemy to the most eligible bachelor in the kingdom.

Look all you like, but do not touch. Robyn was rightly wary of the Wydvilles and their designs on Edward. Last time she saw these three sisters together was a Witches Night séance in Kenilworth Castle, and all three had danced naked at her coven initiation. Wydville women were witches—at least the ones she had met—and these three were daughters of the duchess of Bedford, the most powerful witch-priestess in England and the sorceress who brought Robyn here from the twenty-first century. Twice. Coming in drag to Smithfield must be fairly tame for them.

Last among the challengers was a plain Midlands squire: Master William Hastings of Burton Hastings, in blue-and-purple livery with a black sleeve flying from his helmet, and an ordinary male attendant. "Who is he wearing the black sleeve?" asked Deirdre, who curtsied more to the House of Lords than to country squires, getting to know Saxon gentry from the top down. Robyn shrugged, being new to the nobility herself. Hastings sounded familiar, like maybe a name from Shakespeare, but it might be because she rode against a girl named Hastings in high school.

"William Hastings is my father's second cousin." Edward took unusual pride in his faint relation to the squire of Burton Hastings. "And he descends from the Mortimers through his mother." Edward, too, descended from the Mortimer earls of March, and through them from the last undisputed king.

"So is he champion of Burton Hastings?" asked Deirdre—the awe in her voice made it plain that the world beyond Wexford was largely terra incognita. Burton Hastings might be big as London. Bigger even, and farther off than Scotland. Thanks to Robyn's stories, West Hollywood was more real to her handmaid than Paris or Rome. "He must be mighty," Deirdre ventured, "if they named the whole city for him."

"Burton Hastings is no big place," Edward cautioned, "and was likely named for his ancestors." He always treated Deirdre like someone with a will and an opinion, and not just because the worshipful young redhead treated him like a mythic prince. Robyn had seen him pay the same patient attention to aged archers who served his father in France. Born outranking nearly everyone, Edward had had to learn to talk to underlings or lead a lonely life; so he took pains to be winning, listening to lesser people's stories and never forgetting a face. "Hastings's father and grandfather fought for my family at Agincourt," he explained, "and William himself has been my gentleman since I was first made earl of March. He was sheriff of Warwickshire, and stood with my father at Ludford—so Hastings has shown bravery, but never been to battle."

"Then he is an untried champion," Deirdre stoutly declared, making Master Hastings sound all the braver for riding alongside proven knights and lords' sons. Being Irish, Deirdre saw romance at every turn and magic in the most mundane armed encounters.

Hearing William Hastings was Edward's man—his blood kin and boyhood retainer—buoyed Robyn a bit. Squire Hastings sounded like the perfect surrogate, giving Edward less excuse to ride. All three challengers were chosen for political reasons, each representing a different faction in the recent civil war. Three weeks before, Edward and the Neville earls had camped the rebel army on this spot after London rose to join them. In a whirlwind campaign, they captured King Henry at Northampton and returned him to London, making this their symbolic return to Smithfield. Declaring peace, then offered up mock combat in place of violence, practically apologizing for the shortness of the two-week campaign and for the briefness of the rain-dampened battle at Northampton, which lasted barely half an hour by Robyn's watch. Any knight who felt he had not gotten enough fighting could take a whack at whatever faction he pleased. England meant to have peace, but Grey, Wydville, and Hastings stood willing to accommodate those still wanting to fight.

Turning away from the judges, the three challengers raised their blunted peace lances and rode on toward the pavilions. As they drew closer, Edward ticked off their histories to Deirdre. "Hastings stood with my father at Ludford, surrendering to the king's mercy and accepting pardon. Sir Anthony Wydville opposed us from the beginning and was taken in a raid on Sandwich, held by us some months in Calais, then paroled. Both took honorable parts, on opposite sides, standing staunch in their opinions through defeat and capture. And neither fought at Northampton."

"So there are no blood feuds to settle." Any thoughtful Irish lass saw the sense in that.

"Exactement!" Edward was teaching Deirdre French, in return for
Gaelic. His father was earl of Ulster and lord lieutenant of Ireland,
but that did not mean Edward spoke the language.

Only Sir Collingwood Grey had been at Northampton, but he,
too, had avoided blood feuds, being notorious for fighting in numerous battles and tourneys without killing anyone "except through
mischance." Collin had killed no one at Northampton, not with his
own hand, having been far too busy arranging his king's defeat. Sir
Collin's uncle, Lord Grey de Ruthyn, commanded King Henry's vanguard at Northampton; and when the rebel vanguard under Edward
reached the king's lines, the Greys changed sides en masse. Collin
helped break down barricades and welcome Edward into King
Henry's fortified camp, spending most of the brief battle keeping his
men from killing the enemy by mistake. He certainly bore no animosity to the comrades he just deserted, who only minutes before
had been in the same army. "Betraying them was bad enough," Collin had explained, "without actually stabbing any in the back." But
Edward did not bother to tell Deirdre this. When Lord Grey de Ruthyn decided to change sides, it was Deirdre who took the message
to Edward, memorized in both English and Gaelic—amply repaying
Edward for always taking her seriously.

Sir Collin trotted up to the mounting steps, did a rattling dismount, and handed his horse over to his sister; then he went clanking
into his blue-and-white-striped pavilion. Men walking in armor
sound like someone sorting pots and pans, searching for her favorite
skillet. Sir Anthony Wydville did the same, vanishing into his red-
and-white pavilion, leaving the three Wydville nymphs in drag to
care for his big bay charger. Master William Hastings had no tent,
but Edward escorted the squire of Burton Hastings into his own
murrey-and-blue pavilion—leaving Robyn and Deirdre to care for
Caesar. Her handmaid giggled happily, saying, "He will ride."

"I hope not." Robyn shook her head. At times Edward took way
too many risks, though he often claimed the same of her.

"Do not worry for him." Deirdre sounded more concerned for her
than for Edward.

"Why not?" She often envied Deirdre's easy uncomplicated relations with Edward, who was far closer to Deirdre in age—both of
them being born in the same century. Deirdre never had doubts or

worries, happily worshiping the young Saxon "prince"—glad to get the big bed when m'lady was away. Pure teenage hero worship, a blissful vicarious relationship with her lady's boyfriend, the only Saxon lord who took her seriously, free of sex, betrothal, or fears for the future.

Deirdre took her hand, squeezing lightly. "Do not worry—he will not die before he does what he was meant to do."

She stared at her earnest young handmaid, asking, "What is that?"

Deirdre laughed, saying, "Why, only he can decide."

Never ask direction from the Irish. Trumpets sounded, and Deirdre dropped her hand to clap as the first contestant entered the lists, a knight wearing the Neville saltire, a big white X on a red field—*gules, a saltire argent*. His visor was up, and Robyn recognized a relative-to-be, Sir Thomas Neville, Edward's first cousin. Edward's mother was a Neville, one of a huge brood of children married into most of the ruling families. Robyn was going right from being an orphan only child to someone with relations in all the right places.

Sir Thomas Neville rode to the center of the lists, dipping his lance to the ladies and judges, then cantering over to where the challengers' shields hung on posts before their pavilions—bright heraldic peace shields, made for blunted lances. Showing more courage than sense, he tapped Sir Collingwood Grey's silver wyvern shield with his lance. Sir Thomas was impetuous; at Blore Heath he pursued the beaten enemy so closely that he himself was captured and missed the subsequent fighting. Now to make up, he rashly started at the top. All today's jousts were *à plaisance*, but Sir Collin had killed more men by accident in tourneys than he ever did in battle. And Collin had been on the losing side at Blore Heath, having had his horse killed under him and getting a ghastly wound of his own, which left him no reason to treat Sir Thomas Neville lightly.

Sir Collin came clanking out of his pavilion, and Jo had his gray charger ready. Collin swung aboard and waited while Jo solemnly brought him a tall blunt peace lance fitted with a three-pronged crown to spread the impact. Handing up the lance, his sister stepped silently back as Collin trotted off to face Thomas Neville before the tournament judges. No longer having a horse to hold, Jo strolled over to stand next to Robyn. Jo Grey had her brother's high forehead, dark eyes, and strong, determined nose, making her look more stern than pretty. Leaning close, Jo whispered, "Will Edward ride?"

What everyone wanted to know. Robyn merely repeated Edward's answer: "Mayhap."

" 'Tis certain." Deirdre felt totally sure of her Saxon prince. Robyn smirked at the teenager's confidence. They were three witches in drag, standing by the Smithfield lists, struggling to predict the future with half of London looking on. None of them was a real seeress. Deirdre was a novice at best, having never done the Witches Flight, not even an initiate—more a witch want-to-be. Jo was a coven leader with eons of experience but scant powers of prediction. Robyn was the only one who saw clearly into the future, unfortunately that future was the distant third millennium—five minutes ahead of her was a total blank.

Finishing flowery speeches about the peace of the realm and the honor of Saint Anne, Collin and the young Neville rode to opposite ends of the saddle-high tilt barrier that ran the length of the lists, keeping the horses from colliding, assuring that only the riders were struck. Medieval animals had few rights, but tournament horses were rigorously protected. Blows against horses were banned, and any harm done them was investigated more immediately and thoroughly than a human wound—men put themselves at risk, but horses were just along for the ride. Tension mounted as the herald called out a chivalric ready, set, go. Seeing Collin's visor go down, Robyn looked over at Jo, who was not the least concerned. Jo must have seen Collin ride in scores of tournaments, winning repeatedly—seeing two men killed in the process. Why start worrying now?

Hearing the herald call a third time, Robyn turned to see the steel-clad horsemen spur their mounts and lower their lances, hurtling toward each other, throwing up wet clouds of Smithfield mud. Meeting with an earsplitting crash. Sir Thomas Neville's lance glanced off to the side, but Collin hit Sir Thomas Neville so hard and squarely, the blow lifted him right out of the saddle, sending him flying through the air to splash down in front of the tournament judges. That's for Blore Heath.

Real squires rushed to see if the Neville was as dead as he looked. Holding her breath, Robyn stared at the suit of armor sprawled in the lists, containing her future cousin-in-law. She thought of the man's mother, frumpy old Countess Alice of Salisbury—in whose household-in-exile Robyn had served. Losing a son like this could kill the broken-down old lady, who had seen her share of trouble already.

Happily, this young Neville bounced up before the squires even got to him, still full of fight. Closing her eyes, she thanked Hecate–Saint Anne whose day remained miraculously unmarred. "May the Mother's mother protect us on this, her day, and preserve our loved ones from peril."

Her eyes opened, and her heart sank. Edward emerged from his murrey-and-blue pavilion in full armor—except for helm and gauntlets—grinning happily, looking just like when she first saw him ride up atop his black warhorse: charming, jovial, and totally lost in twenty-first-century Wales, searching for Llanthony Priory and the Vale of Ewyas. It took the longest time to get him out of that armor, and a lot of their early dates had ended in battles. She seriously hoped those days were behind them—what use was peace if you did not stop fighting?

Seeing her disappointment, he nodded apologetically at the Londoners in the stands, saying, "These good commons did come to see a show."

And a free one, at that. A surprising similarity between medieval England and the third milliennium was that folks paid good money to see millionaires slam into each other—only here they did it on horseback, and added in politics. Contestants were not just rich, but the country's rulers, as well. Collin's uncle was in the House of Lords, as was Sir Anthony's father, and Sir Thomas Neville's father and brother sat on the Royal Council with Edward—yet they all risked their necks to keep the commons happy. Medieval England was not a democracy by any means, but the mood of her people still mattered, and the mood of London mattered most. Just this morning, popular approval had saved Robyn from having to make embarrassing explanations to some constables and an undersheriff. London politics was up close and personal; people knew who ruled them, often by sight, and took up arms when government went awry. Twice in ten years London had risen up, joining rebellions against the crown, so any sane government courted her citizens—hence today's politicking on horseback. By opening her gates to the rebels, London helped elevate Edward from a titled teenager in exile to Royal Councillor. Now Edward intended to return the favor.

Trumpets sounded, and another impetuous Neville entered the list,

Sir Thomas's younger brother, Sir John, also wearing the white Neville saltire. Dipping his lance to the ladies, he went and tapped the red-and-white shield of Sir Anthony Wydville. Escorted to the saddle by his winsome squires, Sir Anthony mounted up and rode out to defend the honor of Saint Anne, dipping his lance to the ladies and then turning to face the Neville. Both young men gripped their shields and spurred their horses, thundering toward each other through the mud. Lances dropped, and the knights came crashing together, sparks flying as each hit the other on the helm. Sir John Neville's helmet went sailing away to bounce down the lists, drawing a gasp from folks craning to see if his head were in it.

Luckily, it was not. Dazed and bleeding from the nose, but with his head still on his shoulders, Robyn's future cousin-in-law saluted smartly with his lance and then trotted back out the far gate while Sir Anthony was welcomed down from the saddle by the Wydville sisters. Beaten by the Nevilles at Blore Heath and Northampton, the loyalists had at least got to see a couple of cocky young Nevilles unhorsed and unhelmed. Edward was next.

She had to hope he knew what he was doing, since there was no chance of talking him out of it. Behind Edward's youthful joie de vivre lurked a boy's stubborness in a man's body. And he was born to knighthood in an England with no army, no bobbies, no MI5, no Scotland Yard—just an armed populace and an armored nobility. He had fought pitched battles since he was thirteen, killing men with edged steel. She had seen him do it, too, on the first day they met. Shocking, and then some. Yet she never suffered a speck of harm when she was with Edward—though they had been through battles and sea fights together. And she had been hounded, starved, and nearly torn limb from limb when they were apart—so Robyn found it hard to hold his martial skill against him, especially when he had such a just cause and engaging smile.

Holding Caesar steady while Edward mounted, she was at the starting gate for the second time today—only this time she was not riding, which actually made it worse. Robyn whispered to the black charger that all would be well, telling him to heed his master. Calm excitement shone in Caesar's dark luminous eyes. Caesar was a warhorse and had done this innumerable times, enjoying jousting as much as the boy on his back did—Edward would not be riding him otherwise. At Northampton, Edward fought on foot—never liking to risk his horse. But on the day they first met, Robyn saw Edward and Caesar turn to meet three mounted pursuers. With sharpened weapons and no tilt barrier to separate the horses, Caesar not only bore Edward into battle but attacked an opponent's mount, as well, like a king stallion battling a rival with teeth bared and steel-shod hooves flailing. Mock combat in the Smithfield mud did not much frighten Caesar.

When Edward was ahorsed, Deirdre handed up his helm and white lion shield, then ran to fetch his lance. Letting go of the bridle, Robyn helped him slip the heavy steel gauntlets onto his hands, savoring the feel of his bare flesh under her fingers, willing him to come swiftly back. Sensing her worry, he leaned down to whisper, "Witches are not the only ones needing to show courage."

Too true. Bold boys in armor could risk their lives for peace and the honor of Hecate and Saint Anne. Nor could she complain, not even in her heart—she needed his support in her own mad escapades as much as he needed hers. Maybe more. And by now she was witch enough to know that sending your man off to fight with pleas and weeping was the worst possible omen.

Squeezing his hand and returning his smile, she whispered, "Break your neck, and I will never forgive you." Deirdre returned with his lance, and then he was gone, trotting happily off to salute the judges. Hecate help him.

Londoners in the stands roared their delight as Edward entered the lists; a belted earl and national hero not on the official program made their free show even more of a bargain. Edward had pulled off yet another crowd-pleasing surprise, using Hastings as his stalking horse to stand in his stead, and giving him an excuse to pitch his pavilion. Politics here and now demanded a dramatic flair, which Edward had aplenty, and he courted the citizens of London as boldly and earnestly as he had courted Robyn—leaving her to forlornly remind herself that his reasons for riding into peril were the reasons she loved him. What she most admired was not Edward's wealth or charm, but his willingness to risk this pampered existence to make medieval England a better place, and not just for the nobility.

"Are you worried?" Jo had come up silently as the cheering subsided.

"Naturally." She nodded, still staring at Edward's armored back. "Scared and then some."

Jo smiled at third millennium idiom. "Naturally" did not apply to Jo, a well-born witch-priestess, coven leader, and medieval unwed mother with a baron for an uncle and a knight for a brother. Unconcerned with social standing, Jo was consumed by spellcraft and raising her difficult bastard daughter. "Do not worry," Jo told her. "He is in Hecate's hands. And there has been a miracle already this Saint Anne's Day."

"Really?" Robyn glanced at Jo.

"Seen this very morning by a great multitude in Cheapside," Jo declared. For a world without newspapers or CNN, word spread like lightning, at least in London.

Robyn told Jo all about her wild ride through the Cheapside throng into Saint Martin-le-Grand, dodging pole arms and Saturday shoppers. Deirdre chimed in with details, cheerfully reliving the mad adventure. Setting Saxon law on its ear was an outstanding lark to her.

"Very exciting." Jo smiled primly. Collin's sister much preferred Witches Flights, being born for the broom and not the saddle—still, Jo approved the impulse, kissing them both and saying, "You did well. Wonderfully well."

It was not like Robyn had much choice—no more than she did now, as she watched Edward rein in before the ladies in the stands, giving his lance a dip to them, then to the tournament judges. Titled ladies and merchants' wives threw summer flowers down to him, waving scarves and handkerchiefs, happily offering up their favors to London's new champion. If London's opinion mattered a lot, then these were the women who made up the city's mind. Male society was weirdly truncated, since the richest, most powerful men in London had to scrape and bow before an insane king, and take orders from uppity titled teenagers like Edward. With true political power out of people's grasp, public opinion was the only real check on government. London opened her gates to the rebels not because the city fathers were won over to Edward's cause—mayors and aldermen made lukewarm rebels at best—but because London's citizens liked the look of this respectful, God-fearing rebellion led by brash handsome young nobles promising justice tempered by mercy. Had the women of London feared and opposed the rebels, Edward and Warwick would never have gotten into the city, not even with twenty thousand bowmen at their back and King Henry himself at their head.

Trumpets returned Edward's salute, announcing his entry into the lists. Turning Caesar about, Edward came rattling back toward the pavilions, his lance raised high, with half of London looking on and wondering which challenger he would pick. What shield would his lance strike?

Robyn tried to guess along with the rest. Certainly not Master Hastings—Edward's own man—the crowd would see that as a serious shuck. Fighting your squire with blunted lances was not exactly courting death. Sir Anthony Wydville made a much better target. Not that she wished Sir Anthony ill—the young knight troubadour once stood between her and a pack of witch hunters—but Edward had scores to settle with the Wydvilles. Twice the Wydville witches tried to lay hold of him, first by casting a Displacement Spell sending him to twenty-first-century Wales, then by bringing Robyn to this backward time as bait with which to trap him—even though Edward chivalrously released Duchess Wydville and paroled Sir Anthony when they were taken by the rebels at Sandwich.

But it was Collin's wyvern shield Edward struck with his lance, setting the metal ringing and bringing an answering cheer from the stands—like everything Edward had done since entering London, challenging Collin was immediately popular. Continuing his grudge match with the Wydvilles would have been too easy; he had beaten them in battle, why best them in mock combat, as well? Sir Collingwood Grey was the reigning Westminster Champion, and the man who treacherously welcomed Edward into Mad King Henry's fortified camp. The fight between the vanguard champions that did not happen at Northampton would be restaged at Smithfield—Lord Grey de Ruthyn's nephew versus the duke of York's son—risking their privileged necks to entertain plain beer-swilling Britons. London cheered lustily.

When Collin emerged from his blue-white pavilion, cheers got even louder, and louder yet when he was ahorsed and Jo handed up his lance, shield, and sallet-helm. Heartsick, Robyn stood, watching, in her silly murrey-and-blue squire's outfit as her betrothed and her champion turned armored backs to her and rode toward the tall tapestried stands, where they dipped their lances to the ladies in the

carpeted luxury boxes. Women smiled and applauded in reply, leaning excitedly forward to wave hankies and show their cleavage.
Jousting was one of the most female-friendly contact sports—pro
football might be played for couch potatoes, but tournaments were
put on to impress the fair sex. In "olden days," damsels happily gave
it up for tournament winners, publicly offering themselves as prizes.
First prize, to be precise. That was jousting at its most scandalous,
giving women the illicit thrill of seeing well-heeled young gentlemen
hack at each other with edged weapons just to spend a night in bed
with them. Heady stuff, and naturally banned by the Church.

Robyn was not the least thrilled to see the two men dearest to her
facing off on horseback. Thank God it was not over her. They were
doing it for Saint Anne, flirting with the death crone to win her favor.
After trotting to opposite ends of the lists, they turned to face each
other, lances high. Tension silenced the Londoners in the stands as
heralds sounded the call. Ready . . . Set . . .

. . . Feeling a bare cool hand in hers, she looked down. It was
Deirdre's. "Let them go," intoned the heralds, "in the name of God."
Everything here and now was done in God's name: the good, the
bad, and the merely idiotic.

Edward and Collin spurred their chargers, going from trot, to can-
ter, to gallop, a ton of flesh and steel hurtling together. Her hand
tightened around Deirdre's, drawing strength from the teenager's
touch—whatever happened, Deirdre would be with her. The girl had
literally nowhere else to go. Halfway down the tilt barrier, the two
men in her life met with a horrific metallic crash, both leaning into
the blow, hitting the other square on the shield.

Lances exploded from the impact, sending splinters whirling
through the air. Light tournament lances broke more easily than
heavy war lances, and more spectacularly—a nod toward showman-
ship, showing medievals were already into special effects. Both men
swayed in the saddle, but stayed upright, clutching the butt ends of
their broken lances, momentum carrying them to opposite ends of
the lists.

Edward came right to her, visor back, flushed and exultant. His
white lion shield was brightly scarred by Collin's lance, and Edward
triumphantly held his own shattered stump, ridiculously pleased to
survive his first pass at Sir Collingwood Grey—Westminster Cham-

pion and one of his boyhood heroes. Brown eyes shone with delight. "Held him, by Heaven! Did you see?"

Of course she saw; so had half of London. But it was against the rules to offer advice to contestants—even a simple "Get down, nitwit, before you get spitted" was frowned on. All she could do was return his crazed smile, hoping that was encouragement enough.

"You did, Your Highness! You did!" Deirdre answered for her, dropping her hand and doing a swift little bow, then running to get another lance from spares leaning against the palings—leaving Robyn alone for a moment with Edward. She gave him her best Miss Rodeo Montana grin.

"I held him!" He happily repeated himself, as elated as a young bronc rider who barely believed he stayed on the horse. "I held him, did I not?"

She bobbed her head, sticking with her witless grin, wishing she could say, "Wonderful! Quit while you are ahead!" Now she knew how her high school boyfriends felt, watching her risk her neck barrel racing for bits of ribbon. One boy dumped her when she broke her leg and would not promise to give up riding. He said he would look silly going to the prom with his date on crutches. She never sympathized with him until now.

Collin cantered up, and Jo met him with a new lance. Feeling upstaged, Robyn ran to get Edward's replacement lance from Deirdre, meeting her serving girl halfway, momentarily relaxing her superglued smile. Luckily, ladies did not have to be heroines to their handmaids, or who would catch them when they fainted? Returning to Edward, she handed up the fresh lance with a heartfelt "Here my love, hurry back—and try not to hurt him."

Edward hefted the new shaft, gleefully returning her smile. Why not? Her handsome idiot was living a teenager's dream: he was a real, honest-to-goodness knight in armor sparring on horseback against a famous champion in front of an adoring crowd, while his shapely squire brought him fresh lances. Any boy unable to enjoy that was dead to the world. Closing his visor, Edward trotted off to meet Collin again.

Robyn was left clutching the butt end of a broken lance. She looked over at Jo, who held another shattered lance, and wondered what Collin's sister could possibly be thinking. Jo gave her a grave look, worthy of a coven leader, though at the moment the witch-priestess wore a boy's doublet with a bollock knife between her blue-and-white harlequin legs: an especially jarring ensemble since Jo in drag was the very image of Collin. Smaller for sure, and without the beard—but otherwise a younger, softer Sir Collin, backed by a howling Smithfield mob. When Robyn first arrived in the Middle Ages, she was Jo's confidante and companion, sleeping in Jo's big canopy bed because she did not rate a room of her own. Yet Jo was utterly dependent on brother Collin for shelter and protection. Jo's own noble lover, Edmund Beaufort, duke of Somerset, was killed at Saint Albans—some would say assassinated—in a trap sprung by Earl Warwick and Edward's father, leaving Jo to raise her bastard daughter alone. Yet Jo never displayed the least animosity toward Edward, which showed how contrary witches could be.

Edward rode to the far end of the lists and then turned to face Collin again. Crowd noises quieted as both men waited atop their chargers, lances cocked, faces masked in steel, listening for the herald's call. Then in the name of God and Saint Anne, her errant champions galloped at each other, coming together in another awesome crash.

Again Edward's lance shattered, sending the better part of the shaft cartwheeling into the stands. Collin's lance held, hitting Edward square in the middle of his white lion shield and bowing from the impact. Both men were lifted out of their tall saddles. Collin managed to keep his seat, leaning hard against his lance, forcing Edward to absorb the blow.

Thrown backwards, Edward broke through the back of his saddle, slamming onto his mount's armored crupper, taking Caesar down with him. Mount and man staggered backwards, borne down by Collin's lance, until Caesar's rump crashed into the tilt barrier, tossing Edward clear. Flung through the air, he banged off the broken tilt barrier, landing facefirst on the wet ground in front of the stands, still clutching his broken lance stub. Mud rained down around him, but Edward did not move. Caesar righted himself and trotted straight to the mounting block and stopped, his breath coming in sharp snorts, his saddle empty.

Robyn's booted feet were in motion before she realized she was running. Glad not to be wearing a long trailing gown and headdress, she sprinted across fifty yards of soggy tilting field, the mud pulling

at her leather riding boots. It took her forever to get to Edward—
who still lay facedown in the muck, surrounded by summer flowers
tossed to him minutes ago by admiring ladies. He had hit hard, slamming into the ground, and had not stirred since. Steel plate was so
heavy that fallen knights often smothered in their armor, or drowned
in the mud. At Northampton, more men-at-arms died trying to swim
the swollen Nene than were killed in combat. Edward's own grand-
uncle had died facedown in the wet plowed ground at Agincourt,
and now the Hope of England lay motionless in the Smithfield mud.

Dropping to her knees beside him, Robyn fumbled with the strap
on his sallet helm, desperate to see his face, to make sure he was
breathing. All around her, stands that had been raucous were hushed.
London's hero had fallen, dashing the holiday mood. Ladies stared
down from tapestried boxes, their silk hankies still, all set to cry their
eyes out over her loss—while she knelt in the mud in a squire's gaudy
doublet and particolored hose, tugging at the wet helm strap with
its old-fashioned hand-forged buckle. Still no movement from Edward amid the mud and flower petals—not far away lay a lady's
garter thrown by some enthusiastic fan when he entered the list.

Jerking frantically at the slick sodden strap, she managed to free
the buckle and lift off his sallet. Light brown hair spilled out, wet
with sweat. She tossed the sallet away and brushed aside his hair,
happy to see no blood or bruises. But she could not tell if he was
breathing, and his armor made it impossible to get a pulse or heart-
beat. She kept thinking about how Collin had killed two men at
tourneys—by accident.

With the strength of desperation, she rolled his dented armor-clad
torso over, dug mud out of his mouth, and began CPR. Chest com-
pression was impossible through his muddy breastplate, but
mouth-to-mouth was what mattered most. Her 4-H lifesaving training took over. Miss Rodeo Montana must be prepared for every
emergency—anytime, anywhere. Filling her lungs with air, she leaned
down and tried to breathe life back into Edward. One lungful, then
another.

Nothing. Half of London held its breath, watching her every
movement, wondering what became of the newly proclaimed peace
if Sir Collingwood Grey had just killed the heir to the duke of York.
Robyn alone cared for Edward himself, not for England's hope or
York's heir, but for her sweet hurt love, without whom she was lost,

marooned forever in a medieval nightmare. This was why she so feared today's tournament; she had known in her heart something horrible would happen. Tilting his head back to clear the air passages, Robyn tried again, breathing deep into him. Still nothing.

Hecate help me, she prayed, please do not take him, for I do need him so. Tears welled up, wetting her eyes and catching in her throat, making it hard to breathe for herself, much less for two. Stifling her sobs, she refused to give in to despair, taking another deep breath, then giving it to him.

Heralds in royal livery stepped up, wearing worried looks, like stern-faced jokers from an old-fashioned poker deck. One asked in medieval French what she was doing, implying that squires giving their lords mouth-to-mouth in the middle of the lists was clean against tournament rules. She waved them away with tears in her eyes. Had she been a real squire, they might have tried stopping her, but even king's heralds knew not to disturb a white witch at work.

She leaned down again, tears splashing onto Edward's cheeks. Her fingers dug under his armor, feeling a pulse in his throat. Thank Heavens, he was alive. Trying to fan that fire, she gave him another deep lungful of air, feeling him stir beneath her. Hallelujah! Gulping more air, she bent down, breathing harder into his mouth.

This time he breathed back, expelling her air, then drawing in some on his own. She sat up and waited, breasts heaving, anxiously searching him for signs of consciousness. Folks in the stands groaned, thinking she had given up.

Edward's brown eyes flicked open. He stared up at her for a moment; then his lips curled into a smile. "My lady knows how to bring a man back to life."

Tears of relief streamed down her cheeks as she gratefully cradled his head in her lap, calling him a "godawful fool" and "totally witless idiot."

He grinned up at her, listening attentively until she finished berating him, then asking, "In truth?"

"Only sometimes," she admitted, drying her tears with her dirty palm, ashamed for letting her fear run away with her. Cheers erupted from happy Londoners, seeing Edward speaking and smiling, ecstatic that their young hero had not made the ultimate sacrifice for Saint Anne. Jubilant just to have him alive, Robyn realized she had run through Edward's faults before checking for injuries, showing horribly sloppy bedside manner. She asked, "Are you hurt?"

"Just my pride." Edward put a steel arm under himself and started to push up, struggling to rise, having small practice in picking himself up off the ground. "Naught else seems broken."

She helped him sit, getting thunderous applause from people rejoicing to just see Edward upright. Hankies fluttered in the luxury boxes. Overjoyed to be holding him, feeling for herself that he was not badly hurt, Robyn remembered Jo saying, "The place to see a tournament is from the lists." Trust a witch to know. Bad as this was, it would have been far worse sitting on embroidered cushions in some upholstered box, watching another woman breathe life back into Edward, then tearfully waving her nose-wipe in thanksgiving. She would not have traded places with any woman in the boxes above her, not for a duchy and ten thousand pounds a year.

Helping him stand brought still more cheers, until the lists rang with joyous relief. Sir Collingwood Grey, Westminster Champion and winner of the joust was forgotten—all the cheers were for Edward. And for her, for racing to his side and breathing life back into him, while the people behind the palings could only watch helplessly, expecting the worst but seeing another Saint Anne's Day miracle instead. She steadied Edward on his feet, then let go, settling back into character, no longer the white witch, back to being the dutiful squire. Edward was not going to ride again today, leaving naught to do but limp gracefully off. Which Edward did, drawing more delighted cheers, as though he had thumped Collin handily instead of getting knocked facefirst into the muck. Stamping feet shook the stands as commons chanted Edward's title, "March, March, March, March . . ." Suppressing the urge to do a quick victory dance herself, Robyn solemnly collected the shattered lance butt, tuning out the applause and playing the part of a dirty-faced squire whose knight had just been trounced. Out the corner of her eye she saw Deirdre taking charge of Caesar.

Cousin Hastings came clanking up to meet them, a big bluff Midlands squire, clean-cut and darkly handsome, easily ten years older than Edward—yet he had been Edward's "gentleman" since Edward was a boy. Taking advantage of their tournament roles, Hastings flashed Robyn a smile, accompanied by a friendly pat on the butt, the sort meant to buck up a young squire after a lost joust. And at the same time he signaled playful male appreciation for the actress beneath the outfit. Hastings knew how to do it, bold but perfectly in the moment, showing interest without being lewd or obvious. Half of London saw him do it, but not Edward.

Robyn studiously did not react. Master Hastings of Burton Hastings was plainly bound for better things—if he was not beheaded for presumption first—but she had not come to flirt. Following Edward into the pavilion, she turned and shut the tent fly, tying it closed in Hastings's face, tired of living life on display. This striped windowless tent was about as private as you could get smack in the midst of a major athletic event. It had a clothes chest and an arming stand to hold Edward's armor when he was not in it, and various edged weapons were strewn on the carpeted floor to create a lived-in look. Helping him out of his armor, she loosened buckles and untied "points" he could not reach, feeling for breaks and bruises—three months in the Middle Ages had made her moderately adept at getting men out of their armor. His limbs were sound, but she could tell by his wincing and startled yelps that a couple of ribs were broken. She cooed in sympathy, "Did that hurt, dear? How about here?"

"Mercy, my lady!" Edward grimaced as she probed his ribs. "I did you no harm."

"So, you say." She had been scared silly seeing him fall and not get up. Rolling down his wool hose, she discovered a long ugly bruise on his hip, which explained the limp. That and the bent ribs were the worst of it, plus a possible concussion, along with minor cuts and abrasions, mainly from his own armor. She hated seeing his beautiful body banged and bruised, even in sport—actually in a calculated attempt to win over the London commons, giving new meaning to "the body politic." What a weird world this was, where leaders had to lead with their bodies, performing for the public and leading their men into battle. Strange, though somehow just. Luckily, Edward was young, strong, and likely to heal quickly. Rather than leave him to medieval medicine, she insisted on bandaging his ribs and putting antibiotic ointment on the cuts and bruises—kissing each wound to make it heal quicker.

Edward liked that. Acting frightfully healthy for someone who had lain at death's door, he tried to turn serious medicine into playing doctor, reaching under her doublet to undo her laces and roll down her hose, as well, asking, "Did you truly hate the tourney?"

"Only when you were riding." She twisted her hips to keep his hands off her hose laces. She was glad to see him showing every sign of a swift recovery, but just a thin layer of murrey and blue separated them from thousands of spectators—most of whom happily imagined the worst of her already.

"Yet you did smile and wish me luck," he reminded her.

"Women can be deceitful," she warned, secretly pleased to find him so healthy. Aside from his rolled-down hose, all he had on was his shirt and arming doublet—a padded cotton affair with chain-mail patches trimmed by cords for tying on his armor—which she had shoved up over his shoulder to bare his muscled chest and bandaged ribs. *Très* chic. And the earthy smell of sweat and leather was surprisingly exciting. When she was done doctoring, Edward claimed a kiss from the nurse.

She gratefully gave it to him, using this delightful interlude of tongue-tilting to reach behind her back, undoing the ties to the tent door. Soon as their lips parted, she slid his hands off her doublet, then slipped out to rejoin Deirdre, leaving him to get dressed. Or greet his public in a shirt and arming doublet with his hose about his knees. "Is he well?" Deirdre looked worried for her Saxon prince.

"Too well," Robyn replied, rolling her eyes. Deirdre understood, grinning in delight. Robyn, too, relaxed, thanking Hecate the tournament was over—at least for Edward. Collin could still be challenged by some especially suicidal contestant; but Sir Collingwood Grey could take care of himself. Sipping honeyed café au lait from her thermos, she watched folks have a grand time banging into one another on horseback or wildly cheering those fools who did. All her fears and tears were for naught, just part of the Saturday matinee show in the medieval theater of the world.

Edward emerged, wearing his fashionable purple-gold outfit with slashed sleeves and particolored hose, happy as if he had won the joust. Or as if she had given in. Seeing his delight, she actually felt guilty for not having quick hot sex in the tournament pavilion. How many chances did you get to do that? But she could tell he would have liked it a lot, and would no doubt end up dragging her to every two-bit tourney that came along, just to make sweaty love in his pavilion. Better save it for bed.

Rain returned, drowning the remainder of the tourney, but by then the rebel earls had made their point—England's fighting nobility could win more honor and renown jousting for pleasure than trying to put Queen Margarett and her corrupt court back in power. If Nevilles must ride against Percys, then do it on the tilting field where commons would pay to watch. When the skies opened up, contestants stopped coming, and the stands emptied, sending most folks heading for London through the mud. Riding back to Baynards Castle, she saw Cock Lane doing a brisk business, offering drunk happy men haven from the storm. She wondered how many girls like Mary lived there, abandoned by both city and Church—one less at least, thanks to her. Women had their victories, as true as any won by a Westminster Champion.

It was a wet vespers at Saint Martin-le-Grand when Robyn arrived, wearing a sodden cloak over a somewhat dry gown, blue and white, and trimmed in silver to honor Collin's victory. Her umpteenth costume change today, but Collin had worn her Minnie Mouse favor while knocking more men into the mud than anyone else at the tourney—and that deserved recognition. Edward wore purple and blue, beneath a gold cloak embroidered with white roses. They were a study in contrasts; her silver, his gold, Collin's BMW colors, and Edward's deep royal blue and purple. Robert Stillington, dean of Saint Martin-le-Grand, met them at the church door, showing them to Mary's simple cell, with its straw mattress, washstand, and tiny window. Delighted to see her rescuer return, Mary pushed dirty hair out of her teary brown eyes, barely paying attention to the two men, though one was dean of Saint Martin's and the other earl of March. By now men must have seemed a dead loss to Mary, no matter how exalted their stations—the girl rightly guessed Lady Robyn to be her best hope.

Unable to conceive of a female he could not charm, Edward worked to put Mary at ease, sending away fussy old Dean Stillington and going down on one knee to talk to the girl, who looked half-grown beside his six-foot frame. These two contrasting medieval teenagers might as well have come from different planets. Edward had practically a royal upbringing, with French tutors and fencing practice, while Mary had seen her mother die and then been pimped by her stepfather, getting her tutoring from Cock Lane. Curiously, the one thing they had in common was that both of them had been condemned to die miserable humiliating deaths by Mad King Henry's government—showing the haphazard nature of insane tyranny.

Looking like a prince out of faerie, draped in his shining gold cloak and white roses, Edward coaxed the tiny bedraggled girl into telling a halting story. Mary claimed to have harmed no one, least of all her stepfather, whom the girl still greatly feared. "He is big and wrathful, and wants to be obeyed." Mary seemed amazed that people thought she might have hurt him, or opposed him in anything. "It was hard enough merely to please him."

Robyn hastened to reassure the girl, pointing out, "He is dead and gone now."

Mary shrugged and looked into her lap, her hair falling down to hide her face. "Mayhap."

"How did he die?" Edward asked gently, prodding the girl to tell her side. Had he been callous toward Mary, Robyn could hardly have forgiven him, but Edward immediately sympathized, horrified that this could happen in "his" England.

Mary shook her head in amazement. " 'Tis a mystery much beyond me. So miraculous I can hardly think it true."

"Do you mean he is not dead?" Robyn still hoped the whole thing might somehow turn out to be a ghastly misunderstanding. Just like modern-day courts, Medieval justice was prone to whopping blunders. "Why did the court think you killed him?"

Mary gave a how-should-I-know shrug, eyes downcast. Clearly the court's motives and conclusions were far beyond her ken. "He may be dead," Mary admitted, looking deep into her lap. "But not gone. When a man is that bad, Heaven will not have him, and even the Devil is loath to let him in. Or so he often told me, saying, Hell itself had no pit fit to hold him." Too mean to die, and not ashamed to say it. No wonder Mary paid scant attention to her trial, barely counting the victim deceased. Seeing he would get no sensible answers, Edward settled for soothing the girl, asking how she was treated. Mary brightened at once, saying she had this wonderful cell all to herself, plus two hot meals each day that she did not have to beg or put out for. "And whenever the bells toll, nuns show me the proper way to pray, something I sorely missed. Here I feel safe, safer even than in Newgate jail."

Being whisked into sanctuary was plainly the best thing that had ever happened to Mary, who was not the least concerned with clearing her name. When you wake up at dawn, expecting to be burned alive before noon, facing a future of free meals and frequent prayer must be Heaven—and forty days had to seem like forever. Edward smiled at her enthusiasm, saying he would see they cared for her. "Should you want for anything, tell the monks to send me word."

Mary looked up, bewildered past speaking by such amazing good fortune. Despite having been intimate with a host of men, she acted painfully shy when faced with a handsome young nobleman near to her own age, wishing only to do her favors. Entertaining boat crews on holiday did not prepare her for offhanded chivalry from Edward of March. Robyn took the tongue-tied girl's hand, thanking Edward for her, having far more experience at being indebted to ardent young nobles.

Leaving Mary luxuriating in solitary confinement, they bade goodbye to the dean of Saint Martin's, who sat on the Royal Council with Edward. Dean Stillington complained that though King Henry praised him for "great cunning, virtues, and priestly demeaning" in more than ten years he had not gotten a single penny of the forty pounds a year due to a Royal Councillor. It was typical of Mad King Henry's government that it gave away rich titles and vast lands, but could not pay his royal councillors their forty quid. Edward vowed to change that, greatly pleasing the dean of Saint Martin-le-Grand, who promised to watch over Edward's wayward murderess.

Beneath the dripping church eaves, Robyn paused before plunging into the deluge, where wet horses waited to take them back to Baynards Castle. Edward offered her part of his cloak, saying, "I held him, did I not?"

"Held who?" Her mind was still on Mary and Saint Martin-le-Grand.

"Sir Collingwood Grey," he replied happily, pulling her closer to him. "I held him on the first pass."

"Yes, you did," she admitted, liking his strong arm around her, knowing there were advantages to having a boyfriend who could break lances with the reigning Westminster Champion, especially in this day and age. Last time they were alone was that kiss in the pavilion, and from the firm way he grasped her, she could guess what her next costume change would be—if Edward had his way. He clearly could not wait to strip Collin's colors off her and get one up on her champion. But they were in a church, a house of God, a sanctuary crowded with priests, nuns, political renegades, and common cutthroats, so his hormones would have to wait—though not for long. Mary might not know what to make of Edward, but Robyn did.

Black Dick Nixon was waiting with the horses, bowing to Edward, but giving her a wink as he did. Every felon in Christendom seemed to want to be her friend. Riding home through the rain, people applauded them from doorways and upper windows. Women curtsied to him and called out blessings to her, thanking Lady Robyn for saving London's young hero. Any that still thought of her as Lord Edward's "pretty strumpet" wisely kept it to themselves.

Back at Baynards Castle, light and music poured out of the main hall, reminding her they still had a tourney to celebrate. What a day, and not yet dusk. Feeling like Cinderella coming late to the ball, she fled to her tower room to change out of her wet dress. She entered the celebration in a wide green gown sprinkled with gold fleurs-de-lis, with a matching jacket—summer colors picked to go with Edward's white and gold. Edward's parties were light, happy evenings full of music and merriment, not your usual medieval eating contests with tainted meat. With tables pushed back, dancers whirled beneath battle flags hanging from the tall hammer-beam ceiling, stopping every so often to sip spiced wine, and be entertained by fools and tumblers. Stiff halberdiers stood guard over a fancy buffet laid out along one wall to avail the hungry: minced chicken in green ginger with herb sauce, sugared wafers, date compote, and lamb *en croûte* decorated with angels. When the time came for guests to leave, small boys in rich apparel sweetly sang them out the door.

If you did not count the sewers, cooks, musicians, and grooms they were alone at last. Edward smiled across the empty space, arching an eyebrow to say, "Shall we?"

She nodded in agreement, thinking it had been a long rainy summer's day, and they had hardly been alone, unless you counted the near tryst in his arming tent. But they could not just slip off—everyone gathered at the foot of the stairs, and the boys choir sang them up the steps. In the last month these people's lives had changed drastically. Baynards Castle had been closed down, "in the king's hands," and most of them were unemployed, or serving a lord-in-exile, or on the run themselves, facing a rainy summer and a worse winter. Then in one swift stroke, Edward and the Nevilles landed at Sandwich, rallied Kent and London, and took the king at Northampton, miraculously ending the fighting—turning these people's lives around, giving them jobs and a place to winter. Well worth a song at eventide.

Edward's bedchamber was far bigger than hers, with thick warm carpets and tall sculpted stone windows instead of narrow firingslits. And it could have been half hers. She could have shared Edward's apartments, and had men in Yorkist livery seeing to her every need—but she wanted a room of her own, to share with Deirdre. Some nights, anyway. Tonight Deirdre was going to get the big bed once again. Diligently seeing to her love's wounds, Robyn got out clean bandages and put on more antibiotic, making him promise to take a bath. Hot water was already on order. Stripped to his shirt and bandages, Edward wanted to start right where they left off in the Smithfield pavilion. "After the bath," she insisted, "I will not bed any boy fresh from rolling about in the Smithfield mud."

While servants filled the big tub in Edward's presence chamber, she lounged beside her lord on the curtained bed, still in her green-gold ball gown. These private times were her favorites, when they could be alone together, joking and talking, going over the day's events, and planning their future—just her and him, without Edward's numerous retainers, troops, and relations. Not even dear crazy Deirdre. Robyn took this peaceful moment while the bath was filling to check Edward's head for signs of concussion, still pleading Mary's case. "You can see how innocent she is; no true court would convict her."

"Is that what you want?" Edward asked, drawing her body closer and starting to undo the gold buttons on her dress sleeve. "An honest trial before honest judges?"

Good question. Medieval courts were easy to dismiss, being all male monstrosities, with shifty lawyers spouting bad Latin at bigoted judges, but what did she plan to replace them with? Twelve good women and true? Hardly likely. She did not feel up to reforming the medieval judicial system. "Not really. Though it might have to do."

Truth is, she did not trust the courts. What she wanted was for Edward to make this go away. He could, too. Mad King Henry had given up governing to friends and relations, who corrupted the courts by intimidating juries, passing absurd laws, fining those who disobeyed, and presiding over bogus "treason" trials to profit off their victims. Naturally one of the most popular parts of the rebel program was an end to favoritism and blatant injustice. But what she needed was blatant old-fashioned favoritism. She just did not know how to phrase it.

"Thanks to you, she is in sanctuary," Edward noted, still working on her buttons; she had dozens on her sleeves alone, giving the boy a ways to go. "Exile is now the worst she can expect."

All in sanctuary could confess their crimes and leave the kingdom, being escorted by a constable to the nearest port and taking whatever ship they found. If no ship was sailing, felons had to walk into the sea up to the knees and cry, "Passage, for the love of God and good King Henry!" once a day until a ship took them away.

"That would hardly work for Mary." She had seen that, too, at Sandwich, a man in shirt and trousers standing under guard in the surf—probably the happiest man in England to see the rebel fleet sailing into port. "Mary is far too small and frail to be dumped on a boat bound for Flanders." Though Flanders could be fun, and the Dutch were delightful; she and Edward had spent a superb week in Bruges as guests of Lord Gruthuyse, filled with balls, masques, and boating on the canals—but Mary would not get the royal reception.

Edward smiled at her stubbornness, starting on her bodice buttons, working slowly down her sternum toward her tight tailored waist. Fingers stroked the inner curve of her breasts through her thin silk chemise, then felt their way down her belly past her navel, sending thrilling little shivers through her thighs. Undoing the bottom button, his hand drew up her silk chemise, baring the soft white flesh below her belly. He asked her, "So would you abide by a court's judgment?"

Not likely, but she could always appeal to his honor. "Only if that judgment is applied to me."

He stared at her, looking puzzled as his fingers slid past the elastic band of her third millennium nylon-spandex panties. "Applied to you?"

Ignoring the hand in her pants, she whispered huskily in his ear, "If Mary is guilty, then I am equally guilty for freeing her from the law."

"What?" His fingers stopped, and he looked puzzled.

"Aiding a fugitive and an accessory to murder," she reminded him, thrusting up to meet his hand, letting him feel what was at risk. "If there is no justice for Mary, there is none for me, or anyone. Don't you see?"

"Never fear," Edward assured her dryly, "you make it all too clear." Justice for the weak and powerless was not exactly an aristocratic concept, but Edward was far from stupid—in fact, she was one of the few things that did not come easily to him. It had taken months of hard wooing to get her here, in his bed and in his grasp, an unaccustomed struggle Edward would not soon forget. Compared with bedding her, seizing London and King Henry had been a breeze. "Mary will get my good lordship," Edward swore, "for justice' sake."

Edward might leave some Mary Nameless to an honest judge and sober jury, but not his lady and countess-to-be; no one trusted the law that much, least of all her lord of March. Kissing her hard, he pressed Robyn back down into the soft feather bed, his hand on her pubic mound, laying physical claim to what he could not otherwise control.

Glad to have her hero in hand, she closed her eyes and kissed back, reveling in Edward's reassuring strength, in his solid physical promise to set things right. Politics here and now was intensely personal, and justice was not some blindfolded goddess with scales, but a brawny young warrior you could hold in your arms and taste on your tongue.

Without breaking the kiss, her bandaged warlord shed his sweaty shirt and climbed eagerly atop her, his big firm body smelling of leather and horses, his mouth tasting of ginger wine. Very spry and eager for an invalid almost given up for dead at Smithfield. Hands hardened by sword and lance pulled down her nylon panties, and a firm finger stroked the tip of her groin, sending delightful shivers up her spine. Her hips started to grind almost on their own as that single fingertip slowly traced the lips of her vulva and then slid into the moistness between, making her gasp with excitement. This was what she wanted, what both of them wanted. What was the use of being lord and lady if you could not have just what you wanted, whether in court of law or satin-curtained bed?

Aroused by the cool friction of his finger sliding into velvety smoothness, she ground harder, pressing her pubic mound hard against the heel of his hand, forcing his strong stiff digit in deeper. Yes, this was so much better—living in the Dark Ages did not have to be dreary. Warm waves of pleasure surged through her as his finger went back and forth, faster and surer with each stroke. They were still enthusiastically tangled in the bed sheets, ball gown, and each other when grooms knocked on the door, saying my lord's bath was poured.

3

⟫ Lamastide ⟪

Sunday, 27 July 1460, Height Sunday, Baynards Castle, London

Deirdre's being more difficult than usual, saying the Sunday before Lamas is Height Sunday in Ireland, and we must climb some hill or mountain to pray over the harvest. Hard to do in downtown London. Rain is pouring buckets outside, not the best weather for mountain climbing, especially when you are struck down with acute Sunday morningitis—barely able to stir from bed, much less the castle. After yesterday's near fatal tournament and mad dash down Cheapside, I need to rest frayed nerves, enjoying one last wet lazy Sunday in London. Tomorrow we slog off through the downpour to spend Lamastide in Canterbury as guests of the Archbishop—Mad King Henry's notion of summer vacation.

Still, I must go out to visit Mary, especially since we leave tomorrow. If summer is this much work, what will winter be like? Hopefully, I will be a countess by then. . . .

*R*obyn *stopping typing* and looked at Deirdre, who was staring out a rain-spattered arrow slit at the hills north of the city. Edward was meeting with the prickly Nevilles, whose tempers had not improved by being knocked about at tourney. Good. Edward was great at that, able to talk to the Nevilles when no one else would. But Robyn wanted to forget the fate of England for a day, in favor of cooking appetizing nutritious food for the road under semisanitary conditions while repairing her torn riding dress and worn psyche. Brushes with disaster were bruising, and hand-washing and drying were daylong chores when it rained all the time—with Deirdre being more a distraction than a help. "We must make our sodden way to Greenwich tomorrow," Robyn reminded her maid. "Why not have Sunday be a day of rest? Which was God's plan."

Raised a heathen, Deirdre did not see it that way—to her, the seasons were everything. "Height Sunday is for the harvest," Deirdre insisted, turning about to plead with her. "And the harvest hereabouts needs help."

Her handmaid was right, of course. So what if the king left for Greenwich tomorrow? People still had to eat. How could the mad gyrations of an insane Saxon king possibly compare to the harvest? Here and now, summer was spent getting ready for winter. Battles, tournaments, and royal progresses were exciting diversions that put no food in the larder. Besides, she had to indulge Deirdre, who was her most constant companion. Even Edward lacked Deirdre's raw devotion, being caught up in his duties as boy earl and national savior. Deirdre had only her mistress to worry over. Without saying a word, Robyn went back to typing. . . .

OK. I give in. If today is the day to pray for the harvest, then we should do it. But there must be some limit to Irish impracticality. Leaving London is out. We shall be hitting the soggy roads soon enough. It must be some high holy place in the city, somewhere close to Heaven. Saint Paul's immediately suggests itself, sitting atop Ludgate hill with its fifty-story steeple; but we can hardly use Saint Paul's bell tower for some heathen Irish rite, not on Sunday at least. Luckily I know just the spot—intimately, in fact.

More later . . .

By midmorning Lady Robyn and her maid stood atop the White Tower, the ninety-foot-high inner keep of the Tower of London, nearly three hundred years old and still the tallest secular structure in the city. Wearing Stafford red and gold and a sodden cloak, she had come by boat from Baynards Castle, entering through the Tower's Water Gate, the Traitors Gate—for the first time since Lord Scales's ill-fated attempt to flee the Tower with her in tow. She had King Henry's permission to visit this bloodstained royal keep, for the stated purpose of giving thanks in Saint John's Chapel for her recent release.

Presenting her permission to Lord Fitzwalter, the new lord lieutenant of the Tower, she and Deirdre said their thanks in the chapel,
then ascended to the topmost battlements. There she got a sweeping
view of London, Southwark and the Bridge, Aldgate, and the wet
green fields beyond. On one side of the city wall stood Holy Trinity
Priory, the city's grandest monastery; on the other side were the
crowded tenements of Portsoken, an outcast district beyond the
walls, whose alderman was the prior of Holy Trinity. Medieval
wealth and poverty often went side by side, yet this wall separating
want from plenty was particularly poignant. Heaven's rain fell on
both alike, but the prior's roof looked in better repair. Her red-haired
handmaid was ecstatic, saying this was higher than she hoped,
"Though not so high as an Irish hill."

"William the Conqueror did his best."

Whitewashed walls and towers, fifteen feet thick at the base,
soared above the city walls, rising from a foundation of chalk, flint,
and Kentish rag, bound with mortar and the blood of beasts. Deirdre
said it would do.

Surveying the harvest through the falling rain, it was plain the
green world beyond the walls was not going well; rain had hurt the
haying and played hell with standing grain. The downpour they'd
waded through to Northampton had hardly let up the whole time
she was in the Tower—or so they told her. Robyn's windowless cell
was buried so deep in the White Tower basement she did not know
day from night, much less what the weather might have been like.
Now she looked down on drowned gardens, bare tree limbs, and
streams turned into brown torrents carrying topsoil into the Thames.
Not encouraging. Deirdre sighed, sounding sorry for the Saxons.
" 'Tis bad enough, though I have seen worse. Ireland rarely has three
dry days in a row."

Whatever the calamity, a Wexford girl has seen worse—but things
are plenty bad when the wild Irish began to pity you. "We always
have hope," she reminded her handmaid. "Eight days ago I was buried under these same stones, in a black windowless cell without food
or water, certain I would die." Hopeless and then some. "Yet here I
am." She spread her cloak and did a rain-drenched pirouette. "Alive
and whole, and five pounds lighter."

Deirdre scolded her. "M'lady is too thin by half." Her maid had
fried bacon and scrambled eggs on the morning fire, filling the tower

bedroom with breakfast aromas that practically forced Robyn to eat. Deirdre did not mean to have m'lady starve on her. "We must fill you out again."

"Mayhap." She had eaten the eggs but not the bacon, sending it on to Saint Martin's instead, for Mary and Black Dick Nixon. Already people were eating off her plate; Deirdre, for one, was getting fat on what she did not eat. With a hard winter coming it would only get worse.

So be it. Happy to have gotten this far, Robyn prayed for a break in the rains, and for the harvest, giving thanks even in the face of the flood from above. When Heaven had heard enough, she turned to Deirdre, saying, "In that black basement cell, I swore I would live to dance atop this tower—it sounded awfully forlorn at the time, and now I cannot let the moment pass."

Shedding her sodden cloak, she danced atop the great stone tower that had held her prisoner, turning wild circles in the rain. London, the Tower, Portsoken, gray clouds, and green hills spun about in a wet whirl, with her at the center. She was alive! "Thank you Hecate for not taking me!" And free! And the men who had tormented her were now doing far worse. Lord Scales, former lord constable of the Tower of London, had been beaten to death by London boatmen. Her former jailers, FitzHolland and Le Boeuf, were in Newgate prison awaiting execution on Tuesday—a much anticipated spectacle, which Robyn meant to miss. Deirdre joined in the dance, linking arms with her mistress, laughing as they went to and fro in an improvised jig atop the White Tower, giving thanks for life and praying for an end to the rain.

And the rain did relent. By afternoon the sun shone and the day warmed, shrinking the sparkling puddles and raising clouds of vapor from wet roofs. Robyn took the chance to ride out and see Mary, making sure the girl got her bacon—which she had. Black Dick Nixon got his, as well, tickled that such a "well-spoken southern lady" had taken his case to heart. Let him think what he liked, she had merely sent him bacon—not being able to take more than one multiple felon to heart at a time. Mary had indeed won her heart, but the best Black Dick Nixon could hope for from her was some gold half-nobles and a good horse.

Riding back by way of Saint Paul's, she passed an impromptu street fair as people scrambled to sell their wet wares during the break in the rain. Harpers and pipers came out with the sun, playing for half-pennies, while butchers' boys pushed "hot pigs' knuckles" and "peacock pies"—neither of which tempted her. Where Carter Lane met Wardrobe Place, a strapping fellow in hip boots stepped briskly into the street, stopping smack in her path. Wearing stained blue-gold hose and a yellow quilted doublet, he went down on one muddy knee in front of her horse, doffing his big floppy green beret.

Shocked, she reined in, never having been accosted so abruptly in the street before, not in London at least. Southwark was another matter. Luckily her worst enemies were in custody—in fact, her biggest fear was that this fellow might represent the law, retaliating for the recent fracas at Saint Martin's sanctuary. Deirdre drew rein beside her, set to come to her lady's aid.

But it was Matt Davye who grinned up at her, hat in hand, light brown hair falling across his face, his broad smile full of boyish good humor. Though they usually met under fairly alarming circumstances, the young man always acted pleased to see her. "M'Lady Stafford," he begged, "please halt a moment. Pray let me thank you."

"What for?" she asked, sitting up in her saddle. She felt she owed him thanks, and maybe a gold noble, for that beautiful goal-line block at the gate to Saint Martin-le-Grand.

Matt Davye's smile widened, showing strong white teeth. "For my freedom."

Someone told him about her secret testimony. Matt Davye was one of Duke Holland's men in the Tower of London when they threw wild fire onto East Cheap, killing women and children—a crime London took most seriously. His comrades sat awaiting execution on Tuesday, including Duke Holland's bastard brother, and Le Boeuf, Holland's hated chief executioner—friends and family of his victims were flocking from as far off as Sandwich and Newbury to see how Le Boeuf enjoyed being on the working end of the disemboweling knife. Matt was spared because she swore that he showed pity on the Tower prisoners, slipping them food and blankets, and telling them when King Henry returned. She asked, "Who says you owe me your freedom?"

"Earl Warwick himself, m'lady." Matt nodded enthusiastically, hiding behind a greater man's name. "His Grace swore I had your ladyship to thank."

Figures. Warwick presided over the trials, which suited his petty

vengeful nature, and it must have wounded the touchy Neville to see
Matt Davye get away on her word. Warwick liked to pretend she
was just a pretty face, but in his proud heart the Neville earl knew
she was the one Edward heeded—and that hurt. Having a woman
and a commoner come between Warwick and his most noble ally
insulted the earl personally and politcally, mocking both his manhood and nobility. So this was just the sort of story Warwick relished
relating, piously putting down Edward's clemency by blaming it on
his witchy mistress, making Warwick's own bloodthirstiness sound
manly.

Let the high and mighty Neville snicker—none of the assorted blue
bloods cowering in the Tower were punished, so Matt Davye certainly merited a break. Her testimony was secret to protect her—the
victim. Why should she have to tell the world all the terrible things
done to her in the Tower? It was bad enough having to tell Warwick.
"Now that I am free," the young man in the yellow doublet suggested, "perhaps m'lady might have use for me?"

So that was what this was about; Matt Davye was trying to turn
a timely block into a job in her "household." His former master,
Henry Holland, duke of Exeter, was last seen headed into exile, so
any hope of advancement Matt had from serving King Henry's closest cousin-male was gone. Edward and Warwick's masterly victory
at Northampton left Matt broke and alone on the streets of London.
While Robyn was triumphantly freed from the Tower and happily
lodged in Baynards Castle, Matt Davye had been taken into custody
himself, threatened with hideous death, and then tossed back into
the rain—and told he had Robyn to thank for it.

No wonder he came to her. It said a lot about the Middle Ages
that she had to have a household. Whatever gold or honors Lady
Robyn got did not come free—medieval society demanded she support others with it; serving girls to dress and change her; butchers,
cooks, and bakers to make her meals; cupbearers and sewers to serve
them; laundresses for her washing; seamstresses for her sewing;
grooms for her dogs and horses; and harpers to keep her happy.
Amazingly, folks fought to serve her, eager to live in a manor hall
and "eat at a lady's table." Deirdre had begged shamelessly for her
job. Commoners knew the nobility lived well, too well in fact, wasting money on finery and display, filling out their households with

pretty foreigners, bastard relations, infamous scofflaws, and armed felons. So far, she had only Deirdre.

She glanced over to gauge her handmaid's reaction and saw the Irish girl smirking at this Saxon's presumption—neither horrified nor thrilled by the prospect of Matt Davye in her lady's livery. Turning back to the man kneeling in the mud, she asked, sweetly, "Would you truly serve Lord Edward's whore?"

That is what Matt Davye called her when he first came to change the bucket in her Tower cell. She had learned not to take the word personally—a lot of people she did not know called her *whore* because she and Edward were not married, and would just as easily call her *countess* when they were. *Whore* was merely a title, like *heiress* or *princess*—only you were not born to it; it must be earned.

Matt Davye's grin melted, as he saw that a fortnight ago he had thoughtlessly spoken his mind. Medievals had to watch what they said, even to prisoners locked in a secret cell in the Tower basement, for the wheel of fortune was always in motion, and last week's wretched convict could be next Sunday's friend to the king. Ignoring the crowd that gathered to watch, Matt Davye clung hard to his hat, saying, "I would gladly serve Lord Edward's lady."

So you say. She studied the young man kneeling at her stirrup, noting he was big and healthy, and pleasant looking. Medievals wore their resumes on their faces, and Matt Davye had plenty of spirit. She had hired staff before, but never so personally, nor with life and death hanging on her decision. Without her word, Matt would be sharing a cell with FitzHolland and Le Boeuf, hoping to get off with a hanging. And she had lain for hours in the black Tower basement, despairing of ever seeing the day, wondering if Matt Davye liked her, and what the extra cheese and blanket meant, or how much he might willingly do for her, and at what cost. Thankfully her situation had improved, so she could be more picky—no longer having to pin her hopes on whatever man was least cruel to her. She asked evenly, "Have you anyone to speak for you?"

Happy to see her not holding "whore" against him, Matt's grin returned. "Duchess Anne of Exeter is Lord Edward's sister, and will testify to my many good services." It was smart of Matt to pick a woman; Earl Warwick's word would not be near enough. Political feuds often split the marriage bed, and Edward's older sister Anne was wed to his family's most violent enemy. Not the happiest marriage in the land, and any competent seeress could see a messy divorce in the Duke Holland's future.

She turned again to Deirdre, asking in Gaelic, "What should I do with him?"

Her handmaid surveyed the stalwart young fellow taking a knee in the mud. With armies being disbanded and noble employers headed into exile, footloose jobless men were plentiful, and women could pick and choose. "He looks useful," Deirdre conceded, "if he can be trusted. Beware of a bull's horn, a horse's hoof, and a Saxon's smile."

Too true. Yet Robyn needed retainers, and from the moment they met, Matt Davye had been going out of his way to do her favors, often with no conceivable hope of reward—why? Probably for all the wrong reasons. Still, she had to trust someone, so why not start here? Reaching down, she motioned for him to get up out of the mud, saying, "You have already served me well, most recently at Saint Martin's. I owe you for that, and for a pair of warm blankets."

Matt bounced eagerly to his feet, reaching up to bring her fingers to his lips, saying, "Those blankets were my gift to Lady Stafford."

No doubt. She never questioned where they came from at the time. Had Matt Davye been sleeping under a cloak for her, when she was a doomed prisoner in the basement below? Did he ever dream of such a stunning reversal of fortune? Mayhap he expected it—but that just showed intelligence. Whatever his reasons, his befriending her would pay off handsomely. Taking her hand back, she patted Lily's white neck, asking, "Do you like horses?"

Matt's eyes lit up. "Who could not love horses like these?" Both were beautiful beasts—Lily, with her broad white forehead and pink nose, and strong, patient Ainlee. Edward liked to give the best.

"I am sorely in need of a master of horse," she explained. "On the morrow these two mounts and several sumpter horses need to go by boat to Greenwich, then from there over the roads to Canterbury, where we will stay for several weeks, and then return the same way to London. I need a man to make sure my horses are fed oats and fresh hay, and that they get good rubdowns and dry stalls—also to see the sumpter horses are loaded and unloaded each day, and the baggage safely stowed. Can you do that?"

"My lady has found her man," Matt declared confidently. Giving him the reins, she let her new horse master lead Lily back to Baynards Castle, noting he did have a feeling for the horse. If Lily felt comfortable, so should she.

Edward bravely ordered up a party for their last night in London, with plenty of drink and dancing—like there really was a summer holiday ahead. It was Sunday, so even the beggars at the gate were invited in, to eat in the kitchen and listen to the music. Collin and Jo came up from Southwark, along with Bryn, Collin's Welsh fiancée, making this their good-bye party, as well, since they were returning to Greystone in the Cotswolds. Guards had their halberd shafts covered with blue velvet fastened with silver nails in Collin's honor, showing Edward had no hard feelings about being knocked helm over hind end into the Smithfield mud.

When Robyn presented her new horse master, Edward greeted him by name, saying, "Matt Davye, welcome to our service. My sister, Duchess Anne, does speak well of you." Casually inviting this former enemy into his household, Edward insisted on showing off the stables and introducing his own marshal, seeing the new horse master actually got a horse for the morrow. Edward liked to know his men, by face, name, and deed, and he thought no detail beneath him, especially when movement loomed; the same swift decisiveness that trapped King Henry at Northampton was aiming to get them to Canterbury in record time. So when the dancing was done, Matt Davye would go to work, sleeping the night in the stables—but at least the straw was dry.

Lady Robyn was not sleeping on straw these days—thank Heavens! For her, Height Sunday ended in Edward's big white-and-gold canopy bed, propped atop huge feather pillows and a fat feather mattress, feeling like the princess with the pea, in her best blue satin gown with her head full of spiced wine. Quiet moments like this were when being in the Middle Ages most amazed her, when that "What am I doing here?" feeling was strongest. She took out her notebook, checked the time—MON 7-28-60, 12:02:33 A.M.—then typed

Monday, 28 July 1460, Midnight, Baynards Castle, London
  Monday morning already. And a million things to do—most likely in the rain. Up at cockcrow, Mass and breakfast, then pack up the wardrobe, and see Matt Davye off with the horses, visit Mary and Black Dick Nixon at Saint Martin's, come back, pack

some more, fix food for the road, finish packing, shop for essentials, then hie ourselves down to Greenwich in some tiny coaster to join Edward and the king. Another dawn-till-dusk day. Thank heavens for Matt Davye, or Deirdre and I would be hauling the horses about, as well. But sleep first . . .

She stopped typing, staring over at Edward, who lay stretched out beside her, freshly bathed and smelling of soap, wearing a simple three-quarter sleeve silk tunic fastened with a silver falcon-and-fetterlock broach. Very fetching. This Roman slave boy outfit went with the barbarian motif of carved oak tables, handwoven tapestries, and civet-trimmed coverlet. Pretending to be the pampered princess, with her comely serving boy, she returned to typing.

Does liking Edward's good looks make me shallow? Hope not, because I do. Just seeing him lying alongside me in his skimpy tunic is exciting. You would think that being in 1460 was wild enough, without having princess and slave boy fantasies, as well. Must be the wine.

Bryn was breathtaking as ever, sewn into a stunning gown that made her into a Welsh princess out of faerie. Type casting, but it turned Saxon heads—reminding them why they conquered Wales in the first place. How happy not to be in competition with her—again. While kissing good-bye, Jo whispered, "See you on Saint January's Day." Whatever that means—must get a calendar. Cannot keep taking on the Middle Ages one day at a time. Master Hastings is going back to Burton Hastings, so he, too, got a kiss, much to his delight. Below the party still goes on; musicians, grooms, and servants, drinking and dancing, not missing us better sort in the least. Except maybe Bryn . . .

Edward shifted on the bed, and she looked over at him, finding that his long, clean, scented limbs lying at careless angles aroused her. She smiled to let him know it, and he grinned back over the rim of his gold wine goblet. Then he took an idle sip, saying nonchalantly, "Lord Clinton has landed."

"Landed where?" Lord Clinton was Deirdre's former master, exiled to Ireland with Edward's father. Easygoing, charming, and insolvent, Clinton combined high principles with low tastes, and had an alert eye for the lasses. Deirdre had fond memories of her maid service under him, but was delighted to trade households. Even Robyn admitted the man was cute.

"At Bristol." Edward cocked his head to the west, where his earldom of March hugged the Welsh hills. "Father had him arrest shipping in the Severn."

"Arrest shipping?" Sounds like Lord Clinton had solved his money problems at last. "Taking people's ships at sea is properly called piracy."

"Not when it is ordered by Good King Henry's lord lieutenant in Ireland." Edward raised his gold goblet in honor of his father-in-exile. "Lord Clinton seized three French ships, all piously named *Marie*, a sure sign father means to return soon from Ireland."

"How soon?" She did not look forward to meeting Edward's father, Richard, duke of York, who ruled over the Anglo-Irish, acting as the king's lieutenant, minting coins and calling an Irish Parliament, even though he was an attainted traitor in England. When a king's officer came to arrest him, Duke Richard had the Saxon king's emissary tried for treason, then hanged and quartered—winning the good duke friends all around the island. If the Irish loved him so, why not stay in Dublin, at least until after the wedding? "How long before your father gets here?"

"Maybe a month," Edward hazarded, "two at the most. We are calling Parliament for October, to give him ample time."

She saw Edward was also uneasy about his father's return, since none of her prospective in-laws so much as knew she existed. This same boy earl who captured kings and casually called Parliament hesitated to present his fiancée to his noble parents—teenage life is never easy, even with your own castles, bowmen, and a live-in girlfriend. But there was no stopping the oncoming family reunion. Edward's mother had just been released from genteel captivity in Wallingford Castle, and she would be in London by the time they got back from Canterbury. Fortunately they would not face the full weight of "meeting the family" until the fall—which was fine with Lady Robyn, since so far she had not had much of a summer. Aside from a delightful interlude in Calais and a less delightful week in the Tower, June and July had been spent plotting and carrying out the successful invasion of England. August need not be all work, as well.

"Lord Clinton sent along letters from Dublin." That Edward had his mail forwarded by a pirate said a lot about England's totally private postal system—which worked without stamps, post offices, mailboxes, ZIP codes, or street addresses. Letters found their way however they could, with whomever was willing—common carriers, passing friars, trustworthy vagabonds, touring minstrels, or genteel pirates. Taking another sip, he smiled wickedly, saying, "Father wants me to marry a Scots princess."

"What Scots princess?" She looked to see if he was teasing, having heard hair-curling stories about Scotland, which was more savage even than England, ruled by a disfigured tyrant, King James II, who trusted no one—his father, uncle, and boyhood friends having been murdered by his nobles, some before his eyes. Just the family to marry into.

"I believe her name is Mary," Edward replied airily, as if first names barely mattered when discussing foreign princesses. This was not the first royal bride his father had tried to foist on Edward, so far with scant success. His teasing was actually a compliment; moments before she imagined herself as Princess Robyn, now Edward was passing up a real flesh-and-blood Scots princess for her. "Warwick sides with father," he added in mock seriousness, "saying such a wedding would do us all well."

Warwick would; the noxious Neville delighted in slighting her, and doubtless hoped a marriage of state would reduce her hold on Edward. Foolish hope, since Edward was not about to pick a wife for her political value—he yearned for a soul mate, not a useful foreign alliance. Did Warwick know they were betrothed? Probably not. Neville spies were only so good. She asked blandly, "Why so?"

Warming to his story, Edward slid closer, casually resting his free hand on her silken thigh, seeing if jealousy might rouse her. "King James Stewart of Scotland, James of the Fiery Face, wants our friendship—or so he vows. Which would bar our enemies from seeking safety in Scotland." Right now the queen and the more recalcitrant court nobles were on the run, looking for a place to light. Scotland was a prime spot, lying alongside the most sympathetic part of England, the northern lands of Percy, Darce, and Clifford—all die-hard supporters of the old order. "If we sealed the back door into Scotland, it would make all the difference," Edward pointed out. "We could reduce the castles in Northumberland, and there would be no war in the north."

Nor anywhere else. Peace would be secured, and lives saved, so King James Stewart offered up his daughter to seal the deal, since his sworn word was not nearly good enough. Earl James Douglas had fled Scotland after his brother was stabbed over supper by King James and his dinner guests—showing there was more to be feared at a Scots feast than beetroot soup and haggis. The victim was the king's cousin and under a royal safe-conduct—which Earl Douglas tied to the tail of a winded horse and dragged through the streets of Stirling before burning the town and fleeing to England. Scots civil wars made English contests seem like genteel brawls. Lying back in a rustle of silk, enjoying the feel of his fingers on her thigh, Robyn asked sweetly, "Does she have the family disfigurement?"

"Not at all," he assured her gravely. "I hear she is a comely lass." King James of the Fiery Face got his name from a large flaming red birthmark.

"Too bad." Robyn shook her head sadly, ignoring the hand on her hip. "If she had even a huge mole or harelip, it might be different—there is nothing sadder than a lovely young princess."

"How so?" Edward looked puzzled, clearly liking his princesses young and pretty. His warm hand began pushing up her dress, baring her calf, then her knee, then her hip, sending shivers of pleasure ahead of it.

Pretending not to notice, she replied with mock surprise, "Why if the poor girl were plain or disfigured, she would at least gain a handsome dashing husband. But if she is comely as you say, she could surely find a good enough man at home—being, after all, a princess." Carried away by the wine, she insisted staunchly, "Something should be done about this shocking slave trade in oppressed princesses—being fathered by kings does not make them unfeeling breeding stock."

"Oppressed?" Edward lifted an eyebrow—the word did not have its modern connotations, meaning something more like rape.

"Yes, oppressed princesses." She stopped his hand with hers. "Taken from their families as teens and toddlers, packed off to arranged marriages, or just shopped around to prospective in-laws on approval. Pimped by their loving parents."

"You make it sound so mercenary," he protested, trying to free his groping hand without having to set down his wine goblet.

She would not let go. Holding his free hand in both of hers, she brought his fingers to her lips, lightly kissing them, running her tongue along the tips, feeling him tense in anticipation—unable to touch her so long as he held the wine cup. "But those lands and titles are what count," she insisted softly, liking the way he responded to the touch of her tongue. "Why else would anyone want to marry a child?"

Giving up trying to subdue her single-handedly, Edward looked askance. "Are you mocking my age?"

"Heavens, no!" she protested. "These Middle Ages are most wonderful, if you do not mind the iffy sanitation, and absolute lack of just about everything—"

"I mean my eighteen years." Looking about, Edward saw he had been outmaneuvered for once, drawn too deeply into the bed. He could no longer put the wine down on the floor or on one of the carved oak chests. He had to keep hold of the goblet or spill the cinnamon spiced wine on his civet-trimmed coverlet.

"Tosh," she told him. "Eighteen is not a child. At home you would be perfectly legal, old enough to fight, vote, and marry. Though not to drink." Letting go with one hand, she surprised him by seizing his goblet and whisking away the offending wine.

"What?" Edward tried to grab at the wine, but she was too quick. "Old enough to go to battle or Parliament, but not to an inn! That is absurd!"

"*Exactement.*" She took a sip and set the goblet on the floor on her side, where he could not get at it. But now he had both hands free, and in a moment he was atop her, pinning her to the soft feather bed—more or less what she'd wanted from the start. Robyn relaxed, lying face-to-face for a long rapturous kiss that grew more and more loving until it nearly lifted her off the bed. All this playful talk of foreign princesses was just meant to inflame her. And mayhap it worked. His weight felt warm and comforting, smelling of soap and sweat at the same time, holding her securely in place, while hands worked furiously on her buttons, peeling back the ball gown to get at bare skin, producing a tickle of desire that made her hips squirm pleasantly. When their lips separated, she went on, "And in the end, the same horrid fate awaits each poor bartered princess."

"What horrid fate?" Edward looked down at her, hair falling onto his handsome face, surprised by her solidarity with this far-off Scots princess, who was only supposed to arouse her jealous passion. His fingers continued to work as he spoke.

She rolled her eyes, as if the answer were obvious, lying flat on her back, and half-undressed in her lord's bed. "To be sent totally innocent into bed with a brute she has never seen before, who cannot speak her language and wants only to molest her. Breeding cows are treated better."

"Am I, then, a brute?" Edward asked, though he was hardly in a position to argue, lying atop her, busily undoing her gown, with one thing uppermost on his mind. She could feel his firm impatience through the fabric.

"All men are," she replied primly, making the most of her compromised position. She did not truly believe that, but medieval men had no defense against feminist arguments, since they secretly assumed they were brutes, totally out to get the better of women—one of the few points where Holy Scripture and male hormones absolutely agreed. What surprised them was how readily women put up with it. "Which leaves me with only . . ."

Edward closed her mouth with his, tasting of wine and cutting her off. His hands went under her silk chemise, stroking the curve of her breasts, thumbs brushing her nipples. With her gown open, and his slave boy tunic half undone, she could feel the smooth ripple of his stomach and the firm expectant shaft pressed hard against her, straining to get inside. Stripping away the last of her ball gown, Edward sat up, breaking the kiss to pull off his tunic, revealing his bandaged ribs and splendidly excited body—six feet of shapely muscle topped by an impish drunken grin. Unslowed by bent ribs or a recent concussion, his lordship, the earl of March was about to enjoy himself immensely.

Sighing in feigned resignation, she went on, "Leaving only one way sure to keep you from deflowering innocent princesses . . ."

Eager hands thrust her down, and Edward shut her up with another winey kiss, while one arm went behind her back, drawing her closer. She had meant marriage, but making love must do, at least until after Parliament. Peace hung in the balance, and the enemies of peace prayed some slip would discredit the brash young earl of March—like marrying a witch from the future. How strange that her personal life had become intensely political. Who she slept with and whether she married him had become grave matters of state, with major foreign policy implications. Amazing. Not that Edward aimed to wait for marriage. Despite all the teasing, this tender loving boy atop her was a belted earl, in his own castle, and in his own bed. Her feudal overlord, in fact if not in name—bent on having his way.

So be it. By now she ached for him, as well. Glad to extend his droit du seigneur by yet another night, she opened her legs like an obedient vassal, taking her ardent young lordship inside her, enjoying his animal abandon. Bucking atop her, head back and eyes half-shut with pleasure, the untamed rebel earl, claimed her completely. Her soul went to God, but her earthly lord got her body—thank Heaven. Letting go, she shut her eyes, giving in totally to driving desire, rolling her hips from side to side as Edward rocked within her, thrilling to his power and excitement. Wild piping came up the stairs from the party below.

Legs wrapped around him, thighs tensing in time to the piping, she ground herself against Edward's groin, forcing his stiff muscled shaft in all the way. Her wounded young warlord did not even wince. How utterly magnificent to be free, victorious, and incredibly in love. Things did not get any better. Bursts of pleasure shot through her, pure white flashes of ecstasy starting at the base of her spine, shooting through her groin, and exploding into lightninglike spasms of release, filling the darkness behind her closed eyelids. Glorious and uplifting, her climax went beyond pleasure and into utter mad abandon, so the merest brush of skin on skin seemed unbearable. Only Edward's hard solid body kept her firmly in bed.

Waves of sensation subsided, sinking into a hollow blissful ache between her legs, leaving Robyn spent and happy, lying with Edward still holding her, their hearts beating together. She realized rather irrelevantly that the piping had stopped and the rain had returned. Sex was as transporting as Witches Flight, lifting her up and carrying her totally away, taking her to another world. Earthly worries had to wait—marriage among them. But once Parliament ratified the peace settlement and cleared Edward of treason, then anything was possible—it would literally be up to them. After all the years she spent searching for the right man, who would have thought she'd find him in 1460?

Monday, 28 July 1460, Aboard the Maidenhead, *Off the Isle of Dogs*

Thank Edward for going ahead with King Henry. I hate ponderous royal progresses full of prickly lords and ladies fighting over precedence, trying to get close to the king. Parties like last night's, with all ranks joining in the music and dancing are the Middle Ages at their merriest. Being sung to bed afterwards was not so bad either.

At dawn Matt Davye had the horses ready for the barge trip downriver, an auspicious start. Deirdre sewed scarlet facings onto Matt's yellow doublet, making my new horse master stand out amid Edward's murrey and blue. Then we plunged back into the city, finding just the right red cap for Matt, and saying good-bye to Mary at Saint Martin's. Mary seemed awfully calm about her savior leaving town—merely making me swear by Saint Anne to return. Easy enough. Back at Baynards Castle another dependent was waiting, little Beth Lambert, left in my charge by the Greys. Another flurry of packing, and we bade the beggars at the gate good-bye, boarding this pretty little cog—flying Lady Robyn's red and gold. Making the *Maidenhead* the first vehicle of any kind to bear my colors. Too cool. Until I got here, I did not even have colors.

And *Maidenhead* is worthy of the honor, a shapely little single-masted ship, with broad clinker-built curves coming to a sharp point at the prow. She has castles at either end, and I am sitting in a plush dry chair high on the covered stern castle, looking out over the rain-pocked river. Much safer than some open wherry or row barge, especially in the rain. The lower river can be rough and dangerous, particularly if you have to shoot the Bridge—look what happened to Lord Scales. . . .

She stopped typing to run an eye over her charges, already feeling responsibility for her slowly growing household. Deirdre was an old sea hand at sixteen, having twice run King Henry's blockades; but at nine or so, blond Beth Lambert had never been aboard anything bigger than a rowboat. Little Beth did not look the least intimidated, climbing up to sit in an embrasure on the crenelated stern castle, excitedly calling out sights. Passing beneath the drawbridge on London Bridge, trumpets sounded, and Robyn feared the girl would fall in, but Beth merely called out from the embrasure, "Two big brewer's carts, a lady's horse-drawn chair, and a whole gaggle of pilgrims are waiting in the rain for us to pass." Anything to impress the alderman's daughter.

Beth was the daughter to John and Amy Lambert of West Cheap,

fostered into Edward's household. Her father was a London alderman and sheriff, the sort of man in line to be mayor. Her mother
was Lady Lambert, and she watched the Saint Anne's Day tournament from a luxury box—but was still thrilled to have her daughter
serve in a noble household. No one here and now thought nine too
young to be out on your own and learning a trade. Outside of a
nunnery or a noble home, there were no schools for smart strong-
minded girls; instead you found some woman you admired and
trusted, and you learned from her—be it midwifery or witchcraft.

Below the Bridge lay the Pool—a deep spot dug by the heavy flow
of water off the Bridge, which serving as anchorage for ships avoiding the sixpence toll—filled with cogs, costers, grain hulks, tall carracks, Spanish caravels, Italian galleys, and little ketches reeking of
spoiled fish. Rearing high over it all was the White Tower, where she
and Deirdre had danced in yesterday morning's rain—plainly visible
even as the city walls and forest of ships' masts sank down behind
green spreading marshes. She returned to her typing.

> . . . Tomorrow the men who tortured me in the White Tower
> vaults will be executed—one more reason to be out of town. Hav-
> ing lain in a dark cell expecting to die, I do not wish that on
> anyone, but Gilbert FitzHolland and Le Boeuf have hounded me—
> literally—since the day I got here, setting dogs on me twice, sacking
> the manor where I was staying, and then doing terrible things to
> me in the Tower. Le Boeuf is the worst, a sadist who revels in the
> despair of his victims. Nothing will be done to Le Boeuf that he
> had not gleefully done to others.
>
> Gilbert FitzHolland troubles me more. He is scary and vengeful,
> and a fanatic witch hunter who hurt me terribly. And now because
> of me, he is behind bars waiting to die. But I lack the total killer
> instinct that says, "Whosoever harms my manicure must be torn
> in two." However many murders FitzHolland may have commit-
> ted, he missed with me—which makes all the difference. I came
> willy-nilly out of nowhere into FitzHolland's world, defying his
> customs, freeing his prisoners, and overthrowing his king—and
> now FitzHolland is going to die horribly, while I will live on in
> luxury, or what medievals suppose is luxury. Gilbert FitzHolland
> sitting in a Newgate cell amidst murderers and rapists has a hear-
> twarming ring. Public humiliation and torture, followed by slow

gory execution before a laughing, jeering mob somehow smacks of sinking to FitzHolland's level—if only a little. Luckily I do not have to watch.

Closing her electronic notebook, she said a silent prayer for Gilbert FitzHolland, but not for Le Boeuf. Neither man's death could rightly be blamed on her. Since Northhampton, Edward had followed a policy of scrupulous conciliation, sitting in council with former enemies and pardoning the lords holding the Tower—in part because of a promise made to her before they even landed at Sandwich, since she would not have come with him to London to preside over a bloodbath. Others were not so forgiving. Warwick had a long list of men he desired dead. And London wanted vengeance on the men who threw fire from the Tower, so with their leaders pardoned, justice must fall on the men who carried out the crime.

Putting tomorrow's executions out of her mind, she looked ahead instead, watching as the *Maidenhead* rounded the southern end of the Isle of Dogs, entering Greenwich Reach. Pleasance Manor hove into sight, with its tall watchtower, tiltyard, and palatial mansion set amid two hundred acres of enclosed park and woodland. Windowed galleries, long low walls, stands of trees, landing steps, and private wharves ran along the river. "Ooh!" and "Ahh!" came from the girls, who had never seen Greenwich before. Deirdre demanded to know, "Who lives here?"

"We do." Edward had arranged for her to take private riverside apartments, safely away from the waterfront inns.

Another round of excited *ooh*s and *ahh*s. Then Deirdre looked at her and asked, "But who does all this belong to?"

"Pleasance is a royal manor, but it was not always so." She had the story from Jo, and it was worth passing on to her young charges—who needed to know how ruthless royalty could be. "Pleasance was built by King Henry's uncle, Duke Humphrey of Gloucester, and passed into the king's hands when the good duke met his mysterious death."

"How mysterious?" asked Deirdre, slipping into Gaelic.

She answered in English, so Beth could understand. "Duke Humphrey angered the queen." Everyone knew the queen's anger could be deadly. "On his way to Parliament, the duke was arrested, and in less than a week he was dead—no one knows the cause." The official version was that he fell into a sudden coma at Saint Saviour's Hospital and died a few days later—but hardly anyone believed it. Would a veteran warrior—one who had campaigned mightily in France and who rode briskly through winter cold to attend Parliament—really just curl up and die after a couple of days indoors? "Some say he died of a broken heart."

"Or was smothered in his bed," little Beth suggested. Lurid versions of the Duke Humphrey's death had long circulated in London, this being among the nicer ones.

She shrugged. "Either way, the queen's greatest enemy in Parliament was gone, while Pleasance and many other manors passed into the king's hands, along with the duke's splendid library and astronomical tables—all to be divided among those who ordered Duke Humphrey's arrest." Saying this aloud used to be treason, but tongues had loosened a lot since Northampton. "Good" Duke Humphrey of Gloucester was at best a womanizing old warhorse, always happy to pop a cork or take a misguided whack at the French—but his death had scared a lot of folks, showing just how far the French queen and her favorites would go. If King Henry's uncle could be struck down so easily—who, then, was safe?

"Had the duke no wife or heirs?" asked Deirdre. "No family to avenge him?" With small faith in English law, Deirdre favored direct action by family and friends.

"His family was the king's family," Beth pointed out—as a London alderman's daughter, the girl had seen the parade of politics all her life from between adult knees. "He did have a wife, his duchess, only she . . ." Beth looked at her mistress, unsure how much to say.

"Only she what?" Robyn asked, wanting Beth to say it aloud.

"She was a witch," the little girl whispered.

There was the word. Part of learning to be a witch was admitting you were one; the Tower taught Robyn that. She and Beth Lambert were sister-initiates, taken together into the duchess of Bedford's coven on a Witches Night last May, but Beth was very much the older sister—by about five hundred years—which made it her duty to broach unpleasant topics. "Duchess Eleanor was a witch who married into the royal family, then conspired to harm the king by magic when her husband was heir apparent. When Duke Humphrey died, Duchess Eleanor was already in perpetual imprisonment in Beaumaris Castle on the east tip of Anglesey facing the Lavan Sands, far off beyond Wales. I have seen the place in the Menai Strait, and it looked godawful lonely."

Robyn sang a verse in the popular song about it:

> Farewell, London, and have good day;
>   At thee I take my leave this tide.
> Farewell, Greenwich, for ever and ay;
>   Farewell, fair places on Thames side;
> Farewell, all wealth and the world so wide.
>   I am assigned where I shall be;
> Under men's keeping I must abide.
> All women may beware by me.

Beware indeed. Especially want-to-be witches like her two young handmaids. Both Beth and Deirdre had been at her secret betrothal; and though both were remarkably quick-witted and adept at keeping secrets, they needed to know this was not just some romantic game their mistress was playing. Another witch out of nowhere had once married a noble relative of King Henry's, becoming the lady of this grand Thames-side manor—but she lost everything: titles, riches, noble husband, even her freedom. And the Witch of Eye who aided her was burned. She finished up by paraphrasing their Bard-to-be: "So mind our manners here in Greenwich, least it mar our fortunes."

Both heads bobbed agreement. Hoping she had made an impression, Robyn watched Pleasance Manor draw closer, spread out beneath its hilltop watchtower, where the Greenwich Observatory would one day stand and mark the prime meridian—zero degrees longitude. But Greenwich was not yet the center of the world, just an amazingly pleasant royal manor, acquired through murder.

Wednesday, 30 July 1460, Pleasance Manor, Greenwich
Finally this is starting to feel like vacation. My room here is bigger than at Baynards Castle, with a separate bed for Beth and Deirdre—*très* plush. Matt Davye was here to greet us, with horses tucked safely in the stables, and a light buffet laid out—tart berry pastries, green apples, boiled water, warm loaves, plum jam, and ginger wafers. Perfect. Palatial room, handsome maid service, tasty snacks, and separate beds. Lady Robyn has landed. King Henry makes do with much worse—I have seen his rooms. No wonder

some women give up on keeping a household and just go visiting all the time. Matt got his new red hat as a reward.

Things are so grand, I mean to stay, at least through Lamas. Edward is gone already, headed over the muddy roads to Canterbury with King Henry. I miss him, but we could hardly be together at Court, anyway. Edward is Henry's closest male relative in attendance, while I am an absolute nobody, unconnected to anyone. Entering at Edward's side insults half the women in the room—so why go to their soirées just to see Edward at a distance? One day these people are going to have to accept me as countess of March, and eventually duchess of York. Until we are married, why make a scene? Besides, all that pomp and ritual is godawful boring. If Lady Frogbottom of Swamp-on-Marsh wants to stand for hours watching King Henry look uncomfortable, why get in her way? Things are hard enough on women who marry into the nobility— witness Duchess Eleanor of Gloucester, late of Beaumaris Castle, whose arrogance and pretensions alienated the women of London: "All women may beware of me."

Or Queen Margaret, last seen robbed of her treasure and jewels, riding pillion behind a young page named Coombe, her small son in her arms, headed three-to-a-horse for Harlech Castle on the far edge of Wales. I have enemies aplenty, and the surest way to add to them is to push ahead of Lady Frogbottom, just because my boyfriend is an earl. The best place to see a tournament is from the field, and the best time put up in a palace is when His Highness is away—you get faster service, better food, fewer duties, and a nicer pick of rooms.

And Lamas Day, the first of August, is a huge Christian-Pagan harvest festival, so Holy Canterbury will be a madhouse. It will be Witches Night, as well, and I feel safer having our harvest sacrifice in the quiet rainy countryside, away from hostile scrutiny at Court. Servants here are delighted to have me stay, seeing an excuse to serve the good wine at dinner, and order up minstrels from town— meticulously charging it to the earl of March, making the household books look that much better. (God, I am beginning to think like Lady Frogbottom.) So I kissed my knight good-bye and watched him ride away into the rain, the first we have been apart since I escaped from the Tower. . . .

Thinking about the Tower made her stop, staring out her leaded window at red-gold dawn on the river, seeing her colors spread across the Greenwich Reach—incredibly beautiful. Swans swam through last wisps of morning fog lying on the low marshland. Beth and Deirdre were still asleep, and she looked at her watch. WED 7-30-60, 5:32:06. Two days until Lamastide. She wished she could go back to sleep, but it was light outside and thoughts kept coming. She started typing again.

FitzHolland is dead. And Le Boeuf. Sometime yesterday they were led out of Newgate to Tyburn and executed in ghastly fashion. No matter how richly deserved, their deaths bother me. It is one thing to have your testimony save worthwhile lives—like that of helpful, handsome Matt Davye. Condemning men to squalid painful deaths is altogether different. Four months ago these two thugs were living their medieval lives, happily murdering and kidnapping under guise of law. Then I came and they are gone, doing hard time in Purgatory, waiting for spots to open up in Hell. Hecate help them. And here I am in their place, learning to be a medieval. Weird, when I think about it.

So let's not think about it. She closed the notebook on FitzHolland and Le Boeuf. At least her secret testimony saved them one final indignity. She truthfully said she was not raped—terrorized, tortured, and starved mayhap, but not raped. Which saved FitzHolland and Le Boeuf from having to publicly forfeit the offending member. When it came to forcible rape, medievals could act like rabid feminists.

With Edward gone, she turned her attention to the girls, whose education was supposedly in her hands. At home in Hollywood she had led a relentlessly adult life—career, partying, apartment, cooking, gym, boyfriends, stock options—an only child with no kids, she rarely got to be maternal until she had come to the Middle Ages. Now she was playing Wendy to a lot of medieval lost children who showered her with affection, looking up to her and calling her m'lady, loving her whether she willed it or no. Beth and Deirdre kissed her good morning and good night. Edward meant to marry her. Technically this was summer vacation, but she started the girl's education with Lamas Day, also called Lughnasadh and Teltane. After morning Mass, she took them for a stroll along the river, saying, "Today is Lamas Eve. Do you know what that means?"

"Swan Upping Day!" Beth Lambert replied brightly.

"Swan upping?" Sometimes the translation in her head did not quite connect, especially when a normal-sounding word had some wild new meaning.

"On Lamas Eve they go up the Thames to take up the swans and mark them," Beth explained, happy to show she had something in her curly blond head. "That is why it is Swan Upping Day."

"Mark them how?"

"By notching the cygnet's bills with a bollock knife. Any unnotched bird is wild and belongs to the king."

Sounds gruesome. "Don't the swans object?"

Beth nodded. "Something dreadful. And they say they often get a fearful ducking . . ."

"Who does?"

"The Worshipful Company of Dyers and Vinters."

Robyn guessed there must be booze behind this—the perfect drunken excursion, splashing about in the shallows upriver, assaulting frightened trumpeting swans for fun and profit. Glad to be missing it, she asked, "What else does Lamas Eve mean?"

Deirdre piped up. "Last of the hungry time before the harvest, when Lugh the God of Light holds a funeral for his foster mother, Tailtiu, and she goes into the ground to bring forth the harvest."

"*Exactement.*" She tried to explain some of the science behind it, telling the girls that whether they called it Teltane, Lamas, or Lughnasadh, the day after tomorrow was a cross-quarter day, like May Day, Halloween, and Candlemas—midway between the solstice and the equinox, both high summer and the doorway to fall. "And the seasons themselves are caused by the tilt in the earth's axis as it travels around the sun."

"Around the sun?" Deirdre looked askance at the idea.

"Yes, the earth's path around the sun is tilted. In summer we are tilted toward the sun, and in winter we are tilted away from the sun, and in fall and spring the tilt is even." Stars always fascinated her, in the sky or on the screen—and her semester of college astronomy made her the world's authority on cosmology and astrophysics.

"But the sun goes around us," Deirdre insisted stubbornly. "You see it rising in the east each day, and sinking down in the western sea each night."

"It only looks that way," Robyn insisted. "Our world, Earth, is actually a huge ball hurtling through space, and the sun is an even bigger ball of flaming gas so unimaginably far off it takes a whole year for us to circle around it." Deirdre looked dumbly at her, as did Beth Lambert, getting her first lesson in astronomy in the royal park at Greenwich. "This tilt is why the seasons are different throughout the world. We are in high summer, but the Australians are deep into winter."

"Australians?" Deirdre searched her memory of tales from the future. "Those black folks on the other side of the world, who go around naked and upside down—only it looks right side up to them?"

"The very ones. Right now they are tilted away from the sun, and living in deepest winter."

"Winter? In July?" Her maid expressed amazement.

"Actually August," Lady Robyn explained, "in Australia it is already tomorrow morning."

"Hoo, and they call the Irish liars." The redhead clearly did not believe, or if Deirdre did, it was for Lady Robyn's sake. In a world of miracles, simple truths sounded like the wildest fairy tales, but Robyn meant to muddle on, mixing modernism and magic, hoping not to offend, while knowing that was impossible. Most medievals were amazingly broadminded, with notable ghastly exceptions. Unfortunately, it was the exceptions she must look out for.

Lamas Day began with a real Lamb Mass, a blessing of the animals at the parish church of Saint Alphege, and ended in a midnight ritual. Robyn chose the stables, to be closer to the animals, kneeling around a lighted candle, a tall green taper set in a bowl in front of Lily's open stall. Ainlee looked on from the opposite stall, as did the stable cat, lying cuddled with her kittens. She had given the stable boys a butt of spiced ale to ensure privacy, and Matt Davye had Lamas Night off. There was already an all-seeing eye carved in a stall post, showing the spot had been used before. Witches liked familiar spots, linking them to past women and past lives, and when Duchess Eleanor owned this manor, her coven leader was the Witch of Eye.

Kneeling in the green-smelling hay, hearing doves cooing quietly in the dark eaves, it was easy to feel at one with the animals. It being

Friday, none of them had eaten flesh, and aside from the doves, none of the animals were headed for a cooking pot, making it easy to wish them all the goodness in the world without feeling too hypocritical. The Middle Ages were hard enough on people, on animals they were absolutely wretched. But not these animals, not this night. Robyn included them in her chant, vowing to eat no more dove meat this year—if at all possible. She opened with a West Country harvest prayer Jo taught her:

> Bless each maiden and youth,
> Each woman and tender youngling,
> Safeguard them beneath thy shield of strength,
> And guard them in the house of the saints,
>   Guard them in the house of the saints.
>
> Encompass each goat, sheep and lamb,
> Each cow and horse, and store,
> Surround Thou the flocks and herds,
> And tend them to a kindly fold,
>   Tend them to a kindly fold.
>
> For the sake of Michael head of hosts,
> Of Mary fair-skinned branch of grace,
> Of Bride smooth-white of ringleted locks,
> Of Columbia of the graves and tombs.
>   Columbia of the graves and tombs.

Starting with the youngest, she had each of them sacrifice something special "for the harvest"—to give their prayers commitment and show the seriousness of the winter ahead. Beth offered up a favorite rag doll, saying her child's prayer, then holding it over the green candle until the cloth caught fire. When the flames got too hot, Beth dropped the doll into a waiting bowl. Deirdre gave up a pinch of Irish earth, her most potent charm, useful as unicorn's horn against poisons and venoms, sprinkling it slowly into the flame while they repeated the chant. Tearing open one of her irreplaceable instant mocha packets, Robyn fed the contents to the flame, filling the stable with burnt coffee smell. Only three packets left. By the time she got to Canterbury, she was down to two.

*Sunday, 10 August 1460, Feast Day of Saint Lawrence,
Canterbury*

Seeing Edward again is wonderful. Ten days without him turned
out to be longer than I thought. Even if I have to share him with
the Court, just seeing him every day is a treat—from his smile in
the morning to his warm presence at night. Mother Mary, was
anyone ever so hopelessly in love? No one I know, anyway.

Otherwise Holy Canterbury has been anticlimactic. Last time I
was here was with the rebel army, the day after we landed at Sandwich. We marched straight through the city gates to the cathedral,
across the tall nave and past the choir, to fall on our knees and
give heartfelt thanks at the golden tomb of Saint Thomas à
Becket—cheered every step of the way by the citizens of Canterbury. An impossible act to follow, giving this trip much more of a
vacation feel.

Canterbury is a tourist town anyway, with dozens of deplorable
inns and a thriving relic industry devoted to holy memorabilia—
everything from scented votive candles to saints' hair, bone frag-
ments, and fingernail parings. Edward has leased a tall town house
just off Castle Street, near the ancient parish church of Saint Mil-
dred's, well away from all the commotion at Court. My room is
small but airy, on the top floor, with a splendid view of Canterbury
Cathedral rearing over the rooftops of Mercery Lane, beyond the
Buttermarket and bull-baiting stake. I have sworn off eating flesh—
at least until we get back to London—but the meat-loving Middle
Ages goes easy on vegetarians, treating fish like they grew on trees,
which Deirdre swears they do, though only in Ireland. There is a
stinky fish market, with buckets of fresh shellfish and live catch
from the river Stour.

King James of the Fiery Face still wants Edward for his son-in-
law, and is attacking Roxburgh castle to press his suit, one of the
last bits of Scotland currently in English hands. Poor dear Edward,
put upon by those rough, amorous Scots. Warwick wants to get
out of it with a quickie foreign wedding to the preteen princess—
who is close to being Edward's cousin. But thanks to me, Warwick's instinctive white trash solution will not work, so Edward
will just have to play coy and hard to get. I promised to give him
pointers. Today is the Feast Day of Saint Lawrence, a martyr grilled

to death over a fire, who is said to have maintained his good humor to the end, joking with torturers that he was done on one side and needed to be turned. Medievals made him the patron saint of cooks.

Friday, 15 August 1460, Eve of Assumption of the Virgin, Canterbury

Roxburgh has fallen. But any threat of a Scots shotgun wedding for Edward is gone. According to Earl Douglas, bloodthirsty King James had a love of huge cannons, terrifying his barons and neighbors. His Highness personally sited the guns that brought down Roxburgh and put on a demonstration for the ladies, setting off the great hooped bombard called the Lion—which blew itself to pieces, taking King James with it. The new King James is nine years old, and not likely to lead an army south demanding that Edward marry his sister. I assured Edward it was for the best, since the English have no business being in Scotland anyway. Ask any Scot.

Yesterday the bishop of Chichester preached, rewarding us with a forty days' indulgence just for listening—which should prove handy if I ever make it to Purgatory. King Henry has been passing his stay in prayer and hobnobbing with his bishops; but he appeared in the procession, and at high Mass and evensong pumping up the tourist trade in this damp and depressed summer. Henry will soon be our responsibility. With Scotland safely in the hands of a nine-year-old, Warwick is headed for Calais, where the castles of Guînes and Hammes are still held against us by intrepid young Duke Somerset. Which leaves Henry in our care, with the peace of England depending on getting this strange frail man safely back to London. Having charge of King Henry, along with the great seal and the wooden stamp they use to forge the royal signature, means virtually running the country. Mercifully our reign will be brief, since Warwick will be back soon; then Edward's father will arrive, along with the new Parliament. Still, it looks good on your résumé.

Monday morning, she hit the muddy roads again. Monday used to mean fighting the L.A. traffic to the studio; today it meant getting the king of England back to London along with a mob of lords, clerics, minstrels, men-at-arms, hunting dogs, hawks, carts, and sumpter horses. But now she got to ride up front with Edward, guiding Lily through Canterbury's towering Westgate and across the drawbridge straddling a swollen arm of the Stour, where Saint Peter's Street turned into the London Road and was lined with cheap inns catering to pilgrims arriving after the portcullis closed for the day. Traveling with King Henry meant sharing rutted roads with wagons carting feather beds, fine china, bright tapestries, and the royal chapel—all sunk up to their axles in the muck. One of the many things that first alarmed her about the Middle Ages was the abrupt disappearance of asphalt. Aside from some surviving Roman roads, pavement stayed in towns and cities, and most country lanes were mere bridle paths. Weeks of rain had worn down even the lush English countryside, and she waited in the saddle while men sweated and swore, ferrying baggage across washed-out fords and over roads turned to rushing creeks. Edward apologized for the English climate, claiming, "It is not always so bad. Summer brings hordes of holiday pilgrims to Canterbury."

"This is August," she pointed out, watching someone else's bundles go whirling away in the flood.

"So it is," Edward admitted ruefully.

Despite the dreadful weather, country folk struggled to bring in what was left of their sodden harvest, doing backbreaking work with sickle and scythe for a penny a day—when they were paid at all. Binders followed behind the reapers, tying the grain into sheaves, and after them came the gleaners, children and old folks working on their knees, picking each precious kernel out of the mud. Robyn saw them stop their unrelenting labor to kneel in mud-stained awe, hatless and humble, as their royal master rode by amid his glittering retinue of lords, ladies, knights, heralds, liveried servants, and household retainers. No wonder King Henry was ridden with guilt and spent his days begging God's grace and forgiveness. What feeling person would not? As she rode, Robyn said a fervent prayer for the harvest and the people bringing it in.

At Greenwich the mud and toil ended, and boats draped in royal bunting waited at anchor in the Thames to take them up to London on the morrow's tide. When the sun returned, Robyn tried to wring one last bit of vacation out of the waning day by taking her little household for an afternoon picnic in Pleasance Park, with Beth riding pillion behind Matt Davye. Calling a halt at the highest part of the park, where the watchtower looked down on Greenwich Reach and back over the wooded hills toward Blackheath, Robyn had Matt see to the horses while she took Deirdre and Beth to where the observatory would one day stand. Feeding them petti-cakes and carp quenelles, she described how the Old Royal Observatory looked in the far-off third millennium, with the prime meridian laid out in engraved brass and glowing fiber optics, slicing straight through buildings and courtyards, splitting the world in two halves as it went, finally turning into a thin green laser cutting across the Thames Valley and disappearing into Essex.

Deirdre stared down at the big shining bend in the river, where the Thames looped around the Isle of Dogs. "Ooh, what a miracle to see." By now Robyn was resigned to having the future be a sort of far-off fairy land. Any attempts to make the wonders sound natural and matter-of-fact just made the third millennium all the more astounding and mysterious—like trying to explain color to a mole. It would have made more sense if she just said the Virgin Mary drew the prime meridian with her finger.

Deirdre pointed down slope, saying, "Riders are coming, m'lady. Two royal grooms and a townsman in bad boots."

Three men were cantering up from the manor house, less than a mile away. Two were grooms in King Henry's livery, while the third was older, wearing a townsman's long gown with a rolled hood, over plain black boots and leggings. Little Beth recognized him at once, "M'lady, 'tis the King!"

So it was. Moments later she was doing her best curtsy to the middlemost horseman, with Deirdre and Beth bobbing beside her. Acknowledging their obedience, King Henry dismounted. He was just short of forty, but looked closer to fifty, careworn and put upon, and nothing like a king. Her sovereign's plain coat and round-toed farmer's boots made her feel overdressed in her shimmering cloth-of-silver riding gown with royal blue bars and lace trim. But King Henry hated fuss and bother, avoiding it whenever he could—one of the reasons she and Henry got on so well was that Robyn found it hard to treat him like a king.

Ordering his grooms to watch the horses, Henry invited her to walk with him around the watchtower, taking in the view, an almost unheard of suggestion from the shy, reclusive king. Instantly she agreed, and they strolled off together, careful to keep in sight of her maid—not that Deirdre was much use as a chaperon, but Robyn wanted to make her king as comfortable as she could, knowing Henry hated any hint of impropriety. Something must be preying on the normally silent monarch, who usually disliked being with women or talking politics—the two main preoccupations of medieval princes.

As they walked, they talked about the beauty of the Thames and the welcome break in the rain. Despite their easy relations, she kept her eyes dowcast when speaking to her sovereign, and watched what she said—not just because Henry was king, but because she did not want to burden him with the truth. Edward liked the fact that she was from the future, finding it flattering to have a mysterious magical lady love, delighting in her astounding stories. Henry was not likely to take it so well. To Henry, she always tried to be no more than she appeared, a pretty and polite young woman hanging about Court and aspiring to be a lady, but with no visible means of support. Her past history and present position would no doubt appall King Henry, so why bring them up? It would just put more gray in her king's brown curls. Without warning, Henry cut short the discourse on the woods and weather, asking, "What think you of our young cousin, Edward of March?"

That was a pretty question. Did Henry know they were lovers? Last time they discussed her sex life, she truthfully told Henry she was in a chaste relationship with a young man she might marry—but that was ancient history. Could Henry not know London's biggest bedtime story? Possibly. Did it matter?

She looked into her king's worn brown eyes. Henry was in a hell of a fix, having happily given over governing to his queen, her cronies, and his bastard relations—mostly Somersets and Tudors. Now he was thrust back to being king, under incredibly trying circumstances, with his old nemesis Warwick sitting on the King's Council—the man who massacred Henry's most loyal lords. Twice. And who Henry held responsible for his own arrow wound at Saint Albans. So right now with Warwick away, Henry desperately needed to sound out his "young cousin" of March, to find out what Edward was thinking and hopefully get his support. And like the least of his subjects, Henry hit on appealing to the one woman who clearly knew Edward's heart.

"He is loyal and honest," she assured him, "wanting only to serve Your Majesty, and to protect his king's honor." Alas, that meant defending Henry against his queen and grasping relatives, but that could not be helped. "That is why he risked life and honor to fight his way through your enemies and lay his sword at your feet." Henry nodded soberly; at Northampton the first thing Edward did on entering the royal tent was drop to his knees, pledging fealty to the king he just defeated. Seeing His Highness needed more reassurance, she added her own personal commitment to Henry's kingship, swearing her utmost "to keep and nurture my Lord Edward's love for his sovereign."

With all his warts, she wanted Henry to be king, exactly because he did such a bad job of it. Hating decision making and piously preferring religion to politics, Henry gladly left the real governing to others—making him the perfect figurehead, who disliked fighting and distrusted Warwick, both sterling qualities in any monarch. With Henry on the throne, Parliament and the King's Council had to rule—not a true democracy, but a start. Her sovereign beamed, happy to have won her loyalty, without having to know her reasons. He started to say, "Lady Robyn, your most loving . . ."

Deirdre stepped up, rudely interrupting her king, saying, "More riders, m'lady," pointing toward Blackheath.

Lèse-majesté and more, but what else did you expect from the Irish? Robyn prized Deirdre for her alertness, not her manners. Looking about, she saw that Matt Davye was gone, as was one of the grooms. What was worse, armored riders were coming up from the direction of Blackheath, two dozen at least, big men in sallets and half-armor wearing red surcoats with the white Neville saltire cross. Looking back toward Pleasance Manor, Robyn saw more steel-clad riders emerging from the trees between them and Greenwich, all wearing the Neville saltire. "Forsooth!" she cried, the strongest oath Henry allowed in his presence. "I do not like the look of these Nevilles."

Indeed not. Especially since a blond-bearded, hard-eyed ghost rode at their head—Gilbert FitzHolland, who had been hanged, beheaded, and hacked to pieces at Tyburn three weeks ago, looking unbelievably hale and healthy. Horrified, Robyn could barely believe what was happening, seeing armed terror galloping toward her, rapidly cutting her off from Edward back in Pleasance Manor. Mad Duke Holland's prickly half brother had been her personal nemesis since day one in the Middle Ages; her pert attitude and ill-concealed sense of moral superiority had affronted FitzHolland mightily from the first moment they met. And here he was, back from the dead, the man who swore to see her burned at Smithfield, pounding up Greenwich hill with two score armored riders at his back— putting her, the girls, and King Henry at FitzHolland's merciless hands unless she came up with another medieval miracle.

4

✦⟹ Proud Cis ⟸✦

Seconds counted, and she had a million things to do at once. First she looked to the child in her care and saw little Beth holding Lily's reins, making herself useful like a good medieval infant, awaiting orders from her sister-initiate. Smiling her approval to Beth, she shot her handmaid a sharp look, telling Deirdre, "Withdraw at once— your conduct is inexcusable," adding in urgent Gaelic, "and come back with Edward."

Doing a quick curtsy, Deirdre was gone, leaping onto Ainlee and galloping down the sweep of green hillside toward the manor house. Turning back to her confused king, Robyn grabbed the silver folds of her gown and did a bobbing curtsy of her own, begging Henry's patient forgiveness for her outspoken servant. "She is silly and Irish, but I do fear these Nevilles mean us harm."

Henry nodded in horrified agreement, not knowing what royal command to issue. Never at his best with armed men bearing down on him, Henry had special reasons to fear the Nevilles, whom he blamed for his arrow wound at Saint Albans and for beating his queen at Blore Heath.

Not that these were really Nevilles—she did not believe that even for a moment. Not led by Gilbert FitzHolland, who fought the Nevilles' tooth and nail at Saint Albans and Blore Heath, losing both times. These riders wore Neville colors because they feared to wear their own. Any seamstress could sew white crosses onto red surcoats, and Neville saltires were an excellent excuse for armed strangers to skulk about Blackheath—with Warwick away, they could claim to be his men. Unless she did something, King Henry would fall into the worst possible hands, ruined men bent on reviving the civil war,

mostly for their own profit. "With Your Majesty's leave"—she motioned toward the watchtower—"I would feel far safer within this
stout tower."

Instantly, Henry saw the sense in that, ordering his remaining
groom to bang on the door, shouting, "Entrance, entrance, in the
name of the king."

Surprised watchmen swung open the door, doing deep bows at the
sight of their distressed sovereign. She looked hurriedly about, seeing
no sign of the other groom, or of Matt Davye—two very suspicious
absences. Someone tipped FitzHolland that Henry had slipped his
leash to wander about the manor park on personal business, with
just a pair of retainers. And who better to do it than one of those
two retainers? But seeing Matt Davye gone as well was a personal
blow. Did Matt come begging for a job just to betray her? Damn,
she had saved the man's life.

She helped hustle everyone, including the horses, into the ground-
level chamber at the base of the tower. In the confusion she took
charge of the door, seeing it was locked and pocketing the big iron
key. No one could unlock the door without frisking her first—something the prudish Henry would never allow. Then she begged her
sovereign's permission to signal for aid, saying, "Sire, pray allow me
to run up a flag calling for help. Despite these stone walls, I am still
sorely afraid."

Her king agreed. Henry's most endearing trait was his increasing
aversion to armed combat. At Saint Albans he tried to be a hero in
armor rallying his outnumbered troops—and got an arrow in his
throat—leaving him with scant taste for battle. She had sat through
the brief battle of Northampton with the king, keeping Henry safe
in his tent. Like any right-thinking prince, his instinct was to stay
put and preserve the head of state until help arrived. Thanking His
Highness profusely, she backed up the stairs to the top of the tower,
taking the key with her. From the tower battlements she could see
miles of green rolling downs stretching in all directions, a vast sweep
of parkland, blending into forests and fields, cut in half by big shining
loops of the Thames. A smaller signal tower rose up atop the main
tower supporting the signal mast, and the boy at the base of the mast
was energetically running a red pennant up and down, frantically
signaling to the manor below.

Seeing no need to tell the lad his business, she turned toward Pleasance Manor, searching for signs of alarm—and not seeing any. Were they blind? Forty-odd red riders were converging on the watchtower, but most were coming from the south, out of Blackheath, hidden by the hill from the manor below—which was why they had a watchtower. Deirdre was already halfway down the slope to the manor, but red riders raced to cut her off.

Robyn looked down as the first of the riders reached the base of the tower; it was FitzHolland riding hard ahead of the rest, his blond beard neatly braided and his head still securely on his shoulders. FitzHolland called up, "Open in the name of King Henry!"

"Never," she shouted back, leaning out from the battlements, letting him get a look at her. She must answer him, before anyone else did—a minute's calm conversation would establish that these were not Nevilles, but friends of Henry and his queen, led by a bastard cousin. "Not to any false Neville and traitor."

"You!" FitzHolland looked flabbergasted. They did have a disturbing habit of meeting at inopportune moments. "What a most amazing whore! Never did I hope to snare you, as well."

"How nice to see you doing well." She half meant it—FitzHolland alive lifted a bit of secret guilt from her soul. "Or at least in one piece."

"Small lot you care," FitzHolland spat back. "You have fouled me time and again."

"It is you who have been hounding me," she protested. This all started as a Pleasance Park picnic.

"Not nearly enough," FitzHolland declared angrily. What made the man so mean? Mayhap a hard childhood. Being raised as the bastard relation by a family of homicidal sadists could not have been easy. FitzHolland's grandfather had a youthful career of mayhem and murder before being executed for rebellion, and the torture rack in the Tower of London was named the Duke of Exeter's Daughter—after FitzHolland's philandering father. She glanced again toward the manor, but all she saw was Deirdre being reined in by a pair of armored riders. Her redheaded handmaid struggled at bit, then gave in—no help there.

Suddenly, someone seized hold of her leg. Looking down, she saw it was Beth Lambert, her sister-initiate. Beth whispered earnestly, "How may I help, m'lady?"

"Just keep your head down," she advised, putting her arm around the girl's small shoulder. "And it never hurts to pray."

FitzHolland hollered up at her. "Hear me, harlot, I demand to see King Henry." More of FitzHolland's riders arrived at the base of the tower, ringing her in compeltely. Dismounting, some of the men tried the door, beating on the wood with their sword hilts, but so long as she had the key, they could not get in—none had thought to bring scaling ladders, or a battering ram.

"His Majesty is not receiving at the moment," she replied pertly, playing desperately for time, dragging out the standoff until help could arrive. "Miscreants and traitors must come back on Thursdays." Beth giggled behind her silver sleeve.

FitzHolland failed to see the humor, ordering his men to beat harder on the door, saying, "Damn you, shrew, open up. I am the king's sergeant-at-law."

"You were the king's sergeant-at-law," she shot back. "Now you are a felon."

"Damn you witless, worthless woman. Do as I say." FitzHolland rose in the saddle, shaking a mailed fist at her. "Or by Heaven I shall—"

"Or you shall what? Rack me and burn me?" She could not help adding that last part. The man meant for her to die horribly, even if she obeyed him, taking the bite out of verbal abuse. Mere threats were unlikely to sway her.

FitzHolland answered with more invective, calling her *bawd* and *slut*. She hoped King Henry was hearing this—who never swore above a *forsooth*. She called back, polite and cheery, "Present your petition like anyone else, or await a public audience."

Again Beth giggled, but the suggestion brought more abuse and threats from below, culminating in a command that she open up at once, "Or face dire and fatal consequences." She heard steps on the stair behind her, and the sergeant of the watch appeared, looking wary. Someone below must have realized she had the key.

Doing an awkward bit of a bow, the sergeant asked, "M'lady, if you will? His Majesty wishes to speak with you." Behind him the red signal flag continued to bob up and down.

Beth's grip on her tightened. Though it was death to open the door, she could stall only so long against a direct command from King Henry—who would soon realize that this was not some absurd outrage by the Nevilles. FitzHolland saw it, too, cutting short his curses. He shouted loudly and clearly. "Enough senseless talk. Open in the name of King Henry."

"Look, m'lady." Beth pointed down toward the river. "Look there." She looked, following the little girl's finger.

"Take me to the king," FitzHolland insisted. "I will prove to His Majesty I am no traitor."

"Too late." She waved triumphantly at Pleasance Manor, where men were finally pouring out of the main buildings and stables. "Look behind you."

FitzHolland twisted in his saddle, swearing mightily. Half a hundred riders in murrey and blue were pounding up from the manor, followed by swarms of archers. Edward had his own armored retainers—plus those lords attending the king—but the real threat lay in those knots of archers armed with powerful rapid fire bows; every farmstead for miles had its bows and bills, and a hue and cry would quickly raise the countryside. Thousands of archers could soon be scouring the surrounding counties for treasonous fugitives or whoever else needed apprehending. She called out to FitzHolland, urging him on his way. "Friends of yours, perhaps?" Warwick himself had condemned FitzHolland to death, and no phony Neville surcoat would save him. "They seem most eager to see you."

FitzHolland glared up at her, fuming in helpless fury at the base of the locked watchtower. Now he had to run. Somehow the former sergeant-at-law had avoided his one-way trip to Tyburn, but if these men caught him, they would carry out the sentence at once, figuring they were doing the condemned a favor—a swift dignified beheading, with king and nobles attending, and claret afterwards, being much preferred to agonizing death before a jeering London mob. Turning away from the watchtower, FitzHolland ordered his men to flee for the woods around Blackheath, shouting a hasty au revoir to her: "Damn you, lewd bitch, I will be back."

How comforting. She could not help being in FitzHolland's way; none of this was planned, least of all by her. FitzHolland was the last man Robyn cared to see—in fact, she had thought him safely dead. Clutching the battlements, she thanked the hard cold stones for being between her and him. Thanks to FitzHolland, she knew what it was like to have men seize her and hold her, ignoring her struggles, binding her and hurting her, aiming to kill her but determined to break her spirit first. Shuddering with relief, she hoped never to see the man again, alive or dead.

Behind her, the watch sergeant coughed in embarrassment, adding lamely, "M'lady, His Majesty waits below." She knew that; she just did not care—not at the moment. She badly needed to collect herself, and Henry of all people would understand. Medievals were not likely to hang you just for being late, since everything ran on sundial time. Henry himself once refused to speak or respond to questions for a year and a half.

"Ho, the tower," called a warm familiar voice. "Is His Majesty safe?" Looking down, she saw Edward, splendidly fetching in shining half-armor, heraldric surcoat, and thigh-length leather boots, sitting atop his big black Friesian, surrounded by a knot of excited horsemen wearing his colors. My, but the boy could dress, even in dire emergency. Matt Davye was with him, and so was Deirdre— two red-gold splashes in the mob of murrey and blue. Robyn saw no sign of the wayward royal groom, who was probably riding off with FitzHolland, but everyone else was safe and accounted for, thank Hecate. Edward rose in his high saddle, "My Lady Robyn, is the king with you?"

Again King Henry. Folks had an unhealthy fixation with Henry— his whereabouts, his mental health, his family affairs, and marital relations were all subjects of intense national debate—no wonder the poor fellow flipped out. Robyn was a virtual nobody, and she already felt way too much public attention on her private life. Holding in her hollow stomach, she called down to Edward, "King Henry is here, and here is the key." Taking the heavy iron key from the hidden pocket in her silver-blue gown, she tossed it down. Still clutching Beth's hand, she turned and brushed past the bemused sergeant, lifting the silver hem of her gown and descending the stairs, obedient to her king's command.

By the time Edward opened the door, she was doing her best curtsy to King Henry, with Beth at her side, confessing she no longer had the key. Edward went down on one knee before his king, asking after His Majesty's health and offering an escort back to Pleasance Manor. Henry accepted, and they all rode back down the hill, surrounded by a mob of happy archers waving their bows and crowing over their easy victory.

Riding downhill in a daze—with her handmaid beside her and Beth mounted pillion behind Deirdre—Robyn gladly left Henry to Edward. Tag team king-sitting. Instead she listened to Deirdre breathlessly describe her own adventures trying to dodge the phony Nevilles—the gay way the girl talked about getting caught by armed men sent shivers through Robyn. Edward's bowmen had chased Deirdre's captors off, but the teenager had ridden into mortal danger at the orders of her mistress, carrying a message Deirdre had no hope of delivering. That snap command to find Edward could have been Deirdre's death sentence, depending on what man happened to grab her—Robyn's stay in the Tower taught her that English chivalry did not apply to nobodies. But being Irish, Deirdre knew that already. Robyn did not feel secure until they had King Henry safely in chapel for vespers, still unsure what had happened. Only then did she give her heartfelt thanks.

After vespers, she collapsed on a cushioned window seat in Edward's tapestried apartments, shocked at having seen—and talked with—Gilbert FitzHolland, someone she thought was safely dead. But by now she should have known that the past would not always stay buried. Thrilled with her performance, Edward handed her a silver goblet of warm cinnamon wine, asking, "Are you well?"

"Hope so." She took a soothing sip. Half of England's current problems came from the aristocracy drinking nothing but wine and beer, effectively preventing sober government. No wonder Victorians had to invent tea time, just to keep them from being totally smashed by early afternoon—it must have been amazing, sobering up to discover you were ruling half the world.

Edward settled in beside her, no longer wearing his half-armor, just a wide-sleeved white tunic with gold trim, very choirboyish—never judge a man by the wrapper. Putting an arm around her, he tenderly nuzzled her neck and kissed her cheek. "Unbelievable. You are most amazing, saving King Henry for us in the very teeth of two score horsemen."

"If you say so." She took another sip, still horribly shaken. Edward acted like she had driven the horsemen off single-handed, when all she did was bar the door. And Henry was never in much personal danger. FitzHolland would have whisked his royal cousin off to some friendly castle, then probably out of the country. It was England that was endangered—and her—any harm done to Henry would have been purely accidental. Though Heaven knows the royal family had certainly had its share of happy accidents.

Edward heartily praised Matt Davye as well. "Your new horse master was splendid at every turn. When King Henry's groom shied away, Matt followed the man at a distance. Spying the false Nevilles, he came straight here, insisting on giving his message to me alone." Edward liked servants who showed intelligence and initiative—anyone could be obedient, but real underlings knew when to break the rules. "What a shrewd stable lad you have found."

She had not found Matt Davye. Matt had come to empty the slop bucket in her Tower cell, but she took the compliment as intended. It felt good to be appreciated, even for the wrong reasons, and she was glad Matt had made such a hit. Taking another sip of cinnamon wine to fortify herself, she told her beau, "I recognized one of them."

"Recognized who?" Edward pulled her closer, all set to thank her personally, having come perilously near to losing the king—an unimaginable catastrophe—on his first attempt at king-sitting. Dad and Warwick would have never forgiven him.

Resting her head against his gold-trimmed shoulder, she reveled in his firm security, saying, "Those false Nevilles were led by Gilbert FitzHolland." She saved this for Edward alone, lest it get back to Henry that his bastard cousin had been leading the "Nevilles." Matt Davye was not the only one able to keep a secret.

"Gilbert FitzHolland?" Edward looked askance. "But the man is dead. Hanged, drawn, and beheaded at Tyburn."

"So we hoped." She had felt bad about his death sentence, but now that little bit of guilt was gone—FitzHolland had used his newfound freedom to strike immediately at the peace, and at her. "Yet it was FitzHolland, speaking astonishingly well for someone both hanged and beheaded."

"What did he say?" Edward turned suddenly serious, clearly scared for her.

"Mostly, 'Damn you, open this door.' And the like." She laughed lightly, taking a sip of wine, glad Edward took her cares so swiftly to heart. She had only to show concern, and he was there. "Plus filthy names I will not repeat."

Edward shook his head. "How ghastly. Someone must have freed him, someone with gold enough to open doors in Newgate. And to supply him with men, as well."

Not to mention Neville surcoats. "Unless FitzHolland thought this scheme up to pass the hours in his cell, someone also gave him Henry's schedule and put him in touch with the missing groom."

Edward agreed, mentally reviewing suspects, saying, "Someone very near to the king." Edward could have named everyone with access to King Henry, from cooks to clerics—he had that sort of attention to detail, drunk or sober.

"But not King Henry himself," she pointed out. "His Majesty was royally shocked by the whole business."

Edward kissed her again, glad to hear this, since nursemaiding the king would be infinitely harder if Henry were scheming to escape. "So how did you happen to be with the king?"

"There was no happenstance in it at all," she boasted. "Henry came to me."

"Whyever?" Edward inquired. "Aside from the obvious reasons." His arm tightened possessively about her—even a dashing boy earl could envy his king.

"Alas, I was not the true object of royal attention," she admitted, taking another tipsy sip. Henry was far too timid and pious for that; just getting his wife pregnant had put the man in a coma. "His poor daft Majesty wanted to know your feelings. Heaven alone knows why."

"So His Majesty went straight to the source." Edward took her free hand in his, kissing her fingers and then pressing them to his heart. "And people claim the king is mad."

His hand felt comforting, closed warmly around hers. She told him, "King-sitting is not as fun as I hoped."

"King-sitting?" Her love looked puzzled.

"Looking after King Henry. It is another one of those things—like being cast away on a deserted island—that sounds like a grand adventure, but turns out to be too deathly serious, and a bit boring to boot." Medievals loved this pomp and circumstance, punctuated by outrageous drinking bouts over poisonous meals. When she was duchess of York, she would be unable to duck it, but by then she hoped to be living in the country with Edward, raising kids and redecorating the castle.

Edward laughed, "Worry not, our 'king-sitting' will not last. Enjoy this while we can."

Back at Baynards Castle, things had already changed. She returned to a castle bursting with ladies-in-waiting wearing white and gold, who rushed out to cheer their triumphant return. Edward's mother had arrived—the current duchess of York. Until now, Edward had hardly any waiting women, unless you counted washerwomen, seamstresses, and hangers-on like Robyn and Deirdre. Now a duchess's household had moved in, much to the delight of the men, who thought the liberation of London was going splendidly. First they had the Baynards Castle back, and now women had returned.

Not just women, but kids, as well. Children came running up to greet them, and Edward introduced his younger siblings: sister Margaret—a woman at fourteen, fair and pious like her mother; and two younger brothers—George, about Beth's age, very charming and full of himself, and the youngest, small dark Richard. Here was half the far-flung family, the most that had been together in one spot in almost a year. Last time Edward saw these children he was fleeing into exile, and the kids were being left to the mercy of the queen and court. George demanded of his older brother, "Have you been in battle?"

"Twice," Edward told him, "on land and at sea. And Lady Robyn was with me both times."

Her stock went way up with both boys; George made a man's bow, and Richard gave her a long awed look. Margaret sounded shocked: "Not in armor, I hope!"

"Heavens, no," Robyn assured the girl. "The men were in armor. I was in a velvet dress—but I believe they gave me a break." Margaret smiled shyly, not knowing what to make of her. Too bad. Up until now, Robyn had adopted an easy attitude toward children and teenagers, who happily answered her questions about things everyone should know, applauding her efforts to seem more medieval, more English. Or in Deirdre's case, more Irish. With Margaret, she needed to be circumspect, since anything she said would no doubt go straight to Mom.

Edward went with his siblings to greet the mother he had not seen since he and Dad abandoned her to the enemy. Retiring to her tower room, Robyn ordered water boiled for a bath, foreseeing a close inspection and wanting to look her best for Duchess Cecily. While Robyn washed, Deirdre laid out gowns on the bed and consulted on colors. Murrey and blue would not do. And even her own gold and red was not the best, since her claim to Stafford livery was mere propaganda—most people liked seeing the Yorkist heir with a woman in Lancastrian colors, but Edward's mother might easily take it amiss. So Robyn settled on Collin's blue and silver, displaying her link to the Greys, her medieval foster family. Properly primped and ready, she sat down and waited for word from the duchess.

When the summons to meet Duchess Cecily never came, she was more relieved than insulted. Deirdre returned from chores to say the duchess had installed herself in the master suite, taking Edward's bed and bedroom, his wardrobe and presence chamber. There would be no more gala parties ending with them being sung upstairs to bed. Her handmaid grinned wickedly. "Your betrothed will be without a room, unless we have him here."

"Things are crowded enough," she told Deirdre tartly. Medieval rank and formality were closing in, cutting into her privacy, and she had not even met her future mother-in-law.

Dinner was more of an ordeal than usual. After three weeks at Court she was used to sitting apart, watching Edward eat at the high table—but she had supposed that would end once they got home. Now she saw it would last until their betrothal was revealed. At least she got a good look at Mom, who fairly glittered in a gold gown set off by clouds of white lace, talking easily across the high table with her son. Blond and stately, and still handsome at forty-five—no mean feat in the Middle Ages—Cecily of York was a Neville by birth, Salisbury's sister, and Warwick's aunt. You could see where Edward got his tall good looks and his coloring—halfway between Cecily's and his father's, who was said to be small and dark like little Richard. You could also see where Edward got his proud intensity and his fondness for listening—sitting and sipping wine while Duchess Cecily went on about the visions of Saint Bridget. "People call her Proud Cis," Deirdre whispered in Gaelic, "and they say she spends an earl's income on her clothes."

Both rumors were easy to believe. It used to surprise Robyn that Edward valued her opinion so highly, almost from the moment they met. At best it seemed an obvious ploy to get her into bed—but it was not. Seeing Edward laughing and joking with his strong-willed mother, she realized he had been taught early on to respect female opinion. His mother, nurse, and older sister had raised him, not his always busy father. It sobered her to think that she was probably the first woman he was alone with after leaving home—and he had been under a spell as well.

After dinner, Edward invited her to a private audience with Proud Cis, apologizing ahead of time, "Mother can be infernally proud, and fierce as a bear when the family is threatened. And do not talk to her about religion, or you will not get out until dawn." Edward looked worried, something she had not seen when he was trapped in a ship assaulted by Irish pirates or facing three-to-one odds on horseback—introducing her to his mother easily trumped such mundane emergencies. Those historians who portrayed medieval women as helpless pawns of their fathers, sons, and husbands had to have been men.

"Say something encouraging," she suggested, not having seen Edward this concerned since she set off alone before the battle of Northampton to contact Collin in the enemy camp.

Edward thought for a moment; then his face brightened. "Mother once whipped Warwick's bare bottom with a willow switch."

"Never!" She was descending the keep stairs, wearing her shimmering blue gown trimmed with cloth-of-silver, but that image stopped her in midstep. Edward must be making it up. "Richard Neville, Earl of Warwick?"

"Pulled his hose down to his ankles and left long red welts on his rear. Or so I hear, not being there myself. It was when he was an infant, and mother visited her brother Salisbury, where she caught him bullying the other children."

"Not the noble Warwick!" she scoffed. Actually, it was the obnoxious Neville to a T. She set out again, ready to give Duchess Cecily a chance.

"He was not noble Warwick then," Edward reminded her. Warwick's earldom came from his wife.

Curtsying low—in the same presence chamber where she and Edward used to take their private baths—she waited for Duchess Cecily to give her leave to rise. New hangings covered the walls, and the tub was gone, replaced by a plush carpet. Proud Cis clearly rated appearance above cleanliness.

"Rise, child." Duchess Cecily was old enough to be her mother, but not by much, and sat in a high-backed chair, wearing a cloth-of-gold gown and sporting her husband's falcon-and-fetterlock badge done in silver thread. Robyn remembered when she had first heard of that badge, while hiking in twenty-first-century Wales, and thought it weird at the time. Now it went way beyond weird to stand before a duchess wearing it, in her husband's castle, betrothed to her son. What was she doing here?

Edward introduced her as Lady Robyn Stafford without saying lady of what, skipping straight to the story of how she saved him when he was held captive aboard the *Fortuna,* beset by Irish pirates—leaving out the magical parts, which he had not witnessed anyway. Edward had just that proper touch of "look what I found" enthusiasm, tempered by his need to keep the whole truth from Mom, saying, "She stood up to Owen Boy O'Neill himself, reminding the brigand of his Christian duty to the lord lieutenant, speaking so fairly she won the savage over."

Duchess Cecily gave her a disbelieving look. "You speak their language?" Edward's mother had spent years in Ireland—wild handsome George was even born in Dublin—but Her Grace never thought to learn Gaelic. "How long were you in Ireland?"

"Only a day or so," she admitted, taking the magic out of her life made it sound ludicrous.

Duchess Cecily eyed her evenly. "And you learned their language?"

"She has the gift of tongues," Edward explained. Feeling like a prize parrot, Robyn hoped the duchess did not demand a demonstration.

But Duchess Cecily had heard Gaelic aplenty. "Tut, my son, you make her sound like a popinjay. This is plainly a miracle. Admit it, my dear, you have had visions, as well."

She glanced at Edward, who merely rolled his eyes; then she confessed, "That very night, Your Grace." The first spirit she successfully conjured was an Anglo-Irish ghost called John-Amend-All, who aided her appeal to Owen Boy O'Neill.

"See, I told you." The duchess smiled for the first time, a grin remarkably like Edward's. And like Edward, his mom was no fool, and had already sensed enough to make Robyn uncomfortable. "Thank you for saving my son." Proud Cis sounded truly thankful, adding, "That took courage and spirit. You are young and ignorant, yet you have a visionary eye and a rudimentary religious sense, as well as no means to live. Can you read and write?"

She admitted she could—without saying she could do it in any language Duchess Cecily could name.

Her Grace concluded, "Then you would make a very good nun—a talent for saving men must not be wasted."

Get thee to a nunnery. She had to admire the cool offhand arrogance; clearly Proud Cis was determined to have everything her way, now that she was out of custody. If Duchess Cecily knew her son was betrothed to this young ne'er-do-well from nowhere—best known for seeing things and speaking barbarian tongues—Her Grace would have gone ballistic. Someday soon Proud Cis would have to know, but for now the best Robyn could do was to be scrupulously honest. "I fear I will never make a good nun."

"Women can do wonders if they will it," the duchess assured her. "And I have absolute faith in your ability to amaze."

Duchess Cis was shrewd if narrow-minded, but Robyn had hoped for better from this mystic aristocratic mother-in-law to be. After the uncomfortable interview was over, she sat sewing in her little tower room, wondering what she was doing, desperately trying to please these people. Who could hope to satisfy all their idiot prejudices and superstitions? No one she knew, that's for sure. Her own mother would not have cared that Edward's family were bigoted Catholic hillbillies in armor, former convicts and fugitives who had never heard of indoor plumbing—"Just so long as you love him, dear." Her fingers smoothed the fine satin fabric, making each stitch as tight and true as she could. There was much here she still enjoyed, the mystery and spellcraft, and getting to make beautiful things with her hands—Proud Cis had not put an end to that. Robyn would just have to settle for debauching Duchess Cecily's teenage son.

Edward breezed in on cue, happily complimenting her needlework and announcing he had moved into the big keep bedchamber used by the castellan before the main hall was built. "Which means we will be even closer together."

She saw he would persist in looking on the good side. Edward was not stupid, nor was he one to give up tactical advantage—admit the problem, and he might have to do something about it. But she would not let him off so easy, nor would Proud Cis. She could already see it would be "me or Mother"—Duchess Cecily was not about to give up her son and heir without a fight. Putting aside her sewing, she nodded significantly to Deirdre, who suddenly remembered an undone chore and dashed off to it. Turning back to Edward, she asked, "Why cannot we just tell her? Your mother will know soon enough."

"Tell Mother what?" Edward tried to look innocent.

"That we are betrothed," she reminded him.

His looked turned to pure horror. "Dear God, she would disown me."

"So what?" She felt like telling the incredibly stuck-up Plantagenet clan to keep their two-bit dukedom, with its washed-out roads and Iron-Age amenities—she left a perfectly good studio job to come here, one that paid a whopping lot in this penny-ante economy. She smiled at the love of her life, asking, "Am I not worth it?"

"*Certainement!*" He took her hands in his, saying, "Of course you are," as if it were a statement of fact, not deigning to flatter, merely acknowledging that she was far better than he deserved—making her a countess was merely the best he could do. "Mother judges only by rank or religion," he complained with the impatience of youth, resentful of adults mired in the old ways. "My mother is descended of kings and raised to have her way—yet she shall not tell me who I will marry."

She could see he meant it—this was one fight Proud Cis would lose. "Yet our wedding must wait until after Parliament," Edward added. "Until then I am an attainted traitor, with all my lands and titles forfeit. How can my love marry a landless condemned criminal?"

Hiding behind his death sentence. Some men would plainly rather be hanged, drawn, and quartered than married. But Edward was right; his enemies would delight in using her against him. They could not possibly get married until Parliament confirmed his rights—then if folks took it amiss, they could retire to his earldom of March, where he had castles and manors and thousands of bowmen at his call, letting England lurch along without them. "Please forgive my mother's pride," he pleaded, brown eyes brimming with contrition. "I must give her the main hall for now, but we shall have the keep."

Baynards Castle's keep was the big central tower, with its own lord's hall, presence chamber, and bedrooms—not as comfy as the main hall, but better lodging than most medievals got. She could hardly pout if it was the best her boyfriend could do, having slept in much worse. And he made a fetching figure, begging her forgiveness in his dark velvet doublet with long ragged sleeves that showed the scarlet lining. So far she and Edward had not fought, surviving armed skirmishes, sea fights, and pitched battles without so much as a cross look or unkind word. Heaven knows why, but she had never been this much in love before. Saying it mattered not where he slept, she added wickedly, "Feel free to move in here with me."

He looked around the little room and laughed. "And then receive Warwick in your bedchamber?"

She shrugged. "It is what he thinks already." Warwick would be the least of his worries.

"This all will pass," Edward promised. "Exciting things are coming."

She arched an inquiring eyebrow. "How exciting?"

"Very, but I must not say more, for it touches on the king." He ended the conversation with a kiss, leaving her wondering what was afoot. First his mom, now Mad King Henry? She had thought His Highness was safe at Westminster, someone else's worry for the moment. If it touched on Henry, it could mean most anything; witness how her last "private" conversation with the king went.

Truth to tell, she had more pressing problems. Proud Cis was going to be with her for a while, but Mary in Saint Martin's needed more immediate attention. Early on the morrow, she received Dame Agnes in Edward's presence chamber, his white lion banner behind her. Living in a castle let you receive in grand style, with liveried servants and a sideboard of nuts, wine, cheese, raisins, sugared prunes, and candied ginger set out in silver dishes for her guest's refreshment. Suitably impressed, Dame Agnes would have gladly given a complete survey of the London prisons if Lady Stafford had let her. FitzHolland's escape was simplicity itself, according to Dame Agnes. "Three masked men overpowered the turnkey in the dead of night. Despite the hour, FitzHolland was up and waiting for them, showing he had warning through his jailers. He and his cellmate vanished into the night, not to be seen since."

Until turning up at Greenwich weeks later. "Who was his cellmate?"

"FitzHolland was lodged with a former executioner, also meant to die, the one they call Le Boeuf. Both were boastful and defiant, not fearful in the least. I had thought them brave villains, mocking their fate," Dame Agnes admitted ruefully. "Now it appears they were just well informed."

Le Boeuf, too. Figures. And the city jails could not be trusted—small surprise there. No one even thought to inform Edward that FitzHolland was free, showing how haphazard medieval communication could be. "Who do you suppose helped them?"

"Gilbert FitzHolland was a king's sergeant-at-law, with friends aplenty, some highly placed and owing him favors—even up to the highest," Dame Agnes added significantly. Within the City of London, the mayor was supreme after the king, and mayor William Hulyn was a holdover from the old regime, when FitzHolland's noble brother wielded power over life and death in London. Hulyn sat with Warwick at the Guildhall trials, but he might have approved the death sentences knowing some could be overturned on the sly. Which meant they must keep watch over Mayor Hulyn, though it was up to London to replace him.

Suitably warned, Robyn changed the subject. "What about Mary's crime?"

Dame Agnes said that was something shocking even by Cock Lane standards. "Her stepfather was an evil man, and came to an evil end, hacked to death with a kindling ax before his own hearth."

"How do they know Mary did it?" That still seemed so inconceivable.

"Hearing the man's cries of terror, people called a constable, who battered down the locked door, finding her stepfather dead and Mary spattered with his blood. There was no one else in the room, not even a cat."

Not good, but hardly conclusive. "And what did Mary say happened?"

Dame Agnes shook her head. "The girl would not say, refusing to give a word of explanation, not even to save her life."

"Nothing?" Mary had been talkative enough with her.

"Only that she was innocent." Dame Agnes looked distraught, clearly unable to imagine a reason doing Mary any good.

"Might there be some other way in or out of the room?" she suggested. "Aside from the door they broke down?"

Dame Agnes had plainly never thought of this, shaking her head and saying, "It was raining, so most likely the windows were shuttered. There might even have been a fire in the hearth." Might have been, if anyone had thought to look. Not enough medievals read Agatha Christie, or even Nancy Drew. She thanked Dame Agnes for her help, promising to investigate Mary's case personally.

She got Mary's side of the story, in the girl's tiny cell at Saint Martin-le-Grand. Mary did not need banners or a big buffet to impress her, though she happily ate all the nuts and candied fruit Robyn brought. Between bribes, Robyn begged Mary to tell her side of the story, but the girl just shook her head, insisting, "You will never believe me."

"I will try," she promised. Still the girl would not answer, so Robyn tried another tack, saying, "Do you swear you did not kill him?"

Mary nodded in silent agreement.

"But you were there?" Obviously.

Mary nodded miserably, willing to answer, but not to talk.

Still they were starting to get somewhere. "So you must know who did kill him?"

Mary shook her head. Undeterred, Robyn continued to lead her witness. "Did your stepfather attack you?" That seemed a safe guess.

Another nod.

"With the ax?" Robyn suggested.

"Oh, no," the girl insisted. "He preferred to beat me with his own fists, or sometimes a switch."

"So his hands were empty when he came at you?"

Again a nod. It was a weird game of medieval twenty questions. Drawing the girl closer, Robyn attempted to comfort her while squeezing out the truth. "Did he touch you?"

The teenager shook her head.

"What stopped him, then? Who killed him?"

Mary rested her head on Robyn's velvet shoulder, whispering softly, "His ax."

Well, of course. "But who wielded it?"

Another whisper even softer: "No one."

"No one?" Robyn looked askance, saying, "The ax just flew about the room, hacking at him all on its own?"

"Yes, m'lady." Mary nodded eagerly, glad to be finally understood. Welcome to the Middle Ages. Why had Robyn ever thought patient understanding would produce some sensible answer? Mary gave her a wary smile, asking, "Do you not believe me?"

It was a measure of how medieval she had become that she hugged the poor girl closer, whispering, "Yes, of course I believe you."

Mary thanked her profusely, promising that she never asked the ax to defend her; the dumb wood and iron had just flown up on its own, without so much as a by-your-leave. Mary had been horrified by the spectacle, sure that if she told anyone she would have been burned for heresy, if not witchcraft. Accused of calling on the occult to save her. Holding tight to Mary, Robyn wondered what she would do next. So much for being the medieval Nancy Drew, going over the murder scene for clues—none of this was going to make sense by modern police methods. She tried to picture the new trial Edward promised. Was anyone going to listen to testimony like this? Not likely.

Saturday, 23 August 1460, Saint Bartholomew's Eve,
Baynards Castle, London

My four-month anniversary in the Middle Ages. Edward says he has a surprise to mark the day—as if I could somehow forget. Four months ago I stood looking down on the green sweep of Cam Long Down—feeling like the Fool on a Hill—seeing the M5 motorway replaced by deep plowed medieval fields grazed by great flocks of sheep. Horror battling with denial. What a day that was—Saint George's Day—Wednesday, April 23, 1460. In that one day I met Gilbert FitzHolland, Le Boeuf, Lord Scales, and Sir Collingwood Grey, and ended up going to sleep in the dungeon of Berkeley Castle. Amazing that I did not die of culture shock. Now I am resigned to be the only person who remembers techo-industrial civilization. Who has been to "New" York and "New" England. Who can quote Shakespeare and name all four Beatles.

Edward has vowed to make up for it, saying I should wear my red-gold gown, the one trimmed in bullion, and the cap-of-pearls he gave me at our betrothal. Obviously the boy has plans. . . .

Edward had an ivory-white galley waiting at the castle dock, flying Stafford red and gold from her sternpost—only the second time she had seen her colors on anything bigger than a ball gown. And this sleek shining white galley, with its crimson oars and gilt trim, made the *Maidenhead* look shabby. Edward certainly knew how to impress a date. She turned to him with a puzzled smile, asking, "What is this for?"

"Why, for my lady, of course," he answered innocently, offering a hand to help her board. "Do you not recognize the colors? We must call on King Henry at Westminster."

"Must we?" It was her anniversary, and the first warm sunny Saturday since Saint Anne's Day, making visiting King Henry seem too much like work. Henry could drain the fun out of anything— even being born king—a boating picnic up the Thames would be ten times better.

"Come, do this for me," Edward begged, giving her hand a squeeze. "I have a special surprise for you. To me this is like a four-month birthday; four months ago you were born into my world."

How true. When she first arrived, Jo gave her a *Babee Book*, to teach her how to behave in a lord's manor. How to grovel gracefully and eat politely with your hands. She asked, "How do you know it is not my true birthday?"

Edward looked shocked. She knew his birthday—28 April 1442— but he had never thought to ask hers. "Is it?" he asked. "That would be too astounding."

Way too astounding. "Actually," she admitted, "I was born on the first day of spring, March twenty-first—that is why they called me Robyn."

He laughed, claiming he should have guessed. Boarding under clear bright skies, it felt like a real August weekend at home—an excellent omen. Not as hot as Montana in August, more like California. Rowed by twenty men in red-gold livery, the galley skimmed swiftly up the Thames, past the rose-twined Temple gardens, and tall lordly mansions with great green lawns and private docks. Crimson oar blades dipped and flashed in the sun, sending them slicing through the traffic on the upper river, leaving big row barges wallowing in their wake. Boatmen in little bobbing skiffs cheered as she swept by, seeing Stafford red and gold flying alongside the White Lion of March.

All the way, Edward would not say what lay ahead—which could mean almost anything under Mad King Henry. Any monarch, even a mad one, could give justice, save lives, grant titles, pardon crimes, and cure diseases, or so medievals supposed. Edward naturally reveled in the mystery of a royal surprise.

When they reached Westminster, with its great abbey and gilded angels, Edward escorted her in to see the king in his huge hammer-beam hall, one of the few times they were together at Court with all its pomp and protocol. Not that King Henry kept much state these days, having a mere handful of lords in attendance amid a crowd of retainers and liveried servants—some comedown after the feasts and processions in Canterbury. And nothing like the state the queen used to kept at Kenilworth. Magnificently dressed men in silver-trimmed satin and slashed velvet stood around, with a sprinkling of women trying to be seen—but any Court without a queen was bound to be drab. Warwick and most of his clan were still in Calais, or off dealing with the north, and the only nobles she recognized were friendly types like Collin's neighbor, Lord Saye, and James Douglas, the Scots earl-in-exile, both looking pleased to see her. As she and Edward entered, the multicolored Court fell silent, and the human peacocks looked toward the worst-dressed man in the room, the drab dark figure on the throne. Taking her cue from Edward, she curtsied to her king.

Henry smiled wanly, then nodded to a herald wearing the lions of England quartered with the lilies of France. Unrolling a parchment, the herald reared back and cocked his head, blasting out each word, proclaiming aloud that on this twenty-third day of August, King Henry of Windsor, the Sixth of his name, by the Grace of God monarch of England, Ireland, and France, would reward "Lady Robyn Stafford for her loyalty and support of her king at Greenwich Park and for her bravery at Northampton, both times in the face of his armed enemies. . . ." For this service she was given for life the revenues of the Honour of Pontefract, "including the towns of Bradford, Leeds, and Haworth, and the royal manors of Pontefract, Sayles, Ferrybridge, Castleford, Skelbrooke, and Barnsdale, and rent of the tenantries of Stubbs, Norton, and Fenwick for as long as she shall live." And remained unmarried. There was a strict proviso that should she marry, the rents and revenues would return to the crown and her husband had to provide for her—since a woman could not serve two masters.

Hearing the long list of manors amazed her mightily, more so than

the grant itself. She had expected she would be given something—
that was why people came to Westminster—but she thought it would
be more like a pat on the head and a purse full of gold nobles. Instead
she found herself on her knees, pledging homage and fealty to King
Henry, with her hands pressed together between his. She pledged her
entire faith to Mad King Henry, against all men living or dead. Then
he raised her up, and she repeated her oath on a holy relic, the same
martyr's tooth Edward had sworn fealty on after the battle of Northampton—now both she and Edward served Mad Henry, something
she never expected two months ago when they set out together from
Calais to oppose the king.

Her most bizarre medieval ceremony yet, stranger even than
Witches Night in a stable. Mad King Henry took Christian charity
literally, giving out titles, lands, leases, money, offices, pardons, and
reprieves without consideration of merit, previous grants, or political
repercussions. Driving the King's Council to distraction, until they
saw they had to limit access to the royal person, keeping appoint-
ments and petitioners away, totally separating Henry from the me-
chanics of government—which was most likely what Henry wanted
in the first place. But here he had outdone himself. Aside from wid-
ows and heiresses, women did not normally hold manors. She was
given only the net revenues—what the king would keep after ex-
penses. Actual running of the manors and the royal castle of Pontefract remained in the king's hands—a wise precaution on the Mad
King's part, since Robyn knew next to nothing about managing a
medieval estate. She could not even imagine what the total income
might be—but these "revenues" were hers for life, so long as she
remained unwed. Since she could not pass them to her husband or
her children, the crown lost nothing but current profits, which still
must come to hundreds of pounds a year. In a single royal stroke
her future was assured—such is the power of kings. Even mad ones.

Suddenly she was her own woman, and far less dependent on Edward—though that hardly mattered when they were so hopelessly in
love. In a few months she would give it all up to become countess
of March, making the Honour of Pontefract seem pretty paltry. Yet
the royal grant instantly made her a woman of means, able to say
no even to Edward. If Proud Cis became too impossible, she could
move to a town house. Or retire to her manor of Pontefract, which
was somewhere up north of Nottingham in Yorkshire—she knew it

from Shakespeare—not the least likely, but it gave her options. Was that what Mad King Henry wanted, enthroned in shabby silence? Was this Henry's weird backhand way of bidding for her favor? Hoping she would keep young Edward of March true to his king by making them both swear on the same holy molar?

Edward acted almighty pleased as well, bowing enthusiastically to his sovereign and plainly happy for her. Normally Edward was blasé about titles, mixing easily with everyone, never seeming bothered to be betrothed to a nobody—but he had always wanted to make her a "lady," swearing to do it on the first day they met. She had thought him totally daft at the time. Now she was Lady Robyn Stafford of Pontefract, pronounced *Pomfret* like the cakes.

Lady Pomfret humbly thanked her sovereign, feeling somewhat ashamed to get so much money for nothing—but she assuaged her guilt by remembering all she went through to get here. England might not owe her a living, but these men certainly did. Besides, this was how the medieval economy worked. Practically no one had normal jobs. Most were small farmers, and many of the rest were clergy; only in London and the larger towns did a lot of people work for wages, and many of them worked for a lord or lady who lived on rents and revenues from the countryside. She had literally nothing to do with the money but spend it on someone.

Hearing her thanks, Henry perked up—happy to see her happy. Giving things away was the high point of the royal day, and Henry would have done it every day if his keepers would let him. He gave away provinces to the French and founded Eton College—not all his impulses being equally fortuitous. Great as this was to her, it was hardly anything for him—some royal revenues that might revert to the Crown anytime. Until Edward and Warwick reined him in, Henry regularly spent five times his normal income on the royal household, though he himself dressed in sackcloth. Sitting up in his shabby black jacket, squaring his scuffed boots and grinning good-naturedly, her sovereign asked if there was anything else he could do for her. Henry was clearly in the mood to please.

Seeing a moment to hit up her monarch, she replied swiftly, "Nothing for me, Your Majesty, but there is a poor girl in Saint Martin-le-Grand sanctuary who was sentenced to be burned—and I will stake my own freedom on her innocence."

Henry asked for details, and she gave a medieval version of the abuse defense, leaning heavily on the stepfather-cum-husband's known shortcomings, and Mary's complete helplessness. Finding herself swearing to miracles she did not fully believe in—an ax could have flown about the room, chopping this miserable villain into kindling. It could have. Since coming to the Middle Ages she had seen weirder things happen, far weirder—just being in this time zone at all beat any airborne antics by inanimate objects.

His Highness ate it up, of course. Cock Lane sex and violence heaped with salacious suggestion abounded in so many pious moral lessons you could barely keep count—the sort of tabloid story London ached for, but did not yet know. Henry ordered Mary pardoned sight unseen, hardly believing the trial court could have been so blind to miraculous evidence. "He who made the earth and heavens can certainly make an ax to strike."

King Henry's court applauded her humble piety in the face of outrageous royal generosity, giving her favor to an unfortunate. Uppity young ne'er-do-wells must try not to look the part—ask nothing for yourself, just take what you can get. In a matter of months these people were going to have to swallow her being a countess, then eventually duchess of York. Here in fact was her first step up the social ladder, and the first test of her popularity. Polite applause said she passed.

Later, out of sight of Court, she let herself gloat. Sitting in the stern of her ivory white galley with her colors flapping overhead, she demanded details from Edward. "How long have you known this would happen?"

"Since the day we got back from Greenwich," he admitted, showing an unsuspected ability to keep secrets from her—she had never seen this coming. "It was King Henry's idea, and he swore me to secrecy." Handy, but no doubt true. Henry loved secrets and spying—particularly on women, which came from being taken from his mother so young. His Highness used to have peepholes in the palace, and he'd dressed up as a page to spy on his bride-to-be when Margaret first arrived from France. Such secrecy was more touching than the grant itself. Henry did care for her, enough to snoop about and plot surprises.

"Where is this Honour of Pontefract?" Her Honour of Pontefract, which she had never seen, and had only vague notions of its location. In four months she had been all over the Welsh Marches and seen something of Kent and the Midlands, but Yorkshire was still terra incognita.

"In the West Riding, right near my father's castle of Sandal. Very beautiful country," Edward recalled, "though I much doubt you will see it anytime soon."

Just the royal revenue from it. Putting politics aside, she gloried in the moment—and in the freedom the money gave her. Ever since that first day four months ago, where to sleep and what to eat had been a daily worry. People were more than kind to her, offering her tainted food off their own plates and inviting her to share their louse-infested beds. And Edward was the best, even taking up bathing in her behalf—though she suspected he did it for the sex. But having her own income and her own place, with things just the way she wanted them—that was what she missed most from the third millennium, more than MTV and microwave popcorn. She could really set up her own household and have an impact as someone other than Edward's "constant friend."

Watching the walled city pull toward her, she realized what an exciting time this was to be in London—even if she were not being rowed down the Thames from Westminister in an ivory-white galley with a royal grant in her pocket. This little city pulsed with life and possibilities, attracting the best people from England and footloose adventurers from abroad. Maybe she should open a print shop? She had seen printed books on the Continent, but there was not a single printing press in England. This newly liberated London needed a new voice. Naturally there were no copyright laws. She could reprint Christine de Pizan and old *Saturday Night Live* routines—here and now all the jokes were new. Seeing the way Henry took to her tabloid tale, she could even start a newspaper. Anything too political was treason, but she hoped to change that.

And another woman had won her freedom today. She told Edward, "I must go at once and break the good news to Mary."

"But I have the boat for the day," Edward complained. She saw he was teasing, and did not mean to invite her on a private riverside picnic with twenty lusty oarsmen for company.

"Maybe afterwards," she suggested, "we could picnic somewhere—minus the rowing crew." Mary's forty days were not up for more than a week, but the girl deserved to know right away. What would she do with Mary? Where would the girl sleep? Clearly her tiny tower room would not hold her growing household; too bad Proud Cis had taken up half the castle. Mayhap she would get a house in town. Yesterday that would have been unthinkable; today it was totally within her means.

At Baynards Castle she went straight to the chapel and gave private thanks. Her four-month anniversary in the Middle Ages was truly a day to remember. She managed to pour out her thanks, light a dozen candles to the Virigin, and escape before Duchess Cecily led her ladies in for noon prayers.

Telling Matt Davye to saddle Lily and Ainlee, she changed into a green riding gown and then set out with Deirdre for Saint Martin-le-Grand. Practical worries vied with excitement as she rode through the bustling streets with an eye out for town houses she might someday like to rent. Past Wardrobe Place she saw a couple that seemed perfect, though something in Cheapside might be better, with her print shop below and rooms above—close to the churchyard book market and the law courts, ensuring plenty of customers. At Saint Martin's sanctuary she gave Black Dick Nixon a silver groat to see Lily was not stolen. Bowing, the brigand vowed to do his best. She thanked the outlaw for his faithful service, realizing their relationship was about to end. Soon he would get his horse and be on his way.

As she led Deirdre into the great stone church, excited nuns came fluttering up to her, saying, "M'lady, m'lady, have you heard of the miracle?"

"What miracle?" Tears of rapture rolled down the nuns' faces as they mumbled over their beads, making it hard to tell what was going on. Had they already heard of King Henry's clemency? That would be incredibly fast even for London gossip.

"Mary is gone," the nuns chorused. "Gone to God. When Sister Eudocia came to take her to noon prayers."

"Gone to where?" Little of this made sense.

"To be with God!" the sisters insisted, sounding suddenly cheerful. "We thought you must have come because you somehow heard."

"She's dead?" What a calamity. These nuns had no way of knowing she came bearing the king's pardon.

"Not dead," they told her. "Gone! Sister Hildegard was sewing with her. When Sister Eudocia came to call them to noon prayer, Sister Hildegard answered the door, expecting Mary would come, too, as she did every noontide. When Mary did not emerge, both sisters looked back into the cell, and it was empty!"

Slowly their story sank in, about the time she was kneeling in Baynards Castle chapel, lighting her thanksgiving candles to the Virgin, Mary had disappeared. Vanishing almost in front of these nuns. "No, I had not heard," she told them. "I came to tell her the king had pardoned her."

"He has," the sisters happily agreed, still telling their beads. "Not King Henry, but Our King above."

5

⊷⊷⊷ Halloween ⊷⊷⊷

W*hat do you* think?" Deirdre asked in Gaelic when they were safely away from the Saxons, riding side by side past Saint Paul's.

"I'm trying not to," Robyn admitted, staring vacantly at the Saint Paul's Saturday market, letting Lily find her way home.

Not as ready as the average medieval to proclaim an immediate miracle, she had taken a quick look around before giving thanks in Mary's cell—seeing four bare walls and a window so high and small only a wren could use it. Roof and floor seemed solid, leaving just the doorway where the nuns had been standing. Robyn used to smugly think people could not just disappear—but then she did so herself. Magic was behind Mary's disappearance, powerful magic, full-blown sorcery that sent axes flying through the air and snatched teenage girls from stone cells. She did not have a clue who or what lay behind the magic, or even whom it was aimed at. Lady Robyn reminded her maid, "This is a day for celebration."

"So you believe Mary's in Heaven?" Deirdre said it like she had her doubts.

"Mayhap." Most medievals took random miracles as more proof of God's mysterious ways, but she dared not be so naive—such thinking was what got her here in the first place. "But we cannot be too trusting."

"Why so?" Deirdre gave a wary glance at the churchyard Saturday market, seeing nothing more sinister than tempting bargins—scented wax candles, lace fans, and strings of sweet figs. Both lady and handmaid suddenly had money to spend.

"Because such things happen for a reason." Which Lady Robyn had not yet divined. Four months ago to the day, she sat down on a green hill in twenty-first-century England, indulging in a silly ritual at the invitation of what she thought were amateur witches—and ended up here. She was still unraveling the reasons for that, and Mary was even more of a mystery. "Until we know the why of this, we must be wary."

"Surely this happened for good reasons," Deirdre suggested. "The man who died was a monster, and Mary must be in a better place." So they both hoped.

"Perhaps, but we have been drawn in, and that is suspicious." She went over the events of Saint Anne's Day in her mind, but it all seemed to pivot on her trivial decision to turn into the city, going to Smithfield by way of Cheapside and Newgate. Everything after that had been out of her hands—she had had to do what she did, right up to today, when she pleaded Mary's case to King Henry. "We have magical enemies, adept at laying traps for the unwary."

"Do you mean Duchess Wydville?"

"Among others." Duchess Wydville had laid several traps for her, and she had tumbled in every one—that day on the hill above Cam Long Down, then off the coast of Ireland, and finally in the Tower. Each time she had gone blindly forward, trusting in what she was told, a smile on her lips and glad hope in her heart. And each time she was roundly thumped for her pains—sent back to the Middle Ages, used as bait, and then abandoned in a black hole in the Tower basement. What a fool. She meant to do better next time. "Duchess Wydville is not even the worst."

"Bad enough for me," declared Deirdre, who distrusted the duchess heartily from the first. Robyn nodded in agreement, having learned to use Deirdre's suspicions as early warning radar. Robyn herself had been easily charmed by Duchess Wydville when they first met—never suspecting the kindly old dear could do anything to harm her. Then look what happened. She missed Mary already, hoping she was well.

Dean Stillington of Saint Martin's did not doubt Mary's disappearance was a miracle, but he managed to hint that given time the nuns might turn the girl up. Always possible. Managing a house of God holding monks, nuns, thieves, pimps, murderers, and political outcasts had to be pretty much hit or miss—a minor miracle in itself. So she told Black Dick Nixon to try to turn up word of Mary and what might have happened, promising to talk to him, "Monday, after Saint Bartholomew's Mass."

"As m'lady wishes," he replied with a swarthy grin. "I will not be going out." Her visits had been nothing but profitable.

Monday brought no word of Mary, not from the nuns, or from Nixon, so she gave in to the inevitable, rewarding Black Dick Nixon for his service—seeing him safely out Aldersgate headed for Barnet and the Great North Road. Venetians were happy to lend her money against her manorial revenues, filling her purse with enough silver to buy him a beautiful horse, a big buckskin stallion that looked to have brains as well as body. Nixon liked the look of him, too, saying, "M'lady knows horseflesh."

"I grew up with horses," she told him. "And cattle."

"As did I," replied Black Dick with a smile, his family being infamous stock thieves. "We have much in common, m'lady."

"We do?" There were few medievals she felt less akin to than Black Dick Nixon, mercenary cutthroat and border bandit.

"For sure, m'lady, we both speak good Northumberland, unlike these Southrons." They had naturally enough been using his native tongue. "An' I ken you come by yer Northumberland dishonestly."

"Really?" It came through spellcraft, very much a crime.

"No matter," Nixon hastened to assure her. "I come across my own Northumberland dishonestly, making us both born outlaws."

"I see," she replied primly. Nixons were notorious border reivers, taught from childhood to steal, making a Nixon as natural an outlaw as a sorceress.

Black Dick's grin widened. "An' when these fine lairds find you out an' turn against Yer Ladyship, well then there is sanctuary awaiting you in Tynedale. Just follow the North Tyne until you are near Kielder an' the Borders; then ask about for Nixons, or Crosers, and we will take you in—for thou art a winsome lass who did me more than one good deed."

Thanks, but no thanks. What was it with medieval men that they all had such big plans for her? Pious King Henry wanted her married and cared for, showering her with rents and revenues in the meantime. Gallant young Edward immediately made her his lady. Sadists like Scales and FitzHolland could barely wait to see her punished for her sins, and now this felon on the lam wanted her for his thieves' den. This was the witch hunter's great dilemma: even the worst of men could not help liking a witch who was pretty, pleasant, and obliging—especially when she spoke his language and lined his pocket. She thanked the fugitive felon, promising to remember his offer if ever she were that desperate. Then she gave him a purse with six gold half-nobles inside, wishing him luck.

Nixon knelt in the mud and kissed her hand, thankful as only a cutpurse can be when someone just hands him gold. Then Black Dick mounted his gift horse, saying, "Good luck with yer young earl, then. An' when he tires of you, your ladyship has safe haven in Tynedale."

Then he was off, riding insolently up Aldersgate street, headed north, a border ruffian with a day-old beard, his boots thrust out of his stirrups and a broadsword across his back, whistling a heathen tune through his teeth. Thus ended a strange chance relationship that began in the ironstone village of Hardingstone, with its gothic Eleanor's Cross, on the road to Northampton. Black Dick Nixon came banging on a farmwife's door, along with Mary's Jock, Sweet-milk Selby, and Bangtail Bell, looking for excuse to loot and finding her instead. Something Black Dick never held against her, despite her role in the death of his lord, the loss of Nothampton, and his landing in sanctuary. He always pressed the relationship, pounding on her door and holding her horse; she in turn talked him out of looting that day in Hardingstone, and now sent him home with gold in his purse, one of the only Percy border riders to profit from his trip south. Strange, but somehow fitting.

Back home at Baynards Castle, she moved up to the high table, making for livelier dinner talk. Now that Lady Robyn was idly rich, she could eat with Duchess Cis and her ladies without fear of her commonness contaminating them. Over baked eels and sea bream, Duchess Cecily treated her like a cross between a lady-in-training and wayward servant girl caught playing show-and-tell with her son. Religion was the only topic allowed, being both safe and instructive. "You are young," Duchess Cis informed her, "and no doubt ignorant. Have you ever read the Testaments?"

"Parts of them." But not recently. Her total immersion in medieval Catholicism was heavy on ritual and light on Bible study, but she used to work for the people who made *The Ten Commandments* and *Jesus Christ Superstar*.

"And the Church Fathers?"

"Hardly at all," Robyn admitted.

Duchess Cecily's smile broadened. "Not surprising. Do not blame yourself, my dear; women are woefully taught. Luckily, we are more willing to learn than men will admit." Her ladies tittered lightly. They had the high table to themselves since Edward was dining out with Earl Douglas, and the only men were those serving them date compote and pickled porpoise. "Look at you, almost totally untutored, yet already you see visions."

Only since coming here. She nodded attentively, feeling like some sort of spiritual idiot savant. Most medievals spoke with incredible certainty about religion, because belief hardly had any competition; science was still crude astrology and amateur chemists struggling to turn rocks into gold—most people put far more faith in magic. Duchess Cecily looked her over thoughtfully, saying, "Women's mysticism is no simple thing; our feelings run much deeper and flow more freely than men's, with more twists and turns. We have to look farther within ourselves, and find more devious pathways to the divine."

Devious and then some. Tonight was Witches Night, as well as the Feast Day of Saint John the Baptist. Proud Cis reminded her of the Duchess Wydville; one was a Christian mystic, and the other was Witch-Duchess of Bedford—but both were infernally sure they had a direct line to the hereafter, happily managing whoever's lives most needed meddling. Duchess Cecily told her, "Your precocious spirituality reminds me of the young Catherine of Siena—who could neither read nor write, yet lived the life of a saint. You have her sense of self-sacrifice and service, as well as wit and will, and a power of attraction that brings people to you. Both women and men, is that not so?"

Robyn nodded. All too true. Everyone from Black Dick Nixon to the Duchess of Bedford was overly concerned with her physical and spiritual well-being. Owen Boy O'Neill made her an honorary colleen before she even set foot in the country.

Duchess Cecily smiled in triumph, adding, "And have you a thirst for mortification?"

"Sometimes," she admitted, though not on her better days.

"I see it in how you eat—barely picking at your sea bream, and not even touching the baked eels or pickled porpoise. Eating sparingly, obsessively boiling water, and washing food—all these show a morbid fear of death."

Or of medieval food and sanitation. Being Friday, Duchess Cis had only fish on the table, but eels repelled Robyn, and pickled porpoise was not as bad as it sounds—being a fish and not Flipper—but still did not tempt her. "Your very fear makes you court destruction," Duchess Cis decided, "leaving you dangerously thin. Self-sacrifice is second nature to you, so much so you put yourself in constant peril, telling everyone it is for others." Much of this was annoyingly accurate, but Robyn had no plan to open up to Proud Cis. She missed Jo, far away in Cotswolds, who could talk of anything and everything without fear or censor. How could she seriously examine her life when she constantly had to lie about it? Duchess Cecily asked, "Have you seen the Virgin yet?"

She confessed she had not. "At least so far as I know."

Her Grace nodded, approving her willingness to doubt the senses. "You will."

And soon, from the sound of it. Escaping dinner, she retreated into her tower room, wishing Prince Charming would do something about Mom—but he was far too busy running England. Some thin excuse. Worse yet, she could not even sulk properly, because she had to share the room with Deirdre and little Beth—both of whom impertinently insisted on trying to cheer their mistress. First rule in the *Babee* book, "Keep tales in mind to please your lord or lady." Somehow she needed more space. You cannot have a household without a house.

Monday, 1 September 1460, Labor Day, Baynards Castle, London

September first. Labor Day back home. End of summer, one last picnic then pack the kids off to school. Here fall is still weeks away, and families labor nonstop to bring in the sodden harvest, with children binding the sheaves their parents cut, learning by doing. With rain pelting the standing crops, every hand is needed to reap what can be saved. London can import foreign grain—for a price—but most people live on what they grow or sell. Deirdre says in Kent it rained so hard harvesters were found drowned in the fields. Winter will be even worse.

Which is why I am house hunting in earnest, not just picturing myself in places, but actually looking for something to rent. Wait any longer, and it will be too late. Next month Parliament comes to town, and London will fill up with lords, ladies, and MPs from the countryside, plus all the hangers-on it takes to keep them happy. I have looked for places in Cheapside and around Saint Paul's. And even Saint Bride's beyond the wall, which seems perfect for a print shop, though I want to live in London, or at least Southwark.

Monday, 8 September 1460, Nativity of the Virgin, Baynards Castle, London

Friday would have been Mary's forty-first day in sanctuary, and since it was Witches Night, I prayed for her. No answer. And at the Virgin's birthday Mass this morning, as well. Again, no answer.

Edward has sworn to take me away from all this, at least as far as the Southwark Fair. He promises another surprise. We shall see. . . .

Southwark Fair turned out to be a low dirty affair of jugglers and street vendors. Edward looked happy to escape Mom's pious grip, clearly missing the good old days when London was newly liberated and they were free to throw wild parties and free tournaments. Southwark still had that liberated feel, with its floating population of peddlers, street players, pilgrims, prostitutes, and scofflaws living under the forgiving rule of the bishop of Winchester. She saw a delightful puppet show and a monkey acrobat doing cartwheels on a tightrope, wearing a skirt and carrying a basketful of eggs. Meat roasting on the street corners smelled heavenly, forcing her to give in and eat some hot off a spit. It was delicious and thoroughly cooked. Edward's younger brothers George and Richard came with them, and having been raised in the country, they were all agog, staring wide-eyed at the acrobats and whores.

Secretly, Lady Robyn eyed a tall half-timbered three story standing empty, with a shop below and living quarters above. Wondering who owned it and why it stood empty, she decided to ask when Edward was not with her.

He led her past pilgrim's inns and public baths to Falstaff's Place, the Southwark mansion the Greys used, and where she stayed in July when the rebels marched up from Sandwich and Southwark welcomed them in. Falstaff's Place took up most of a block, with a gated courtyard, stables, and baths, as well as the stately mansion, putting it far out of her price range. Warm baking smells came from tenements in front.

Edward had arranged for them to dine in the great hall, with its carved oak furniture, liveried footmen, and live music. Going out with Edward always meant the unexpected. It used to be battles and derring-do; now it was royal grants, masked balls, and surprise buffets. Terribly inventive. Sitting back in his carved oak chair, dressed in his own murrey and blue, he asked, "What do you think of this place?"

"Absolutely awesome," declared George, with berry jam spread on his noble face. Young Richard agreed. They were thinking of Southwark as a whole, with its beer gardens and bear baiting.

Robyn smiled. "I have loved this house from the first day you brought me here, and I saw London out my window." She had spent those first heady July days here, before the battle of Northampton, enjoying herself immensely. Oddly enough, the mansion's former owner—the late Sir John Falstaff—was one of the few fifteenth-century people she had heard of before coming here. Falstaff was a character out of Shakespeare—there was even a whole play about him, *The Merry Wives of Windsor*—and he had owned various properties around town, from this pretty mansion to the Boar's Head Inn. The old knight had died some months before she arrived, and now the mansion belonged to his lawyers, the Pastons, pushy Norfolk gentry who sought Edward's "good lordship." The sharp contrast between this opulent manor of a successful old warrior and Shakespeare's drunken buffoon always reminded her not to prejudge the Middle Ages. Literally anything was possible. She told Edward, "This hall holds many warm memories for me."

"Good," Edward declared, pouring himself some wine, "for I have asked Hansson, the Pastons' agent, to let me have it, until next Michaelmas."

"For me?" She could not believe it; this mansion was far beyond Lady Pomfret's means, with a main hall you could play handball in, hung with pious tapestries and captured battle flags, plus enough objets d'art to start a museum. Upkeep alone would sink her, even if she got the place for free.

"You? Whyever for?" Edward looked at her like she were mad. "For my mother, the duchess."

"Your mother?" Proud Cis, duchess of York, living in wild Southwark amid tavern wenches and Winchester Geese? "Would she, really?"

"Yes," Edward replied airily. "I think mother would be far happier out of that cold, dank castle. Winter is coming, and this is an astonishingly handsome manor. Besides, things seem far livelier south of the river, which mother might well enjoy. Do you not think so, boys?"

Brother George immediately agreed. "Oh, yes, Mother will love it, with all the music and dancing."

Little Richard was more circumspect, saying, "There are many amazing people here, though some seem very low fellows."

Hiding her smile, Robyn solemnly agreed with him, "Certainly, Southwark has many souls in dire need of religious instruction." The riotous medieval fair going on outside, and its drinking, dicing, music, and whoring made the perfect forum for a serious examination of women's religious mysticism.

"*Exactement!*" Edward declared, pleased that everyone agreed. "And all under the gentle guidance of the good William Waynflete, bishop of Winchester. I do not think where Mother could be happier."

"But will she really do it?" Proud Cis was not the type to be easily pushed around.

"*Absolument,*" Edward assured her, "with Parliament coming, we will need to have the castle ready." Clever use of politics. Parliament could mean confrontation if the beaten lords brought hostile retinues to town, so naturally the castle must be in a state of defense—any boy who could capture his king could certainly outmaneuver Mom. Edward added softly, "And I thank you for taking mother's religious lectures sans complaint; that alone makes you a saint."

She laughed at that suggestion. "Not hardly—I have been pricing town houses for over a week. If your mom had not been gone by this Michaelmas, I would have been."

"Then it is well I moved in time." Edward toasted his success; in its own way, this was as deft an operation as his landing at Sandwich or his march on Northampton—swift, timely moves taking even his family by surprise. Now he had turned his prompt ingenuity to domestic affairs, with resounding success. Edward meant to have her for his countess, despite family feeling and feudal tradition—if medieval England could not deal with that, then the country would just have to change with the times.

Thursday, 18 September 1460, Saint January's Eve, Baynards Castle, London

Duchess Cecily and her ladies are in Southwark, and I have my castle back. Edward dutifully visits his family daily, ten times happier with the broad river Thames running between him and Mom. Life here has returned to the normal routine of impromptu parties, late-night scented baths, heathen Irish singing, and witches' Sabbaths. Tomorrow is the last Witches Night of summer, and after that comes the fall equinox. With Proud Cis safely across the river, celebrating the change of seasons will not be such a religious juggling act. Duchess Cecily's Christianity clearly works for her—and I am far more Christian now than ever before—but I still need to practice my own women's mysticism.

Who knows how long this idyll will last. Edward's father finally landed in Chester, and will make his way to London anon. And it is the good duke's digs we are living in. Suits me right for dating a teenager who must ask Dad for the keys to the castle. Edward radiates optimism, saying there is much to do in the west, and the roads are drowned in rain—so Dad will not likely arrive before Parliament. Edward is too polite to say it, but he moves much faster than his father; it having taken the good duke more than a month to make the short sea crossing from Ireland. Faced with that exact same trip, Edward got us to Calais in days, then landed at Sandwich, marched on London, and seized the king in less time than it took Dad to get to Chester.

After Parliament Edward claims we will do as we please. We shall see. I am asking Dame Agnes to suggest women for my budding household. They are building a whole new wing at Ludgate just to house families jailed for debt—someone there must need a job. . . .

Friday was Saint January's Day, the subject of her Witches Night sermon to Beth and Deirdre when the three of them were alone in her dark tower room, kneeling in white shifts around a single candle.

She asked her witches-to-be, "Why does Saint January's Day come in September?" Neither pupil knew, slowly shaking heads crowned with wreaths of wheat.

"Saint January was a Christian bishop and a martyr," Robyn explained, "but before that he was a Roman god, Janus, god of boundaries and beginnings. And before that he was Diana, witch-goddess of birth and death—our first beginning and ultimate boundary. Which was why the Romans began their year in January, with gifts and winter feasting."

Both nodded solemnly, but Beth observed, "Our year begins with Easter." Putting the rebirth of Christ above the mere birth of the new year.

"But that will not last," Robyn explained, "the New Year will return to January." One prophecy sure to come true. "And just like January is the boundary between one year and the next, Sunday is the fall equinox, the boundary between summer and winter. Which makes this the last Witches Night of summer, the last night we will wear white. After tonight we will wear the black shifts of fall and winter."

She felt them shiver. Winter was an icy ravenous beast here and now, with frigid claws and cold fangs, devouring the young, the sick, the old, the unlucky, and the unwary—and this dark, wet winter looked to be worse than most. But it was not here yet, she reminded them. "Right now the wheel of the year is in balance, with equal hours of dark and daylight—this is called the equinox. But darkness is winning. Each night is a little longer, each day a bit shorter. We cannot stop it, no more than we can stop the sea with our hands, but we can ready ourselves, by welcoming in winter and welcoming in the darkness."

This sort of talk got witches in trouble. Honest folk were rightly afraid of darkness, with its death and demons. Witches' talk of "welcoming in the darkness" or "taking back the night" sounded to them like appeals to evil, smacking of pacts with Satan. She asked her charges, "What do we need to welcome in the winter?"

"Food," Deirdre suggested, eyeing nuts, berries, and newly baked loaves that ringed the candle to represent the harvest.

"Yes." Robyn nodded solemnly. "That is what all England prays for. What else do we need?"

"Warmth." Beth nodded at the bolt of black fabric set aside for their winter shifts. "And friends and family," added the alderman's daughter, who like most medievals associated warmth with closeness.

"Food and warmth is what we are offering. Friends and family are who we will call on," Robyn told them—or the closest thing she had to family here and now. Casting her circle, Robyn began a keening chant, calling on Joanna Grey, far off in the Cotswolds—who had taught her the chant and who promised last July to see her on Saint January's Night. Deirdre was not yet ready for a Witches Flight, but mayhap the Cotswolds could come to them. Both girls joined in, and the chant ran around the small circle as they focused solemn faces on the candle flame. Dark flickering shadows danced on the walls behind their wheat-crowned heads.

Slowly the candle flame grew in the darkness, broadening out, starting to look like a distant night fire floating in the air between them. Without pulling the girls from their trance, Robyn raised the chant, filling the tiny tower room with song, pushing back the walls, and letting in the night. Black air rushed in out of nowhere, fanning the candle flame.

Growing ever bigger, the flame became a fire, widening the circle, throwing bigger, wilder shadows on the wall. Women appeared in the shadows, wearing white shifts and chanting along with them. Robyn saw Jo and Joy sitting in the front row, their long black hair showing against their bright white shifts. Behind them, she could dimly make out a dark hilltop, recognizing Shenberrow Hill on the Cotswolds Edge, where she had celebrated May Eve with the women of Greystone manor. Some of these same women were visible behind Jo, their faces flickering into and out of focus. Jo's daughter, Joy, sat in front of her mother, holding something yellow in her lap, a small straw and cloth bundle.

Jo's stern voice came to them all the way from the Cotswolds, cutting through the keening chant. "Give your offering to the fire."

Reaching out, Joy placed the straw bundle in the fire, making it flame up even higher. So high Robyn could feel the heat on her face. Her eyes smarted and stung, and her chant faltered.

Instantly the flame flickered and went out, plunging the tower room into darkness. Beth and Deirdre barely missed a beat, bravely crooning away in the blackness. Keeping up the chant, Robyn fumbled inside her shift, finding her lighter. Reaching into the darkness, she relit the candle.

Too late. Jo and Joy were gone, along with Shenberrow Hill and the Cotswolds Edge. She was back with Deirdre and Beth in her room at Baynards Castle, but lying on the carpet by the candle was a cloth-and-straw harvest doll.

"Look," Beth pointed at the doll, "she is the straw doll Joy burned in the fire." And now "she" lay on a castle carpet in London, a hundred miles from Shenberrow Hill. Not even singed.

Robyn picked up the straw doll from the Cotswolds, finding it cold in her hand, like it just came from a chilly hilltop—a gross violation of quantum physics that made a total hash out of cause and effect.

Deirdre pointed to their ring of harvest food, saying, "two loaves are missing." Her maid was right, two of their little loaves were gone. And far away atop Shenberrow Hill the women of Greystone saw their witch-lady and her daughter feed a straw doll into the fire, getting back two fresh baked loaves.

Women had power in the Middle Ages, in ways Robyn never expected. She could not vote, or sit in Parliament, but she was also not bound by the laws of physics, literally able to walk on air. Or see all the way to the Cotswolds from her castle in London. And while men were holding their elections, and preparing for Parliament, women across the country were getting ready for a cold, wet winter.

Tuesday, 23 September 1460, Baynards Castle, London

Five months in the Middle Ages. Unbelievable. When I first arrived I thought another day here would be too long—and that I would never survive a week. Yet here I am, whole and healthy, and reasonably sane. And happy. Not only is Edward's father dawdling in the west, but Duchess Cecily is also headed off to be with him, riding in a four-horse chair covered with blue velvet. Putting even more miles between me and Proud Cis.

Dame Agnes has come up with a cook, a forty-something woman named Hanna, tall and white-haired, with a husband in prison, four sons, and a mountain of debt. Hanna has an excellent humor and does not mind my mania for cleanliness, gladly using boiled water and washing with soap—so happy with her new job, she would have done it on stilts. Her sons have the run of the castle, playing knights with Edward's brothers. Helping Hanna out and sharing her quarters is a dreamy young seamstress named Alice, a waif from Kent who appeared at the castle gate, offering to help with the sewing and washing, "Or any honest work." Word must be getting out that Lady Robyn is a soft touch.

Sunday, 28 September 1460, Michaelmas Eve, Baynards Castle, London

Edward and I went to see John Lambert, Beth's father and a stalwart Yorkist, sworn in as sheriff of London in the Guildhall, where he was given his golden chain of office and a sumptuous banquet of gilded meats basted with egg yokes, saffron, and gold leaf. This weird fare was consumed almost in silence by a thousand banqueters, a sign of the wealth and solidarity of the men who rule London. How incredible that such men allow themselves to be ruled by a crazy-quilt nobility, headed by Mad King Henry and his feuding cousins? But the answer is of course that they do not. These men rule London, and King Henry's Court—only recently back from Coventry—must be on its best behavior if it means to stay. There was meat aplenty, since Michaelmas marks a depressing killing off of the animals people cannot afford to feed over the winter—hoping instead to live off their beasts' flesh, salted and saved as sausage. Winter is looking to be a savage endurance contest.

Sunday, 5 October 1460, Saint Faith's Eve, Pleasance Park, Greenwich

Even King Henry does his bit to lay in meat for winter, by hunting at Eltham and Greenwich, riding over rain-soaked hills slaying deer for the royal household—the closest kings come to honest work. Though not today, for it is the Lord's day, and since he was a toddler, Henry has refused to do anything that even smacks of work on a Sunday. I have come with him, not for the hunting, but to play Hollywood Yankee at King Henry's court, keeping an eye on Henry and getting a break from London, which was filling up for Parliament. Neither Henry nor I get to vote, so we make a perfect match. Happy to have Lady Pomfret dress up his drab court, Henry feeds me tibids off his plate during otherwise silent dinners—but no one thinks that any madder than normal.

Parliament will soon put an end to the fun, since Henry has to make a brief appearence at the opening, though neither of us are attending. Parliament is an all-male affair, and even the Commons is for land-owning heads of households only, leaving out women, children, foreigners, lords, clergy, servants, laborers, copy-holders, kings, and lunatics—close to all the country. There are no election laws, or secret ballots, and the only parties are York and Lancaster. Despite the many flaws, I am all for calling Parliament, so Edward's lands and titles can be restored and his death sentence lifted. Still, it is hard to get terribly excited over an institution that excludes you on principle. My future rests with the most undemocratic parts of the government, being a royal pensioner, then marrying into the House of Lords.

And the good side is that those who do not vote do not pay taxes—so all my income is tax free. And if Parliament ends in catastrophe, we women cannot be blamed. Saint Faith, whose feast is tomorrow, is one of my favorites, the patron saint of prisoners. Too often she was all I had. . . .

Thursday, 9 October 1460, Baynards Castle, London

Edward's father arrives tomorrow! The good duke of York, along with Duchess Cecily, and Edmund, earl of Rutland, Edward's younger brother, backed by a small army of supporters from Wales and the west. Dad sleeps at Abingdon tonight, and will be here on the morrow. He has sent for trumpeters and clarioners to escort him to London, and we will go with them to greet him.

Naturally I expect the worst, especially after Duchess Cis. Dad was supposed to be the touchy one. Marrying into the proud Plantagenets seemed so much saner when they were represented by smart dashing Edward, earnest young earl on the lam. We were so busy eluding capture and staging coups, I stupidly assumed "happily ever after" was the easy part. Now I know better. And tomorrow will be Witches Night, as well. Figures to be a lively weekend. More later . . .

Go forth she did, riding out of Ludgate under gray clouds—she in her most splendid red-gold riding gown, Edward in his murrey and blue—escorted by two score men-at-arms. Luckily the morning proved dry, and the colorful little cavalcade made good time, leaving London and Westminster far behind, meeting Duke Richard of York on a straight stretch of Roman road south of Saint Albans, scene of his great victory five years before. Dad was visible at a distance, backed by a mob of horsemen sporting gay banners—half the Welsh marches were seeing their hero to London. First sign of disaster was a man walking before the duke holding a bared sword, point upright, the sign of a king in his own country. Behind him, the duke's banners bore the royal arms of England, the lions and lilies "undifferenced"— arms borne only by the king. A chilling sight. If Duke Richard was serious, it meant renewed civil war.

She had the same helpless feeling she felt on seeing Black Dick Nixon and his merry thugs ride into Hardingstone, realizing these men meant to fight—no matter what. War and strife were riding toward her, with no way to stop them, and all she could do was glue on a smile and pretend not to notice. Did Edward know this was coming? Gadding about with King Henry in Greenwich, it was easy to lose touch with government, but if a coup d'état was on the way, she would like to have known—if only to complain.

Dismounting, she did homage to her future father-in-law. Any qualms at meeting Edward's famously stern dad were submerged in the catastrophe about to engulf England. Dressed like a king and wearing the arms of England, Duke Richard of York looked small and dark, like the son named for him, lacking Edward's build—and good sense—but he seemed much more like a monarch than Mad Henry of Lancaster. All he needed was the crown. With characteristic tact, Duke Richard declared his delight at meeting her. "So this is my son's whore? Would that I had seen you sooner, for I now conceive his interest."

His flunkies all laughed, claiming they "could conceive it, too."

Edward stepped blandly in, explaining how she saved his life at sea and helped secure Henry at Northampton. "Lady Robyn Stafford has done much and suffered more than most, all to see your safe return."

"For which you have seen her well rewarded." Richard winked approval of his son's pretty dalliance. Black Dick Nixon had treated her better. Remounting for the ride back to London, she fell in with the earl of Rutland's retinue, mostly teenagers in smart new livery. Only a year or so behind Edward, Earl Rutland was completely different from his big brother, smaller and slimmer, more like a boy than a man, but pretty enough to be a girl. Riding back amid cocky young men in Rutland's colors—who joked and carried on for her benefit—she worried about what would happen when they got to Westminster with one king too many.

Marching straight on into London, accompanied by trumpets and clarions, they were met by the mayor and aldermen—including John Lambert, resplendent in his new sheriff's coat and chain. All looked roundly shocked to be greeting not just a returning duke, but a pretender to the throne. After an uneasy scene, Duke Richard headed for Westminster, where Parliament was meeting.

Here Robyn took her leave, gladder than ever to be excluded from the sessions, riding back to Baynards Castle through sober streets. People had turned out for a succession of triumphs—the entrance of the rebel earls, the return of the king, and the new freely elected Parliament—now London was seeing something less to her liking. Happy crowds that had come out to welcome home Duke Richard were aghast to have him return as king, since in their minds, two kings could only mean more war.

Rain returned in the afternoon, and Edward came back wet from Westminster, describing the dismal scene in Parliament. "We dismounted and father strode into the hall with his bared sword borne upright before him. He marched straight to the king's dais beneath the canopy of state, bowing to the lords, then putting his hand on the empty throne. . . ."

"Where was Henry?" she asked, worried for her frail unstable king, who was bound to be bullied by the duke.

"Heaven knows?" Edward shrugged off his sovereign's absence. "Cowering in the queen's apartments most likely, which was where they found him later. When father seized the throne, lords and commons alike rose to get a better look, and he turned to face them, his hand on the throne, expecting cheers and acclamation." Edward grimaced, sitting in a chair in his plush bedchamber, dripping rainwater onto the carpet.

"What happened then?" Robyn asked, selecting a dry crimson robe, edged with gold. Her gift, hand sewn with Deirdre so Edward could wear her colors for once.

"Nothing." Edward shook his head sadly. "No cheers. No applause. No angry cries. Lords and commons looked incredulous, or embarrassed, knowing he expected them to proclaim him king—but not one of them would make a peep. After months of happily awaiting his return, they were all reduced to dumb blank-faced cattle. What a fair farce!"

"How did your dad take it?" Duke Richard's months of exile in medieval Dublin had left him seriously out of touch.

"Father was absolutely furious, stepping away from the throne and declaring he claimed the realm of England as heir of King Richard II, demanding to be crowned on All Hallows Day."

Trick or treat. Halloween was three weeks away, and Richard of York already had his costume picked out, the royal regalia. "Did no one say anything to him?"

"His holiness, the archbishop of Canterbury had the temerity to suggest father consult with King Henry, who also claimed the crown. Father declared, 'I know of no one in the realm who should not more fitly come to me.' Then father proceeded to do just what the archbishop suggested, marching out of the hall in search of King Henry."

"It would have been a long wait for King Henry to come to him," Robyn observed, knowing how Henry hated public scenes. Had Duke Richard kept to his original resolve, he would still be standing by the empty throne.

"No doubt." Edward had long ago given up waiting on King Henry. "Father broke into the royal residence at Westminster, found Henry hiding in the queen's privy chamber, and beat on the door until Henry let him in. There in the queen's abandoned bedroom they both laid rival claims to the throne." Dueling mad monarchs, a national nightmare come true.

"Here, let me get you out of those wet clothes." Dragging him out of the chair, she started helping him strip.

"Father is being a fool." Edward shook his head, struggling out of wet finery. "Throwing away all we have won in an insane desire to be king. What was the point of taking Henry at Northampton? Why did we fight that battle? If we wanted to make my father king we should have just done so—leaving Henry with his kin. Then people could freely choose, father or Henry, who do you fight for? This way we look like idiots, fighting for one king, then offering up another. If we keep Henry as king, we are rejecting father for his addle-headed cousin. Yet if we make father king, we have stolen the crown from a pious madman we swore to protect."

And a deposed Henry was most likely a dead Henry, making them murderers, as well. Edward was right, why could not Henry be Queen Margaret's problem? But the battle of Northampton could not be undone; they had Henry and would be judged by what they did with him. Seeing Edward's linen undergarments were dry, she pulled the red-gold robe over his shoulder, asking, "Why did you not tell me this was coming?"

Not warning her was not exactly a lie, but it was a serious omission from someone who never before deigned to deceive. They had ridden out of London together in high spirits, yet he must have known his father was coming as king. Edward looked her straight in the face, not trying to duck his duplicity. "I knew nothing could be done about it, and did not want to dampen your day. I wanted you looking forward to seeing Father."

Fat chance of that—but at least he tried to think of her. She knew his dad would be trouble, just not how much. Arranging his robe just right, she asked, "What does Warwick say?"

Edward rolled his eyes. "Warwick is so incensed, he will not speak to Father, only to me."

"Lucky you." She pulled the sash tight, rose on her toes, and kissed him—trying to show the advantages of siding with political outcasts.

For once she sided with Warwick. Edward's father was mad to think he could barge in and bully Parliament into making him king, throwing aside a peace settlement people bled and died for. Londoners favored the peace, and actually liked having a daft, pious, gentle, unassuming king—a sort of national mascot unlikely to make trouble so long as his mad impulses were restrained. Which Warwick and Edward had been doing admirably. For the first time in Edward's young life, England's needs and his family's were not the same. She consoled him, saying, "Thank goodness for Parliament."

"Why so?" Edward looked puzzled. "It has been a prime farce so far."

"That is the true beauty of democracy," she pointed out—medievals still had a lot to learn about popular politics. Why worry about opinion polls when a poleax will do? "If a problem proves impossible, you kick it back to the voters. Then if it ends in disaster, folks know who to blame."

Saturday, 18 October 1460, Saint Luke's Day, Baynards Castle, London

London is appalled at happenings in Westminster. Here and there I hear people say Duke Richard would make a fine king—for London is still a very Yorkist town. But most wonder where the good duke left his marbles. Who needs a new king just when the old one is becoming manageable? Henry has been king nearly forty years—longer than a lot of folks live here and now. To most Londoners Henry has always been king. But Duke Richard continues to press his case, showing he does not care whom he offends, going back before the House of Lords, even sitting on the throne and lecturing his fellow lords on their duty—without much danger of winning them over. His direst foes, men like Holland, Clifford, and Percy, were busy honing their knives in the north, not even bothering to come. The men York is turning off were the moderates who thought he deserved a hearing.

It is easy to understand Duke Richard's anger. He is by far the better choice for king—wise in council and brave in battle, thrifty when need be, and on most days a just compromiser who won the heart of England and the backing of everyone from Italian bankers to the wild Irish. How galling to spend twenty-odd years watching a witless cousin drag the country from one disaster to the next—the loss of France, bankruptcy, popular revolt, fleet mutinies, repression, and judicial terror, followed by more revolts—the only decent government came when King Henry was catatonic, and Richard of York himself was Protector. You could hardly expect Duke Richard to just drop to his knees, thanking Henry for letting him come home. But Mad King Henry is the biggest prop to peace, and now Richard of York means to kick him aside.

Naturally Parliament prefers the easy calls. Commons annulled all the acts of Queen Margaret's "Devil's Parliament" held last winter in Coventry, returning Edward's lands and titles, and overturning his death sentence. Meaning we can now marry—for what that is worth. Edward's family considers even King Henry beneath them; picture what they will think of having me for a daughter-in-law. And it is too late to fly off in a huff and rent some place in town—London is full up for Parliament.

Thursday, 23 October 1460, Baynards Castle, London

Half a year in the Middle Ages—who would have thought it. I do not feel "at home" here, but I am in the same state of uneasy suspension as the rest of medieval England. The House of Lords' decision affects me more than many people who have lived here all their lives, since if Duke Richard of York becomes king, Edward will be heir apparent—unable to marry without royal consent. Worse yet, if we did wed, I would be in line to be queen, right behind Proud Cis. What a ghastly thought.

With every reason to want Duke Richard rejected, I must admit he has a case. By now the genealogy is thoroughly familiar. Duke Richard's mother, Edward's grandmother, was Anne Mortimer, the last of the Mortimer heiresses—a couple of whom died in the Tower for daring to carry the blood of Lionel of Antwerp, second son of King Edward III. King Henry is descended from John of Gaunt, Lionel's younger brother, making York's claim plainly superior. In fact the only real objection is that his claim comes through a woman—but even the most sexist medieval finds that argument weak. King Henry's claim to France comes through a couple of women. Duke Richard is not just the best man, but he has the best claim, as well.

Refusing to rule for Duke Richard but not knowing how to rule against him, the Lords made vain attempts to pass the buck, first asking King Henry what he wanted done. Henry could not come up with a coherent reason for being king—much less a plan of action. Appeals to the chief justices and king's attorneys proved equally useless. Commoners all threw up their hands in mock despair, asking how could they hope to judge their betters? Being the king's closest kin, the Lords must decide—earning their keep for once. So after spending most of a rainy October trying to avoid it, the Lords are finally getting set to vote.

Saturday, 25 October 1460, Saint Crispin's Day, Baynards Castle, London

Despite all Duke Richard did to hurt his case, he came just five votes short in the House of Lords. They will not make him king, not yet at least. In a split decision that angers nearly everyone, the

Lords decided Henry is king, but York is his heir, disinheriting the infant Prince of Wales. An exceedingly poor deal for Duke Richard—ten years older than Henry and unlikely to ever wear the crown. Called the Act of Accord, it is bound to provoke war, and worst of all, Edward is as much an heir as ever. Everyone expects he will be the one to succeed Henry, the only truly popular part of the Act of Accord. Except with me.

Though there is little for Dad to celebrate, Edward is throwing him a Saint Crispin's Day banquet—which I shall have to sit through, showing there are no hard feelings, however much I hurt. At least Edward swears we shall sit together. . . .

Family only sat at the high table—Plantagenets and Nevilles—but Edward arranged for them to sit together anyway, putting Robyn at the head of his retainers and bringing the tables together, making the height difference nominal. She wore a crimson sleeveless surcoat over a white-gold bodice with slashed angel-wing sleeves, topped by a high scarlet collar and a pearl-studded gold coif—defiantly showing her colors. Edmund of Rutland sat on the far side of Edward, and they had a fine time talking among themselves, ignored by the older folks, and hero-worshipped by the younger ones. George and Richard kept staring down the table at their older brothers—who went into exile and fought in battles, living beyond the reach of lessons and tutors. Leaning past Edward, Robyn had fun filling in Rutland on all their adventures in Ireland and Flanders.

Too much fun. Seeing his sons' attention diverted, Duke Richard demanded to know, "What is so amazing at the lower table?"

"Lady Robyn Stafford." Proud Cis nodded her way. "She has hidden powers of attraction."

"Really?" Duke Richard sounded unconvinced.

"She has visions, too, even seeing the future."

Duke Richard scrutinized her carefully, the cold stern gaze of frustrated royalty. "Is that why our sons find her so fascinating?" He called down to her, "Come, share your stories. What have you to say to us on this Saint Crispian's Day?"

People turned to look at her, the source of the trouble. Saint Crispin's Day was hallowed to them—the glorious twenty-fifth of October—"When Good King Harry slaughtered all those French."

Good King Harry was King Henry's father—Henry V, Henry of Monmouth, the warrior king who annihilated the French at Agincourt. Brave, bold, and decisive, Good King Harry was everything his son was not. As might be expected, this touchy young paladin left a trail of bodies behind him, dispatching religious dissenters, Welsh rebels, French prisoners, and hapless civilians—even executing Duke Richard's father for treason. However, Good King Harry's chief failing was to die young, leaving a brain-damaged baby in charge of a bankrupt country, setting the stage for the current hysterical crisis over kingship. Hereditary royalty was a lot like picking heads of state out of the phone book, since you were stuck with whoever turned up.

Rising slowly, she did a polite curtsy to the high table, determined to make Duke Richard sorry he ever called her whore. Luckily, she knew most of Shakespeare's Saint Crispian's Day speech by heart. Or at least well enough to fool folks who had never heard it done right. Shakespeare would not put Stratford-upon-Avon on the map for another hundred years or so, something she had learned to use to her advantage. Hollywood loved *Henry V*, filming it again and again, with this showstopper speech given by the hero king when the tiny English army faces the huge French host at Agincourt. She started simply, saying loud and clear: "This day is call'd the feast of Crispian . . ."

Tolerant smiles broke out at the high table—like she was a child reciting her piece, who had started well by getting the day right. Only Edward had heard it before and knew what to expect.

> He that outlives this day, and comes safe home,
> Will stand on tip-toe when this day is nam'd,
> And rouse him at the name of Crispian.
> He that shall see this day, and live old age,
> Will yearly on the vigil feast his neighbors,
> And say, "To-morrow is Saint Crispian."
> Then will he strip his sleeve and show his scars,
> And say, "These wounds I had on Crispin's day."

Smiles froze in surprise at the words of their unborn national bard, knowing she spoke of Agincourt, the forty-year-old battle to possess a muddy field in France that still weighed heavily on these folks. When his overweight uncle smothered in his armor at Agincourt, it made young Richard Plantagenet the Duke of York.

"Old men forget..." She reminded them, skipping ahead in the speech:

> But he'll remember, with advantages,
> What feats he did that day. Then shall our names,
> Familiar in his mouth as household words,
> Harry the King, York, Bedford, and Exeter,
> Warwick and Talbot, Salisbury and Gloucester—
> Be in their flowing cups freshly rememb'red. . . .

She stuck *York* in there out of deference to her hosts. This roll of heroes showed how far England had fallen. Today's King Harry was mad, and the new Duke Exeter roundly hated. Gloucester had been murdered at Parliament, and Bedford was survived only by his witchy widow. The heirs to York, Warwick, and Salisbury sat about the table—all lately acquitted of treason. And England had been roundly beaten by the French.

> This story shall the good man teach his son;
> And Crispin Crispian shall ne'er go by,
> From this day to the ending of the world,
> But we in it shall be rememberèd. . . .

Here she turned sideways and spread her hands out, palms up, smiling wide, careful not to put her back to the high table, but including everyone in the hall, reaching out to the lower tables, light shining off her golden angel-wing sleeves. This last was Shakespeare at his most subversive, preaching the end of nobility and a single English nation, where bravery and sacrifice eclipsed empty rank. She sounded every word, speaking clearly and solemnly to those seated below the salt:

> We few, we happy few, we band of brothers;
> For he to-day that sheds his blood with me
> Shall be my brother. Be he ne'er so vile,
> This day shall gentle his condition;

And gentlemen in England now abed
Shall think themselves accursed they were not here,
And hold their manhoods cheap whiles any speaks
That fought with us upon Saint Crispin's day.

Stunned silence greeted her performance. Everyone stared at her, amazed by the unexpected burst of iambic pentameter. Then Edward started to clap, loudly and alone. Rutland seconded him, as did George and little Richard, then the lower tables joined in, applauding wildly, their cheers turning to hoots and whistles. Toasts were drunk to King Harry's victory, and the French were damned out of hand. No white-haired bowman rose on tiptoes to show off his scars, but she saw tears in the eyes of old men who might have been there, plus looks of surprised respect from Salisbury and Duke Richard. She had spoken eloquently of their heroic childhoods, and how seriously things had gone wrong since. Nor did it hurt to gently remind the men at the high table that most of them had been safe "abed" while commons like her were taking the king and suffering in the Tower. Even Warwick gave her a wink that was only half-lewd.

"See," Duchess Cis declared, "she has strength of will and almost a man's wit."

Acknowledging the thanks, she confessed it was a man's wit, but "William Shakespeare" meant nothing to them. Weird in a way, because most of the folks at the high table must be in Shakespeare. How could Shakespeare have written three plays about poor mad Henry VI and not included this wild crew? Three plays Robyn did not know all that well, thank goodness, since she did not want to know what happened next. Duke Richard, on the other hand, ached to star as *Richard III*. When the evening ended, they parted with a kiss, Duke Richard Plantagenet of York, pretender to the throne, and Lady Robyn Stafford of Pontefract, the poetess strumpet. Then she kissed Proud Cis, as well.

She did not get Edward alone until they were in his big canopy bed, not a prime spot for political debate—whatever Londoners might think—especially when you are half-naked and much the worse for wine. She told Edward the Act of Accord was a disaster for everyone, predicting, "Queen Margaret's supporters will be livid, harping on the rights of the Prince of Wales. And many will listen. Folks like King Henry, when he is properly looked after, and hope for better from the Prince of Wales when he is of age." Comfortably far off at the moment. "They do not want a world in which the richest strongest noble gets to be king."

"Henry is still king," Edward noted wearily. "Weak and bankrupt though he may be."

She would not let Edward wriggle off so easy. "So for his pains your father gets the worst of both worlds, not to be king and have a war anyway?"

Propping himself up on a muscular arm, Edward stared hard at her. Many rich and powerful men lost a lot of their aura in the nude, but Edward always looked like a bold medieval warlord, even in bed. Not the worst fate a wayward lady could face—too bad they were fighting. "Yet he is my father," he reminded her—not just his father but his feudal overlord to whom he owed service, his sire in every sense of the word. "And I cannot go against the family."

Great. She was Diane Keaton in the Shakespearean-language version of *The Godfather*—Dad had committed the family to war, and young Edward had to fight. Visiting Italians invariably swore that Englishmen were too clannish and violent for them, addicted to feuds and liable to kill without warning—though they liked how English wives greeted guests with a kiss. One moment all was well, with Henry under control, Parliament in their pocket, and Mom off in Herefordshire. Then Dad comes sauntering in from exile, and suddenly love, peace, and happiness fly out the castle window. "Well, beware," she warned him, "because your family is bound to suffer most from this so-called Act of Accord."

Edward shot back, "Do I have your witch's word on that?"

She shook her head. "That is just plain karma."

"Karma?" Edward gave her a puzzled look.

"Balance, totality, ying plus yang," she explained.

From the look on his face, she might as well have said *witchcraft*. "You wanted to leave it to Parliament," he reminded her. "This is what Parliament has decided."

That hurt, especially for being true—she had gotten what she asked for, just not what she wanted. "We cannot just blindly follow Parliament back into war."

Edward sighed, not at all enjoying the fight. "War will come whether we will it or not—if war is what worries you?"

"Of course it is." She snorted at the self-evident. "Who would want war?"

"Holland, Clifford, Percy, Somerset . . ." Edward swiftly ticked off their most prominent enemies.

"What woman would?" She dismissed the opinions of disgruntled nobility spoiling for a fight—though they were the ones with knights and bowmen on call.

"Queen Margaret," Edward suggested smuggly, knowing he had her there.

Right, Margaret the Anjou Amazon, evil Frog Queen, Robyn was starting to rue the day she and Edward overthrew her. "I am beginning to have much sympathy for Queen Margaret."

"Really?" He arched an eyebrow. "Margaret of Anjou?"

"As I would for any woman dragged to this savage island and told to somehow set it right."

"Are you worried that might be you?" Edward asked.

"Might be? It will be if I marry you." The one clear advantage Londoners saw in the Act of Accord was that it made Edward heir to the throne. The Prince of Wales had just turned seven—a prince in a poke, like his father had been. England shuddered at the thought of yet another child king, in an age when many kids never saw puberty. Part of the fond affection for Mad Henry was the pious hope he would live long enough for his son to grow up. Now the Act of Accord put Edward in the infant prince's place, making an heir apparent out of the most popular young lord on the Royal Council— free of the family insanity and ready to rule. "If we even can get married," she snorted. "No Norman king has ever married one of his subjects."

Edward smiled at the word *Norman,* a dig at his being from Rouen—by birth neither of them were native Britons, though that did not stop them from arguing over the crown. "Except one who married an Englishwoman before he was king. I swear on all that is holy to marry you before Father and Henry are dead."

"I am not an Englishwoman, thank goodness." She still claimed allegiance to a country that did not yet exist. Currently Montana belonged to the Crow and Blackfoot—but she had grown up with Crow, always finding them friendly, and now she even spoke their language, no doubt they would be happy to have her. There was nothing like dealing with Brits all day to make you feel Native American. "I do not want to be queen," she told him. "Countess is bad enough."

Reaching over, he drew her closer to him. They had not made love since Dad arrived—two entire weeks—something of a record, not counting the time she spent in Greenwich. "What woman would break an engagement because it might make her queen of England?"

"I would," she warned him, though it did not exactly sound like grounds for divorce.

"Thank Heavens it is out of our hands." His own hands pulled her next to his strong, naked chest—pushing up her long silk chemise. Her amorous drunken boyfriend had just been made heir to the throne, and he meant to celebrate.

"How can it be out of my hands?" She used hers to keep him off her, braced against his naked chest. Edward could not just make her be queen—women had some rights, even in 1460.

Excelling at hand-to-hand combat, Edward deftly pinned her to the bed, seizing her wrists and holding them above her head. Trapped beneath his naked body, she ceased struggling, glaring up into his grinning face. "We are betrothed," he reminded her. "Nor will I let you break your troth, for I do love you, and I have given you no grounds. Soon we shall be married, and by this All Hallows Eve the Act of Accord will be the law of the land—to deny it would be treason."

Trick or treat, marriage or treason. She said nothing, angry at being manhandled. She did not like to have him atop her, callously holding her down. She was not the only one who would be tempted into treason. From all the cheers and tears at dinner, it would be no easy thing to disinherit the healthy young grandson of Good King Harry—just to please Edward's haughty family. Northerners would not stand for it, and Wales might rise in support of her prince. Sure he had the upper hand, Edward asked, "What is so bad about being queen?"

"What is so bad?" She laughed in his face, shocking them both with her vehemence. "Are you daft as well as drunk? Look what you did to Queen Margaret—now lodging in Scotland. You took her from home as a teenager, marrying her to a madman ten years older, insisting she bear a son—all the while insulting her for being French, maligning her morals, and murdering her favorites." No wonder the woman acted seriously mad at times. "Now you have driven her into exile, solemnly disinheriting the son she dutifully produced—if that is being queen of England, then I would far rather be a barmaid at the Boar's Head Inn."

"What a barmaid you would make"—Edward examined the half-nude body he was holding—"lecturing Duke Richard of York at his own table—at Saint Crispian's, no less. 'Gentlemen of England now abed, shall think themselves accursed they are not here . . .' "

"Hah," she gave him a shove with her knees. "I would do better at the Boar's Head."

"But you must be queen," he told her amiably, holding her helpless with only half his strength.

"Must I?" Again she tried to push him off, but she might as easily have moved Saint Paul's.

"*Absolument,*" Edward insisted, "for it is plain there will be no peace in the family until you outrank my mother."

There's a pleasant thought, Proud Cis forced to serve and curtsy, bringing her toast and herb tea—that almost made it worth being queen. Almost. "War in the north and Wales is a high price to pay for family peace," she warned him. "Which you will not get anyway."

"We shall see." He kissed her, hard and passionately, once more taking possession of her mouth. Despite her anger and sadness, she kissed back when she could have bitten his tongue. She did love him; he was why she was here. Even now, her body responded, aching to give in, glorying in the feel of his long firm form forcing her down into the feather bed. Taking this as acquiescence, Edward deftly pushed the silk chemise past her breasts, slipping his knee between her legs, his groin pressing hard into her hip. Even drunk, he knew what he was doing.

Still kissing, she slid sideways, slipping away from his knee, keeping her legs together. Adept at maneuvering, Edward rolled over to stop her, without letting go her hands or breaking the kiss. She rolled back again, feeling like their lips were making love while their lower bodies fought. From the very first she had refused to give in to him. Edward outranked virtually everyone in England, and she curtsied and called him "my lord" in public—but they both knew that was politeness. Privately they were equals, even when she was a penniless witch on the run. And now she was Lady Robyn of Pontefract, friend of the king, with a Westminster Champion to defend her. Though she hardly looked it now, thrashing about in an earl's bed with her chemise up around her shoulders.

Seeing he would get only a kiss, Edward relaxed and made the most of it, playfully exploring her mouth, letting her feel his excitement, reminding her how much fun they might have. And it was fun, but that only made her start to cry, thinking of how wonderful things had been, and could be—but weren't.

Startled by her tears, Edward stopped kissing, letting go of her hands and rolling off her. He took a long drunken look down the length of her half-naked body, stymied by her resistance—knowing all he could do was look. Edward was not the sort to force women—and if FitzHolland and Lord Scales could not break her in the Tower basement, what hope did he have? No good would come from trying to force her, either in bed or at the altar. Unable to have her, Edward comforted her instead, holding her in his arms as she cried, softly asking her what was wrong, and why she was so sad.

She did not answer. Her hurt was deep enough already, without having to say it out loud. Edward has sided with his family against her and against the peace they had made, betraying their love and everything they had built together. However much they were betrothed, Edward could not make her marry against her will. Mother Church protected her right to say no. No one could force her to be queen, not even dear, sweet noble Edward—not if he held a knife at her throat.

Sunday, 26 October 1460, Saint Lucian's Day, Baynards Castle, London

Our first fight. Fitting it is over the issue ripping England apart. This "Act of Accord"—still waiting to be signed—will cost people's lives, plunging the country into war when we should be getting ready for winter. What a fool! To think that somehow Edward would be different—the medieval man with a modern mind, ready to forget rank, family, and upbringing, all for me. Some silly fairy tale.

And I fell for it. Amazingly hard. Throwing away my life at home, every friend I ever had, an awesome Hollywood apartment, hot showers and indoor plumbing—all for a footloose young earl-in-exile, with broad shoulders and a charming smile. What could

I have been thinking? That I could just waltz into this weirdly male world and have everything I wanted—magic powers, the man I fancied, and a title to boot? Welcome to the Middle Ages.

What now? Edward is my reason for being in this millennium. Without him, medieval England is a rainy low-rent excursion with chancy food and worse facilities—one any sane woman would avoid in a snap. But I do not have to be here being rained on— thanks to Mad King Henry, I have money and am free to run from my problems. Lady "Pomfret" can winter in Italy if she wants. Leonardo da Vinci lives there; so does Columbus. We could rent an old Roman villa on the sunny slopes of Vesuvius, overlooking the Bay of Naples. I must poll my little household. Matt and Deirdre are always ready for adventure. But Beth and Hanna have families to think of, and who knows where spacey young Alice is at— last Friday she hinted she would like to learn witchcraft. Am I so obvious? Suppose so.

Monday, 27 October 1460, Saint Jude's Eve, Baynards Castle, London

Jo has arrived! Bringing Joy with her, doing a mother-daughter Halloween pilgrimage to Saint Albans. Collin saw them as far as Wallingford, where they hired a boat to take them to London. Having Jo here for Halloween means a chance to learn more spellcraft—something to look forward to, love and politics being a dead loss. And magic always holds out the hope of returning to my "own" time, now that I have far less reason to stay here.

Beth is ecstatic to have Joy back, showing Jo's daughter the straw doll they passed through the fire on Saint January's Night, saying, "Thank you, thank you. I burned by own rag doll for the harvest, this is like having her back."

Jo got the big keep bedroom with its Lion of March presence chamber—Edward having moved back to the main hall when his mother left, continuing the medieval game of musical beds. Once Jo settled in, Robyn spilled the whole sad story, starting with Proud Cis and the duke's pretensions and ending in the disastrous Act of Accord. "What can Edward do?" Jo asked as her look-alike daughter combed Mom's long black hair. "Parliament has voted this monstrosity, and even King Henry is powerless to stop it."

"Henry is perpetually powerless—but Edward could at least refuse to sign it." The Act of Accord's main advantage was to make Edward the likely heir—put fey young Rutland in his place, and Parliament might think twice.

"And give up the kingship?" Jo asked evenly.

"He would if he loved me," Robyn complained. How could England's "Hollow Crown" compare to her?

Jo smiled at her plight. "Yes, I see your problem. Edward is bold, handsome, and vows he loves you. He gives you gold, gowns, a beautiful horse, and a castle to live in. Worse yet, he wants to marry you—and you suffered all this to happen?"

"Graciously," Robyn admitted, least anyone think her ungrateful.

"And now the heartless young knave proposes to make you queen of England, as well?" Jo shook her head dolefully, saying, "Some men are just insufferable."

"I will not have my children made heirs to the throne," Robyn insisted. "Hereditary monarchy is a travesty. Look what it did to King Henry, taking a perfectly fine fellow with *monk* written all over him, and making him a fumbling head of state, committing high crimes and comic misdemeanors, forcing the shy retiring soul into a very public marriage and sex life. All for the supposed good of England." Jo had to admit that kingship had done Henry small good, driving him catatonic at times.

"Who would want that for her children?" Robyn demanded. "Three of the last four kings were either deposed and murdered, driven insane, or died on campaign—that is if they even get to be king. How many royal heirs have been murdered or abducted?" By making his line regal, Duke Richard turned his entire family into targets.

"You make me happy my daughter is a bastard." Jo gave Joy a hug and kiss, her daughter beaming happily to hear it was better to be a bastard than a princess. Jo told the news from the Cotswolds, saying Greystone was recovering from its looting last May, when FitzHolland's Swans fired the hall and barns. "Collin has a roof up on the main hall, and the crops are in and under cover, though most of the outbuildings are still in ruins. Winter will be wet and hard. Collin has bought grain from Brittany, and Welsh cattle, but he does not have money for more."

"I have money now! Can you believe it?" Lady Robyn spent her first month in the Middle Ages living off the Greys, getting handouts from farms and abbeys, and being fed by the Welsh. "Now I can pay back some of what I owe."

Jo did a mock curtsy. "My Lady Pomfret, you have come up in the world."

"You mean since you first took me in out of the rain?" Some of her newfound money had to go to Greystone—hopefully in the form of food, which was harder than it sounded with grain scarce and the wretched roads awash. Jo's week-old letter announcing her visit had yet to arrive by common carrier. Medieval England's private postal system was totally swamped.

All Hallows Eve was on the regular Church calendar, celebrated by a special Mass—but it was also the start of the Fools' Season, Samhain, the Celtic new year and the Druid festival of the dead, the doorway into winter, when the gates between the worlds opened and fairies, pixies, ghosts, and witches escaped to spread terror. Providing a perfect excuse to start Saturday night revelry early, while the breweries worked overtime getting ready for the Fools' Season. All Hallows Eve also fell on Witches Night this year, which was why Jo decided on the pilgrimage—honoring Joy's father, who died at the battle of Saint Albans.

To make the Halloween mood complete, this was the day Duke Richard and Edward swore to uphold the Act of Accord and took over in Westminster. Edward looked very much in costume, donning the lions and lilies of England instead of his murrey and blue—but Robyn was boycotting the ceremony, as well as his bed.

Rising early and dressing in deepest black, she rode with Jo and Joy up Watling Street all the way out to Saint Albans. Hela, Joy's talking magpie, flew ahead of them, leading the women to the Castle Inn at the corner of Saint Peter's Street and Shropshire Lane. There they dismounted, saying a prayer for Joy's father, Edmund Beaufort, duke of Somerset, who was killed on this spot five years before—some would say assassinated by Warwick and York. "I told you we would go to Saint Albans," Joy solemnly reminded her. Being here fulfilled Joy's offhand promise of a pilgrimage, made six months ago in a Cotswold pig farm on Robyn's second day in the Middle Ages, when they were on the run after escaping Berkeley Castle.

"And I did not believe you," Robyn admitted. At the time Robyn thought the promise was an obvious child's fantasy, aimed to throw off their pursuers. Yet here they were, half a year later, laying red October roses alongside the Castle Inn.

"Predictions are difficult things," Jo told her daughter, "coming true in unforeseen ways. One Witches Night I dreamed your father died beneath a castle, so I warned him to shun castles and avoid sieges. Good advice in any event." This was the first time Jo ever laid claim to foresight. "Alas, he took the prophecy too literally, becoming rather reckless so long as there were no castles about. This battle came unexpected, and though outnumbered, your father disdained surrender, fighting fearlessly—until he looked up and saw this sign overhead." To aid illiterate customers the Castle Inn had a crude painting of a castle hung above the main door. "He faltered and was cut down at once, some say by the earl of Warwick."

Warwick and Duke Richard took King Henry's unpopular Court by surprise. Unable to hold a hostile London, Henry and his lords had to fight at Saint Albans, outnumbered and unprepared—with typically disastrous results. Henry's people were no better at war than they were at governing. On a May morning five years ago, this sleepy little street, with its churches, market, inns, and great stone Eleanor Cross, was barricaded for street fighting and strewn with armored bodies. Besides Somerset, the dead included Lord Clifford and Henry Percy, earl of Northumberland—all three had sons who had not come to Parliament, wanting only vengeance. King Henry was wounded in the neck here, totally losing his taste for battle—in some ways Henry had a very sensible insanity.

At the nearby abbey, Joy lit candles on her father's tomb, whispering the witches' prayer for the dead, inviting him in for Halloween. Seeing this bastard girl praying to talk to her dead father reminded Robyn just what price England would pay for the Act of Accord.

By the time they returned to Baynards Castle, All Hallows Eve was upon them. Bonfires burned on Surrey hilltops, and masked celebrants wandered the streets, tapping windows, stealing gates, blocking doorways, accosting their betters, and demanding alms—even from witches on horseback—forcing Lady Robyn to empty her purse just to get them home. Deirdre told her that others fared even worse. King Henry lost his home completely. Costumed like a king, Duke Richard rode to Westminster backed by torch-bearing retainers, taking possession of the palace in a wild Halloween scene—going from visiting second cousin to master of the house. Henry was booted out—still king, but confined to the bishop of London's palace.

Dreamy Alice the seamstress had sensed big things were afoot, and asked Deirdre if she could join the coven this evening. Men might make and unmake kings in Parliament, but an imaginative young seamstress aiming to better herself had to seek other ways of bending the world to her will.

Jo would not have it. "We have too many novices already, and we face a trying winter—it would not be safe. If the girl really wants to be a witch, she will wait. Keep her with you, and mayhap when spring comes the coven will grow."

While nightwalkers stalked the streets, pulling pranks and assaulting drunks, Jo cast a Hallows Eve circle in the presence chamber adjoining her borrowed bedroom, seating each of them at the point of a five-pointed star—Jo, Robyn, Deirdre, Joy, and Beth in that order, all wearing winter black—with a single tall black candle burning in the center. "We are at the gate of winter," Jo told her tiny coven, "the land of darkness, cold, and death. Though without winter there could never be spring." Jo started a chant, sending it singing around the circle:

> Samhain's door leads to winter,
> Days draw inward,
> darker, shorter, colder.
> Trees turn bare and leafless.
> All is dead, all is dead.

Relaxing into the chant, Robyn let herself go, happy to have Jo here, glad not to play coven leader to novice girls, letting worries and responsibilities slide away into the emptiness of winter. Edward had made his choices. England must care for herself. So must poor lunatic King Henry. So must Duke Richard and Proud Cis, who so richly deserved each other. She must think of herself now. Letting go of problems she could not solve, she freed herself for the counterchant when it came her way:

> Life sleeps, life sleeps,
> Beneath the ground,
> Beneath the frost,

Seeds quicken in the cold,
Ready for the returning light.

When the counterchant came back to her, Jo did her invocation,
inviting in the spirits of the night, the souls of the dead. This was
necromancy, the most feared form of spellcraft—presided over by
Hecate, the death crone—yet totally appropriate to the season. With
herself as Mother, and Joy as Maiden, Jo called on the Crone.

Giving in to the ritual, Robyn opened her mind to the night, letting
her soul drift, floating where it willed. Light appeared ahead of her,
white and bright as spring, beckoning warmly. At first she thought
it was the candle flame, but it was sunlight falling on a rose garden—
a rose garden she recognized, the Temple gardens, just up the
Thames beyond the city walls. On sunny days she could see them
through the northernmost arrow slit in her room. White and red
rosebushes bloomed at either hand, and she let her mind drift farther,
enjoying the delightful out-of-body stroll through the sunlit white-
walled garden.

Men appeared ahead of her, talking loudly. Too bad. Rich and
clean shaved, they were dressed in black velvet and crimson taffeta
with splendid tooth-cut sleeves. Broad feathered berets and velvet
rolled hats pinned with family badges topped neat pudding basin
haircuts. Worse yet, they were arguing, making an enormous racket
beside a tall ornamental fountain. And she knew them. Warwick was
there, wearing red, with closed hanging sleeves trailing nearly to the
ground. Duke Richard was with him, looking dour and dressed in
black velvet trimmed with tiny white silk roses. Arguing with them
was a forty-something noble in blue satin, trimmed with gold, good-
looking in a rich affluent way, saying, "Let him that is no coward
nor no flatterer, pick a red rose with me."

Warwick smirked. "I love no colors, and pluck this white rose
with Plantagenet." By which Warwick meant Duke Richard, who
was holding a fresh-plucked white rose to go with the tiny silk ones
on his gown.

She was in a scene out of Shakespeare, the famous Temple-garden
scene that sets off the Wars of the Roses, where the great nobles
choose sides by picking roses—white for York and red for Lancaster.
Henry VI, part I, act II, scene iv, to be exact—Robyn had stage-
managed the scene once, scrambling to find real roses during a Mon-

tana winter. But now she was seeing the scene in the Temple gardens she knew, cast with the real nobles, some of whom she knew, and some she did not. It dawned on her that the ones she did not know must be dead—killed at Saint Albans. One of these talking dead, a white-haired noble wearing a white ape's clog badge with a gold chain, picked a red rose, saying, "I pluck this red rose with young Somerset."

Which made the noble in blue and gold Edmund Beaufort, duke of Somerset—Joy's father. And Jo's lover. She tried to imagine Jo with him, which was hard, having never known Jo to have a man, not in this millennium or the next. Still, she could see it: Somerset had energy, wit, and clever good humor, and when someone took his opponent's rose, he warned him, "Prick not your finger when you pluck it off, least by bleeding on it you join me."

Duke Richard got the most roses—though some of his "lords" were Temple lawyers. He immediately tried to bludgeon Somerset with his majority, saying, "Now Somerset, where is your argument?"

"In my scabbard," Somerset replied hotly, "where lies the means to make every white rose red."

Duke Richard scowled, the same frown he had turned on her, "Hath not thy rose a canker, Somerset?"

"Hath not thy rose a thorn, Plantagenet?" Somerset shot back. He threw York's father's execution for treason in Duke Richard's face, then stalked off, calling York a yokel and swearing to "find friends to wear my bleeding roses!"

Add impulsive and intemperate to Somerset's character—but he was the object of Joy's pilgrimage, so Robyn followed him into a deep recess of the dream garden, winding her way through thorny green hedges. Somerset lingered beside a red rosebush, letting her catch up, looking cool and smart despite his late outburst. Gold lining shone inside his slashed blue satin sleeves, and he wore an open satin hood that sat on his head like a cleverly folded cap. Smiling broadly, Somerset asked, "Who are you?"

She did a deep curtsy, seeing how Jo could love this man, and why Warwick had to kill him. "Lady Robyn Stafford of Pontefract."

Somerset laughed loudly, "Lady Robyn of Pontefract? King Henry must have done that. Serves me right well for leaving His Majesty alone and unchaperoned." Reaching into his open blue-gold sleeve, Somerset produced a curious ivory white statuette, a foot tall and trimmed in gold. "Give Joanna a kiss for me, and have this to help you on your way."

Reflexively, she reached out and took the statuette, knowing as soon as she touched it that she had made a tremendous mistake. What had looked like ivory felt like wax, and what had seemed like gold was merely gilt paint. She looked up at Somerset, but he, too, was changing, turning into a woman before her dreaming eyes, a woman Robyn knew. She found herself staring at a duchess in drag, Jacquetta Wydville, the witch-duchess of Bedford, still wearing Somerset's blue-gold gown and cap hood. Blond and stately, with sly, heavy-lidded eyes, Duchess Wydville laughed at her. "How good to see you Lady Stafford, and to wish you a joyous All Hallows Eve."

Before she could reply the witch-duchess was gone, vanishing with a smile. Robyn realized she had been tricked by Duchess Wydville, thinking she was seeing the shade of Somerset, led down the garden path by an older, better witch. She spun about, trying to retrace her steps, frantic to somehow warn the rest of her little coven that they were under magical attack. White walls and thorny rosebushes closed in around her, cutting off retreat. Feeling like Alice lost in the Queen of Hearts's rose-garden maze, Robyn ran down long green lanes sprinkled with roses that led nowhere, searching for an open gate or a gap in the hedges, finding herself hopelessly trapped. Duchess Wydville had played her perfectly, and worse was sure to follow.

Abruptly the Temple gardens vanished, and she was jerked out of her dreamworld by the presence chamber door banging open. Light from flaring torches flooded the chamber, falling on the white-chalked star and the women and girls kneeling upon it. Shock washed over Robyn like ice water, and she froze, kneeling at her star point, knowing she was caught.

Strange men burst into the presence chamber, accompanied by stinging torch smoke, real men armed in leather and mail—not dead dream lords—men wearing the duke of York's silver-blue livery, except for one dressed like a London constable. All were armed with swords and ugly bollock knives dangling lewdly between their legs; they looked like demons in some weird Halloween scene. For a confused instant Robyn thought this, too, must be a joke, an All Hallow's prank by costumed party goers, who would presently shout, "Trick or treat!"

Only they did not even grin, and they had a woman with them. Sweet, dreamy Alice the seamstress looked sharp and aware amid the men, with a black iron key in her hand—reminding Robyn what century it was, and that this was really happening. Cold, primal fear coiled in her gut. Men were invading Witches Night. Armed men who had barged in on an incredibly incriminating scene: two ladies, their serving girls, and a bastard daughter, all dressed in black, kneeling at the points of a big pentagram chalked on the presence chamber floor, ringing a tall black burning candle. Hard to pass this off as a semi-innocent slumber party gone berzerk. Indeed, the London constable loudly announced that they faced arrest.

Jo asked blandly, "What for?"

That stumped the constable—staring at little blond Beth still kneeling on her pentagram point—not sure what to call this Halloween scene. But a well-dressed busybody stepped forward, answering for the constable with the usual list of high crimes—witchcraft, heresy, treason, and a host of lesser offenses. This was the first man she recognized, John Fogge, a Kentish landowner and member of Parliament, also a Wydville cousin—small wonder there. Nobody bothered to read them their rights, since they hardly had any, and everything would certainly be used against them, including what Robyn held in her hand.

By the light of the sputtering torches she saw she was holding a wax image of Duke Richard of York, with a white rose carved on his chest and a gold falcon and fetterlock done in gilt paint on his wax surcoat. Driven right through the white rose was a silver pin, piercing the statuette's heart. Shifting light from the torches made Duke Richard's crude wax face seem to laugh at her, a parting little illusion by Duchess Wydville and a fair start to the Fools' Season.

PART 2

Fools' Season

From Ireland thus comes York to claim his right,
And pluck the crown from feeble Henry's head:
Ring, bells, aloud; burn, bonfires, clear and bright . . .
     —Shakespeare, *Henry VI, Part II*

    Shall we their fond pageant see?
    Lord, what fools these mortals be!
—Shakespeare, *A Midsummer Night's Dream*

6

⤙⚬⚬⚬ Night and Fogge ⚬⚬⚬⤚

*B*usted. *Shocking, but* hardly surprising. She had been taking things far too fast, running way too many risks, hobnobbing with dead nobility when she should have been watching her back. While she sounded off against the Act of Accord and planned her happy Halloween, Duchess Wydville had planted Alice as a spy, setting a trap with this evil little wax statuette. Silently Robyn cursed her own thoughtless complacency and her overweening stupidity.

Gloating over his catch, the busybody MP looked stern and prissy, with his neat bowl haircut, long straight nose, and thin, mean hyphen of a mouth. Thoroughly Yorkist, John Fogge helped hand Canterbury over to the rebels, and had been at the Saint Crispin's feast— yet he was a Wydville cousin, and the one with the list of charges ready. Witchcraft, heresy, treason—as if he knew ahead of time what he would find. His fellows just stood blinking in the torchlight, amazed at what women will do when men are not around, especially on Halloween. How often did they get to see a knight's sister and an earl's mistress kneeling in black shifts on a chalk pentagram, communing with the dead?

Jo jumped up, snuffing out the tall candle and demanding the men leave immediately. "This is my night chamber; be gone at once." But it was not really her chamber, being borrowed at best, and the armed men did not budge.

Still holding the wax statue of Duke Richard, Robyn got up to stand alongside Jo, attracting the attention of Master Fogge, who pointed at the waxen image, saying, "Seize that ungodly thing." Nervous bowmen shuffled forward, and she gladly gave up the grotesque voodoo statue—not hers to begin with and bound to be no end of trouble. Surrendering it with a smile, she deftly palmed the silver pin that ran through the statue's heart, sticking it in a fold of her black shift. One less bit of evidence—plus she knew from previous incarcerations that once locked in a cell everything you had became precious. Her VISA card got her out of Berkeley dungeon. Bug spray had freed her from the men in the Tower.

Gingerly the bowmen took the wax statue over to Edward's carved oak side table, set it down and stood guard on it, fearing to touch it too much. Who could blame them? This wax image was wickedness incarnate, and Robyn wished she had never laid hands on it herself. Seeing the statuette safely under armed guard, the London constable asked, "What are your names?"

"Lady Robyn Stafford of Pontefract." She tried to look the part— even barefoot in her black shift—smiling encouragement to the little girls still kneeling on the pentagram. "If you will kindly send for Edward, earl of March, all this may be easily explained."

No one ran to fetch Edward. Presumably he was in the main hall's master bedroom, sleeping off his exciting day. She no longer knew for absolute fact where Edward slept, since he now had a suite of rooms at Westminster, as well. "Who are these others?" asked the constable warily—wanting to know who he was arresting—looking especially hard at tiny Beth Lambert, kneeling blond and barefoot at her star point. Attempting to arrest the wrong person had gotten lawmen drawn and quartered of late.

She nodded at Jo. "This is Lady Joanna Grey, a guest, and her daughter, Joy, and this is my maid, and our fosterling, Beth Lambert." Daughter to John Lambert, newly elected sheriff of London— despite the two ladies present and the duke's natural daughter, it was the littlest among them that gave the constable pause—no lawman liked collaring his boss's daughter on capital charges. "Pray send for Edward of March," Robyn suggested pointedly. "He will set everything right."

"We need not bother his lordship," John Fogge assured them, hoping to make this a fait accompli. "There are cells waiting at Newgate, and the sooner these women are in them, the sooner we may all be asleep."

"You are not putting any of us in Newgate," she told the obnoxious MP, "not the children, not my guests, not the servants, or me." If they were going to fight about this, then best do it here in what used to be "her" castle. She would not be hauled off somewhere to be tormented in private, not without a battle, anyway—she had been there already. "I demand you send for Edward of March, who is the lord of this keep." It was his father's castle, but she was willing to stretch the point to get Edward here. "Or he shall know whom to hold responsible."

"And who is that?" asked Master Fogge haughtily, sure it was not him.

Who, indeed? Duchess Wydville? Duke Richard? Alice the seamstress? There were so many hands in this awful business, she hardly knew who best to blame.

Boots sounded on the stone steps leading to the hall below, turning heads toward the open door. Someone was coming. Even the girls still kneeling dutifully on their pentagram points craned their necks to see, hoping for a Halloween miracle.

Edward breezed into the room, cool as a breath of spring. Holding a lantern to aid the torchlight, he took in the tense scene in the presence chamber: the armed men, the women and girls in black, the perplexed constable, the wax statuette and tall black candle, rolled back carpets, and the huge pentagram chalked on the wooden floor. Despite the witching hour, he was wearing a wine and azure gown with open ragged-cut sleeves, over gold-and-black hose—all he lacked was a cap to cover his tawny hair. The others wore feathered bonnets or big floppy berets to go with their grim looks.

She shot Edward a rueful smile, signaling that she was sorry, but what could she do? Smiling broadly in return, he told the presiding MP, "Well done, Master Fogge, how fine to see you here. You seem to have things most admirably disposed."

Fogge bowed deeply, glad to find Edward approving. "Thank you, my lord of March."

Edward beamed satisfaction—adept at dealing with disaster, he surveyed the room with approval. "Master Fogge, you have things so splendidly disposed, I fear we no longer need your alert assistance, invaluable as it has been."

"My lord?" Master Fogge went from relieved to taken aback. "But these women are—"

"Under my authority," Edward announced airily, lowering his lantern to show he had seen enough. "Dangerous though they may seem, I will take my chances alone with them." Edward had no problem wielding power, being trained to it all his life by steely willed parents—just how steely willed Robyn had recently discovered. He gave crisp, simple orders backed by his hearty smile and knack for connecting names and faces—remembering John Fogge was nothing, he could as easily have named every MP from Kent, and their wives.

But behind his happy bonhomie lurked naked force; Edward habitually fought in the front rank, and he had never lost a battle. So far.

John Fogge bowed, then strode officiously over to the table; he picked up the wax statuette, declaring, "Your sire, the good duke, should see this." Richard of York's wax face glared at Robyn from atop the wax statuette—no longer laughing. Nor did she find it at all funny, though she did her best to smile.

Edward nodded absently. "Pray give the good duke my warm regards, and tell him I have things well in hand here. Father will understand."

"As Your Lordship wishes." Fogge bowed stiffly, still holding the statue; then he scooped up the tall candle, as well, and left with the much relieved constable in tow, trailed by the silent bowmen. Seamstress Alice vanished with them, still clutching the key to the room.

Edward winced. "Makes me most glad I came alone."

"How did you know to come at all?" Robyn asked, weak with relief, happy her love had found her, even under these difficult circumstances.

Flapping loudly, a black-and-white bird flew into the presence chamber through the open door. Joy's magpie familiar proudly screeched her name: "Hela! Hela!" Flying twice around the room in triumph, the bird landed on Joy's shoulder, doing a little bobbing bow. "Hela!"

Hela, queen of the dead, was in her element on Halloween, and while Robyn said a fervent thank-you for the rescue, a bit of warning would have done even better.

Shutting the heavy presence chamber door, Edward did not bother to turn the lock—it being far too late for that. He was getting his first look at a Witches Night, and she could see it was an eyeful. Even without the statue and candle, the presence chamber still made some scene by lantern light, with his White Lion of March looking down on women and girls spaced around the chalk star wearing Halloween black. Jo did a dignified curtsy, seeing no point in a closing prayer—the ritual was ended and the circle dissolved as soon as men entered the room. "Thank you mightily for coming so promptly to our aid."

Edward politely acknowledged her curtsy. "Pardon my intrusion, Lady Grey. I am glad to be of service, though I came to speak with Lady Stafford—alone if that were possible."

Jo bade the girls rise from their pentagram points, where they had knelt silently throughout the ordeal, doing their training proud. Standing up, they did deep grateful curtsies, thoroughly shaken, and thankful to Edward, who was already their shining hero. Robyn told her maid to take Jo and the girls to her tower room, adding, "Make sure you bolt the door." No sense making that mistake again. With more curtsies to Edward, they trooped out, the girls holding tight to Deirdre and Jo. Hela went, too, leaving Robyn alone with Edward for the first time in days.

Too bad it took catastrophe to bring them together. Doing a deft curtsy of her own, she thanked him for showing up when he did, apologizing mightily. "Please forgive me, had I known it was unsafe, I never would have had the ritual here." The locked presence chamber of a castle keep seemed perfectly secure.

Without saying a word, Edward set his lantern on the table, then locked and bolted both doors. When he had secured the room, he strode over and took her in his arms, giving her a kiss that almost lifted her out of her black linen shift. Their first real kiss since Saint Crispin's—shocking, intimate, and sexy—not at all what she expected after making an astonishing mess out of All Hallows Eve. Thinking they were on the verge of their second fight, she found herself tongue locked instead, nearly necking atop the pentagram. When he relaxed, letting her speak, she asked, "Why did you do that?"

"I have very much wanted to take you in my arms," he admitted, smiling in triumph, "to hold my true love close and to kiss you long and deeply. And did I assume that right now you would not stop me." Edward knew all about strategic advantage. Now that he was standing between her and prison, she could hardly complain about his being heir to the throne.

What was the use of having a knight if he never came to rescue you? She rested her head on his big velvet shoulder, thrilled to feel his hard arm around her waist, knowing he would cheerfully put his strong agile self between her and any danger. "I am just amazingly glad you came when you did."

"But for that bird, I would not be here," Edward confessed. "Things have been most busy for me—though all through the day I thought of you."

"Indeed?" she whispered, reveling in the security of his embrace.

Edward's long fashionably slashed sleeves enfolded her lower body, feeling incredibly comfortable against her thin shift, warming her legs on what was now a cold November night.

"Oh, yes—my day has been a total triumph," he assured her. "Lords and Commons declared my father heir to the throne, amid much pomp and ceremony. I was cheered by commons, serenaded by bards, and feasted extravagantly at royal expense. Bishops prayed for my well-being, strange women showered me with flowers, and servants threw coins at the poor in my name. I finished the day at Saint Paul's, hearing evensong with King Henry, followed by a lavish Westminster supper—trout quenelles, lamprey en croûte, minced crab, and crayfish."

Quite a day, especially compared to hers. And he had taken an oath before Parliament never to "consent to abridge the natural life of King Henry the Sixth, nor to hurt nor diminish his reign and dignity royal." Or so she heard, having taken no part in any of it— not so much as seeing Edward since yesterday noon. "But I missed you mightily." He tightened his hold, pressing her against his velvet covered chest. "Most of all when I lay down in bed, tired and alone."

Alone? Admirable restraint when half the women in London would have been ecstatic to console this poor abandoned heir to the crown. Sad young royalty are so tragically attractive. But Edward claimed to have been pining for her. "And when Joy's raucous bird woke me, I came straight here, bringing beer so the keep guards could toast my elevation." Winning made Edward popular; touches like that made him loved. How many modern commanders would take the time to make sure their loyal guards were drunk at their posts? "Hearing the porter had passed a London constable, I went right here, thinking you would want a warning."

Nice to know that when the law arrived, loved ones thought naturally of her. Robyn had to rethink the whole concept of living in an era where she was illegal. "Thank you for thinking of me," she whispered, still clinging to his shoulder; beneath his breezy manner, Robyn could see he was worried. Was she the only thing in life that gave him such grief?

Edward looked past her at the white pentagram, shining in the yellow circle of lantern light, saying, "This bit of foolishness will bring no end of trouble."

"This is just a harmless Halloween ritual, meant to unite a girl with her father, who was killed in the wars." Just because she was defeated was no reason to back down; Robyn had to make her case as hard as she could to Edward. "No harm has been done here to anyone. This is a private ritual done for a willing girl, with her mother's consent and direction."

"People will call it harm," Edward declared, "and claim it is aimed at my father."

"Joy has no father," she pointed out, "because your father took up arms against the king. This was just a ritual to help her deal with her loss. The real foolishness is the Act of Accord, which is like to create more orphans, making more trouble even as we speak."

"You make a very persuasive case," Edward admitted, "especially to one who loves you." He kissed her anew, more tenderly this time, then he nodded at the pentagram on the floor, saying, "Strangers will still find this devilish hard to explain."

"All it is now is chalk, which washes right off." Warm soapy water sat waiting in a bucket.

"Not yet." Edward solemnly walked her over to the pentagram, guiding her with an arm about the waist, stopping when they stood together in the center of the star. Edward looked about, obviously enjoying the effect in flickering lamplight. "Most impressive, even if this is but chalk."

Edward was clearly intrigued by the only sort of power denied him by birth—women's power. Here was the one thing he could never totally control. When she was first whisked away to medieval times, Robyn assumed she would die of plague. Coming in second was ending up enslaved to some man. Instead she found a world weirdly in touch with its female side. When she arrived, England was ruled by a young woman in her twenties, Queen Margaret, leading armies and dominating her shy, retiring husband. Ironically, Robyn helped unseat Margaret, turning power over to the all-male Royal Council—something she was just now coming to regret. But even when not ruling directly, women had tremendous advantages. Violence against men was a given. She had seen rich, successful, politically connected men casually put to death for wearing the wrong livery or voicing unpopular opinions. Violence against women was universally abhorred—unless the law called for it. But in general women were meant to be immune from war and assault, and they suffered far less at the hands of the law, getting all manner of special rights and protections, some of them quite useful. Men still got the best of everything, but medievals made sure they got the worst of it, too.

Witchcraft was the great exception. Spellcraft was not men's magnanimous gift to women, making all the difference. Witches did not have to be good, obedient, or marry well, nor must they submit to the Church; witches just were, their power coming from themselves and the cosmos. Naturally men made it illegal, imposing savage penalties—but crimes committed in secret by women were peculiarly hard to repress. Men did magic—dull, plodding turning of lead to gold, or telling fortunes for the rich. For real in-your-face dancing-naked-under-the moon magic, men must turn to witches, and even the most godly could be swayed by a pretty, quick-witted witch. Pious witch-hating King Henry thought the world of her—though this Halloween night might change the royal mind.

Edward had other notions about dealing with women's power, some of which would shock King Henry senseless. Reaching down, he found the hem of her shift, lifting it with his fingers, feeling for the bare flesh beneath. Her skin shivered at his touch. Women with power did not frighten him; in fact, Edward found it exciting, and a challenge. Bunching the fabric in his fists, he dragged the hem up her calf, past her knee, then slowly up her thigh.

Chills ran ahead of the steadily rising fabric, though now was plainly not the moment to get amorous. As usual, Edward had let his hormones get ahead of him. When the hem got to her hip, she tried to stop him with her hand, whispering, "Wait."

"For what?" Edward asked innocently. This was the farthest he had been in weeks, and she could hardly say no now. "Seems to me, we have waited overlong."

"This is not the time to . . ."

Edward stifled her protest with a long, tender, luxurious kiss, while he finished lifting her shift. Robyn kept her hand on her hem, but she could feel her resistance fading. Her young warlord was going to get what he wanted. She needed Edward desperately, craving not just his power and protection, but also the feeling of having a loving soul mate on this mad adventure, one who knew her needs and matched his words with deeds. Most days, Edward was all that and more, and only her foolish infernal pride kept her from being safe in his arms. How could she ever hope to survive the hard winter ahead without him?

When their lips parted, Edward went down on one silk knee, the way a knight knelt before his liege—offering up his body by putting his hands between those of his lord, preparing to kiss a holy object. Just as she had knelt before Mad King Henry when His Majesty made her Lady Pontefract and had her kiss a holy martyr's tooth. Only Edward's strong hands slid between her legs, his fingers separating her inner thighs, while his lips kissed the soft swell of her belly, producing in her an astonishing surge of pleasure. Moving purposively downward, he spread her legs still wider apart, meaning to put his tongue where it would do the most good.

"No, wait . . ." Her hand went to stop him, but Edward was not to be put off. She must submit to her lord or the law; this Halloween night left her no third choices. Trick or treat, thanks to Duchess Wydville. Her hand ended up playing with his honey-brown hair, pushing him closer to where he was headed. Enjoying the cool feel of his tongue gliding down her bare stomach, she closed her eyes, emptying her head of fear and dread, trying to anticipate nothing but where his kiss was going.

Witches wear nothing under their shifts, as Edward was delighted to discover. Lips and tongue played with soft curls of pubic hair, while his hands reached around to grasp her buttocks, fingers pressing into her flesh, pulling her closer to his hungry mouth. Edward had what he wanted, and she was amazed at how good his touch felt after weeks of going without. Why keep pretending this was not what she wanted, too? Relaxing into Edward's strong grip, she sagged slightly, letting herself sink onto him, opening her thighs while his tongue teased and tickled and searched out just the right spot.

When he found it, she felt the shivers all the way to her toes. Edward's sturdy deft strokes produced a warm rush of pleasure that lifted her up again, until she was practically straddling him, standing on tiptoe at the center of the white chalk star, her black shift wrapped about her waist. Breathless with delight, held upright by Edward at the heart of the pentagram, the five chalk points radiating out from them, Robyn felt raw sensual power surge through her like never before. Not your normal Witches Night. Not in her coven at least. Hecate help her—this was magic of another sort, pitting passion and hope against the hard cruel Fools' Season ahead. Power flowed out of the black night into the five star points, rising up through Edward to her, the hidden power of the dark naked seed that sleeps through winter. Here was the secret of the sacred marriage, the wedding of beauty and beast, of sacred and profane love, enclosing the warm bud of life that women held safe within them, aching to blossom again in the spring.

He licked harder as his kiss went deeper, probing and teasing, licking around her most sensitive spot. Robyn moaned in response, pressing herself against his lips. Keeping one hand on her butt to hold her up, Edward brought his other hand around, resting his hard warm palm right on her pubic mound, his fingers reaching down, holding her up for his tongue. Each long wet stroke felt like lightning shooting through her thighs. Jerking in wild abandon, Lady Robyn Stafford of Pontefract came in her young lord's mouth.

Edward let her down lightly, keeping hold of her while he rose to his feet, wiping wet lips on his gaudy sleeve. He looked very pleased with his own Halloween magic, while beneath her bare feet, the center of the pentagram was a white chalky mess. Edward asked solemnly, "Does her ladyship not feel better now?"

She admitted she did, swaying weakly in his arms, legs together, wishing the feeling could go on forever.

"Well, there's a start," Edward declared happily, grinning to have gotten his way yet again. This was how medieval men liked to see their women, totally wanton beneath all the pretense of purity. "Would that the rest of this unlucky night could as easily be undone."

Amen. This part had been extremely painless, particularly compared to what was coming. Now she had to tell her sweet talented love how badly she had been fooled. Sighing heavily, Robyn sank into Edward's embrace, loath to admit her stupidity. "There was no luck in this, bad or good. I was set up."

"What?" Edward looked to her, puzzled by her modernisms.

"This was all arranged by the duchess of Bedford," she explained. At Greenwich she had dutifully warned her novices not to end up like the duchess of Gloucester; now she was caught in the same way, holding a wax image of a political enemy standing between her and the throne. If Duke Richard were gone, she would be engaged to

King Henry's heir apparent, and the biggest impediment to her royal marriage would have been removed—the disapproving father-in-law that she had publicly opposed. And this all happened the very day "conspiracy against the life of Duke Richard of York" had been made high treason—Duchess Wydville was nothing if not thorough. "John Fogge is a Wydville kinsman, standing for her husband's manors in Kent, and Duchess Wydville or one of her daughters told Fogge where to look, and what to find. They undoubtedly planted Alice in my household, as well, to spy on me and get a key to this room."

"And the wax statue?" Edward asked, mentioning it for the first time. Medieval England was like a hillbilly Haiti, since the very same people who wrote the Magna Carta and the King James Bible absolutely believed in voodoo. Especially the sympathetic magic part, thinking that you could hurt and kill by sticking pins in wax dolls, or by melting them slowly. Personally, Robyn remained a skeptic—despite being a witch herself—having never actually seen it done. But that level of proof was beyond most medievals.

And this wax Duke Richard doll would certainly do her no end of ill. "It is not mine," she vowed. "I swear I never saw it before tonight."

"Never?" Edward looked relieved to hear that, his grin widening again.

"Not once," she assured him, happy to be totally honest—at least about this.

"How, then, did it get into the keep presence chamber?" Edward asked with the same patient seriousness that she had shown to Mary, asking how the ax was able to fly around the room.

"That is a woman's secret," Robyn admitted, to his immediate disappointment.

"Why did I not see that coming?" Edward rolled his eyes. "Do you not mean a witch's secret?"

Same thing. English witches rarely admitted men to their circles, another sign of the remarkable solidarity Englishwomen showed toward an intensely male world. From nuns to barmaids they banded together, asserting their right to make their own rules and to say no to men. "Normally I would not name witches to any man," she warned Edward, "but I have told you about Duchess Wydville because her spells were aimed at you."

"How do you know?" He listened intently, not out of doubt, but

with curiosity. Witchcraft was one of the few sources of power denied to the highest nobility—naturally Edward wanted to know
more.

She tried to sound nonchalant. "Believe me, I know. Duchess
Wydville and her daughters have designs on you." What sensible
woman did not?

"I see." Edward still looked mystified. "Why would the Wydvilles
do this?" When Edward and Warwick had the Wydvilles in their
power at Calais, they chivalrously let Duchess Wydville go free and
later paroled her son, Sir Anthony, as well—hoping to win the Wydvilles over by doing so. "Do they really fear me that much?"

"No"—she hid her smile—"of all your enemies, Duchess Wydville
fears you the least. What can you do to her? Challenge her to single
combat? You had her in Calais, and you let her go. Duchess Wydville
is a witch descended of witches, with ways of striking at you that
you cannot see coming, and you will not know when you are hit.
Jacquetta Wydville thinks men were made to be manipulated, which
is how she got to be duchess of Bedford in the first place—far from
fearing you, Duchess Wydville means to eliminate you, or put you
to use. I am the one she fears."

Edward laughed, and hugged her tighter. "Her Grace is a wise
witch, indeed."

"Really, you must believe me." She did not mean to boast, but it
was the blunt truth. "I am your witch alarm, warning you when
magic is used on you. To Duchess Wydville, that makes me a traitress, not just to King Henry, but to witches, as well, using my powers to shield a man and letting you in on our secrets." Some of them.

Edward shook his head, admiring the neatness of Duchess Wydville's coup, saying, "What shall we do?" For the first time ever,
Edward had no plan to offer. From the moment they met on that
grassy ridge top in twenty-first-century Wales, Edward had been an
absolute font of astonishing ideas, starting with the absurd notion
that he was a medieval earl and she ought to be his "lady." No
matter how hopeless the situation or impossible the odds, Edward had
some audacious scheme to turn the tables, and it all came astound-
ingly true—until now.

"Here, I will show you what to do." She gave him a kiss and then
slipped out of Edward's arms, fetching the soapy water. "We can
start by washing up."

Hating inactivity in the face of danger, Edward Plantagenet stripped off his finery and got down on silken knees again, and instead of defending her, sword in hand, he helped wash away what was left of the chalk pentagram. No longer magic, the big five-pointed star succumbed easily to soap and water. When they were through, they rolled the carpet back over the damp boards, returning the presence chamber to normal. Edward looked happily at her, glad to have done something useful, however menial. Standing where the star had been, he wrapped his wine-and-azure gown around her cold shoulders, saying, "May I see my lady safely to bed?"

She nodded, but she would not let him steer her downstairs toward his apartments, insisting on mounting the steps to her tower room. Edward wanted to finish what he had started atop the chalk star, but she could not just give in completely. Indeed, she dared not. Surprised at her resistance, Edward asked softly, "Have you not missed me?"

"Very much," Robyn admitted; she had missed him intensely, and not just in bed. She missed the whole feeling of being in this together, of having a lover and confidant, of making a future with Edward, even if it was in the past. In the last month Medieval England had turned viciously against her. When October opened, she was Lady Robyn of Pontefract—King Henry's friend, London's heroine, and Edward's betrothed, eating off the royal plate, loved by the commons, and destined to be a duchess. Now it was November, and she was back to being Edward's "whore" and a witch-traitress awaiting trial, whose future was confined to four walls and a stake. "Most of all, I miss my lord of March, who promised to make me his lady."

"Here he is!" Edward was overjoyed to hear he was what she missed most. "I am he."

"And more. You are also King Henry's likely heir. I was willing to be your countess—but never queen."

"Come, being queen is not so bad." He tried to cajole her. "After all, I will be king."

That was a consolation, but not enough. "Even if I could suffer being queen, I cannot let my children be royal heirs." At the rate they were going, there had to be children. For medievals it was abstinence or motherhood, everyone being Catholic, with birth control very hit or miss and abortion unsafe but legal. Getting into bed with Edward would be rolling dice with her future, and her children's future. "I will not have sons taken away at five, like Henry was taken from his mother. Nor have daughters packed off in their teens to a foreign marriage like Queen Margaret." Shakespeare was chock full of weeping queens who lost their children to politics.

"No one will take our children from us, not until they are ready to leave." Edward sounded supremely confident that there would be children, and that he would always be there to protect them. His grip on her tightened. "Nor will I let anyone take you away."

"And Jo, Deirdre, Joy, and Beth?" She was not the only one caught in Duchess Wydville's web.

"Nor them either," he swore. "Not if I have to hold this castle against all of London." He meant it, too. What others said, Edward did. He would defend her against all comers, head high and sword in hand. This gave Robyn a heady feeling, but it was hardly practical. They already had one civil war on their hands. Beset by enemies, Edward could not sit helplessly in London keeping his girlfriend from being arrested. She laid her head back on his shoulder, saying, "I cannot fight both Duchess Wydville and your father at the same time."

"No one expects you to fight them," Edward protested. "Our enemies are Queen Margaret, Duke Holland, Clifford, and Somerset. . . ."

"Our open enemies," she reminded him, "just the ones brave enough to pick up a sword." She was tired of arguing. None of this was necessary, not the Act of Accord, or his father's absurd pretensions, or the renewed war. How could Edward have such a cunning tongue, and not know the truth in what she said? Holding him tight, she whispered into his shoulder, trying to make her words go through the fabric to his heart. "Protect yourself, my love. Times are coming when I cannot be there to guard you."

He laughed lightly. "And all this time, I thought I was guarding you."

"Which only shows how mistaken men can be." Without her, Edward would be led by his father from one folly to another, turning his talents against folks whose only crime was not wanting Duke Richard as king. She raised her head and pressed her lips to his, putting an end to the argument. Unable to complain, Edward turned it into a long, lingering kiss good night, not wanting to let her go. His kiss was lovely, and the boy could not help it that his dad was

Darth Vader, but he was not going to have her in his bed until he broke with the dark side.

Untangling from her love, she entered her little tower room, finding Jo and Deirdre waiting up for her, along with the two little girls—making for another medieval slumber party—no one wanted to sleep apart, not tonight. Thanking the girls for their courage, they made a bed for them in a corner away from the door. Beth asked softly, "Will we be burned?"

"Not tonight," Jo assured her, kissing the two of them good night, adding, "Tomorrow is All Saints' Day, and there will be a special Mass—so you must get your sleep." Being caught at a witches' Sabbath did not get you out of morning Mass.

"Do not worry," Joy told her blond bedmate, "you cannot be burned without a trial. And we have not even been arrested yet." At nine Joy was an experienced prisoner, having been imprisoned in both Berkeley Castle and the Tower. Wincing at the girl's nonchalance, Robyn wondered why women's religion was illegal. How horribly unfair. Especially since most medievals were so relentlessly normal, worried about work, the kids, and who was doing whom—but Heaven forbid you should be a witch. Or a Jew. Or worse yet, a Baptist. Puritan preachers were burned alongside the women they condemned, in a blaze of evenhanded bigotry. Much more of this might make her mad.

Deirdre believed in direct action, making her bed by the door, with Robyn's sharp saxe knife tucked under her pillow. Seeing the door securely bolted, her maid lay down and blew out the light, leaving Robyn lying in darkness alongside Jo in the big canopy bed. She wished she were with Edward. How bad was this going to get? How far did she have to fall? Hearing a rustling in the linen, she felt Jo's hand slide easily into hers, offering support and comfort. "What are you thinking?" Jo whispered, pulling herself closer.

"Honestly?" Robyn asked, and her bedmate answered with an affirmative squeeze. "Mostly, I am wishing you were six feet of handsome young warlord, with a brawny sword arm and thousands of loyal bowmen at his back."

Jo chuckled in the blackness beside her. "I will do my best."

"Good," Robyn replied, "because I am scared. Very scared."

"Tell me what happened," Jo whispered. "Where did the wax image come from? I did not see it until it appeared in your hands."

Jo's sole advantage over Edward was that Robyn could tell Jo everything, the whole story of her Halloween visit to the Temple garden, and getting the wax statuette from Jo's dead lover Edmund Beaufort, duke of Somerset. Jo divined immediate meaning from the weird Witches Flight. "Edmund hated Duke Richard, and Duchess Wydville used that to power the spell, mixing in truth with deception. Having Edmund give you the statue was only half a lie."

Fooling Robyn completely. Duchess Wydville was the last person she needed playing around in her head. "How could she invade my mind so easily?"

"It is not so easy," Jo assured her. "Duchess Wydville had to wait for the right moment, when we were most open and least suspecting, using our own spells against us. I invited in Edmund's ghost, so all the Duchess need do was to imitate him."

"What will happen?" Robyn asked, still holding tight to the hand in the dark, wishing it were Edward's.

"Formal prophecy?" Jo asked lightly. "Or mere hopeful surmise."

"Wild guess. Whatever." With Jo, you could never be sure. Robyn recalled Jo's warning to Edmund Somerset—which had come home beneath the Castle Inn sign at Saint Albans.

Jo weighed their chances. "We English witches are traditionally protected by the laziness and indulgence of the English Church— renowned throughout Europe for lenience and frivolity. You know our bishops: a pious collection of kindly old men and shrewd younger sons with secret mistresses. They have neither the desire nor the power to prosecute women en masse—being too busy promoting miracles and dabbling in astrology to point fingers at us." Catholics understood sin, and the English Church aspired to be rich and respected rather than militant. "Moreover, most people are unwilling to see women and girls done to death for slight offenses," Jo added thankfully. "Which is why Duchess Wydville chose Good Duke Richard as the 'victim'—someone so sympathetic, his case cannot be overlooked." Even casting fortunes for the royal family was a high crime.

"So what does that mean for me?" Robyn tried to read her fate in the darkness

"Stay out of court," Jo advised, "unless we get a jury of friends and relations."

She nodded silently. Court was something she wanted to avoid at all costs. "Edward swears he will not give us up."

"And you believe that is so?" Jo asked.

"So long as he has a sword to hold. He is an obstinate boy, and right now everyone needs him." Warwick and Salisbury signed the Act of Accord under duress, leaving Edward the only one that everybody trusted, or would talk to. "But it is nuts, kicking off the new administration with a fight between him and Dad over me. Just picture the headlines. SON'S WITCH MISTRESS OUT TO MURDER DUKE! LOVE BIRDS IN CASTLE DEFY LAW! Totally ludicrous."

Jo sighed. "Joy and I will not be burdening him further, for we are returning to Greystone. We should be safe there through the winter—since a lot of the west will be laughing off writs from London courts this Fools' Season. Duke Somerset is at Corfe Castle, openingly defying the Act of Accord, and no one dares go against him. In Wales, the Tudors hold Harlech, Denbigh, and Pembroke for Queen Margaret and their prince." Like many Greys, Jo had men in both camps—having a daughter by a Lancastrian duke, and a brother who delivered King Henry to the Yorkists. "Tomorrow will be taken up with parades and processions, and special Masses, and the day after is the Lord's day. No one will come for us until Monday, and by then we can be past Wallingford and well into the Cotswolds."

"What if I came with you?" Robyn asked, knowing Jo would certainly have her, but wanting to hear her say it.

Jo squeezed her hand again. "Would you? That would be most amazing. Greystone faces a cruel winter, and we need all the help we can get."

Not sure how much help she could be with the coming winter, she promised, "I will do my utmost." Much as she hated leaving Edward, she had to start over somewhere else, so why not at Greystone, where this all had begun? Stay here, and she would be a prisoner in Baynards Castle, unable to enter London without risking arrest—not the sort of life Robyn wanted. She would not be the millstone around Edward's neck. "Clearly I've done all the damage I can around here."

Jo sighed in the dark. "Witchcraft used to be legal, did you know?" When Jo or Collin got this faraway lilt in their voice, Robyn wondered if they were remembering past lives—both claimed to be immortal witches, reborn again and again throughout the centuries. The Greys had made Robyn a reluctant believer in reincarnation, since she had met exact twins of Jo, Joy, and Collin living at Greystone five hundred years from "now." She had even slept with Jo's brother in both the fifteenth and twenty-first centuries—which must be some sort of record—finding the medieval Collin to be in far better shape, barring the odd battle scar. "Not just legal," Jo added, "it was the religion. Then for a long time we were merely denied, then tolerated, and now prohibited."

Most medievals thought witchcraft was "wrong"—even though they themselves used folk cures and cast fortunes—but few wanted to see little girls hanged for it. Still, you did not need to be a seeress to see where things were headed. England did not have a general witch law—a law making it illegal just to be a witch—but one day there would be. Witch hunters were out there, misogynistic bigots happy to spark a holocaust. Jo did not believe it would come to that. "Not here, not in England—we shall not stoop to mass burnings."

"It will get worse," Robyn warned. She knew there would be mass burnings, maybe not here in England, but somewhere in Europe for sure, with thousands, maybe millions of victims. Only she did not know when it would be. Clearly it had not happened yet—so far the lackadaisical Middle Ages had been remarkably kind to witches—but the burning time would come. It might start tomorrow for all she knew—and that made her feel like a half-wit. She broke down and sobbed, overwhelmed by worry. Her worries. Edward's worries. England's worries—now the fate of witches, as well. Why was she the only one who knew what was coming? She never wanted to be a seeress, that's for sure.

Robyn cried big racking sobs at the unfairness of it all. She stayed here to be with Edward, and now the whole mad medieval world was coming between them. What an unbelievable waste. She remembered once seeing a harried woman at an airport ATM—not LAX, but a U.S. airport somewhere far to the south, maybe San Diego, or while changing planes in Dallas. Holding back tears, the woman was bent over, grimly writing on her ATM slip, gripping a maple leaf key chain, while apologizing in a soft French accent, "Forgive me, I must note this money is American. I came here to marry an American—but he is a bastard. Gave up a perfectly good apartment in Toronto, and he turned out to be a crud." Finishing, she stalked off toward the ticket counters. That was just how Robyn felt—get me on the next fucking flight to Toronto. Or even Dallas. Only that was not happening.

"Do you miss him?" Jo asked, cradling her shoulder and soothing her shaking. Robyn nodded silently, tears subsiding. She was here in the Middle Ages, and she'd better get used to it. Jo gave her a comforting squeeze. "I know, so do I."

Jo was not talking about Edward, but Edmund Beaufort, late duke of Somerset. So far as Robyn knew, Jo had had no lovers since Edmund was killed at Saint Albans. Jo certainly never spoke of anyone—mayhap five years without sex is nothing to an immortal. Robyn came to the Middle Ages determined to be celibate, and she'd barely made it five days—her only defense being that it was a most difficult week. Catastrophic culture shock. But Jo was a witch-priestess and coven leader, totally into playing fairy godmother to her flock of women and girls. Weird even by medieval standards. Aside from the virtuous few still sleeping with their spouses, all sex was sinning—so medievals did not draw as hard a line between "normal" and not. Add to that the common practice of sleeping naked in the same bed, and most of medieval England was comfortably in the closet. But all Jo did was say, "À *bientôt, ma chère*," then kiss her goodnight.

Saturday, 1 November 1460, All Souls' Eve, Baynards Castle, London

London formally opened the Fools' Season today, with a fitting All Saints' Day procession. King Henry wore his crown, looking more than ever like a penniless cleric done up as King of Fools. Warwick bore the sword of state, and Edward held the mantle train—having two of the men running the country doing menial tasks made it doubly a farce. Bringing up the rear, wearing lions and lilies, was the disgruntled duke of York, who came from Ireland hoping to be crowned Richard III today, and instead was stuck playing heir apparent to a lunatic. Still, Londoners enjoyed the show, glad to see everyone marching in step behind their Fools' King—too bad it has to be to war. Children came to the castle gate begging All Saints' cakes, promising to say prayers for the dead.

Jo wants us to leave London ASAP, before the witch hunters are in full cry, so I met with Edward after Mass, to tell him I am going. He took the news badly, sitting nonchalantly in the presence chamber where all the trouble started, boot heels resting on a cushioned stool. Neither of us had gotten a good night's sleep, fueling our second fight. I pointed out that with local law and order solidly against me, I had to leave—noting he could always come west with me, Greystone was next to his earldom of March. Or he could stay here with the folks who had threatened and humiliated his love.

Of course, Edward had no good answer, calling the whole witchy business ridiculous, adding tartly, "Any enterprise involving more than three women is bound to be chaos. I would be better off herding cats."

I informed him this was one cat he no longer had to herd about, but Edward merely shrugged, saying, "Go to Greystone if you wish. I shall not hold you against your will. You cannot hope for a better champion than Sir Collingwood Grey."

That last hurt, sounding like I was leaving him for Collin, and I informed him that were it up to me, I would be going nowhere but with my love. When I spun about to go, he grabbed me before I got to the door, as if he meant to stop me from leaving the castle, keeping me for another private tongue lashing. Not exactly what I wanted—but the show of interest would have been appreciated. All he said was, "Wait until I can at least arrange an escort."

Just wanting to be away, I claimed no escort was needed, saying that last July, Deirdre and I rode from London to Northampton on the eve of battle, accompanied only by Hela the talking magpie. Edward scoffed at that. "All you needed fear then was outlaws. Now there is the law, as well."

Edward is right, as usual. I must get used to being an outlaw again. Darn, I so enjoyed being legal. Paying a secret early A.M. visit to the Venetians, I got another loan against future revenues, before these sweet, friendly Italians could find out how far Lady Stafford's stock has fallen. Sometimes it helps to speak the language.

Then I went straight to the walled Thames Street fortress of the Hansa merchants, the Steelyard, the main Teutonic trading post among the savage English. Normally women are not allowed inside the Steelyard, but the Hansa made an exception, liking that I spoke German and offered Italian ducats up front, paying for a shipload of Baltic grain to be delivered to Bristol, to supplement Greystone's dismal harvest. Medievals can be incredibly haphazard about contracts and schedules, but the Steelyard's grim Germanic efficiency is encouraging—merchants are all disciplined bachelors, doing their own housework and keeping a suit of armor in every bedroom instead of a woman. This is one ship very likely to arrive.

We shall see if I am there to meet it. At least my period came this morning, another medieval miracle—considering how often we made love. Oh, my love—I do miss you so. . . .

To Jo's dismay, it took days for Edward to organize an escort, so long that Robyn suspected him of stalling, never knowing Edward to dawdle. While they waited, formal charges arrived at the gate, accompanied by a king's sergeant-at-law. Medievals had much to learn about legalese, and the capital indictment had fewer clauses than a rent-a-car agreement. Robyn read the whole document aloud to those most concerned, translating law court English into Cockney and Gaelic.

As suspected, there was no indictment for Beth Lambert; in fact, no mention was made of her at all—the least of them had already gotten a walk. While Beth disappeared, the silver pin reappeared, "piercing the wax idol's heart"—a sign the charges were drawn up ahead of time. Medievals set the bar low for false statements and forgery; anything done in a fair hand got the benefit of the doubt. As if high treason, necromancy, and attempted murder of the king's heir were not enough, there was the usual hodgepodge of additional counts, including flouting the law in the rescue of "Mary of Cock Lane." Deirdre was disappointed to get small mention, appearing only as "Dearie a Welsh maid." Despite the inconsistencies and absurdities, Robyn did not doubt the indictment would stand, based on the alarming physical evidence and her known opposition to the Act of Accord—which Duchess Wydville also opposed, but gladly used against her.

Edward finally announced their escort ready, saying he would accompany her as far as Wallingford. Robyn realized Edward had been stalling until he could get away from London—keeping her with him as long as he could. Touching, if pointless, since they must part in the end. So she bade good-bye to her tower room, with its narrow views of Old London, and to Hanna, her cook. Edward promised to keep Hanna on, but Robyn felt compelled to pay the family debts, getting Hanna's husband out of prison. Dame Agnes claimed he was a drunken wastrel, chronically bankrupt, but Hanna clearly felt different, falling to her knees and thanking the employer who had just let her go.

Which soon had Robyn in tears, as well, as she turned her back on the dream castle where she spent her first night with Edward, where she was sung to bed in the evening, then wakened in the morning by the bells of Saint Paul's. The castle in whose chapel she was betrothed and in whose presence chamber she was betrayed. Beggars at the gate wept to see her go.

Beth Lambert stayed behind with her family—being safer in London with her sheriff father than fleeing to the west with indicted witches—but Deirdre, Jo, and Joy went with Robyn. Matt Davye came, too, an aquitted traitor following his mistress back into treason. Edward went with them by boat and horse to Wallingford, the huge triple-moated fortress rearing above the Upper Thames. Here Proud Cis and her children had been imprisoned while Robyn was in the Tower. Women in politics needed to be connoisseurs of prisons, and Wallingford looked elegant, with its tall donjon, towers, and castle town; moreover, Edward's mother had proper apartments instead of a dank dark cell, making all the difference. Their escort waited at Wallingford's north gate, under the castle walls, where a solid stone bridge and wet wretched road headed off for Oxford. Half a dozen mounted bowmen were led by a Yorkist sergeant named Henry Mountfort, whom Robyn first met in King Henry's tent at Northampton. With them was William Hastings, squire of Burton Hastings—Edward's stalking horse at the Saint Anne's Day tournament—who brought along a pair of sturdy brothers, as if expecting trouble.

When time came to depart, Deirdre helped Jo and Joy mount, while Matt Davye saw to the sumpter horses. Hastings hung about, hands empty, wearing Edward's livery and looking coolly in charge, his younger brother Thomas holding the reins of his horse. Edward held Lily's reins while Robyn mounted, getting a kiss for his troubles.

He tried to make light of their parting, saying, "You will be safe, I am sure." Edward just had his own "death for treason" conviction lifted without spending a day in jail. "One of us seems always fated to be under capital sentence."

Too bad it was her turn. And her brave sweet love was not willing to come be an outlaw with her. She worked his silver-rose ring off her finger, the one he gave her before Northampton, the ring that magically took her to twenty-first-century London and back to him. And the ring that had signaled Collin's betrayal of King Henry. Reaching down, she returned the silver ring to him, placing it firmly in his hand.

Edward tried to refuse it, protesting earnestly, "My lady, please. There is no need—"

"Yes, there is." She had to give him back the ring for a whole host of reasons, not the least being that she might be headed places where a white rose was not welcomed. If he could not offer her protection, she could not wear his colors. More than that, she was setting him free, to do as he willed. If he was going to be heir to the throne, there was no future in it for her, and she wanted no claim on him. She closed his fingers around the ring, cupping his hand in both of hers.

There was another reason. If he ever needed to see her, if he was in danger, or had somehow changed his mind, she wanted him to know he could call on her—so that was what she told him. "If ever you have need of me, send this, and I will come."

Reluctantly Edward took the ring, giving her the reins, saying, "I will soon be coming west."

"Will you be coming as heir apparent?" She hid her misery behind pertness—but if he came west as heir to the throne, nothing would have changed.

Edward rolled his eyes, as if to say he was who he was. "I will be coming as myself, to my earldom of March."

"All the Marches will be delighted at your return." She truly meant it; only die-hard Lancastrians like Somerset and the Tudors would dare oppose him in person. And woe to them if they did. Greystone was glad just getting *her* back; imagine if Edward returned in triumph to the west.

"And what of you?" he asked pointedly. "Will you be delighted, as well?"

"When that happens, my lord will know where to find me," she replied coolly, "then you may know for yourself." He must decide between her and the throne—anything less was wishful thinking. And she very much feared he would choose the crown over her—his only complaint was that he could not have both, not being a boy to do things by half. With nothing more left to say, she turned Lily about and set off up the Oxford road wearing her own red and gold, bells jingling on her saddle bow.

She fought to keep her composure—no sense having another crying scene like at Baynards Castle. Women got a lot of leeway here and now; no one thought the worse of Queen Margaret for fainting in the face of calamity—of which Margaret had seen her share. Keeling over in moments of crisis did not keep the queen from commanding armies and calling Parliament. But it did no good to get known as a weeper—excessive public crying got Margery Kempe accused of heresy, for her implied criticism of the Almighty. Passing her mounted escort, Lady Robyn straightened in the saddle, nodding to the lead archer. "Henry Mountfort, I have not seen you since Northampton. You look to have done well."

He nodded cheerfully back at her, touching his helmet. "Yes, m'lady, I am a gentleman-sergeant, owning a farm in freehold, with a wife who eats off silver."

"Lucky woman, from the sound of it." Forcing out a laugh, she added softly, "Thank you for your brave service, both here and at Northampton."

Henry Mountfort beamed, honored Lady Robyn remembered him. They had met just once, each profiting immensely; she had been in King Henry's tent at Northampton, virtually alone with King Henry, and Henry Mountfort was the first Yorkist archer to enter the tent. Together they saw that no harm came to King Henry, and that His Highness landed safely in rebel hands, for which they were both rewarded with the proverbial king's ransom. Henry Mountfort became a gentleman-sergeant, and she was made Lady Robyn of Pontefract. Sergeant Mountfort was too tactful to ask how m'lady Robyn was faring.

Hastings fell in beside her, followed by the rest of their little cavalcade. Grief, shame, and despair all weighed on Robyn, while the land around her got wilder, the roads worse, the houses fewer, and the skies gloomier. And she would face it all without Edward. Hastings was no substitute, though he stalwartly met her gloom with good humor, introducing his younger brothers Ralph and Thomas, merry felons recently pardoned for political thuggery and now happily escorting witches in broad daylight along the Oxford road. Having recently escaped the law themselves, they made light of her indictments. "With Lord Edward's good lordship, all can be made right. Look at us!" Ralph preened for the ladies. "Who would believe we were once guilty of treason and rebellion?"

"And murder!" Thomas added eagerly. "With our family lands forfeit, and living at the king's mercy. And now . . ." He waved his arm to indicate they had it all back, and were earning an earl's silver taking young women of doubtful reputation from Wallingford to the Cotswolds. Absolute proof that God was an Englishman.

As noontide approached, Master Hastings liked the look of a low inn in Dorchester, a little brick-and-tile village by a bridge, but Robyn insisted on stopping at Littlemore Priory. Located just outside of Oxford, the nunnery was glad to have paying guests, being poor and none too pious—the prioress had a daughter by a priest, a bright little girl about Joy's age, which pretty much set the tone for the rest of the convent. Littlemore was short of sheets, pillows, candlesticks, pocket money, and even pots and pans, but her erring prioress was allowed to stay in office since someone had to run the convent, however badly.

Rain kept them in Littlemore several hours, providing entertainment for the nuns and giving the fugitives and their escort a chance to relax. Like everything else in the Middle Ages, being on the run was a sometime thing, having to observe holy days, the Sabbath rest, and the changeable English climate. Unless someone was out tracking you in particular, the chances of getting caught were slim, with no national police, no TV news, no Medieval England's Most Wanted, not so much as a post office to put your photo in. If they had a photo. Ironically, because of the system of hue and cry, the case of a hated high-class fugitive was a hundred times worse. Both the duke of Suffolk and Lord Scales had king's pardons, but they were put to death by common people before they could flee the country. These same folks, so friendly and obliging to her, were death on those who mistreated them. When time came to mount and go, the younger Hastings were in fine spirits, boasting about their high time with the nuns, "playing and romping in the cloisters."

"Really." Robyn looked askance, having seen no such goings-on herself, finding the older sisters friendly and some of the younger ones quite devout. "What did the prioress say?"

"What could the bawd say?" Ralph replied, his breath reeking of beer—half of England's troubles came from drinking beer breakfast, noon, and night. "Except to threaten them with the stocks."

Thomas laughed, claiming the nuns he dallied with had no fear. "They swore they would burn the stocks and run away if their prioress beat them."

"It is being near Oxford that makes the nuns hereabouts so giddy," Squire Hastings observed, "always taking 'religion' with young university clerks instead of tending their gardens."

Robyn observed that Littlemore's gardens looked well tended, and none of the nuns were giddy enough to run off with the Hastings brothers. Heading north and west under leaden skies, she rode past Oxford with its gray walls and tall spires, then the royal park at Woodstock, and then Charlbury, a market town at the edge of Wychwood. Gaunt leafless trees, their skeletal branches clutched at the slate sky, showed she was riding into winter. Witchy woods, indeed—especially on a wet Wednesday vespers in November. Luckily it was Saint Leonard's Eve, the saint who kept you safe from robbers. Passing the night at a sympathetic manor high in the limestone hills near Chipping Norton, Robyn rode out the next day through Over Norton. Topping a ridge, she saw a circle of dark, ragged standing stones, the Rollrights.

She drew rein, brought up short by a medieval first; without warning, she had suddenly come on someplace familiar. This was the Warwickshire border, and the village beyond the ridge was Long Compton. Hastings reined in beside her, saying, "This stone faerie ring is the remains of an ancient king and his men, tricked by a witch—or so people hereabouts swear." Like Edward, Hastings was intrigued by her witchy reputation.

Having heard the story before, Robyn repeated the witch's prophecy that fooled the stone king: "If Long Compton thou canst see, / King of England thou shalt be."

Hastings smiled at her having the words ready—some men liked women with hidden powers, probably for much the same reason other men feared them. Master Hastings was not the fearful type, being supremely confident that no women had powers he could not handle. "I see my lady knows the spell."

"Only by repute," Robyn was not the sort of witch that turned kings into stone. But she had been to the Rollrights twice in May, and could easily find her way to Greystone from here, thought it was still a day away—showing how thoroughly medieval she was getting.

Next came the Four County Stone, where Worcestershire, Gloucestershire, Oxfordshire, and Warwickshire met; and after that Barton-on-the-Heath, Moreton-in-Marsh, and Bourton-on-the-Hill as the land rose up toward the Cotswold Edge. Rain fell near Snowshill manor, but Robyn ignored it, rising higher in her saddle, searching for Greystone on the hill above. Through the blur of rain, Greystone almost looked the same; but as Robyn drew closer, riding past the ancient burial mounds at the base of Shenberrow Hill, she saw the solidity was deceiving. Greystone's stonework was intact but gutted, its timber floors burned clean through and the main hall's massive roof only semi-intact. All that remained of the once lively outer bailey was a line of lean-to shelters set up against rain-soaked walls, housing stables, kitchens, and bird coops. Half a year ago she had ridden into Greystone just ahead of the rain, looking over her shoulder for witch hunters. Now she had come full circle, again on the run, back where her medieval misadventure began.

Greys and their retainers rushed out, hailing Lady Joanna's latest escape from London, brimming with glee despite the devastation. Dismounting, Robyn found herself embracing a brawny young Grey she barely knew, who got a quick kiss and feel for his effrontery. Women kissed her, as well, welcoming home the Queen of May. She had been Marian Queen of May for that spring's May Day games, a singular honor, especially in the Fools' Season, when such fanciful titles turned real. Children seized her gold skirts, calling her Your Highness and Marian, celebrating the queen's safe return.

"Home again," Sir Collin declared cheerfully, getting a kiss himself, looking as fit as when he knocked Edward facefirst into the Smithfield mud. Bryn stood by his side, Sir Collin's beautiful Welsh wife—annoyingly thin, with big brown eyes, a wide sensuous mouth, and shining chestnut hair cut short in Welsh fashion. Collin had a knack for getting the best of everything, and it had taken Robyn several centuries to get over being jealous of Bryn. Theirs was a Welsh "trial" marriage, a lot like Robyn's secret betrothal to Edward; since everyone was Catholic, divorce took divine intervention, so secret engagements were all the rage. Robyn wished her champion luck, for Bryn was a savage at heart, the same Welsh witch who had given Robyn her saxe knife. Bryn, too, got a kiss.

Invited inside, Robyn saw that only the first-floor basement and the stone second floor had survived the fire; all the family rooms above had burned, including Collin's sumptuous bedroom, with its silk hangings, Italian paintings, and priceless Chaucer manuscripts, as well as Jo's cluttered garret, where Robyn had spent her first weeks in the Middle Ages—all torched by witch hunters led by Gilbert FitzHolland. Collin had repaired the roof and made the surviving floors livable, turning the second floor into an old-fashioned lord's hall, with his men sleeping along the walls. He and Bryn slept in a big curtained bed, living more like King Arthur and Guinevere than "up-to-date" Londoners—but they looked happier than in Falstaff's garish Southwark mansion. As Bryn explained, "Just being away from Court does wonders for your good humor."

How true. Robyn felt freer already, liberated from Parliament, national politics, and the long arm of London law—tucked so safely away in the boonies that the coming civil war could easily pass her by. But she still missed Edward. Even chronic medieval overcrowding could not keep her from feeling wretchedly alone, abandoned in the Dark Ages by the man she loved. Single women slept in a makeshift loft above the surviving stone pantry, and Jo had curtained off one end for gentlewomen and their attendants. Lying on a straw mattress, listening to rain on the patched roof, Robyn thought of how far Greystone had fallen—almost as far as she.

None of which stopped Greystone from celebrating the Feast of Fools on Sunday with drinking, dancing, and costumed debauch. Officially, it was the Feast Day of Saint Maturinus, but at Greystone it was a chance to combine Sunday Mass and a saint's feast with Fools' Season revelry. Jugglers dressed in animal skins cavorted with Welsh tumblers and dancing bears to the tune of fiddles, harps, and hurdy-gurdys in a fall Mardi Gras, full of crude flashy tricks and athletic buffoonery—some of it tremendously funny and some of it remarkably cruel. All enjoyed by people happy to have survived a summer of rain and bloodshed, grateful to be dry and alive, even under a patched roof.

And Robyn danced with them, on a sunny day for once, finding herself paired with Matt Davye, who was back to sleeping in the stables. But he cleaned up nicely for the Sunday feast—much to Master Hastings's dismay, who disliked losing to a stable lad. Dancing out of doors on the manor green, they kept time to a bawdy ballad with clappers and finger cymbals, their right arms holding up goblets of honey wine. Just the sort of cavorting condemned by the Church, but this was the Fools' Season, and Feast of Fools itself, when a banished lady could dance to lewd tunes with her horse master, even in Godly Gloucestershire.

> It fell about the Martinmas time,
>   And a gay time it was then,
> When our goodwife got puddings to make,
>   And she's boiled them in the pan . . .

As they linked arms and spun about, trying not to spill the goblets, Lady Robyn reminded her horse master how they met. "Four months ago I asked you the day."

He nodded happily, saying as they spun apart. " 'Twas the Dismal Day of July, and the Lord's Day, then, as well."

> The wind so cold blew south and north,
>   And blew onto the floor;
> Quoth our goodman to our goodwife,
>   "Gae out and bar the door. . . ."

Bar the door, indeed. Robyn took solace in how far she had come, saying when the dance brought them back together, "Dismal days they were. I sat in a stone cell, learning to kill fleas in the dark. . . ."

"While waiting for me to bring wine and bread," Matt recalled.

"Only to have me badger you for blankets and boiled water." Anyone who held her prisoner had to expect complaints. The dance sent them spinning in opposite directions, still holding their goblets high:

> My hand is in my housework,
>   Husband, as you may see;
> An' should it be barred this hundred year,
>   It'll no be barred by me. . . .

When the dance brought them back together, it was time to take a drink. They linked arms, and Matt Davye gave a toast, "To being out of jail."

"And staying out." She seconded his sentiment, sipping warm honey wine. It said something for the Middle Ages that even in times of national crisis, prisoner and jailer could live to dance together under sunny November skies. Hastings had small chance with her, being too smart and smooth by half—if she wanted a brawny unmarried shoulder to lean on, she needed look no father than Matt Davye, who was honest and diligent, and always devoted to her good interests—even in those dismal days when Lady Robyn was just a pert, opinionated witch from the future, waiting to be burned.

Tuesday, Saint Martin's Day, dawned fair and warm, and Robyn went riding along the Cotswold Edge with her horse master, going over Shenberrow Hill to where she could look down on Gallop Wood, and Godly Gloucestershire. Here the limestone ridge underlying the Cotswolds fell away dramatically, forming a grassy escarpment overlooking holy ground, studded with chapels, abbeys, convents, standing stones, and burial mounds. From her high saddle, Robyn could see steeples rising from village churches, and the broad ecclesiastical estates of Stanway, Hailes Abbey, Tewkesbury, and Evesham. Sacred land touched Sir Collin's holdings on three sides, enclosing vast pastures, and making these "wool churches" monuments to the wealth of the Cotswold wool exports which fed the cloth fairs in Flanders. Matt pointed out gray geese flying in a straggling V, headed south—winter visitors from the frozen Arctic. "Just in time for Martinmas."

Robyn nodded, knowing Greystone looked forward to a great goose dinner with the neighbors. At home November 11 was Veterans' Day, dedicated to the dead of two world wars that had not yet taken place—but here the day was sacred to Saint Martin the Magyar, a Hungarian who quit the Roman army to serve God, the patron of farriers and blacksmiths. Sir Collin came from a family of witches, but he never skimped on Christian ritual, from daily Masses in his private chapel to the traditional Saint Martin's Day goose. Being a warlock in Godly Gloucestershire required both public piety and generosity.

As they rode, white gossamer webs blew up from the Vale of Isbourne below, drifting aimlessly in the breeze, filling the air above and covering the grass beneath the horses' hooves. Catching some of the fine white fibers in her hand, Robyn found a tiny spider clinging to them. "This is the *gaze de Marie*," Matt Davye explained, "threads from the veil of the Virgin, or from her winding sheet."

Medievals saw miracles in the normal workings of nature, but

Robyn did not blame them, entranced by the windblown veils. Why should the work of spiders, and the changing of the seasons, not be counted as miracles? Arachne and Mary were both names for the Veiled One, the Goddess in her winter aspect, represented by crones, nuns, and spiders; the death goddess who offered final comfort for afflicted souls. Robyn said a silent prayer for Mary of Cock Lane, who vanished from the company of nuns on the day that she became Lady Robyn. Then she and her horse master turned back to Greystone to greet the Martinmas goose.

After the goose feast, Hastings remembered he had business in Burton Hastings, settling for a good-bye kiss. His rambunctious brothers, Ralph and Thomas, got kisses, as well—they had gotten her here safely from London, or at least Wallingford. Master Hastings made his final bow by the courtyard mounting block, adding, "If my lady ever should have need . . ." Hastings left it for her to decide what need he might fill, mounting with a flourish and then trotting out the gate followed by his well-armed brothers. He headed north on the Cotswold Way, disappearing behind Littleworth Wood, as gone as Saint Martin's goose.

On Saturday next, Saint Cecilia's Day, Robyn performed a miracle of her own, going to Bristol with Collin and Jo to take possession of her grain shipment. Built between stone-bound quays stretching along the Avon, Bristol felt like a fresh sea breeze, bracing and invigorating, reminding Robyn there was a wide medieval world out there that did not much care who sat on the English throne. Bristol's symbol was a ship, and she heard chanteys sung in the streets, and Welsh and Irish spoken, as well as French and Breton. Tall-masted carracks crowded the quays, bringing in hides and fish from Ireland, Gascon wine, Spanish leather, olive oil, dried cod, and little blond slaves from Iceland.

Her heart went out to these wide-eyed frightened children, the first real slaves she had seen in medieval England. How weird to think that these few helpless towheads would grow into a great African flood funneled toward countries yet undiscovered. She bought them food and milk, and she passed out some of her carefully hoarded chocolate, welcoming them to England in their own tongue. Though she now had the money to buy their freedom and send them home, she knew better than to try. Medievals would take her silver, praise her pious generosity, kiss her hand, and then peddle the children somewhere else. Unless she did it herself, it would be like asking them to put the milk back in the cow.

Robyn spoke with merchants, and shipwrights, who knew of lands beyond Iceland; some had been to the Danish Greenland colony at Eiriksfjord and had seen the coasts of Canada to the west. Fisherman claimed to have wintered on what must be Newfoundland. Clearly America was just aching to be discovered. Mariners were intrigued by her tales of pre-Columbian America, though she doubted many of them really believed there were two land masses out in the Atlantic, each bigger than all Europe. "M'lady must not believe everything she hears about lands beyond the sea."

Collin inspected the grain cargo, finding the Baltic wheat ripe and unspoiled, arranging for it to be shipped by barge to Evesham, where wagons would haul it to Greystone. Bristol merchants liked dealing with the Hansa, since Easterlings paid in grain and silver, while Londoners tried to settle their debts in cards, tennis balls, and silver tassels. Collin thanked her profusely for the gift. "This will save not just people, but animals, as well. Without this grain we would be slaughtering our breeding stock and dairy cattle."

She thanked her knight with medieval modesty, giving the credit to Saint Cecilia, whose day it was, a noble virgin martyr who gave her possessions to the poor before being beheaded. Cecilia was one of Robyn's favorites, a lover of music, who refused to be forced into marriage, even if it meant losing her head.

Sunday, 23 November 1460, The New Inn on Northgate Street, Gloucester

Seven months in the Middle Ages. Not bad. When I first arrived, I did not expect to last seven days—yet here I am, alive and reasonably whole, living in what passes for medieval luxury. This "New" Inn is only a few years old, built by monks out of brick and plaster with huge chestnut beams. My own room is dry, spacious, and charmingly rat free, but I still cannot sleep—just because I miss my rich overbred boyfriend. Instead I lie listening to the rain, vainly searching for something I could have done different. Always coming to the same conclusion: I did what I could. So long as Edward blindly follows his father, there is no future for anyone, least of all yours truly.

So what next? Will Duke Richard of York dispose of King Henry and make himself Richard III? That seems the logical next step, despite all the sworn oaths not to do helpless Henry any harm. Is this where Shakespeare's greatest villain comes from? Another play I never read. Of course, I have a thick paperback history of this period; I am just afraid to open it. Some seeress—too frightened by the future to even take a peek.

Deirdre says I should shut my notebook and get some sleep. Suppose I should, tomorrow we return to Greystone. . . .

Now at least they would not starve. Robyn rode back with Sir Collin, Jo, Bryn, and their retainers, breaking their journey at Sudeley Castle and Hailes Abbey. Baron Sudeley fed them dinner in his magnificent high-windowed banqueting hall, and Robyn saw the oak park where Sir Collin had fought Gilbert FitzHolland for her freedom. She lit candles of thanksgiving in Sudeley church. From Sudeley they followed the Cotswolds Way to Hailes Abbey, past bunches of pink and white bramble flowers braving the incessant rain, along with a few red campions blooming low down on the hedges where they were safe from the weather.

She arrived at Hailes Abbey a bit before vespers, finding lay brothers pruning the abbey's hedges, cutting back the brambles and redigging the banks. Hailes was a Cistercian abbey, and the Cistercians were great farmers and wool growers. Oddly enough, she found most of the "modern" things done in the Middle Ages—mass production, record keeping, public health, and education—were done by the Church. Secular governments were too busy whacking at each other with edged weapons. Monks met them at the abbey gate by the fruit trees and fish ponds, inviting them in. With Greystone just over the hill, Collin agreed to stop for a drink with the abbot, his most influential neighbor now that Chief Justice Fortescue was a fugitive.

Nuns helped her dismount, welcoming them in for vespers, always happy to have ladies call. Cistercian nunneries were notoriously strict, and this was a big chance to hear gossip, to touch silk embroidered with ermine, and gasp at the latest London fashions. Butterfly headdresses were back in style, accented by bold bared shoulders. Staying in nunneries was a trick Robyn learned from Collin; they were cleaner than inns, the food was leaner but better, and nuns were good company, less inclined to drunken brawls. A young novice wearing a plain habit and head scarf pushed her way to the front, asking Jo, "Is Lady Robyn of Pontefract with you?"

It was the first time anyone outside London asked for her by that name. Was her reputation spreading? Undoubtedly for all the wrong reasons. When Jo pointed her out, the fresh-faced novice bobbed before her, saying awkwardly, "M'lady Stafford?"

"Yes, I am she," Robyn admitted, sure she had never seen this novice before—unless it was last April, when she dined at Hailes on her way to Greystone.

"Pardon, m'lady, I should have known," the novice apologized, recognizing the red-gold Stafford riding gown, which stood out amidst the blue and white of the Greys. Looking nervous, the nun-in-training nodded toward a bend in the hedge that would hide them from view. "I have something for m'lady. Something I got in the herb garden, which she alone must see."

Wondering what this was about, Robyn followed the novice over to where the hedge hid them, warily holding out her hand. Something found in the herb garden? Hoes and trowels were always turning up strange curios, bits of coarse pottery, Roman coins, and stone spindle whorls lost by long dead women. Trembling, the young nun-to-be took her hand, putting something hard and cold inside it—Edward's silver white-rose ring.

7

⊶⊨⊙ Somerset ☞⊶⊷

*U**ntil she had* the ring in her hand, she did not realize how much she had hoped to get it. Giving it to Edward as they parted had been practically a plea to call her back. And now the time had come when Edward needed her. What other explanation was there? Excited and scared at the same time, she asked the novice, "Where did you get this?"

"In the herb garden." Nodding toward the far side of the hedge, the novice tried to show where she had gotten the ring.

"But how?" Medievals often took you too seriously.

"It was given to me, m'lady. Is it yours. . . ."

"Yes." She clutched it tighter, asking, "Who gave it to you?"

"M'lady, it was a woman." Cistercians were more strict than most, and a novice would not be seeing much of men. Not alone in the herb garden.

"What sort of woman?" That baffled her a bit—what woman would Edward give her ring to?

Shaking her head, the novice could not say. "Her face was veiled, and she spoke in a hush, but I could tell by her manners she was a gentlewoman. And young."

Really? Robyn did not know what to make of this veiled mystery lady. Was this witchcraft at work? What young gentlewoman would Edward send? "This woman told you to give the ring to me?"

"Yes, to Lady Robyn Stafford of Pontefract." Nodding enthusiastically, the novice added, "And she gave me a message to go with it."

"What message?" She had been so piqued by this faceless young "lady" she had forgotten to ask if anything came with the ring.

Closing her eyes to concentrate, the novice repeated the message from memory, "Go south of Farmcote, past the long barrow, to where a small stream winds along a wooded lane. Follow the lane through Guiting Wood, until you come to a ford by a spring—there a boy you know will be waiting to show you the way."

Clear enough, Farmcote was only a couple of miles off—but dusk was on its way, and things were suitably vague after the boy at the ford, that "you will know." Did that mean Edward? She hoped so, all this hide-and-seek made her nervous—the last time she let go of caution was Halloween, and look where that landed her. Robyn realized the novice was fingering her gold-and-scarlet riding gown while clinging to her free hand, the one without the ring, holding it tightly and telling her, "Good luck, m'lady Stafford."

She looked into the girl's eyes, which were big, shining, and wide open with concern. Medievals treated love and romance as life-or-death matters—more so, really, since they touched your immortal soul. Gently, Robyn leaned forward, giving the novice a kiss and a blessing, saying, "Good luck to you. And if ever you have need of aid, seek out Lady Robyn Stafford."

Robyn meant it. Whatever happened to her, this poor girl faced a strict future behind stone walls, and she was thrilled by this small glimpse at the life of a lady in silks, who got silver rings in secret and then went slipping off into the woods to meet with mysterious boys—though both of them fully expected that an ardent young man lay at the end of all this, anxious to do ungodly acts that no priest would approve of and nuns could but dream about. Bobbing and blushing, the novice departed, leaving Lady Robyn standing alone by the hedge.

Or it could all be yet another trap craftily laid by the Wydvilles, with witch hunters waiting at the ford in the woods. Deirdre rolled her eyes at the sight of the silver ring, telling Matt Davye not to unsaddle the horses.

Her maid was the only one she showed the ring to, the only one with a need to know, but she could not hide that she and Deirdre were about to ride off into the afternoon. Her formal champion, Sir Collin was already cloistered with the abbot, so Matt Davye suggested he come along "to at least see to the horses." Lily and Ainlee had already carried them all the way from Gloucester, and they deserved attention, but Matt's real concern was protecting his lady.

Promising Matt she would spare the horses, Robyn got a big thick blanket roll from their packs and tied it to the back of Lily's saddle—in case her traveling cloaks were not warm enough or they had to spend a night in the open. Deirdre did the same. Telling Jo to give her regrets to Collin, Robyn added that he ought not dally with the abbot. "Deirdre and I will be along when we are able. I have been given a sign—one that could mean danger. Best be home as quick as you can."

Jo was witch enough not to ask questions, just kissing them both good-bye and wishing them Godspeed, since they were on hallowed ground. Matt Davye made one last attempt to be taken along, for safety's sake, saying, "Night is coming on, and you will need protection from wolves and footpads."

Wolves did not worry her, and footpads were one more reason to be on horseback—besides if she really needed a champion, one of the greatest lances in Christendom, Sir Collingwood Grey, was within easy call. But Edward had sent her the ring in secret, so she meant to answer it in secret. And one true beauty of being a lady was never having to explain your motives, so all Matt got for his pains was a good-bye kiss. From both of them—which would have to do. It was a strain on this bold young horseman, who had landed himself an easy job in a female household, just to be left holding the sumpter horses.

Riding up Salter's Lane, she got out her copy of the *Cotswold Way Guide*, a thin guide to the area printed in the next millennium, and looked for the long "barrow." She found it easily about a mile south of Farmcote; roads and towns had changed, but the land was much the same. Unfortunately the detailed map ended there—beyond the barrow was a blank, crossed by some nonexistent motor roads. Halfway up Salter's Lane, she turned east through orchards and fields headed for North Farmcote, following the line of where the Cotswold Way would be five hundred years from now. Larks rose singing from the grass before their horses' hooves, but they did not explode upward in jangled song like they did in the spring, having no nests to protect, and no young to hide.

Her heart rose up with them, though, not exploding like during the spring or summer—but lifted up nonetheless. She had been going nowhere here in Gloucestershire, hiding out in Greystone, flirting with her horse master, and playing fairy godmother with borrowed money. With nothing much to look forward to besides a hard winter. Now she had the ring, but what did it mean? Was Edward in danger? Or hurt? Or just lonely? It seemed too much to hope that he might at last be willing to listen to her. Whatever the reason, at last she was headed somewhere. And Deirdre was there to demand direction, twisting in the saddle and asking, "Where is this Guiting Wood?"

"Ahead, hopefully." Robyn rode with the map in her lap, trying to match modern contours to the old landscape.

"We shall see." Deirdre sounded dubious. Third millennium maps were a total mystery to her maid, who knew most maps made here and now were utterly worthless, and she had a healthy distrust of the written word—calling it "lies on paper." Even her capital indictment listed her as Dearie.

Hitting on a lane that ran the right way, and might even be the Campden Lane on her map, Robyn followed it past open pasture and deep-plowed fields to a tumulus that was on the map, then to the long barrow. There they dismounted, saying a prayer for the ancient dead, who were still able to give directions.

Freed from the map, she mounted up and set out southward toward the line of what looked to be Guiting Wood, gaunt skeletal trees and a smattering of evergreens. It was daubed with faded fall colors—pale yellow, rusty brown, tarnished silver, and old gold. Finding the stream, Robyn followed the soggy footpath beyond— hardly the *lane* mentioned, but at least not a game trail. Winding in and out of the wood for more than a mile, the downhill path kept to the south side of the stream, showing no sign of a ford. Shadows lengthened, chilling her and making her wary. What if this daft adventure ended in a dark, rainy night in the woods? Fortunately she had her blanket roll and a heavy wool cloak to go over her gold riding dress and crimson jacket.

Spotting a patch of color ahead, she came on a woman's rose pink gown draped across a tree branch; above it hung a red riding hood and a white veil, billowing in the breeze. Weird. She looked about for the embarrassed woman in a shift that should go with the stray ensemble, but all she saw were tree trunks and some low brush along the stream. Deirdre took this mystery dress as another bad omen, reining in Ainlee and peering into the darkness between the trees. Cautiously Robyn urged Lily onward, not sure what to expect.

Immediately the stream curved southward, and the footpath crossed it at a small steep ford. Sitting on the slope at the far side of the ford was Edmund, earl of Rutland, Edward's younger brother, wearing a silver-and-blue doublet decorated with a gold fetterlock, over blue-white hose—but instead of boots, he had on red leather dancing shoes, matching the dress in the tree. Delicate, with fine dark hair, he could easily have passed for a veiled woman, even in a convent. Dismounting, Robyn did a deft curtsy, counting on Deirdre to do the same, saying, "Your Grace, how good to see you again."

Rutland casually acknowledged her curtsy. "How good to see you, too, Lady Stafford." Slim young Edmund of Rutland lacked his older brother's easy confidence, but he, too, was a teenage earl, outranking almost anyone and politely condescending, asking archly, "Is my lady lost?"

"Seemingly." Or at least off the map. This was as far as her instructions ran, Rutland was the boy at the ford, and apparently the lady in the Hailes Abbey herb garden, as well. "Where are we now?"

"Locals call this Louse Hill." Rutland indicated the wooded rise behind him. "On the far side lies a church where you may find solace and shelter in what looks like a rainy night. Come, I will show you the way."

Robyn obeyed, reassured by Rutland's presence, knowing this was not a trick of the Wydvilles, and that Edward could not be far off. Remounting, she guided Lily through the ford, with Deirdre splashing behind her on Ainlee. Rising from his seat, Edmund of Rutland happily led the way up Louse Hill, through hazel groves and open pasture. Just out of his father's keeping, Edmund was still counted an earl—at least in polite company—though not surprisingly, his county of Rutland was the smallest in England, tucked between Northampton and Lincolnshire. Small as the place was, Edmund could hardly be said to rule it, no more than she commanded Pontefract. She doubted Rutland had so much as set foot in his earldom since his elevation—yet this frail carefree lad was now third in line for the throne, thanks to the Act of Accord.

But the boy did have promise, being smart, friendly, and gentle, noble without being absolutely full of himself, showing genuine concern for her and Deirdre. He had waited patiently by the ford for them to appear, and now he took his time climbing the hill, seeing them safely up the steep wet slope. Like Edward, he was plainly Proud Cis's son, respectful of women and enough in touch with his female side to slink about Guiting Wood in red leather shoes and a rose pink dress. England could certainly have a poorer king than young Edmund—indeed, the country had been making do with far worse for nearly forty years.

From the top of Louse Hill, Robyn got a splendid view of the valley of the Windrush and the wooded rolling hills on either hand. "There is your destination," Rutland declared, pointing to a church at the base of the hill, beside the little river. "Temple Guiting."

"Temple Guiting?" Robyn saw that the "temple" was a simple village church backed against a bend in the Windrush, with a manor lying to the north, both connected to the town by a bridge.

"Named for the Knights Templars," Rutland explained, "who once owned the manor. Now only their name remains." Having no idea who the Knights Templars were, or where they went, Robyn merely nodded. It was strange to still not know some of the simplest things about medieval England.

Earl Rutland led them down the hill to the churchyard, where Caesar was quietly cropping the wet turf, looking for green shoots. Her heart lifted at the sight of the charger, knowing what would come next. Dismounting, she was glad to be back on holy ground, since all churches had an aura of sanctuary, where sex and violence were banned. Her travels were often spent hopscotching from one bit of sacred ground to the next. Earl Edmund nodded at the tranquil church and tall bell tower, saying, "What you seek is inside."

"Salvation is what we all seek, my lord," she politely reminded the young earl, curtsying deeply, trying not to seem too eager to start sinning with his big brother.

Rutland smirked at her pious homily, knowing she had not come here from Hailes Abbey looking for a place to pray. "Go then, and find the salvation you seek."

By now she had seen enough medieval architecture to know the church was at least a couple of hundred years old, ringed with ancient oaks and decorated with stained glass and leafless vines. A side door stood open, and inside, a holy silence greeted her. Standing by the tall ornate rood-screen, with its carved panels of saints and apostles, was Edward, wearing chain mail and Mortimer colors, a barred blue-gold surcoat with an empty white shield in the center, the same surcoat he wore when they first met on the grassy ridge above Llanthony, some five hundred years from now. He had the same confident smile, as well, the same obvious delight at seeing her.

Seeing him in Mortimer colors again made her realize how much the Edward she missed was the one she first met, the footloose earl of March, teenager in exile, her lighthearted knight-errant, charming, thoughtful, and ardent—in love with life and her. Not the Edward heir to the throne, the national hero of a divided country, with his heart hemmed in by the Act of Accord. She wanted the Edward who cared only about winning her and taming King Henry—not necessarily in that order. His smile of welcome broadened, and he told her, "My most gracious lady, how good it is to see you."

She knelt to the railed-off altar, crossing herself, and then turned to Edward, doing another deep curtsy. "My lord, I came as soon as I could." All this "my lord" and "my lady" no longer thrilled her, not when what she wanted to hear was "my love." But he had sent the ring to her, so it was up to him to say why.

Ignoring her formal curtsy, he strolled casually over to where she stood, trying to sway her with his physical presence. And succeeding rather well. Love and longing rose up within her, and she wished there were some way he could just sweep her up and start over again, doing everything right. Despite all that had happened, she still wanted and needed him, craving his protection by day and his hard strong hands on her at night. Edward took her hands, pleased she did not resist, sensing physical acquiescence and hoping to presume on it—he had gotten his way often by acting while others stopped to consider. He told her, "My lady will remember, I promised to return to my earldom of March?"

"Indeed you did, my lord," she agreed amiably, enjoying the touch of his hand, even though it came from a mailed sleeve. "And my lord has gotten as far as Gloucestershire." Temple Guiting was pretty much on the road to nowhere, unless you were headed for Greystone, or Upper and Lower Slaughter.

Edward smiled at her habitual impertinence, since she alone treated him like a real person, an equal, giving her love and respect freely not because his father was duke of York—in fact, she was under indictment for trying to do away with Dad. His grip tightened, and he told her, "First I had to see you."

"And here I am, my lord." Letting go of his hands, she spun about, showing off her gold satin gown, with its big crimson Stafford chevrons. "Look all you please." She wanted him to see just what he was missing by being obstinate. "I would not have you come all this way for nothing."

Edward applauded her riding outfit, saying, "Every bit as beautiful as I had hoped."

She thanked him with another curtsy, adding, "And now that you have seen me?"

"Then I have to hold you." He took her suddenly into his arms, pressing her hard against his mailed chest, his firm embrace feeling both foreign and familiar. She looked up at him, wondering what would come next, not wanting to fight, but not willing to give in, either. Leaning down, he kissed her, a warm thrilling kiss, lifting her up and drawing her out of herself. Excitement and desire struggled with common sense as she kissed him back, enjoying the strength of his mail arms. When the kiss was finished, he said simply, "I still want you for my countess."

"Your countess, yes." She could not totally deny him. "But not your queen-to-be."

He continued to hold her close, reminding her, "Two hale and hearty men stand between me and the throne."

Not nearly good enough. Edward would hopefully outlive Mad

Henry and Duke Richard, who were both bent on self-destruction, each in his unique way. "I will marry you only if you renounce the kingship."

Edward looked puzzled by the concept, as if it were something he had never considered. "For who?"

She shrugged, saying, "His Royal Highness the Prince of Wales comes to mind."

Edward rolled his eyes. Even he could not make England accept Queen Margaret's son as king, a seven-year-old likely to share the family insanity—unless by some lucky chance he, too, was Somerset's bastard, making him Joy's half brother, but no fitter for the throne. "Who else?"

"One of your brothers, then." That was surely possible, if Edward renounced the throne, his claim would naturally fall to his brothers. They both glanced toward the door, thinking of fey young Rutland outside. Would he even want to be king? Mayhap Rutland was what England needed, another gentle unambitious sovereign like king Henry, but sane.

Edward laughed a bit, saying, "George would love it. Though Richard would probably make the best king, better than me, even— he is the serious one."

"Fine, Richard, then . . ." Poor mad Henry was proof that anyone could be king.

Edward kissed her again, cutting her off in midsentence, substituting love for reason, at the same time undoing the laces on her gown. He bared her shoulder, pressing lips against smooth skin, saying, "Here is what I truly came to see."

"Really?" She looked askance, surprised at how far he was getting on sheer audacity. "My shoulder? How sweet, I have another just like it."

He smiled at her pert reply, saying, "Look at how far we have come against all expectations—and our only quarrel is whether you shall be queen. Anything is possible if we will it. Father might even be made to see reason."

"And if he will not?" She could not let him get away with such an obvious absurdity.

"He will have no choice," Edward assured her, slipping in a little pitch for matrimony, "once we are married."

"If we are married," she corrected him. "No one can make me marry without my consent."

"No one can make me king without my consent." His grip tightened, pressing her closer. "When time comes to inherit, my father will be dead. Hopefully that day is far away. I never wanted my father to be king, and I certainly do not hope he dies anytime soon." Edward grimaced, clearly not liking the notion of taking the crown from his dead father's brow. "But when that day comes, I will be heir apparent, able to do as I wish."

"Then you will not take the crown?" She could barely believe what he was saying. Who ever heard of a right-minded young noble turning down a throne? Especially one as good at ruling as Edward?

He solemnly shook his head. "Not if you say no." Edward plainly meant it, his brown eyes looking straight into hers, not wavering in the least. Why bother to lie? She was what he wanted, more than fame, more than wealth and power—all of which he already had. She was what he lacked. He had missed her as much as she missed him—that was why he sent the ring.

"My answer will always be no," she warned. Edward was clearly hedging his bets, putting his father's death off into some distant future where anything was possible. Used to getting his way through charm and force of personality, she had seen him talk ships into mutiny and enemies into laying down their arms. "Do not think you will talk me into changing my mind."

"Would I be that silly?" he asked innocently, as if miracles would not move her. "So long as you say no, I shall never be king. I will gladly give up the throne for the woman I love." Edward meant it— she could see it in his eyes, feel it in his embrace—Edward of March, who could have anything, wanted her. Wild intoxication welled up, making her feel like a priceless treasure more precious than the crown, freeing her to hope. After all, both King Henry and Duke Richard had to die before the question could even come up. Who knows, by then Rutland might be ready to be king, grown wise, calm, and caring—relying on Edward's strong right arm. Whatever the decision, they would decide together. What more could she want?

He leaned in and kissed her again, and she kissed back, losing herself, body and soul, in her lord's embrace. Barriers between them dissolved, quickening her heart and loosening her tongue—the Middle Ages was back to being an adventure, not a prison. His hand slid down from the small of her back to her rear, pressing her against the hard bulge in his tights. When she got the use of her mouth back, she whispered, "We are in church."

Edward looked around, realizing she was right, seeming surprised that he had picked a house of God for this tender reunion. Which did not stop him from kissing her some more, sliding his hand inside her half-open gown, hiking up the fabric of her slip, his fingers feeling for flesh—a pious medieval Englishman at heart, Edward assumed that if the woman was willing, the Lord Christ would surely under-stand, being a man himself.

It was equally hard for her to resist. Having him holding her and kissing her was so much better than being alone and on the run. For the first time in weeks she felt free to offer herself up, totally and completely, and it had to be in church. Was Holy Mary trying to tell her something? Temple Guiting was consecrated to the chaste pas-sion of a saint for her savior, like Mary Magdalen's love for Jesus—but Robyn was in no hurry to take her profane love outside, where her servant, Edward's brother, and all the horses stood waiting. Clos-ing her eyes, she decided if she had to sin, better to do it in private, with only God watching.

"M'lady, pardon me, my lady." Gaelic in a girlish Wexford accent penetrated her hazy euphoria—as it took a moment to register that it was not Edward talking. Opening her eyes, she saw Deirdre stand-ing beside her, politely ignoring her bared shoulders in a house of God. Her handmaid did a hurried curtsy, saying, "Please pardon me, m'lady, but I must speak with you."

Now? Really? Still entwined with Edward, Robyn stared dumb-founded at her maid, asking, "Whyever for?"

Deirdre did another quick bobbing curtsy, saying, "Riders are coming, my lady. Armed riders."

"What is she saying?" Edward asked, his hand still inside her gown, fingers tensing on her breast.

Alarmed, and trying to close her riding gown, Robyn asked, "What riders? How many, and how armed?"

"Oh, a great many, m'lady." Deirdre looked very much at a loss. "Many more than I can count. Hundreds, for sure, and all of them armed for war, with bows, swords, and ugly big axes."

"Tell me what she is saying," Edward demanded, not knowing near enough Gaelic to follow the conversation.

Removing his hand from her breast, Robyn began to frantically lace up her gown, telling him, "Deirdre says there are riders coming. Armed riders."

"What armed riders?" Edward straightened immediately, his hand returning to her back to steady her. "Who can it possibly be?"

"Does it much matter?" Robyn asked, frantically tying up laces—love and danger seemed totally inseparable here and now. "Which enemy would you prefer? Duke Holland? The Tudors? Or maybe just the law after me?" Armed men were always a bad omen, worse than kissing in church.

Taking his hand, she knelt beside him before the altar, giving hurried thanks; then she asked Edward, "Will you swear with me to Holy Mary that we will decide about the crown together? Neither one of us overruling the other?"

It seemed important to somehow mark the promise. Edward nodded solemnly. "May Holy Mary help me, I so swear."

She swore, as well, and they left through the open door, emerging into the afternoon sunlight. Rutland was with the horses, keeping anxious watch at the edge of the churchyard trees. Through the trees she could see a column of armored riders coming up the road from Kineton, knights and mounted archers headed north, trailed by carts and wagons, followed by footmen, low sunlight glistening on their big razor-edged polearms. "Duke Henry of Somerset," Edward decided immediately. "See his lions and lilies?"

Several of King Henry's cousins used that royal motif, and Robyn could not see how Edward could tell them apart at this distance. "Isn't he at Corfe?" Robyn asked. Somerset had been holding out in Corfe Castle, an impregnable royal keep on the Dorset coast.

"Apparently not." Edward glanced about, calculating his odds. Now was hardly the time for heroics, with him half-armed and responsible for two women and a frail younger brother. Even flight looked chancy, having only three horses between the four of them.

"What will we do?" she asked, wanting to be in on any decision before things got too out of hand.

He looked hard at her. "This is most dangerous. So long as Somerset was safely locked up in Corfe, we had little to worry. Now he is on the loose, but with less than a thousand men; somehow we must discover what he means to do, and who he would attack. And then stop him before he makes mischief or gets away into Wales and joins the Tudors. We have loyal troops at Wallingford, and word can go down the Thames from there to London—but someone must get word to Lord Saye at Broughton, and to Hastings . . ."

"And the Greys," Robyn added. Somerset's thousand men were headed straight for Greystone.

"Yes, the Greys," Edward agreed, "and their many relations. And the Marches beyond, to cut Somerset off from the Tudors until I can get men here from downriver." Edward believed in swift, decisive strokes delivered before his enemies even knew he was coming, disarming the opposition. Calais, Sandwich, Canterbury, and London had all come over without a struggle. Only at Northampton did he actually have to resort to battle, however brief. Right now Somerset had an armored gang at his back, and he had to be reined in before he gathered up a real army.

"I gave warning to Joanna Grey," she told him, "as soon as I saw the ring."

His brown eyes widened in surprise. "You are a seeress."

"Not really," she admitted. "My warning was vague."

"Vague warnings are better than none, and make you alert for anything." Edward pointed out a glint of metal on the far side of the Windrush. "Somerset is on alert, as well—see, he has foreriders out watching the bridge and scouting Louse Hill." Following his finger, Robyn saw more riders descending from the forest lane that led to the long barrow and Hailes Abbey, headed straight toward them—ten or so mounted bowmen, led by a sergeant wearing Somerset's red, white, and blue. "They must have come up through Critchford," Edward concluded, "under cover of Guiting Wood."

Edward did not look in the least worried, though Lily's and Ainlee's fresh crisp tracks led right down the hill to where they stood. While Somerset's main body was headed straight for the patch of trees around the church and more riders moved to secure the bridge behind them, Edward acted like he had Somerset trapped and outnumbered, totally intent on snaring the errant duke—unworried by what Somerset might do to him. Somehow warnings had to go two ways, down the Thames to summon troops from London and deeper into the Marches, cutting Somerset off from the Tudors. Edward summed it up tersely: "Someone must get word to Wallingford and London. And someone must raise the Greys."

Robyn nodded, knowing that second someone had to be her. Deirdre alone would not do; a handmaid on horseback bolting from the woods would only attract unwanted attention. Somerset must somehow be kept occupied, and be led away from this spot—for so far as Duke Somerset cared, Edward and Rutland were still under death sentences that needed only to be executed. She told him, "Deirdre and I can warn the Greys. You and your brother can stay here and take the news downriver when Somerset passes."

Her suggestion turned Edward's attention from Somerset back to her; taking hold of her hands, he asked, "Will you be safe?"

"Me, safe?" She scoffed at that silly concept. "I am the treasonous outlaw now—accused of numerous capital crimes." Robyn of Pontefract, Lady on the lam. "I am far safer facing down Duke Somerset than I am carrying word to London."

Ruefully, Edward admitted she was right; she was safer riding off into the wilds of the Cotswolds than breakfasting in his apartments in Westminster. Still, he hated to let her go again, and he tightened his hold on her hands. "What if Somerset seizes you anyway? How would you get word to the Greys?"

"Remember, I am a witch, as well." Robyn had her plans; she just did not want to reveal them to him until it was too late for him to stop her. "But I must hurry—armed men are heading this way."

He kissed her, taking his time, and when he was done, he begged her, "If you can, keep track of Somerset. We must know where he goes. Right now he has some few hundreds behind him, but if he gets into Wales and links with the Tudors, then there will be hell to pay."

"On one condition," she promised.

"What is that?" Edward had learned to be wary of her outlandish conditions.

She looked straight into his brown eyes, speaking slowly and clearly so there could be no misunderstanding. "That you will not kill him."

"Kill who?" Edward looked quizzically back at her. "Somerset?"

"Yes." She motioned for Deirdre to mount up, wanting to be gone from the churchyard before the mounted bowmen arrived. "Swear you will do your utmost to spare him, either in battle or pursuit, unless he is convicted in a real court, of real crimes."

"Why?" Not for the first time, she succeeded in surprising her love. "Do you know him?"

"Not at all." Somerset was Joy's half brother, but the whole time she had been in medieval England, Duke Somerset had been holding one isolated castle or another, first for Mad Henry, then for Queen Margaret. When Robyn attended Court at Kenilworth, Duke Somerset had been in the swamps of the Calais Pale, guarding Guines Castle for the king. "I have never so much as seen him, but I will not help track a man just to have him killed. I could not stand to see his face and hear his words knowing I was secretly leading him to his death. You may catch him and defeat him, but then you must spare him and use all your wiles to win him over."

Edward shook his head in amazement, since it was no small boon his lady was asking. Somerset was a Beaufort, another of King Henry's cousins, with his own claim to the throne. Not only did Somerset despise the House of York, blaming them for the death of his father, but he was also a direct male descendant of King Henry's grandfather—heading a bastard branch of the royal tree, and unlike the Tudors, one untainted by the family insanity. If anything happened to Mad Henry's line—which was doing horribly at the moment—Somerset had a rival claim to the crown. Edward asked hopefully, "What if he dies in battle?"

"So long as you do not kill him, I do not care." Not totally true, since she would just as soon no one died in combat. "Battle is a risk men glory in taking. Somerset has come looking for a fight, so far be it from me to stand in his way. But when you win, you must promise to spare him."

Edward grinned at the second oath wrung from him in this short meeting. "I do promise."

"And any others that ask for quarter," she added hastily. He had wanted her back, and knew right well what he was getting into.

"And those that ask for quarter." He kissed her in agreement to keep her from adding new clauses. Mindful that armed horsemen were coming, she made the kiss a short one, then quickly mounted Lily.

"Be safe for me," he told her, taking Caesar's reins from Rutland, "I will be back as soon as I can with troops to deal with Somerset." He led Caesar into the lee of the church, where he could not be seen from the road, and disappeared into the grove of trees. Just like that, he was gone, and she turned to face the trouble at hand. They had hardly been together an hour, but they had met, kissed, made up, sworn two oaths, and very nearly committed sacrilege. Not shabby for an age that ran on the sundial.

Best of all, she had Edward's promise that he would not be king, not so long as there was someone to put in his place—be it Henry, or Dad, or Rutland. Which meant back to kingmaking—with a vengeance—but right now she must see Edward safe. She told Deirdre, "Have Ainlee ready to run. As soon as we break from the trees, ride straight to Greystone and warn the Greys."

"And you, m'lady?" Deirdre did not like being separated, and she drew Ainlee close alongside Lily.

"I will be along presently." Or so she hoped. "But do not tarry on my account—word must get to Greystone."

"I understand." Deirdre leaned over and kissed her good-bye, saying, "Take care, m'lady."

She promised her maid she would try, trotting Lily out into the open, where the riders by the bridge could see her, hoping to draw them away from where Edward and Rutland had to cross. As soon as they shouted for her to halt, she spun Lily about, racing back down the road toward Somerset's advancing banners, while Deirdre cut across the pastures, headed north for Greystone. Hopefully her maid's turn north would hide Deirdre from the mounted bowmen, while Robyn rode right down the muddy road, splashing toward Somerset's main body like a lark breaking cover to hide her nest. Loudly proclaiming her presence to the world, she offered herself up to lead the armed riders away from her love.

With no hope of getting away herself, Robyn started going over her story, rehearsing what she would say to Somerset. Reining in before the knot of armored horsemen beneath Somerset's lions and lilies, she spotted the duke at once. He was wearing a big blue beret in place of a helmet, and looking much like his cousin, King Henry— only younger and fitter—but with the same long nose, sharp clean-shaven chin, serious brown eyes, and dark hair. Unlike King Henry, Somerset took care to wear the gaudiest surcoat and ride the best horse, a big white-gray Andalusian stallion, tall and proud as a Lipizzan.

Dismounting, she curtsied to the duke, saying, "Your Most Merciful Grace, I am Lady Robyn Stafford of Pontefract, and I plead for your protection." As she did, she remembered Edward's white rose ring was still on her finger, proudly proclaiming her allegiance to the House of York.

"Lady Robyn Stafford?" Somerset had not heard of her elevation; in fact, he had clearly not heard of her at all. "Of Pontefract?"

"By act of His Majesty," she explained, clasping her hands together, to hide the hated white rose, "our most august and sovereign King Henry."

"Ah, that explains it." Somerset laughed at his addled cousin's latest extravagance. "You are most welcome to our protection, m'lady. And who was that riding off?"

His Grace meant Deirdre. "That is my maid," Robyn confessed, wringing her hands in simulated distress while struggling to get the ring off her finger. "She is Irish and startles easy. You might have scared her."

"Where is your frightened maid going?" asked Somerset, amused by Deirdre's full-out flight.

"Greystone." She nodded to the north as she pocketed the incriminating ring. "That is where we were headed."

Pleasantly returning her smile, Somerset failed to notice the ring, merely asking, "Why Greystone?"

"To get away from London," she confessed, rattled by her slip with the ring and struggling to keep lies to a minimum. She already liked Somerset, who was her age or slightly younger, with wry good humor and an easygoing manner—a lot of royal dukes would not give stray ladies the time of day, much less protection.

"London's loss is our profit." His Grace looked her over, pleased with what had come riding out of nowhere, vowing, "I cannot imagine what someone as gentle and lovely as you could have done in London that London should have you leave?"

Somerset clearly wanted to hear something salacious. Breathless ladies begging protection at the roadside owed their saviors some worthwhile story. She solemnly bowed her head, trying not to make it sound like boasting. "Your Merciful Grace, pray forgive me, I stand accused of opposing the Act of Accord, and plotting the death of Duke Richard of York."

Somerset's companions cheered her initiative, saying all London ladies ought to have her pluck and imagination. They themselves had sallied out of Corfe Castle to oppose the Act of Accord and kill Duke Richard, if they should be so lucky. "Any lady showing such enterprise well deserves our protection," Somerset declared. "Do you not say so, Devon?"

Thomas Courtenay, Earl of Devon, agreed with Somerset, giving Robyn yet another chance to curtsy, begging his protection, as well—taking up yet more time. Finally Duke Somerset cut short the formalities, saying, "Come, Lady Stafford, let us catch your excitable handmaid."

She had been holding up Somerset's little army with her pleas, trying to give the Greys time to prepare for hundreds of armed rebels descending on them. As she remounted, the sergeant and his bowmen pressed forward, waving the pink dress and veil like tokens of the chase. Somerset turned to her, asking, "Is this yours, Lady Stafford?"

"Not at all, Your Grace." She shook her head, happy not to have to lie. "Last I saw, it was warming a tree."

Somerset's men laughed in amused disbelief, insisting her fleeing handmaid had dropped it. "You know how clumsy the Irish can be. My lady is brave to have one for a maid." She did not mind their sallies, so long as they did not go searching for the real owner—certainly none of them thought the earl of Rutland had been wearing it. Glad to see them so thoroughly misled, Robyn fell in behind Duke Somerset as they set out after Deirdre, with absolutely no hope of catching her.

Past Temple Guiting, Robyn relaxed, seeing the churchyard falling behind them, with Edward and brother Rutland tucked securely among the trees, if they had not already crossed the Windrush. Distraction complete. She had been afraid something might make Edward break cover, or that Somerset would come up with a reason to search the churchyard, but for once everything had gone as she hoped and prayed. These men in satin and mail might be Edward's enemies, but they were thoroughly friendly to her, and totally unaware that London considered her Edward's "lady." In a civilized age, her name and picture would have been all over tabloid TV, complete with telephoto shots of her and Edward at play—but here the nearest thing to a national media was word of mouth. Having spent the summer in Cornwall and the Calais Pale, these men knew next to nothing about events in London, and what they knew they did not like. So far as they were concerned, she was King Henry's pretty extravagance and a possible multiple felon—being traitors in arms themselves, they thought her excellent company. Somerset invited her to ride beside him, asking, "Did you truly plot to kill Duke Richard?"

"No." She shook her head decisively. "I am absolutely innocent." Of attempted murder, anyway—the charges of witchcraft and defying the Act of Accord hit nearer the mark.

"Too bad," Somerset chided her, "but you have my protection nonetheless. I have imagined Duke Richard's death a million times in the years since my father's murder."

"Then my lord truly does hate him?" Proper respect resulted in talking to nobles in third person, like they were babies or lapdogs.

"Duke Richard? I do despise him." Somerset's good humor faded, showing the family hatred Duchess Wydville had tapped to set her trap—he looked just like the shade of his father, defiantly flourishing his red rose in York's face during that Halloween dream scene. "Duke Richard imagined by father's death, then made it real at Saint Albans."

She told Somerset how she had burnt candles on his father's tomb at Saint Albans that Halloween. "Alongside Joy Grey, Your Grace's bastard sister."

"How wonderfully pious and thoughtful, Lady Stafford." Touched by the gesture, Somerset told her, "I look forward to seeing Joy when we get to Greystone."

Emboldened, she asked, "And Edward of March? Do you hate him, too?"

Somerset laughed at the suggestion. "No more than I would hate a viper threatening to sting my king."

She pointed out that Edward had not harmed King Henry, "When he and Earl Warwick surely could have."

Somerset dismissed that as, "Pretended mercy, a ploy to win sympathy from fair damsels. Mark my words, Edward of March means to be king." She had just gotten Edward's word that he did not, but it was hardly tactful to say so. "And one day he will murder King Henry," Somerset added, "unless we stop him."

Clearly there would be no moving Somerset when it came to the House of York—Duke Richard's spawn were evil incarnate. Luckily, Edward had the task of winning him over; she merely had to keep track of him. She asked, "What about Earl Warwick?"

"Him I hold most culpable for my father's death," Somerset declared. "Duke Holland and I meant to take him on the London road, just as he murdered my father, but someone warned Warwick."

At least they agreed on one thing: Warwick was an odious insect—though Robyn did not think armed assault was the right recourse. With Edward safe, she felt well disposed toward the world, and even if she could not win Somerset over, she could at least get to know him. She asked about his trip, trying to worm out where this duke on the loose was headed, but Somerset would only say where he had been, describing the ride up from Corfe, by way of Bath and Cirencester, making it sound more like an autumn jaunt than a military campaign. "We have had a splendid journey, were it not for the rain. Welcomed all along the way, without the least hint of opposition."

No doubt. So far Somerset and Devon had come through hill country, avoiding cities like Bristol, and the populous Thames valley. So long as they paid their way and kept on going, who would think to oppose them? Things would get harder if they went on into Wales or the Marches, where the land was less friendly, and most castles were held against them. Not that Somerset seemed to care, joking gaily with his companions and laughing aloud at her tales from London, giving no sign he expected trouble. Long chill shadows came out of the trees as the old winter sun sank down beyond the Cotswold Edge. Somerset was being the perfect gentleman, and it saddened her that he and Edward were at war, making her doubly glad she had gotten Edward's promise to spare him. Her last attempt at peacemaking landed her in the Tower, yet she had the great advantage of knowing the nation was behind her. England wanted peace, and someday this feuding nobility had to give in.

Ahead, she saw Greystone lit by torches, its bailey gate thrown wide open, with no attempt having been made to put the half-burnt manor in a state of defense. Joanna Grey had been old Somerset's mistress, making them bastard relations; but at Northampton, Collin and his uncle had gone over to the Yorkists, taking King Henry with them. Somerset and Devon counted that betrayal as treason, and they could easily hold the lord of Greystone responsible for the lost battle and the deaths of Duke Buckingham and Lord Egremont. Luckily, they knew nothing of Robyn's role at Northampton, except that she had served King Henry during the battle and reaped a royal reward.

Jo greeted them at the bailey gate, wearing the family blue and white trimmed with cloth of silver, and topped by her horned-moon headdress. With her was Bryn and Joy, and her most trusted serving women, all dressed in blue and silver. None of them were armed, unless you counted Nest, Bryn's giant nurse-cum-bodyguard, who had her big armor-piercing bow strung and ready—but that was just because no one dared take it from her. No men were in sight. Addressing them as guests, Jo led her ladies in a curtsy to the duke and earl, saying, "Welcome, your most gracious and merciful lordships, pray accept our poor hospitality. There is food and shelter for Your Graces' men in the bailey, while wine and music await my lords within. Please come, rest and refresh yourselves."

Men appeared—stable boys to take their horses, and older servants bearing beer, boiled beef, and hot porridge for Somerset's riders—but males of military age were conspicuously absent. The meaning was clear; the men were under arms in the hills, watching how the women were treated while word went out through the night to their kith and kin. There were two ways of dealing with overwhelming numbers, either fort up and try to stand a seige, or open your gates and offer up a feast. Too weak to do the former, Greystone had to defend herself with food and smiles.

Which suited Somerset wonderfully; hiding any animosity he might feel for the Greys' betrayal at Northampton, he briskly mounted the steps, giving his bastard sister a kiss and a gift—two ivory combs for her hair—saying, "Here is an early Christmas present." Their father used to send Yuletide gifts to Joy, and Somerset had taken up that duty along with his earldom. "I will not be here for Christmas, so I must give you this now."

Joy was just as glad to get her present early. Somerset and Devon disappeared into a robing room to change out of their armor, while harpists started playing in the main hall and servants set out supper. Robyn retreated upstairs to the loft above the pantry, where Jo helped her dress for dinner and dancing, thanking her for Deirdre's warning. "Collin has sent word to Sudeley and Lord Saye at Broughton, and given warning to the Greys in the Marches, in case Somerset goes that way."

Struggling into her best cloth-of-silver gown, Robyn told Jo, "We must find out what way he is headed. If this ends swiftly, Edward has sworn to spare Somerset's life."

"He has?" Jo's grave eyes went wide—she had been as worried

for Somerset as she was for Greystone. Seeing her lover's son riding to war must have brought back memories of his father's death. Jo asked softly, "How do you know?"

"How do you think?" she whispered back, furiously adjusting the hang of her shining silver sleeves. Downstairs a tinny dulcimer had joined the harps.

"Edward is here?" Jo sounded aghast, not the sort of reaction Edward hoped for on his return to his earldom.

"Was here." By now Edward would be headed down the Thames to lay hands on the troops to face Duke Somerset. "I made him swear to do his utmost to spare Somerset, and any others that want quarter. Otherwise I would not help him."

Hope and fear played across Jo's stern face, weighing Somerset's chances while she sewed protective silver bells onto Robyn's bodice. Having a brother on one side and a lover's son on the other must have been hard on her. Jo whispered tersely, through pins in her teeth, "Can you make Edward keep his promise?"

"He will." Robyn wished she were as sure as she sounded. "Especially if it ends soon, without bloodshed, and I am there to see Somerset is safe. But if there is a full-blown battle . . ."

No one needed to tell Joanna Grey how chancy battles could be. Stitching the last bell in place, Jo stood up and kissed her, saying, "Thank you, thank you. Losing him would be like losing his father again. I will help, so long as word goes only to Edward, not to Warwick or York. And we must try to be there, to see Edward keeps his promise."

Some tall order, but Jo doted on impossible tasks. Somerset had not said where he was headed, except that it was nowhere near here, so Robyn tried not to get Jo's hopes up, just saying, "Let's at least see if he is headed west or north." West meant he aimed to cross the Severn at Tewkesbury and plunge straight into Wales. North meant he would cross at Evesham and then make for the Marches, or somewhere even farther north.

Robyn adjusted her heart-shaped headdress, thinking of her secret paperback history of the period, which even Jo did not know about. Would Somerset's march be in it? Probably—if it was important. On the back, some proper British historian swore it was "a complete and readable popular history of the Wars of the Roses." But Robyn had no time to secretly consult the book, and she feared what she might read in it. If Somerset somehow succeeded in laying hands on Edward, or if Edward killed him, Robyn did not want to know ahead of time. Better to get her information on Somerset the old-fashioned way.

Jo stepped back, saying she looked "wantonly beautiful." Bryn had on the green faerie-queen gown that broke hearts in London. Jo herself had on a blue ball gown trimmed with more silver bells. With their men off gathering reinforcements, the women of Greystone descended the stone stairs to the sound of harps and the tinkle of tiny bells on their dresses, all set to dance with the enemy—much to the delight of Somerset and Devon. Since they could not personally confront Sir Collin with his treason, then the next best thing was to dance with his sister and his pretty Welsh lady. Twirling about by torchlight, they turned elaborate circles, twining and untwining to music that filled the two-story hall. When they stopped to catch a breath and drink spiced wine, Jo went back to being hostess, asking Somerset, "Will Your Grace be staying on the morrow?"

Somerset looked genuinely sorry, shaking his head and saying, "We are leaving, I am afraid."

"Really?" Robyn saw her opportunity, taking a slow sip from her silver goblet. Hot ginger spiked wine tasted warm on her tongue, heating her within on a cold November night. "What a truly wonderful chance."

"How so?" Somerset sounded disappointed to find her delighted at his departure.

"Because, I must be leaving, as well," she explained, taking another sip of ginger wine. "And I could most dearly use an escort, if Your Grace could be so kind."

Somerset's smile returned. "To where, my lady?"

Where indeed? Since Somerset had said nothing about where he was headed, she would have to guess. Greystone was perfectly positioned for either heading straight west through Tewkesbury and Hereford into Wales, or for going north through Evesham. Tewkesbury or Evesham? Since Somerset would not say, she had to decide. So far, there had been no talk of Wales, or of joining the Tudors, nor could she picture Duke Somerset disappearing into central Wales, not with the Greys, Vaughans, Tiptofts, and Baskervilles beating the bracken for him. Somerset rated himself higher than that. Why bother leaving Corfe? Corfe Castle had a banquet hall, library, and soft feather beds, just a day away from France by sea, far more inviting than skulking about Powys in the rain—Robyn knew that firsthand, having been a fugitive in the Welsh hills herself. Whatever Somerset was after had to be bigger than that. "At least as far as Evesham," she suggested, "if that is not too far."

"Not in the least," Somerset declared, "we would be happy to see you safely to Evesham. Or even farther."

"How far north is Your Grace going?" Robyn tried to make the question sound innocent.

Somerset laughed, "How far does my lady wish?"

Only one answer came to mind. "I have yet to see my Honour of Pontefract." Actually King Henry's Honour of Pontefract, but all land in England technically belonged to the king, and all landowners held from him—so she was not exaggerating by much. "In these unsettled times, it is good to see to your holdings. And as a woman wanted by the law, I have nowhere else to go."

"An unjust law," Somerset noted amiably. How strange to have this handsome young "enemy" so ardent in her cause. Nor was it all show, meant to impress a wayward lady in distress; Somerset truly hated the Act of Accord, and hardly thought it treason to oppose Duke Richard, who stole a kingdom from an infant prince. He told her in all seriousness, "I would see my lady safely to Pontefract, if she wishes."

"Many thanks, Your Grace. You have been wondrously kind and courteous to me." She meant it, too. He had been very humane toward her, and the protection he offered was real, which made her feel guilty for plotting against him. She had to find a way to pay the good duke back—besides the obvious one. "But I would not be a burden to you in this time of troubles."

Somerset scoffed at that. "No lady in need of succor is a burden to a knight. You would make delightful the dreary road to Yorkshire. Here, let us drink to the Honour of Pontefract."

She drank, wondering what she had gotten herself into—a trip to Pontefract from the sound of it, unless Edward returned in time to stop them. But it was worth it, if she could serve as a peacemaker and keep Edward and Somerset from killing each other. She already had Edward's promise to spare Somerset, and so long as she was there, she had confidence that he would keep it. Worming a similar promise out of Somerset would be far harder, maybe even impossible—but she was counting on Edward to beat him. A safe bet, since her love had beaten every other opponent he had faced, and spared them when he could—including Collin, King Henry, and the lords in the Tower who had fired on London.

Secret word went out that night from Greystone, with a trusted servant riding hell-for-leather toward London, carrying a message for Edward alone, saying, "The dove you spied on the road to Temple Guiting flies north, followed by a robin."

Rutland was right; it rained that night, but the roof held, and the day dawned clear but cold with the smell of snow in the air. Riding north meant riding deeper into winter. Jo and Joy were going with her, at least as far as Coventry, to make sure that Somerset did not double back toward the Marches. They were playing a double game, and there was nothing to stop Duke Somerset from doing the same. Though Robyn thought that very unlikely, since Somerset was openly in rebellion against a government he hated—why would he have to lie to pretty women he met on the way?

Bryn stayed to await Collin's return, giving Robyn a heartfelt kiss good-bye. Bryn knew that Robyn and Collin had tested the limits of Sir Collin's "trial" marriage, and though no one expected that would happen again, Bryn was always glad to see her go. Deirdre and Matt were coming with her, bravely wearing her scarlet and gold, amid Somerset's royal red, white, and blue.

Heading north along the Cotswold Way, she looked back from the saddle, saying a private good-bye to Greystone, which twice had given her sanctuary. This time, at least, the place did not suffer for it. She had expected to winter here, at least through Yule, but now it was not even Thanksgiving, and she was as gone as the Martinmas goose.

8

⤙ Robin Hood Hill ⤚

Evesham was a quiet abbey town, with its market, gardens, and or-chards, surrounded on three sides by a long loop of the Avon. Riding up from the south at the head of Somerset's tiny army, Robyn crossed the Avon on a narrow bridge at Bengeworth, dined at the

Benedictine abbey, and then climbed the low plateau beyond. Already she missed Edward mightily, hoping he would be back soon to take ardent young Somerset off her hands. At the top of Green Hill, she paused with His Grace to survey the rolling woods and fields ringed by the shining river. Somerset told her, "This is where Simon de Monfort's rebels were crushed by Edward Longshanks. Earl Simon was a fool to fight with a river at his back. Mortimers blocked the bridge behind him, and the Avon penned him in on three sides—they sent his head to Wigmore as a gift to Lady Mortimer."

Marcher lords had a rough sense of humor. Having lived some weeks in the shadow of Evesham Abbey, Robyn knew the whole two-hundred-year-old tale. Like her Edward, Simon de Montfort had been the darling of London and the commons, and also had a king named Henry in tow. Knowing they would all die, de Monfort made the king fight in plain armor; but His Highness saved himself by crying, "I am Henry of Winchester, your king. Do not harm me." He shouted it over and over again, until some kind soul led him from the slaughter. Deserted by Llywelyn's Welsh and sorely outnumbered, Earl Simon and his rebel knights died fighting—as the chronicler says, "Such was the murder of Evesham, for battle there was none."

Somerset clearly hoped the same would happen to Edward—if he could be lured away from London and into the west or north, then ambushed by superior forces—something Robyn dearly meant to prevent. "Common folk call Earl Simon a martyr," she reminded Somerset, "a hero who defended the power of Parliament against the king."

"They say a black cloud blotted out the sun when he died," declared Joy, who doted on such gruesome stories. "And people who drank from the pool he bled into were blessed with miraculous cures."

Medieval chemotherapy. Somerset merely smiled, saying, "Monks hereabout spread these stories, profiting off the credulity of the commons."

"At Alnwick, they kept Simon's foot in a silver shoe," Joy added eagerly, "blessed by the monks in secret."

Alnwick was far up near the Scots border, showing the cult of Simon the Martyr was more than local. Credulous or not, folks were wont to make heroes out of those who died defying unjust authority.

The victor at Evesham was Edward Longshanks, conqueror of the Welsh and the Hammer of the Scots, the king who gruesomely executed Mel Gibson in *Braveheart*. In his spare time, Edward Longshanks was a great hater of wolves and Jews, as well, ordering them driven from the kingdom. Killing Simon de Montfort did not end people's desire for a king that gave justice and listened to Parliament—but she doubted Duke Somerset saw it her way.

Though not for lack of trying, since Somerset went out of his way to get to know her, asking about her upbringing in "Staffordshire"—which she admitted was somewhat abnormal, without actually saying it was in another century. When he asked her what her favorite pursuits were as a girl, she confessed to "horseback riding and acting."

Somerset arched an eyebrow. "Not prayers and needlework?"

"No." She shook her head, though she had taken both up with a passion since coming to the Middle Ages. Prayers and needlework were what kept her whole and clothed. "In fact I find myself wishing I had learned more of both."

"I can see you are an accomplished horsewoman." He nodded at Lily, who ambled along beside his charger, enjoying the stallion's company. "That flying dismount and curtsy you did the day we met was most astonishing. I doubt that I could have done it in silk skirts."

"Your Grace is too kind," she told him. "I am sure your lordship could do it quite handily."

Somerset laughed, saying he would stick to armor. "Did you practice those flying dismounts back in Staffordshire?"

"Sometimes in bareback riding, but I much preferred barrel racing. I was all-state champion as a teen."

"How does one race a barrel?" Somerset asked. "By rolling it down a hill?"

"By racing around the barrels, Your Grace." She tried to explain the basics of the game, saying, "You have to circle three barrels on horseback, as fast as you can. Knock over a barrel, and you are penalized five seconds."

"Five seconds?" Medivals timed themselves with water clocks.

"Five heartbeats." More or less.

"That does not sound like much," Somerset objected.

"Your Grace would be surprised." She resisted the impulse to show him her digital watch and prove how long it was. "But I tried not to hit the barrels."

"She was Miss Rodeo Montana," Joy declared proudly.

"Young women in Staffordshire get unusual educations," Duke Somerset decided. "What is this acting you mentioned?"

"Mostly plays and low-budget movies, though I was in a national TV commercial. For Nike." Her one big-bucks endorsement as Miss Rodeo Montana—it paid for college.

Somerset was unimpressed. "You mean like passion plays?"

"In a way. I played a nun in *Measure for Measure*." She quoted from Shakespeare:

> When you have vow'd, you must not speak with men
> But in the presence of the prioress:
> Then, if you speak, you must not show your face,
> Or, if you show your face, you must not speak.

Easy enough to remember, since those were almost her only lines. The big parts always eluded her—until now. Here she was, riding along the north bank of the Avon, a dozen miles from Stratford-upon-Avon, playing Lady Pontefract opposite the duke of Somerset.

"Well said." Somerset approved of England's Bard-to-be. "This Holy Wood you come from must be most pious."

"Not so you would notice." Hollywood "piety" would make Somerset's hair stand on end. Even an arrogant outlaw duke from a bastard house had more piety than your average studio exec.

Somerset smiled at her. "Well, I am glad you can both speak to me and show your face. For both face and voice are passing fair."

"Your Grace is too terribly kind." At least his interest was honest, there being no duchess of Somerset. In fact, young Harry was a catch any footloose lady of dubious means ought to snap right up: rich, young, handsome, and pleasantly engaging, with a good deal of wit and energy. He had a disarming smile and a dancer's body, looking very dashing in tunic and tight hose. And if, God forbid, anything happened to the young Prince of Wales—in an age when children died with appalling regularity—then the Lancastrian heir would either be smart, young unmarried Duke Somerset or the marginally sane Henry Holland, duke of Exeter, unhappily married to Edward's older sister. Not a hard call at all.

But she was already betrothed to one heir to the throne, and did not need to dally with another. All she wanted was to see Duke Somerset safely into the hands of the law—though that did not mean they couldn't have fun first. There was a certain charm to flirting with a man you hoped to see arrested; it served to even the odds.

Riding up the once pleasant Vale of the Avon, Robyn saw what the rains had wrought, passing ruined orchards, drowned meadows, and marshy fields. She was reminded of how medievals described the black thundercloud that swept over Evesham the day Simon de Montfort died, blotting out the summer sun so that monks could not read the sheets of plainsong set before them. This rain was not that black, but it was relentless. Bidford-on-Avon, with its fine stone bridge and tall church tower, looked wet and shabby, and Stratford-upon-Avon, which was so delightful last spring, seemed barely worthy of being the Bard's birthplace. They passed great castles held against them, Warwick and Kenilworth—but no troops fresh from London issued out to apprehend Somerset. Plainly there had been no time.

Despite the swollen fords and washed-out bridges, Somerset moved much faster than Robyn thought he would. She had been deceived by the leisurely way King Henry made war. Edward had marched rings around the king, but Somerset was a real soldier, swift and decisive; loaded down with infantry, baggage, dogs, camp followers and talkative companions, Duke Somerset still made Coventry in a couple of days, and the city opened its gates to him—the first important place to let him in.

Which figured. Robyn did not expect much resistance. Coventry was Queen Margaret's old capital, a splendidly walled town surrounded by a great sweep of soggy common fields, ruled by a few families that formed The Scarlet, the self-elected oligarchy filling every civic office. Margaret used to make the mayor carry his mace of office before her, as if she were king. To these wealthy magnates, Somerset represented the good old days, when Margaret's court squandered the royal revenues on food, drink, and finery, keeping goldsmiths and furriers forever busy—Somerset's father having been one of the worst offenders. While Somerset was splendidly received by supporters of the old regime, Robyn stayed in a Benedictine nunnery north of the city, right next door to Burton Hastings, sharing cramped apartments with Jo, Joy, and the serving women. That night she conferenced with Jo in a hard, narrow nun's bed, whispering over Joy lying asleep between them. No word had come from London, but there had hardly been time. She tried to make that sound encouraging, saying, "If Edward is force-marching north to meet us, he could easily be here before any messenger."

"True," Jo humored her hopeful assessment, "but still I must go back soon. With Collin gone, Greystone needs me." Bryn, being Welsh, was no real substitute, since Saxons were loath to obey her. "But I worry over what will happen to Somerset if Edward catches him. Or even if he does not. Why could he not have stayed safe in Corfe, where no one could get at him?"

Because Somerset was not made that way. Already Robyn could see the young duke was too forceful and restless to stay penned in Corfe or to dally on the way to Coventry. And rash, as well, leaving an impregnable keep to plunge deep into the Midlands with a few hundred men at his back. Yet Somerset had been the soul of chivalry, humane and gentle toward her, and he deserved to come out of this alive. If at all possible.

"What should I do?" Having family on both sides of this "Cousin's War" was driving Jo to distraction—taking her away from her usual problems, such as a raising a willful daughter, and preparing a half-ruined manor for winter.

"You should go back to Greystone," Robyn decided. There was only so much Jo could do for her lover's son. "I am the one who most needs to be here, and I will go on, at least as far as Nottingham. If Edward intercepts him, it will most likely be between here and Nottingham." Nottingham was just over a hundred miles from London, and by marching night and day Edward could possibly cut them off. Past Nottingham, Somerset would turn straight north into Sherwood Forest, which did not sound nearly so promising.

"What if Edward does not come?" Jo looked concerned, the candlelight throwing her worry lines into sharp relief. "What will you do?"

"I will know when I get to Nottingham." Hopefully. Whatever happened, Jo and Joy ought to turn back here at Coventry, where they could be safely home at Greystone in a couple of days. If there was to be a confrontation with Edward in the near future, she would just as soon meet it on her own—with Deirdre and Matt there to help hold the horses, of course. How comfortable it was to be Lady

Pontefract, easily including others in your plans—where else would Matt and Deirdre be but with her? Still, it meant setting out with Somerset sans chaperon, a risk in itself, though that could hardly be helped.

Jo shook her head, saying, "Well, they have put themselves in Hecate's hands." Jo meant the men who had taken up arms against one another; but with winter coming on, they were all in Hecate's hands.

Luckily, Robyn had a newfound friend nearby, a forward Midlands squire who had shown inordinate interest in her welfare. "Burton Hastings is just down the road," she reminded Jo. "Tell Squire Hastings that Somerset is in Coventry—if he does not already know—and to send one of his nimble-footed brothers to Edward, telling him I am with Somerset, headed north for Nottingham." That was as good a plan as she could devise, given the circumstances, though it seemed horribly chancy. "Hastings will at least see you safely back to Greystone, or give you shelter until Collin can come for you."

Jo nodded solemnly, saying, "Good luck in the north." Then she added thoughtfully, "Somerset has a lover."

"He does?" No one had mentioned this before, not Jo or Joy, and certainly not Duke Somerset.

"Her name is Joan Hill," Jo explained, "and I do not know her, but they have a bastard together, a boy."

"Thanks for the warning." She had not told Somerset about her boyfriend either, but she had sound political reasons for not proclaiming her undying love for Edward to his rich and powerful enemies. Somerset had no similar reason to avoid mentioning Joan Hill and the joys of fatherhood, aside from the usual one.

"Thanks for all the wheat," Jo whispered, and kissed her good night, then lay down to sleep alongside her daughter.

Next morning, they parted at the nunnery gate, where she gave Jo a bolt of Coventry Blue cloth to take to Collin. His gift to her when she first arrived at Greystone that spring had been a bolt of blue cloth, and she did not want to go into danger owing any debts—not if she could pay them.

Thursday, 27 November 1460, Thanksgiving Day, Nottingham

No Edward. Cannot say I am surprised. Edward may be a miracle worker, but Somerset has moved much too fast, especially for a medieval. What happened to holy days? And big sit-down meals in the afternoon? Today is Thanksgiving, and I am the only one missing the turkey. Somerset stops here and there, usually to hobnob with local nobility, but then it's right back to the boggy road north. I was sure that Edward would intercept us by now—but he did not.

Now what? Is there any sense to staying with Somerset? I am nowhere near winning him over. At best he thinks I am naive and good-hearted, hoping for peace through compromise. Cannot say I blame him. I feel naive, if not necessarily good-hearted. Somerset is certainly wrong about that, not knowing that I am secretly betraying him to Edward—yet. Another scene to look forward to, assuming we all live to see it.

Logic says I should hie myself back to Greystone while I still can. Hope says that if I stay with Somerset, Edward may yet overtake us, and this may all end without bloodshed. But tomorrow we dive straight into the depths of Sherwood Forest, making successful pursuit unlikely. How can I even be sure Hastings and his felonious family will get word to Edward? On the other hand, safety at Pontefract is only fifty-odd miles ahead, a couple of days, at the rate we are going. There I can bid a fond good-bye to Somerset, leaving him none the wiser. To turn turn back now, I must invent some excuse, which means more lies—something I hate. Somerset actually likes me.

Luckily, I do not have to decide. Since today is Thanksgiving, tomorrow is Witches Night. So I will leave it at that—I will have my Witches Night in Sherwood Forest, and that will decide it. When nothing else works, kick it back up to Hecate.

Nottingham is everything I hoped for, with a huge open air market where robbers' loot is sold alongside silks and spices brought up the Trent from overseas. I can really believe Robin and Marian lived here and loved here—it is that sort of place. Dirty and romantic, full of poachers and ne'er-do-well forest folk, right off a Hollywood back lot. Burning sea coal keeps the place from ever being clean, despite all the rain. Nottingham castle sits on a sandstone crag honeycombed with caves, including the Trip to Jerusalem Inn, where brawny alewives serve home brew to the sheriff's bowmen and shifty-looking friars. They used to call the place Snottingham! Swear to God. Named for some Saxon bigwig called Snot—literally "home of the Snots." Normans made them drop the *S*, a French refinement, like using forks or tongue-kissing.

Prayed today in the Church of Saint Mary, the mother church of Nottingham, where Robin Hood was once taken, after killing a dozen of the sheriff's finest. Here in forest country, the cult of Mary has an outlaw tinge, like Diana of the greenwood—dangerous, untamed, and deadly to men. And just beyond the city gate lies the greenwood itself, twenty-odd miles of forest stretching halfway to Pontefract. . . .

Just beyond Nottingham's north gate the forest began, a great green barrier bringing the open rolling Midlands to an abrupt end. Robyn rode beneath huge gnarled oaks hundreds of years old, the last survivors of vast forests that covered the Midlands when the Romans first arrived. Between the bare oaks, she saw birch and beeches, dark evergreens and thick bracken stretching for miles in every direction, the shadowy haunt of poachers, footpads, wolves, and outlaw forest folk. Or so everyone said. Sherwood lived under Forest Law, which made many normal activities a crime. Medievals had already accepted the triumph of law over reality, and the "king's forests" was a legal concept, not a botanical one, applying to some lands long cleared of trees, but not to woods falling outside the forest boundaries. Irksome and silly in some cases, the Forest Law was designed to preserve game for the king's hunting, but like any good law, it was also milked to produce royal revenue. Beasts of the forest, the fallow and red deer, the wild boar and roe, were protected, as were the trees that sheltered them, making it illegal to cut so much as a green branch, or be seen with an unslung bow. Clearing and planting virgin land was prohibited. Dogs had to be "lawed" by having three claws cut from their forepaws.

Like a lot of King Henry's laws, these were enforced more in theory than in fact—whole villages grew inside the protected forests, complete with homes and fields and churches. And the folks in these forest hamlets liked the royal game laws about as much as Montanans liked the federal Bureau of Land Management, figuring conservation was a plot by London lawyers to make their lives miserable. Hated and evaded as it was, the Forest Law did preserve the royal deer, which Robyn saw in astonishing numbers. Herds of them grazed by the road, looking confidently back at her, curiously alert, but relaxed and unafraid—while outside of the protective forest, folks had been living on salted meat since Michaelmas, when they had meat at all. Hearing a view halloo from his men, Somerset laughed when the deer did not even look up. "They know they have naught to fear."

Being big, beautiful, and meaty did not make deer particularly dumb, and in Robyn's estimation, they knew all about game laws, fearing one lone poacher stalking through the woods more than Somerset's parade of armed hooligans. "I saw the same thing in Montana growing up."

"Mount Anna?" Duke Somerset asked, never having heard of the place.

"Montana, a land across the sea," she explained airily. "Beyond Greenland, and north of Brazil—I visited it as a girl." She stoutly maintained the fiction of being born in Staffordshire, but most folks guessed she had been raised somewhere strange.

"You had a most adventurous girlhood," Somerset observed.

"In some ways." Though not near so adventurous as now. "In Montana there are antelope called pronghorns, like deer only faster. Pronghorns knew to the day when hunting season started, and when it came, the males disappeared. All you saw during pronghorn season were females, which could not legally be taken—but as soon as the season ended, the bucks came back." Medieval deer could just as easily figure out the Forest Law.

Somerset smiled to have found a woman who could talk hunting with him, saying, "These pronghorn must be marvelous creatures."

Marvelously frustrating. Who would have thought growing up in the boonies made her better able to talk to a duke? "Wait until you see the jackelopes."

"Jackelopes?" Again, Somerset looked puzzled.

"Big pronghorned rabbits, Your Grace." Too bad she had not brought a postcard.

"Outstanding!" Somerset was entranced by the notion. "Montana must be a hunter's delight, when even the rabbits put up a fight."

"Sportsman's paradise," she agreed. Absurd monsters always fired the medieval imagination—even attack bunnies.

Sighing, Somerset went back to eyeing the king's deer. "They well know this forest is theirs, given to them by God and good King Henry."

"And only His Majesty may hunt them." She told how she had gone hunting with Henry at Greenwich, admitting she took care not to be in at the kill. Blood sports were never her favorite, but she had eaten Bambi off the royal plate.

"Was His Majesty well?" Somerset asked warily, meaning, was Henry in his right mind? It was treason to actually say it.

"Most well." Henry had been happy at Greenwich, putting up meat for the winter—not having to be king. "His Majesty seemed merrier than I had ever seen him, either before or since." Afterwards came Parliament and Duke Richard's return, followed by the Act of Accord—none of which much improved the royal mood.

Woods were not all deer and royalty. Forest Law preserved the forest, as well, as did the dry coarse sandstone that made most of Sherwood too poor to farm. Even if locals did not poach the deer or cut the greenwood, they, too, profited from this immense patch of woods, which provided everything from beeswax to pig forage. Local crofters used forest moss to chink their walls, charcoal to warm their cottages, and deadwood to cook their porridge. Their meals were supplemented by small game, birds' eggs, nuts, berries, honey, medicinal herbs, fungus, fennel, and forest greens in season. None of this bounty stopped them from damning King Henry's plump deer, and the law that kept acres and acres of good woodland from falling under the ax. If Robin Hood waylaid rich travelers and then feasted them on royal venison, no one north of Nottingham much cared—not with a wet, hungry winter ahead.

She spent the night on a manor near Oxton belonging to the archbishop of York, set at the edge of the forest by the base of Robin Hood Hill. King's deer came down at dusk to feed on the fallow, which also fell under Forest Law. Though she was not sleeping on consecrated ground, the land still belonged to an archbishop, and she did not feel right doing anything to offend her host. Witches Night had to be a sedate late-night ritual, just her and Deirdre, using Christian names. She did not attempt a Witches Flight, praying instead to the Holy Virgin Mary and to Saint Anne, Mary's mother, begging for guidance. Should she head on north to Pontefract? Or should she turn back, now that there was no hope of Edward catching up with them? These were hard and dangerous times, and she wanted to do what was best, not just for herself, but for the people around her. For Edward, of course, and for her little household. And for Jo and all the Greys of Greystone. And for fierce, handsome Duke Somerset, and for even sorrier cases like Mad King Henry and Duchess Wydville. Everyone needed a break with winter almost on them.

Candle shadows played on roughcast walls, but Holy Mary sent no answer back, no sign to say which way to go from here. North or south. Back or forward. Deirdre also felt nothing, just a vague odor, "That smelled very much like summer."

Encouraging, but Robyn had hoped for something more useful. Hecate had just kicked the decision back to her, a perennial hazard of asking Heaven's advice. Well, if it was up to her, she was going back to Greystone, where she would be warm and safe. Without Edward, what use would she be in the north? Whatever Duke Somerset was doing beyond the Trent would be done with or without her. Better to be in Greystone, awaiting Edward's return to the west. Only what should she tell Somerset? Deciding to sleep on that last part, she thanked the Goddess for listening, then snuffed out the candles and curled up in her borrowed bed.

Up before dawn, she lay awake for a while listening for the bells at prime, feeling cheated. Today she had to turn about and head south, having spent Witches Night in Sherwood Forest in a dingy borrowed room. While just beyond the archbishop's pasture lay the dark fabled woods, full of magic and king's deer. No wonder nothing came to her. Looking at her watch, she saw she had about an hour left on Witches Night—why not spend it in the woods? Maybe she would find the sign she missed last night.

Wrapping a warm robe and heavy cloak over her silk nightgown, she slipped on her boots, then stepped over Deirdre, who lay asleep by the door. She considered waking the girl, but decided to let her handmaid sleep. This morning had to be hers, and hers alone. Lifting the latch, Robyn quietly let herself out, slipping down a back hall to the cold dark kitchen, and then out the kitchen gate into a garden full of bare brush and pale grass withered by the first frosts. Hedges stretched off into morning mist, which hid the forest beyond. Finding a gap in the fogbound hedge, she climbed the sloping pasture leading to Robin Hood Hill.

Pale murk enveloped her. Halfway up the slope, she heard the dead grass rustle, and she realized that something big loomed just ahead of her in the fog. Something that moved slowly through the mist toward her, looming larger as it got nearer. She hesitated, peering into blank whiteness. Being born in Montana, she was not much worried by wolves, so she said a silent prayer and then set out again, meaning to go wherever the morning took her.

Fog parted, and she saw it was a big buck, quietly cropping the grass as he came on, eyeing her placidly without a hint of fear or suspicion. Standing stock-still, she waited to see what the deer would do. Raising his head, the deer looked her over with huge liquid eyes, chewing contentedly, at peace with the morning and with her. His breath smelled of new-cut grass. Turning slowly, he ambled off uphill, vanishing into the white wall of fog.

She followed at a respectful distance, guided by the buck's soft footfalls, seeing where the deer would lead her. As the slope leveled out, banks and ditches appeared out of the mist, the slumped and shadowy outlines of an ancient ring-fort, fading into the fog at either hand. Robyn realized the deer was leading her along what must have been a sacred path, laid down ages before Edward's Norman ancestors set foot in England. But the beast could hardly know that, and was merely taking the shortest route over Robin Hood Hill.

At the far end of the ring fort, a huge round barrow loomed out of the white mist, and the deer's footfalls turned downhill. Robyn followed, leaving the ring fort behind, and as she did so, the fog began to lift, revealing a wet green hillside leading down to the Dover Beck. Through layers of shredding mist she saw trees ahead, the first fingers of Sherwood Forest stretching along the stream banks, where the rain-swollen Dover Beck wound its way to the Trent. She saw deer as well, a small herd of does and fawns stepping carefully through the predawn gloom, drifting down to the water to drink, their shadowy forms sliding into and out of each other.

With them was someone walking upright, a graceful bare-legged girl wearing a tanned deerskin and carrying a longbow. She was striding nonchalantly among the king's deer, followed by a big black wolf. Hanging from a leather strap slung over the girl's shoulder was a curved hunting horn, and the girl had a fistful of arrows in her bow hand. Robyn froze, barely believing what she was seeing, especially since the royal deer paid absolutely no attention to the huge wolf walking in their midst. Just carrying a strung bow was a crime according to Forest Law, but this wild child did not seem in the least concerned.

Watching in silent awe as a dawn breeze blew away the last bits of fog, Robyn saw there were rabbits hopping along at the girl's feet, only steps ahead of the wolf. Birds came fluttering down, alighting on the girl's shoulders, equally oblivious of the big black carnivore. Trailing behind the girl was a wild tusked boar, bigger than the wolf but meek as a mouse. Such unnatural behavior was astonishing—as amazing in its way as men laying down their swords for the Christmas season—and it renewed her hope in the impossible.

Something soft touched her hand, and Robyn looked down to see a tiny roe deer licking her fingers. Staring soulfully up at her, the little roe licked one digit then the next, delighted by her salty sweat. With each wet lick, the deer drew her deeper into the circle of magic, inviting her back to an innocent primal world, a forgotten Eden before people brought fear and shame into the world, remaking it in their own image.

This was the sign she had hoped for, though Heaven alone knew what it meant. Stepping cautiously forward, she refused to think about it, giving herself up to the moment, forgetting her awe and fear, joining with the animals. Light showed between the trees, shimmering off the winding stream, spreading slowly over the grass tops. Kneeling by the stream, the girl cupped her hands, dipped them into the shining water, raised them to her lips, and drank. Beside her, the wolf thrust his black snout into the stream, lapping up the water, while deer drank daintily on either hand.

As the sun broke out above the treetops of Sherwood, Robyn saw the girl finish drinking and look up at her. First shafts of daylight fell upon the girl's face, bringing Witches Night to a close—it was Mary of Cock Lane. Mary smiled at her, saying, "Lady Robyn, how wonderful to see you here."

And you, too. But before Robyn could manage a reply, Mary stood up, waved good-bye, and then turned and ran back into the woods, with the black wolf loping at her side, followed by the lumbering boar. Rabbits bounded off in all directions. Amazed and confused, Robyn ran after Mary, though she had no hope of catching up. Still, she kept going, unwilling to let Mary just vanish again. As the sun rose higher, driving back the shadows, Robyn saw that patches of flowers were springing up wherever Mary stepped. Soon all she saw of Mary and the wolf were the miraculous flowered footprints leading northward, away from south and safety, deeper into the woods and winter.

Saturday, 29 November 1460, Saint Andrew's Eve, Oxton, Nottinghamshire

Holy Mary, mornings like this are when the Middle Ages get really out of hand. Just when I have things here and now half figured out—wham!—I am hit with some new astounding impossibility. Serves me right for thinking things could ever be simple. This has to be the same Mary who vanished from the sanctuary of Saint Martin-le-Grand. She certainly had the same face, and she knew my name; which can hardly be coincidence, since twin phantoms would be twice as hard to explain. Far safer to say that Mary from sanctuary is here in Sherwood Forest running with a big black wolf, leaving flowery footprints.

Whatever this is about, I doubt that Duchess Wydville is behind it. This morning's stroll had none of the out-of-body feel of my Halloween dream. This was in-body, in your face, true-at-first-light real, as believable as that mad Saint Anne's Day ride down Cheapside. Were I a true medieval, I would just file it under *miracle* and get on with my life. But that nagging rational part of my mind, the part that remembers a millennium run by cause and effect, makes me wonder, What does this mean?

For one, it means I am headed north. I asked for a sign, and this has to be it—unless I hold out for blazing letters in the sky, flashing GO NORTH, YOUNG LADY.

Even as I type, fresh yellow blossoms are lying on my lap, smelling as sweet as spring. May the Goddess guide me, but that goes without saying. Today is Saint Andrew's Eve, when young women and old maids pray for prospective husbands, one problem I do not have. Thank Mary . . .

However, the sign had only come to her, and she was not yet lady enough to automatically include others when she was headed into unknown dangers. When Deirdre got up, Robyn told her handmaid the whole tale, and got a strong rebuke, "M'lady must not leave me behind like that. . . ."

"I wanted to be alone," she protested, knowing pleas for privacy would get small sympathy.

"Whatever for?" Deirdre demanded. "Anything could have happened."

And did. She shook her head, saying, "I had questions that I needed answered. Personal questions."

Deirdre rolled her eyes. "How will I ever learn to be a witch if you keep leaving me behind?"

How, indeed? She still had pangs of guilt about turning this Irish foundling into a treasonous witch, but clearly Deirdre was going north with her. Whatever dangers lay ahead, her handmaid meant to be there, to see Lady Pontefract got through them. There was still the hope that Matt Davye might show some sense of self-preservation and realize that marching north to Pontefract with men he had betrayed at Greenwich might not be the safest—but all he did was smile and bow, saying, "Worry not, m'lady, I will gladly see to the horses."

"But you need not go at all," she explained. "You may await me at Greystone, just leave us Lily, Ainlee, and a couple of the sumpter horses." If they fell into enemy hands, she and Deirdre could demand decent treatment, and the Church at least would back them—but Matt could expect to be killed out of hand.

Matt merely bowed again, saying blandly, "Where m'lady goes, I go." He was not about to lose sight of his pretty meal ticket, but it sobered Lady Robyn to think that Matt could easily be killed for *her* politics. She used to scold Sir Collin for fence-sitting between King Henry and Edward, refusing to commit to the side of right and justice. Now she saw how much harder it was to be principled when you were risking other lives as well.

Heading north beneath the gaunt gray limbs of Sherwood, Duke Somerset rode part of the way beside her, exuding that easy confidence of a young warrior going into battle. Happy and excited, he was thrilled to ride and flirt with her. The same Act of Accord that ruined Robyn's life made Somerset's much easier. So long as the new government stayed within the law, it had been hard to stir up rebellion, but by disinheriting the Prince of Wales, Parliament turned Somerset's private vendetta into a viable cause, putting the good duke in high spirits. Robyn hoped to see Somerset sorely disappointed, but she wanted it done bloodlessly and to somehow see him spared—not an easy order to fill. No matter what happened, she meant to be a peacemaker and to stop the war from spreading, though that did not mean her role would be respected. Somerset liked her, and he plainly hoped to get closer, yet unless he got what he wanted, that would go only so far. Somerset was a handsome young duke, unused to taking no for an answer, and any warmth between them could backfire badly on that inevitable day when Somerset found out she was marrying Edward of March, son of his biggest enemy.

"Honor, family, and inclination would all bind me to good King Henry's cause," Somerset explained, "even if they had not murdered my father, and stripped us of offices. Everything that men hold dear makes me York's enemy."

And Edward's, as well. Just when she thought there was no hope of hearing a friendly word from him, Somerset smiled at her, saying, "And yet I walked arm in arm with Earl Salisbury on Lady Day in London—though Salisbury's son killed my father."

Robyn had heard about this "Love Day" in London, when the direst enemies walked arm in arm to Saint Paul's—Somerset with Salisbury, Duke Holland with Warwick, and York with the queen—while hundreds of liveried retainers stood armed and ready, watched over by mounted Londoners in armor. The surreal day was topped off by a mass of reconciliation and thanksgiving, and a tournament for peace and Our Lady held at the Tower. Collin had ridden in that Lady Day peace tournament, winning a suit of armor and a ruby ring, but it was all for naught.

North of Nottingham was another country, full of deep dark trees and thick northern accents. Robyn rode for mile upon mile through a cold weeping drizzle, beneath gaunt oaks and wet evergreens, emerging at the northern end of Sherwood to find snow on the ground—not a lot, just dirty-white patches in the shade and ditches, but a sure sign of what lay ahead. Passing a peaceful Sunday night at a Worksop priory, she rode north again the next day, crossing over into Yorkshire, Lady Pontefract's home away from home.

So far people had not rallied to Somerset's banner the way they flocked to Edward's during last summer's march on London—be-

tween landing at Sandwich and entering London a week later, Robyn
had seen thousands, maybe tens of thousands, join Edward and Warwick's line of march. Far too many recruits for her to count. Somerset's force had hardly grown at all, merely picking up some local
knights like Sir Grey of Groby, who was married to a Wydville—
most of Somerset's men came from his Corfe garrison, and Devon's
west country retainers, whose accents sounded more out of place the
farther north they went. She found herself translating between De-
vonshire knights and the locals as word spread that Lady Pontefract
spoke good Yorkshire. Even if folks did not flock to join Somerset,
they did not try to stop him either—and for Duke Somerset that was
enough, since he was more than willing to do the fighting himself.
So badly wounded at Saint Albans he had to be taken home in a
cart, Somerset recovered to carry the war to Calais, and was now
marching the length of England to be in the fight.

Near Tickhill, they came on one of Lord Audley's manors, and
Somerset abruptly ordered the men rounded up and the manor hall
burned. Mounted bowmen set to work combing through the village
for men, while the more thrifty-minded knights looted Lord Audley's
doomed hall. Women wearing white wimples and colorful low-
waisted dresses came running out, pleading in Yorkshire accents to
spare the barns and granary. Seeing Robyn sitting on horseback
wearing red and gold—Audley colors—instead of royal red, white,
and blue, the women went down on their knees before Lily, begging,
"My lady, have mercy. Ask them to spare the grain and kine, for
children hereabouts already go hungry."

Trying to calm them, she promised to intercede with Somerset.
None of these women had heard of Lady Pontefract, but the Yorkshire accent cinched it, along with the Audley colors, convincing
them they had found someone to take their case to Duke Somerset.
Lady Robyn wished she shared their confidence. Somerset had been
humane and gentle toward her, a cheerful traveling companion—but
this was war. Nonetheless, she made their case, saying, "There is
already snow on the ground, and winter will be hard enough on these
women as it is."

Somerset looked sternly at her, asking, "You know what Lord
Audley has done?"

She nodded, saying she knew Lord Audley, "I met him in Calais, finding him both polite and thoughtful." Like Sir Collin, young Audley's crime was changing sides, going over to the rebels along with most of England.

"Too thoughtful, perhaps," Somerset suggested. "He was supposed to go to Calais to support me, not to join Warwick and York. His betrayal will cost Audley this fine manor hall."

Robyn watched as Somerset's men stripped the hall of its silver plate and tapestries, setting fire to the furniture and hand-carved ceiling. Lord Audley's story was an example of the comical incompetence plaguing King Henry's partisans. Audley had been dispatched to aid Somerset's attack on Calais, but sailors in the royal fleet were notoriously Yorkist, never trusting landlubberly lords who thought seamen should risk their lives for short pay and love of King Henry. So when a storm blew up, Audley's crew put into Calais and turned his lordship over to the rebels, adding him to the growing list of high-born captives. With time on his hands, Lord Audley began to wonder if he was on the wrong side, risking his noble neck for overlords that could not sail from one port to the next. Edward's easy honesty and sensible answers eventually won Audley over, along with thousands of others from Ireland to London. And for that bit of uncommon sense, Duke Somerset meant to make Lord Audley pay. Or at least his tenants. She reminded Somerset, "Your Grace, Lord Audley lost a father too."

"So he did," Somerset admitted. Lord Audley's father had fallen at Blore Heath, fighting for King Henry—where Collin was grievously wounded, as well. Both suffered like Somerset, yet both were able to make peace. Only pride and family ties kept Duke Somerset from doing the same. Exasperated, Somerset refused to be swayed, saying, "My lady has a way with words. Explain to these people that I want able-bodied men, five from each village, to come with me to Kingston-on-Hull and fight for King Henry and Queen Margaret."

Friendly as he had been to her, Somerset had small patience with underlings—be they these women, his forced recruits, Lord Audley, or the crew who delivered Audley to the foe—all were supposed to serve Somerset faithfully and without question, or suffer dire consequences. Any notion of "winning" their support was totally alien— in fact, something of an insult. What royal duke needed to justify his actions to sailors and serving women? Edward gladly did, but that was what made Edward an exception. Robyn told the women what His Grace wanted, evoking more cries of woe. Women complained that freezing rains had destroyed grain in the fields, fruit in the trees, and vegetables in their gardens—now they could not lose their men, as well. She begged Somerset to reconsider. "Your merciful Grace, these women are mightily sick of war. Feeding their families will be hard enough this winter, even without more fighting."

"Then we must win before winter," Somerset declared cheerfully. "Come, my lady Robyn, tell me what your peacemaking won you in London?"

She had to admit she had left London one step ahead of the law, accused of attempted murder and treason.

"There, you see," Somerset declared smugly. "I have at least given you a fair hearing, instead of holding your womanly timidity against you. Indeed, I find it most fetching." Proud of his broad-mindedness, Somerset repeated his demands to the manor bailiff and a crowd of frightened copyholders. "Five men from each village in the manor, wearing mail and armed with bows or bills, a week from now at Kingston-on-Hull, or I will be back to burn all the homes and barns."

Having done his level best to spread the war to Tickhill, Somerset ordered his troops to head northward, driving Lord Audley's stolen cattle before them, sticking to the wooded uplands, avoiding the heavy clay floodplain of the Don, where rains had turned the roads to muddy creeks lining flooded fields. Those distraught women of Tickhill were right: Yorkshire was worse off than the south, even less ready to face a winter war—though you could not have told it from Somerset's smiling confidence. Revenging himself on Audley had raised His Grace's spirits, letting him strike back at those who had betrayed him.

Much as she tried to sympathize, Robyn found a dreary consistency in Lancastrian complaints, which were always about what they had lost, their families, their honor, their prerogatives, their revenues, even "their" king. Despite being from the wealthiest families in the land, they felt irreparably harmed, robbed of the right to be even richer and more powerful. It never occured to Somerset that the average English person had anything to gain by his victory—aside from the satisfaction of being ruled by all the right folks.

Striking the Roman road where it crossed a low valley, Somerset reined in beside a swollen creek that led down to the Skell, saying, "Lady Pontefract, here is your honour. That is Barnsdale, and beyond that lies Pontefract."

Barnsdale was one of the manors listed in King Henry's grant to her, so was Skelbrooke, the little washed-out hamlet just up from the bridge. She was shocked at how poor and bedraggled the place looked, with bare fields, blighted orchards, and roads turned to mud. Skelbrooke had been no big place to begin with, and the flood had carried away two homes, the town mill, and several garden plots, so the locals said. On the far side of the bridge they drew water from Robin Hood's well—this, too, was Robin Hood country, or so went the verse: "My name is Robin Hood of Barnsdale, / A fellow thou hast long sought. . . ."

But even the quaint connection did not tempt her to drink—not with a thermos of herb tea in her saddlebag—though locals swore the well had great healing value.

At Wentbridge, where Watling Street crossed the deep cut River Went, they stopped to rest the horses and have peasants serve them tepid beer flavored with berries. She sat for half an hour where the wet road wound down to the Went, sipping her beer, surveying the Honour of Pontefract. Downstream lay Sayles, Norton, Stubbs, and Fenwick, while Ferrybridge and Pontefract were just up the road on the far side of the Went—all of it royal lands, with the rents and revenues going to her. Weird. Until now it had just been money in the bank, borrowed from the Italians. Now it was so awfully real, full of cold sodden farms and impoverished people. Feeling guilty, she tipped the woman who brought her the beer, giving her a fat Venetian silver *grosso*.

Going down before her, the big blond-braided woman thanked, "My Lady Pontefract."

Taken aback, Robyn asked, "Do you know me?" She was sure she had never seen the woman before, who looked to be forty-something and spoke pure Yorkshire.

"Yes, my Lady Pontefract." Looking pleased, the fair-skinned woman bobbed her blond head happily. "Word came up from Skelbrooke that you were traveling with the good duke. People tell how you stood up for the tenants at Tickhill when the manor was burned." Tickhill was twenty miles away, but news of a thousand armed vandals looting and burning, and led by a duke had to travel fast. "May God bless my lady, and see her safe. We have much need of mercy in these hard times."

Medievals continued to amaze her. She was reminded of the ale-wife in a red dress who had given her some beer on her first day in the Middle Ages, coming to her defense and defying FitzHolland. Totally unexpected. Here she had paid for her beer with some of this woman's rent money, and the woman went down on her knees, blessing and thanking her. Other tenant women, observing from a safe distance, gave her bobbing good-byes as Matt helped her mount up.

Nor did it stop there. Bailiffs and reeves met them at the bridge, not just from Wentbridge, but from Barnsdale, Sayles, and Norton, as well, bowing and scraping to Duke Somerset and the earl of Devon. And to her, too. Duke Somerset gave them a short speech, reminding them of their duty to King Henry, who was not just their God-given ruler, but their landlord. Then he told them to give utmost respect to Lady Robyn Stafford of Pontefract, an especial friend of His Majesty, who had bravely served the king in this time of peril.

Somerset was laying it on for her benefit, and his men must be laughing up their mailed sleeves, but the tenants on the bridge all took it as gospel. Or at least appeared to—no one wanting to deny a royal duke backed by men-at-arms, mounted archers, and the whim of Mad King Henry. Though hardly no one had heard of her before today, they happily welcomed Lady Robyn to Pontefract.

When she had thanked them in their own tongue, they crowded forward, asking, "Will we have to send men to Kingston-on-Hull, my lady?" Clearly looking to her to say no.

She looked to Somerset, asking, "Will they, Your Grace?"

"Only if Her Highness Queen Margaret commands. This is a royal manor," Somerset reminded her. All this heady talk made Lady Robyn forget that she did not own the place; since Wentbridge still belonged to the daft king, and hereabouts Queen Margaret spoke for him.

"My Lady," they begged, "pray implore Her Highness to spare us?"

"When next I see her," Robyn swore, a safe promise—since the last time she saw Queen Margaret was months ago, and only at a distance.

Duke Somerset deftly took charge again, saying they were on their way to York, "Where Lady Pontefract will be presented to Her Highness."

They were? She was? This was a surprise. Having brought her all the way from Temple Guiting, Gloucestershire, Duke Somerset was not going to let go of her at Pontefract. She had played her act too well, and Somerset was not just fooled but hooked, planning to have her company all the way to York, whether she willed it or not. His Grace's command was literally the law, as those poor tenants at Tickhill found out, so all she could do was smile her thanks to the duke, as if she were angling for an audience with Queen Margaret all along. Worrisome as this might be for her, it was welcome news to the men on the bridge, who gave a lusty cheer for Lady Pontefract, King Henry's friend, who stood between them and military service.

Robyn acknowledged their thanks, barely believing her reception. Seeing how poor they were, she had expected suspicion and resentment, or at best indifference. Why should they care what Mad King Henry had done with their fines and rents? How could impoverished people not hate some frivolous overdressed idiot living off their hardearned pennies? But folks in Wentbridge were happy to have a flesh-and-blood Lady Pontefract in their corner, a friend of the king, who went pleasure riding with heavily armed dukes and took their complaints straight to the queen. Nor did it hurt that she was pretty, and a handsome tipper.

Across the Went, Robyn climbed the limestone escarpment, passing Darrington and reaching Pontefract at dusk, seeing the hilltop castle's eight tall towers framed against the sunset, huge stone rectangles and a massive rounded keep, totally dwarfing the rained-out hovels in the town below. Trumpets sounded as the bailey gate swung wide, and she passed two twin-towered gatehouses, noting that Pontefract's outer wards swarmed with Percy riders and bowmen in the queen's livery, more troops than it took to defend a castle no one threatened. Having Matt see to the horses, she followed Duke Somerset into the great hall, with its tapestries and gold embossed tables, feeling the same sense of wild unreality as when she first entered Kenilworth, trading rain, cold, and privation for warm sheets and frog-leg buffets.

Weirdest of all, she was the only one who seemed to notice this amazing transition. Duke Somerset casually presented her to the surprised castellan, who had never heard of Lady Pontefract, but hastened to put her up in a suite he had been readying for Queen Margaret, with warm rich hangings, silver-studded furniture, soft carpets, glazed windows, and a hugely soft canopy bed. In this weird looking-glass world, nothing was too good for "special" friends of Duke Somerset.

Still hoping to be left behind, Lady Robyn declared herself totally unworthy of attending the queen—trying to sound too insignificant to trifle with. "Though should Her Majesty have time for me, I would be delighted to pay homage to Her Highness."

Somerset insisted. He was going to see the queen, so she would, too, with no more say about it than the men ordered to gather at Kingston-on-Hull. "Her Highness will certainly have time to see my lady; for you are the last person I know who has talked to King Henry."

He was right, of course. She had not thought about it that way, but neither Queen Margaret nor any of her trusted confidants had talked to Henry since Northampton, or been able to see him. They must be desperate for news of his condition. Fighting a war for a king who was in enemy hands had to be hard, especially when you doubted His Majesty's sanity to start with. For all they knew, Henry could be catatonic again—in a way, it was a wonder he was not. Of course the queen would want to see her, even talk to her in private; so Lady Robyn must make the best of it.

Riding north, she returned to the real world of rain and woe, where manors were looted and men impressed. Nothing had been burned so far in her Honour of Pontefract, whose people were protected by being royal tenants, but Robyn saw tall thin pillars of smoke rising off to the west, toward Wakefield—known for its miracle plays. South of Wakefield was Sandal Castle, the duke of York's chief keep in the West Riding.

Farther north, she faced the first freezing blast of winter. Snow came down, big fat beautiful flakes, reminding her that winter should be a time of fun and holiday, made for skiing and snowball fights, a Fools' Season, where your worst worry was the mob scene at the malls. Snow was piling up by the time she got to York itself, turning the walled city into a white-capped faerie castle, rising from snow-clad heights where the Foss flowed into the Ouse, surrounded by the low, white Vale of York.

Crossing the Ouse, Robyn entered through Micklegate Bar, so

called because the city gates barred people, as well as letting them in. Ouse Bridge, the only river crossing between York and the sea, was not as grand as London Bridge, but it had a chapel and a council chamber built into it. Within the walls was a city of churches, stone wharves, and timber inns on crooked narrow streets with quaint names like Swinegate, Pavement, and the Shambles. All dominated by massive York Minster, the huge half-complete Gothic cathedral, towering above the city walls. Called Eburacum by the Romans, and Jorvik by the Danes, York was the capital of the north, where Constantine the Great was named emperor of Rome, and where King Harold the Saxon heard that the Normans had landed. And now it was Margaret of Anjou's new capital, having already lost London, Coventry, and everything in between.

Robyn found lodging in a Benedictine nunnery, where she would be tolerably safe from whatever designs Duke Somerset might have. As usual, the nuns were glad to have her, flocking about, offering to carry her things, wanting to hear about goings-on in the world of men—far happier to have her with them, than she was to be there. Lovely as York might be, lying under the fresh blanket of snow, she had not meant to come nearly this far north. And all the while this faerie city was filling up with armed men wearing Queen Margaret's daisy flower, the Percy crescent, and the looping Drace knot. Even more troops were gathering downriver at Kingston-on-Hull, including Scots mercenaries, which made even Margaret's supporters nervous. No one in London knew that Queen Margaret had such an army in the making.

On her second morning in the city, Robyn went riding beyond the walls to breathe clean air and get some escape from nuns and the narrow crowded streets, returning through the Monksgate Bar, a heavily fortified gateway with a big ironbound portcullis. At the nunnery gate a man stepped up, wearing a Percy crescent on his russet-and-yellow doublet. Doffing his feathered bonnet, he did a big sweeping bow, saying in broad Northumberland, "Lady Stafford, how good to see you again."

Reining in, Robyn was not nearly so pleased. Standing before her was Black Dick Nixon, whom she had last seen riding out Aldersgate headed for the Great North Road. Now here he was in York, wearing Percy colors and a broad border-bandit grin, surprised and happy to see her. All she could think to say was, "Master Nixon, it is good to see you looking so well."

"Has young Lord Edward tired of you already?" he asked hopefully.

Exactly what she most feared to hear. Nixon knew all about her relationship with Edward. Never actually seeing them together, being in sanctuary the whole time, Nixon had to rely on stories told by monks and miscreants, and such tales only grew in the telling. She tried to retreat behind propriety, asking, "What makes you say such things?"

He nodded to her left hand, still grinning. "You no longer wear his silver ring."

Trust a Nixon to note that. The man must mentally appraise all her jewelry; but at least he did not deign to hide it, and appreciated more than her body. Seeing no way out but the truth, she confessed, "I had to leave London."

His grin widened, as he had recently fled London himself. "Whatever for, m'lady?"

None of Nixon's business, but if she did not tell him, he would make it his business to find out, and Heaven knows what would become of that? "I was charged with treason."

"Treason?" His grin showed that he did not think much of the charge; half the healthy young men in York had come here to commit treason, or worse.

"And attempted murder," she added, so he might not think the less of her.

That piqued the cutthroat's professional interest. "Whom did m'lady try to kill?"

"No one," she replied tartly. "I am utterly and completely innocent."

"As are we all," Black Dick Nixon agreed piously, wagging his head at the sins of the world. "Who was my Lady Stafford of Pontefract so falsely, basely, and slanderously accused of designing to harm?"

"His Grace, the noble duke of York," she admitted wearily, knowing what Nixon's reaction would be.

Black Dick Nixon's bearded face broke back into another gaptoothed grin of delight, and he doffed his bonnet again. "Well done, m'lady, well done. Yer bold imagination makes my grandest ploys seem but rude and feeble. Here am I, happy to have the Percy moon back on my chest, while m'lady is angling to make herself duchess of York."

"I told you, I am totally innocent." Indignant ladylike protests made her story all the more convincing.

"Of course m'lady is innocent." He bowed once more, then clapped his bonnet back on his head; the one nice thing about Black Dick Nixon was that he cared far more for her than for any crimes she may have committed. "And when Ye Ladyship tires of playing the game of kings, remember there is safe haven awaiting you in Tynedale. It may not be the duchy of York, but I know a farmstead there that is snug an' warm in winter, an' passing beautiful in spring."

If they made it until spring; winter was getting harder by the moment. Seeing Black Dick Nixon again was a shock, reminding her what a small place medieval England could be. Who else might pop up out of her checkered past? Gilbert FitzHolland? Sir John Fogge? Le Boeuf? God, she hoped not. She thanked the brigand, saying, "I do remember." Then she slipped Lily through the nunnery gate, retreating into the world of poverty, chastity, and obedience.

But not for long. After vespers she had another unwelcome visitor out of the past—this time a woman, a proud, pale, silver blonde, with sleepy bedroom eyes and a sly witchy grin. Elizabeth Grey was the wife of Sir John Grey of Groby who came north with Somerset, eldest daughter of the witch-duchess Wydville, as well as a lady-in-waiting to Queen Margaret. Tonight Lady Grey came in both capacities, coolly bearing a royal summons for Lady Stafford.

Deirdre helped her into a flowing green gown trimmed with gold lace, but did not go along, since Welsh-Irish maids were not presented to the queen, not unless they had done something truly amazing—like composing Latin poetry or talking with the Virgin. So Robyn set off with just Elizabeth Grey for company, one of the few times they had ever been alone. She had first met Lady Grey while out of body, on the same Witches Night that she and Beth Lambert were inducted into Duchess Wydville's coven; in fact, Elizabeth Grey had led her to the altar and danced naked around the bonfire afterward. Tonight Lady Grey acted more demure, leading her through quiet musty convent halls toward the prioress's apartments, wearing

Wydville red and silver embroidered with black-and-white magpies.

Following in Lady Grey's silken wake, Robyn felt the odd tension that always existed between them. She did not fear Elizabeth Grey the way she feared Duchess Wydville, and unlike her younger sisters, Lady Elizabeth was married, and seemingly indifferent to Edward's charms. On top of that, this cool, beautiful duchess's daughter had welcomed her into the world of spellcraft, for which she had much reason to be thankful—still, there was a strangeness between them, as though they shared a deep secret neither dared broach.

Lady Grey led her to the prioress's presence chamber, but when a nun opened the door, the prioress was nowhere to be seen. Nor was the queen. Waiting inside was Duchess Wydville herself, pagan high-priestess, and dowager duchess of Bedford, an older, sterner version of her daughter, dressed in a flaming scarlet gown trimmed in silver and topped with an elegant white lace headdress. Beneath that lace were the same sharp pale-white features Robyn had last seen laughing at her from atop the wax figure of Duke Richard, when Duchess Wydville had sprung her Halloween trap.

Doing an immediate deep curtsy, Robyn hid her chagrin behind medieval formality, bowing her head until the duchess gave her leave to look up. She had hoped not to see Duchess Wydville; in fact, she had hoped the duchess was back home at Grafton, brushing up on her voodoo—but here the witch was, attending to Queen Margaret. Damn. An interview with the queen was tricky enough without a hostile witch looking over her shoulder.

"Rise, Lady Stafford," Duchess Wydville commanded in her continental accent. "You are more lovely than ever, for the cold has put color in your cheeks."

"Her Grace is too kind." Her Grace was a horrible hag who twice betrayed her to witch hunters—but she struggled not to blurt that out. "As Her Grace will recall, I spent some days of summer indoors."

"*Ach,* that stay in the Tower?" Duchess Wydville dismissed dark days of terror and despair as if they were a weekend at a national monument. "Do you still blame me for that?"

"*Absolument.*" It sounded so much more polite in French, and she would not give Duchess Wydville the satisfaction of an insult—they both knew who was in the wrong.

"My Lady Stafford just did not believe enough." The spell that would have kept Robyn safe required her to have absolute faith in her high-priestess, practically impossible under the circumstances. "But you are still a novice, *nein*?"

"Horribly inept," she agreed, well aware of her limitations; trying to claim equality with Duchess Wydville was ludicrous. "Look what happened to me on Halloween."

"Halloween?" Duchess Wydville cocked her head, looking like she never heard of the holiday. Then a look of comprehension dawned on her, and she laughed. "Silly fool, you should thank me for that."

"Thank you?" She could not think what for, having been made a fugitive, charged with treason.

"For showing you where your true interests lie," Duchess Wydville sighed, as if it were obvious. "You do not want young Edward to be king, no more than I do. Therefore, Duke York will always be your enemy—I only made it manifest. Magic rests on truth, or it would not work. Try as you like to disguise it, you hate Edward's father for what he has done to you, and to your cause. Is that not so? Better to say it boldly and strike right at him than to snivel about trying to live a lie."

True, from some points of view. But there was more to her than hating Duke Richard. She actually believed in peace and justice, and hesitated to use murder and mayhem for personal gain—most days of the week, at least. And any foreign witch-priestess who "charmed" her way to the top, becoming duchess of Bedford and confidante to a witch-hating king and queen, could hardly lecture her on leading a double life.

None of which worried the duchess, who concluded cheerfully, "Now that you are one of us, it is time you reaped the rewards. Tonight you will have a private audience with Queen Margaret, a singular honor for a *lady* of your slight standing, *nein*?" Duchess Wydville arched a blond eyebrow to remind Robyn of her dubious claim to ladyship, something Her Grace could sympathize with— neither of them even being English. "Be obedient and obsequious to Her Majesty," Duchess Wydville commanded. "Give brief respectful answers, saying absolutely *nothing* to upset Her Majesty." Her Grace laid special emphasis on that last part. "Say nothing that would cause strife between Her Highness and those who stand loyally beside her, resolutely opposing York and Warwick's treason."

Robyn nodded obediently, knowing that meant, "Go easy on how the ladies-in-waiting include power-hungry witches with no real allegiance to queen or country." Duchess Wydville had originally married into the royal family with hopes of making herself queen—and who knew, much could still happen. Duchess Wydville had daughters aplenty, several of them blond and beautiful, and the right combination of deaths and marriages could easily make one of them queen. Unless Robyn spilled the magic beans to Queen Margaret.

Which was why Duchess Wydville ended with the word *treason*, reminding Robyn that she, too, hid dangerous secrets. Lady Robyn's hapless attempts at neutrality and pacifism had put her in the unenviable position of being a traitor to both sides. Pretty damned amazing for an amateur, or so she thought, this being her first serious stab at politics. Before coming to the Middle Ages, Lady Robyn had barely bothered to vote.

Vowing to be good, she followed Lady Grey into the next room, which turned out to be the prioress's private dining chamber, where she could entertain guests with less austerity than the Rule of Saint Benedict allowed. Tonight it had been given to Queen Margaret, who sat unattended in a comfortable chair, with a buffet of boiled quail eggs, cheese, wine, and sugar wafers set out on the side table. Bright red coals glowed in the hearth, warming the room. For the second time that night, Robyn did her deepest curtsy, bowing her head before Margaret of Anjou, queen of England.

Margaret was born to be queen, proud and regal, with majestic bearing and royal self-absorption, nodding absently for Lady Grey to leave. Duchess Wydville's daughter did a deep curtsy of her own and then backed out of the room, leaving Robyn totally alone with Her Highness—for the first time ever. Acknowledging Robyn's presence, Queen Margaret told her, "Rise, my child, and be at ease."

Margaret was not much older than she, thirty at most, but the queen was her royal mother, just as King Henry was her royal sire. Robyn rose to stand solemnly before her queen, there being not so much as a stool for her—no one had wasted a moment worrying over her comfort. Queen Margaret sat in crowned splendor, wearing the lions of England and the lilies of France on her gold-trimmed gown, backed by rich royal tapestries hung for the occasion, her slippered feet resting on royal blue carpet—yet her cushioned chair and the hand-carved buffet table were the only sticks of furniture in the room, making Robyn feel like an audience of one at a royal exhibition, which was the effect intended. Margaret asked, "Is it true you have seen His Highness, the king, in London?"

"Most true, Your Majesty." She fought the urge to do another nervous curtsy. "I last saw him in London, two months ago, but before that I was with him twice at Greenwich, and at Northampton in July." Queen Margaret had not seen her husband since Henry headed off to disastrous defeat at the hands of Edward and Warwick.

"Is His Majesty well?" Queen Margaret asked hesitantly, the same dangerous question that Somerset broached. What Her Majesty wanted to know was whether her royal husband was again off his rocker. All Margaret knew was that her husband was in enemy hands, going along with the new government and accepting York as his heir—none of which must sound good to Margaret, who already had ample reason to doubt Henry's sanity. Which was why Her Majesty wanted to hear the answer alone, at a secret night audience in a cloistered convent.

Answering an unasked question is fraught with peril, and a cheery, "Don't worry, your husband's no more nutty than usual," would not do with Queen Margaret. And whoever else was listening. Duchess Wydville would be a pretty poor witch if she could not devise a way of hearing what was said in the next room.

Robyn took a deep breath and replied carefully, "His Majesty was most well when I saw him." Which meant sane. "And striving manfully to deal with the many hardships thrust on him." Or brought on by his own idiocy, though she did not dare say it. Robyn guessed that one of the many drawbacks to being queen was never getting to hear the truth spoken, not even in cloistered secrecy. "His Majesty spoke of Your Highness and the Prince of Wales with heartfelt love and concern."

Her Majesty's voice softened, glad to know her husband still remembered her—literally, there being times when Henry had not even recognized his wife and child. "You were with His Highness at Northampton?"

"I sheltered in His Majesty's tent during the brief battle." She tried to make the fight before Northampton sound less harrowing than it had been. "And His Majesty was most brave and considerate in my defense."

Luckily Her Majesty had absolutely no interest in what Lady Robyn had been doing at Northampton, instead Queen Margaret ordered her to pour wine for both of them, asking, "And you saw His Highness again at Greenwich?"

"Twice, Your Highness—once in August and again in October. Both times he was most well, and most considerate."

"His Highness has been most condescending to you," Margaret noted as Robyn served the wine. They were discussing this woman's husband, as well as the God-given ruler of England, France, and Ireland.

"Most condescending," Robyn admitted, acknowledging that Henry was not just king, but also her personal lord and benefactor. With typical Mad King Henry generosity, His Highness had granted her royal revenues from some rain-soaked manors, so she, too, could profit off the misery of his people. Which seemed so charming at the time, but now left a terrible taste in Lady Pontefract's mouth. "And most generous," she added, not to slight his gift, "more so than I ever believed possible."

"And what have you done for His Royal Highness?" asked Queen Margaret tersely, showing some of the steel that cost men their heads, and families their homes.

What, indeed? Robyn could not just reply, "Not to worry Maggie, I am making it with Edward of March." Fortunately Henry was not the type for casual affairs, not when the stress and strain of getting his lawful wife pregnant had put him in a coma. Margaret of Anjou must know that more than anyone. Robyn could truly say, "His Highness is my king, and I would have no other. So I have tried to give him all the love and support that faith and honesty allows." Which meant she would not think of sleeping with Henry, but also that she would not hesitate to betray His Highness when Mad Henry was in the wrong and innocent lives were at risk. She told Queen Margaret, "It is Your Highness's aid and comfort that His Majesty misses most of all."

Margaret nodded, knowing her husband well. If Henry turned to another woman, it would not be for sex, but for reassurance and support. Accustomed to having his wife managing things, Henry must feel fairly helpless surrounded by brash warlords who no longer took him seriously. Her Highness took a sip of wine and smiled, asking, "Is it true you defied the duke of York in his own hall?"

"On the feast of Crispian." She nodded shyly, letting Queen Margaret assume it was done for her and for the rights of her son, the

Prince of Wales—the irony was that Robyn had done it because she herself did not want to be queen, and did not want her own prospective children to be royal. But she could hardly expect Her Highness to understand. "In London, in the banquet hall at Baynards Castle."

Queen Maggie wanted to hear all about it, and about the vote on the Act of Accord in the House of Lords—not realizing how close it had been, or what the act exactly said. Or how badly Duke Richard had hectored the House of Lords, only to get this dismal result. Rain had all but obliterated the primitive postal system, and Her Highness had no idea what was really going on in London, any more than London knew about Queen Margaret's great armed host gathering at Kingston-on-Hull. This civil war was like a Jingling Contest, the medieval game played by children and spirited young folks—where both sides were blindfolded. Robyn felt like the bell-capped Jingler—the fool and target of both sides, who alone was allowed to see.

Her Highness was alternately amused and aghast by goings-on in the south, and soon they were having a grand time blackguarding Earl Warwick, and laughing at prickly Duke Richard's pretensions, even trading King Henry stories with a smile and shake of the head. One thing she and Margaret shared was tolerant affection for the hapless monarch, and both knew what a handful he could be, especially for a young woman who was not even English to begin with. And both of them knew what it was like to be loved by London, then booted out—when Margaret first arrived, Londoners wore her daisy flower on their caps. So more wine naturally led to a bit of Brit bashing. Queen Maggie thought her subjects were rude and opinionated, "without the least talent for serfdom." Both agreed that the food was vile, and the weather even worse. Lady Robyn could sympathize with Queen Margaret, hauled off to a foreign land at fifteen, married to a madman, forced to govern a bankrupt nation peopled by her born enemies. What an impossible task—that Margaret had made a horrible botch of the entire business was almost incidental.

Pouring still more wine, Robyn discovered that Margaret had an unsuspected love of the theater, secretly going to miracle plays—ironic, since Margaret herself must be a character in three or four Shakespeare plays. When Queen Margaret found Lady Robyn had trod the boards, she wanted to know all about it—so Robyn entertained her with a string of scandalous "Holy Wood" stories, with the names and dates rubbed off. Finally, Margaret brought fond reminiscing to a close by thanking her and then asking, "Does Lady Pontefract have any requests for herself?"

"None for me, Your Majesty," she replied solemnly, knowing one of the reasons she got along so famously with the royal family was that she never wanted anything from them—when most sensible English people desperately hoped for their favor, or their overthrow. Coming from somewhere else altogether, Robyn treated the royals like real people, being as honest as prudence allowed, and they had rewarded her reticence royally. "But I would beg that His Majesty's tenants from the Honour of Pontefact not be forced into the army gathering at Kingston-on-Hull."

Margaret stiffened, offended that impoverished tenants balked at risking life and limb in the dead of winter to put her back in power—showing just how hard it was for the English to please their demanding monarchs. For a moment, it seemed like things might end badly, but Her Highness forgave the affront, saying she would see that, "none will come from the Honour of Pontefract, except those that join us willingly."

Thanking Her Highness profusely, Robyn fell to her knees, knowing she had risked royal displeasure, but glad to have done something for the hapless folks whose rents paid for her silks and satins. Rising from her seat, Queen Margaret lifted her up and gave her an equally thankful good-bye kiss, saying, "Should you see His Highness again, tell him of my love."

Swearing she would, she backed out of the queen's presence with her heart high, happy to have escaped with a promise of help for her people. Until coming north, she had thought of them merely as royal tenants, or as money to be spent, but by now they were only too real. Her people in more than name. Duchess Wydville was smiling like the Cheshire cat when Robyn emerged from her private audience, a sure sign the witch-duchess was somehow listening in, and knew how famously things had gone. "Welcome back to the fight against Duke Richard," Duchess Wydville declared. "This time I foresee we will win."

Some seeress. Robyn curtsied and said respectful good-byes, not at all meaning to join Queen Margaret's crusade against the House of York. Blind and bigoted as Duke Richard might be, he at least had goals going beyond plundering the country at his leisure; while Queen Margaret and Duchess Wydville were in politics for what they could get, having no other hope of income. Even proud, vengeful Duke Somerset was but a bastard relation, relying on the royal government to enrich him at public expense. Which was why the queen never "took her case to the people." Most folks were mortally sick of paying high prices for bad government. Only the noose and disemboweling knife would convince London to put up with Queen Maggie again. The irony that this hideous policy was driven by women was not lost on Robyn, who had discovered that Englishwomen in politics were deadly to trifle with. Margaret of Anjou reminded her of stories told about Margaret Thatcher, who ruled England with an iron fist in the bad old twentieth century; but Queen Margaret was younger and prettier. Picture Maggie Thatcher and Princess Di rolled into one, with a vengeful army of genteel bandits, border reivers, and Scots mercenaries at her back, set to loot their way south. Someone ought to warn London.

Thursday, 4 December 1460, Saint Barbara's Eve, York

Bitter cold today, but clear, and the muddy roads are frozen solid. I have to get word to Edward. He thinks Somerset has a thousand men at most, but there is a huge army gathering at Kingston-on-Hull, ten thousand at least, and more coming every day. If Edward comes north after Somerset, he will be riding into a trap. But how to warn him? Magic springs to mind, but Jo is far off in the Cotswolds, and even if I contacted her, there is no guarantee that word would get to London in time. The only coven member in London is Beth Lambert, but I cannot depend on anyone listening to her. Edward might. But who else would pay attention to a little girl who had a vision of an army gathering at Kingston-on-Hull? Not Warwick, or Duke Richard.

Somehow I must contact Edward directly, something I have never done. But even to attempt it, I must get away from here. I cannot do any serious magic in a Benedictine nunnery with Witch-Duchess Wydville looking over my shoulder—that would be begging for trouble. Tomorrow is Saint Barbara's Day, the patroness of gunners, miners, and anyone who must deal with explosives. How appropriate. I must be sure to light a candle. . . .

But candles to Saint Barbara could not get her out of York, not with Duke Somerset and Duchess Wydville determined to keep her there. Somerset warned her it would not be safe, saying, "There are armed strangers on the roads, and looting and burning, as well. Wait until a proper escort can be found." She could not argue with a royal duke, though the "armed strangers" out looting and burning were Somerset's friends and relations. He was using their lawlessness as an excuse to keep her around, leaving only one thing to do—get thee to the nunnery, girl, making it impossible to contact Edward or anyone else.

Saturday was Saint Nicholas's Day, and the king's birthday—how fitting that Henry was born on Santa Claus Day, with all he had given away. York turned out to celebrate, with riotous processions through the slushy streets, toasting Mad King Henry, and the "boy-bishop" chosen by the choristers of York Minster. Between Saint Nicholas's Night and the Feast of Fools on Holy Innocents' Day, the boy-bishop would go about, solemnly blessing and preaching in childish terms to delight the congregations. More holy days followed: first Saint Ambrose's Day, then the Conception of the Virgin, and a week later, Saint Lucy's Eve.

Lucy was the saint of light, so naturally her day came in midwinter, when light is needed most. And prayers to Saint Lucy were also prayers to the Goddess, for the martyred virgin was the Goddess in her winter aspect, when the earth maiden seems dead but is really a girl waiting to be reborn, a virgin spirit that would warm and grow, finding love in the spring and bearing fruit in the summer, then dying again in the fall. She and Deirdre lit candles to Saint Lucy, chanting, "Lucy-light, Lucy-light, shortest day, longest night . . ."

Lighting candles to Saint Lucy was like saying prayers to Persephone, the Dark Destroyer, Queen of the Dead, the death virgin dragged down to Hades, just as martyrs like Saint Lucy died rather than marry. Despite official denial, the death virgin had a tremendous hold on people's imagination, and long after the Middle Ages were history, she would still be sleeping her winter sleep under names like Snow White, Sleeping Beauty, Cinderella, and Thumbelina, all awaiting love's first kiss to bring them back to life.

As she chanted, Robyn closed her eyes, shutting out the candlelight, searching for her light within. Wary of Duchess Wydville,

Robyn did not actively seek out Edward, but just let her soul drift, knowing where it would naturally go. Blackness enveloped her, frigid winter night, colder and blacker than even a December nunnery had any right to be. This was no ordinary darkness, but the black soulless gulf separating her from her love, and Robyn dived blindly into it, not fearing what she might find, embracing Saint Lucy's night.

Breathing broke the cold blackness. Not her breathing but someone else's. Deep rhythmic breathing and the musty smell of wet canvas with a hint of mint, like the sprig Edward chewed before bed. Sinking deeper into her trance, she saw she was in a tent, pitched out in the cold and damp beneath the stars, with moonlight showing on the fabric in distinctive light and dark bars. She could not see colors, but the design was the Mortimer coat of arms, with the empty shield showing clearly amid the blue-gold bars. From beyond the tent fabric came the sounds and smells of a night camp, sentries stamping their feet in the cold, the warm crackle of a watch fire, the odor of wood smoke mixed with horse manure.

Following the sleeper's rhythmic breathing to the back of the tent, Robyn felt a low cot lying against one sagging fabric wall. Wrapped in a feather comforter was Edward; she could tell by his fresh young smell, by the sound of his breathing, and by the dreamlike certainty of the spell. Robyn had no idea where he was, except that she was in Edward's tent and alone with him—the close personal connection between the two of them could not be counterfeited the way Duchess Wydville posed as the ghost of Somerset's father.

Sitting down on the edge of the narrow cot, she felt him beside her, solid and reassuring, full of life and hope. Here lay safety, comfort, and understanding—everything she needed most—far away at the moment, but thanks to Saint Lucy, near enough to touch. Beneath the quilt and blankets he was naked. Edward always slept that way, tossing off anything to do with the day and throwing himself enthusiastically into sleep, just as he threw himself into his waking deeds.

Excited by his nearness, even at a distance, she leaned down, guided by his breathing, feeling the alternating warmth and coolness of his breath on her cheek, then on her lips. His breath tasted cool and minty. Her lips touched his, first a dry feel of contact, then warm thrilling flesh pressed against hers.

She woke up, still able to taste Edward on her lips. How utterly amazing. They had kissed in the living flesh, despite distance and the depth of winter. What a wonderful Witches Night, wandering out-of-body into Edward's dark cold tent, never questioning where she was, or feeling the least bit chilled. She had wanted to give a warning, but it was not safe with Duchess Wydville so close. Any communication beyond a kiss could easily be intercepted, possibly even twisted to suit Duchess Wydville's designs. Love could power a spell as easily as hate.

Glad for what she had been given, Robyn gave heartfelt thanks to Saint Lucy, praying to meet Edward soon, and in the flesh, for more than just a kiss. All the while she solemnly chanted along with Deirdre:

> Lucy-light, Lucy-light,
> shortest day, longest night . . .

Saint Lucy must have heard her prayers, because word came the next day that Somerset's troops were headed south to war. Suddenly the frozen road to Pontefract was open, and she rode out of York in Somerset's wake, escorted by Baron John de Clifford, who gladly welcomed her company. She found young Lord Clifford to be in excellent spirits, happily looking forward to the fighting ahead. By now she had seen up close how war made some men positively light-hearted, especially the young ones. Committing to combat meant giving up earthly cares, taking each moment as it came, and finding what joy you could, especially in female company. Give any young knight-errant a woman and he is happy and attentive, knowing she may be the last female he will ever be with. Very flattering, in a weird sort of way. War brought out the worst in men, but often the best, as well.

It surely brought out the worst in young Lord Clifford, who was fond of saying things like "Patience is for plowmen" and "Wounds cannot be cured by words"—straining an otherwise pleasant ride. Medieval war was not yet the mass murder of innocents that "modern" war would become—it was more like a deadly athletic contest between conceited young men. But this one was spilling over onto everyone, and by the time they got to Ferrybridge, the first of her manors, Lady Robyn had heard enough, asking Clifford if he was not afraid to die?

"Of course," his young lordship replied with a smile. "Who would not fear death? But fear of death does not stop me from seeking revenge for my father, for I would far rather burn in hell than leave one of York's line alive."

"You cannot mean that," she protested, appalled that the young baron beside her could be so bloody-minded.

Lord Clifford laughed at her naiveté, swearing, "If I fail, may Our Lord above let me die right here in Ferrybridge."

She fell silent, surveying what the rain had done to the once prosperous manor. Ferrybridge owed its name to a stone bridge that replaced the original ferry, making this the lowest dry crossing of the Aire, taking trade and tolls away from Castleford, four miles upstream. But this winter there were few travelers to feed and shelter, and most of them were armed, more inclined to plunder that to pay. Worse yet, the Aire had overflowed its banks, flooding pasture and garden plots, even undermining the bridge, threatening the town's existence. Women came up, offering her thin ale to wet her throat, bringing their children out to see the great lady. Several were sick, and Lady Robyn gave out antibiotics for what sounded like walking pneumonia—these pills often worked wonders, since medieval germs had no resistance against them. Good thing, because this wet hungry winter preyed on the young and infirm.

South of the Aire, freezing rain replaced the snow, and the way was slick and treacherous. Her work in the north was nearly done, and she meant to head south as soon as she could, carrying a warning for Edward and wintering in Greystone where she would be safe and welcome. But Pontefract was a solid gladdening sight, standing out against the southern sky, not likely to be washed away, with her deep foundations dug down into the hill, full of subterranean chambers and passages. Medievals built to last when it came to churches and castles—seen up close, the Tower vaults had been terrifyingly solid. Passing through the great double gates, she returned to that unreal world of wealth and plenty, a high dry island looking down on the sodden countryside. Reining in, Lady Robyn felt guilty for such undeserved privilege, but nonetheless relieved to be safe and dry for the night.

Matt Davye helped her dismount, nodding as he did so toward the bailey gate. "Beware, m'lady. Trouble comes our way."

Shocked by Matt's concerned look, she turned to see the castellan coming to greet Lord Clifford, accompanied by several men in leather and mail. At their head was the blond-bearded ex-sergeant-at-law who gave her that involuntary look at the White Tower vaults, Gilbert FitzHolland, wearing the livery of his half-brother, the mad Duke Holland.

Before she could decide what to do, FitzHolland looked her way; as his gaze met hers, she saw surprise and disbelief turn to malicious delight. Forgetting totally about Lord Clifford, FitzHolland turned and strode toward her, his hand on his sword, his smile widening, as he called a cheery greeting. "Lady Stafford, what outstanding luck. I thought I would have to go clear to London to see you got what is due you."

9

⊷⊜ The Honour of Pontefract ⊜⊶

S he could barely believe such misfortune; a moment before, Pontefract had been her safe haven, where she could make magic, reach out to Edward, and then head south. Suddenly, everything was at risk. Last time she had seen FitzHolland, he had been at Greenwich, heading hell-for-leather into Surrey. Now, without warning, here he was at the opposite end of England, hostile as ever and set to do her harm. Out the corner of her eye, she saw Matt Davye's hand drop to the dagger in his belt, getting ready for the worst. Deirdre stepped up and took Lily's reins so the horse master would be free to defend his mistress. Pulling herself together, Robyn looked levelly back at FitzHolland, saying politely, "Good day, *monsieur*. I desire no quarrel with you."

FitzHolland smirked at her. "Too bad, witch. We already have one."

Why could he not just leave her alone? She warned him, "Do not think you can molest me with impunity. This is a royal castle on a royal manor, and I am a friend of His Majesty." And Her Majesty, for that matter.

Her nemesis laughed at that. "Our Gracious King Henry is far away, thanks to you. You fouled my attempt to save him."

Wishing she had not taunted him half so rudely from the Greenwich tower, she told the former sergeant-at-law, "King Henry may not be here, but that does not make you free to do ill. Duke Somerset thinks most highly of me, as does Her Majesty, Queen Margaret, and Lord Clifford has promised me protection." Clifford and the castellan were headed her way, thank goodness.

FitzHolland scoffed, "None of them knows you like I do." Then he turned his glare on Matt, who stood calmly to one side, his dagger sheathed, but his hand resting on the knobby pommel. Matt's former master asked, "What of you, traitor? Are you mounting my lady strumpet?"

Matt's hand tightened on his dagger as he replied easily, "Only when Lady Stafford desires a mare to ride." She was glad to have big strong Matt Davye standing close at hand, remembering how he had accosted her on the street on Height Sunday, and she had wondered if he could be trusted. Now here he was, deep in enemy territory, calmly facing down his old master, when Matt had as much to fear as she did—maybe more.

Clifford strolled casually up, looking askance at the commotion, saying, "Beware bastard, Lady Stafford lies under my protection."

FitzHolland bowed to his better and said, "My most worshipful Lord Clifford, that can easily be remedied. This lewd lady is a traitress, deserving no one's protection."

Lord Clifford laughed, "Only if you count York as king. She stands accused of trying to kill Duke Richard of York, the foremost traitor in the land."

"She spoiled my attempt to free King Henry," FitzHolland protested. "Were it not for her, His Majesty might be with us even now."

"All by myself?" Robyn asked innocently. "Or did my maid perhaps lend a hand?"

FitzHolland had no ready answer; having failed to take King Henry with two score armed riders at his back, he looked silly trying to lay the blame on her. Nor did his family history of insanity help his case. Switching his tactics, he told Clifford, "My lord, she is a witch, as well."

"Bewitching, you mean"—Lord Clifford smiled at her—"that I would very much believe."

She did a quick bobbing curtsy, thanking Lord Clifford for the timely compliment, trying to stay on the baron's good side. Clifford was arrogant, willful, and easy to anger, and FitzHolland was a fool for arguing instead of trying to win his lordship over.

"And she is Edward of March's whore," FitzHolland added spitefully, seeing the charge of witchcraft would not stick.

"Truly?" Clifford looked her over, as if seeing her for the first time; then he turned back to FitzHolland, saying cheerfully, "The young knave has far better taste in women than I ever thought possible."

FitzHolland fumed. "My lord, do you not see? She has come here to spy on us for him."

Clifford cocked an eye at FitzHolland, asking, "What shall she tell Edward of March? That all of the north country is about to descend on London, beating his vain usurping father into the ground? We shall eagerly show young Edward that ourselves as soon as we can."

Barely containing his anger, FitzHolland complained, "My gracious lord, how can we allow—?"

Clifford silenced him. "Enough, gentle bastard. Cool your indignation. We did not come together to make war on pretty women. They are the proper prize of battle, not the foe."

She did not want to be a prize of war, but she kept silent, knowing better than to argue with Lord Clifford—FitzHolland proved the utter futility of that. There was no way the witch hunter would get a fair hearing from his lordship. Much as she hated the blind, stupid arrogance of the medieval lords, there were times when she owed her life or freedom, or someone else's life and freedom to that same arrogant privilege. Pontefract's castellan came and took Clifford's side, suggesting FitzHolland take his case against her to Somerset, where he would fare no better, maybe worse. Witch hunters faced the perpetual problem that their targets were women, and their quarry could count on some sympathy just by being cute and personable. No wonder the "wicked" witches were always old hags, who could be hanged or burned without evoking pity, at least from the men.

Seeing FitzHolland getting nowhere with Lord Clifford and the castellan, Robyn thanked the men for their keen interest in her physical and spiritual well-being and withdrew, taking her tiny household with her. Matt protested that he must look to the horses, but she insisted he come, too, begging the castellan to have the stable hands feed and water their mounts. FitzHolland would strike at anyone close to her, and Matt was too important to risk. Curtsying to Lord Clifford, she thanked him for his protection, both on the York road and in the Pontefract stable yard, rewarding him with a good-bye kiss that pleased the young baron immensely. FitzHolland did not even get an au revoir, since she heartily hoped never to see him again.

Fat chance of that. FitzHolland's being here changed everything. She was no longer safe here, even with Clifford's sympathy and Duke Somerset's protection. FitzHolland had his own friends in high places—being half brother to a royal duke—and he had an abiding hate of her.

Robyn retired to her sumptuous suite off the castle's main hall; any friend of Duke Somerset and King Henry got royal treatment, which in Pontefract meant a spacious bedroom, a solar with a window seat, a presence chamber, and a private pantry. Matt slept on the window seat, and Deirdre slept by the door, meaning she had the bedroom to herself. Amazing, especially in winter, when medievals clumped together for warmth. Aside from her Tower cell, she had hardly ever had a room of her own, and this big private bedroom beat anything yet, with a walk-in fireplace, warm carpets, a huge feather bed, and floral hangings shot with cloth of gold depicting the Garden of Eden. Her pantry was right next door, smelling of cinnamon and dried apples. To complete the picture, she had a tub hauled into the presence chamber, converting it into a private bath.

Such luxury made the wretched condition of the people around her all the more real. She had to do something for the Honour of Pontefract. Duchess Wydville or Duke Somerset could surround themselves in furs, rich food, and fine incense, figuring God or Hecate would comfort the afflicted—but she could not. Even Mad King Henry, who had made a fine career out of overlooking the obvious, sensed the injustice around him—much of it done in his name—so he dressed in black and prayed constantly, trying vainly to give his guilty wealth away, including the revenues of Pontefract. Now she was stuck with them. Many thanks, Your Majesty. Henry had an incredible talent for making a mess out of anything he did, no matter how well intentioned.

Watching from her window seat, she saw more men pour in from Kingston-on-Hull, turning the whole area into an armed camp. Percy border riders in half-armor and steel bonnets, Fenwicks, Robsons,

Milburns, and Darces, riding ahead of raw Yorkshire recruits carrying bills and pikes—though none from the Honour of Pontefract. To support themselves, they had sacked manors belonging to York and Salisbury, beggaring their neighbors to support civil war, making a bad winter worse. Even King Henry's enemies sheltered in his castle; Scots spearmen joined Grahams and Nixons that had crossed the borders to aid their English cousins, carrying looted chickens thrust through their belts. Robyn asked her maid, "Does Queen Margaret think she can win back the country by plundering her way south?"

" 'Tis hard to say what the Saxon queen thinks," Deirdre ventured, forgetting for the moment that Margaret of Anjou was technically French. "Being that Queen Margaret is in Scotland."

"So she is," Robyn agreed. Margaret had taken this moment of crisis to pass Christmas with Queen Mary of Scotland, giving new meaning to "out of touch." Who knew what Queen Margaret thought? There was a weird disconnection in everything the Lancastrians did, which began by insisting that Mad King Henry was the wisest, saintliest man in England, and the fittest to be king. Swallow that absurdity, and you will admit to anything. Rather than face the thankless task of financing a winter war, Her Highness made herself a Yule guest of Queen Mary, leaving her army to loot her subjects. Merry Christmas from Queen Margaret.

Monday, 15 December 1460, Saint Valerian's Day, Pontefract Castle

Saint Valerian is supposed to give protection against the snow and cold, and the day did dawn warm and sunny, starting a thaw that has the Went bursting its banks again.

To find out just how much I am in for, I called together the bailiffs, feasting them in the solar on smoked herring, mutton pie, minced goose pastries, pickled eels, and date compote ordered up from the castle kitchen and charged to the crown. Between courses, I proclaimed Queen Margaret's promise not to draft them, an overwhelmingly popular announcement. In return, they explained why the moneys due me are so meager—crops ruined, fish weirs destroyed, milk cows and breeding stock butchered that could no longer be pastured over the winter. Rents are in arrears, and there is little to seize in their place. Actual money revenues barely cover my Italian loan—both the Venetians and I having grossly over-estimated what the manors can produce in this wet miserable winter.

Much against my will, I am learning a lot about medieval estate management. Few of the people hereabouts are freeholders, since everything belongs to the king. Most are customary tenants, either descendants of serf families owing feudal dues and labor services, or copyholders holding their land under contract and paying rent to me. Rents are a burden, but generally accepted as fair payment, since they live on king's land and do not expect to plow it for free. It is the arbitrary fines and dues that are hated, things like heriot and marchet, payments demanded when a tenant dies or when their children marry. Such obnoxious fines have no purpose except to line my pockets, and are rightly resented. My absolute favorite is leyrwite, pronounced *lay-right*—a fine paid by "unchaste women" for having sex out of marriage, a real potential moneymaker so long as it is not leveled on me. Such extortionate fees seem more heavy here than in the west; at Greystone they no longer exist.

Whatever their status, copyholders, cottagers, wanton bonds-women, or day laborers, everyone here is nearly destitute. Clearly the Honour of Pontefract cannot support me or my sudden bursts of generosity. And the main means of improving manorial incomes is to convert farmland to pasture, raising sheep and cattle for market while turning out your tenants to starve—not an attractive option.

Thanking the bailiffs, I told them to take goose pastries home to the kids, and I sent them off into the December sunlight, promising an even bigger feast at Wentbridge, on Thursday, on what people call Saint Adam's Eve.

Several bailiffs brought sick children to show me, claiming my few pills and kind words had produced miracle cures at Ferry-bridge. "Lady Pomfret" is not just learning estate management, but becoming the local pediatrician, as well. People here are so starved for leadership, they will follow a perfect stranger, so long as she is going their way . . .

With civil war topping off a wretched winter, the only thing to do was party. Buying more shiploads of grain was totally out of the question, though Robyn could still order up beer and eels, a cartload of bread, and an ox big enough to fatten a village, spending yet more of her dwindling silver. Days of blithely charging things to the crown were gone, and soon she would be counting silver pennies. Damn.

But she had enough for one last feast, since this was the season of giving, the Saturnalia, the great pagan solstice giveaway, when ancient nobles feasted their serfs and retainers. Wentbridge was the middlemost of her manors, smack on the Great North Road, and folks came primed to eat, braving light snow in wool cloaks to gather at the church and manor hall. Wednesday had been a fast day, as were Friday and Saturday, making this their big chance to gorge at the manor's expense. And tomorrow was Saint Adam's Day—which was not on the liturgical calendar, but a folk holiday nonetheless, dedicated to sex and frivolity, and best appreciated on a full stomach.

At the height of the festivities, bailiffs called for silence, and Britons respectfully doffed their hats as Robyn rose from her seat at the high table. Speaking loudly in the hush, using her best stage voice, she announced that all remaining feudal rights such as marchet, leyrwite, childwite, heriot, and boon services were abolished. From now on all customary tenants would become copyholders, paying only a money rent negotiated with the crown, free to sell their tenantry if they found a buyer. People stared at her in stunned silence, amazed at how much their lives had been changed by a single sentence. Furthermore, she told them, "All debts owed to the crown this year are abolished, including the rents due me at Michaelmas."

That turned shocked silence to wild cheers. Waves of applause forced her to stop, standing there in her crimson and cloth-of-gold gown, smiling as people in stained homespun cheered her heartily, hardly believing what they had heard. Meager harvests meant debts to the crown had soared, with scant hope of repayment. Suddenly, all these debts were gone, along with their feudal dues and fines, turning these people into free tenants, which made their meat all the sweeter, and my lady's beer even better.

When they were done applauding, she added, "And all moneys collected for me so far will be returned to the tenants who paid them."

More drunken applause erupted, this time from those thrifty souls who had managed to pay their rents—now they, too, stood to profit from her ladyship's unbelievable fit of generosity. Cheers were followed by toasts to "Our Lady Robyn of Pomfret" their angel from the south. Minstrels struck up Christmas music, and people started to dance, beating out the tune with clappers and knackers hanging from their belts. Banqueters sang carols to the music, while dancers mimed the words, spinning in circles with hands clasped or arms linked, committing sins of sight, song, intent, and touch—but way too happy to care. There was always something subversive about the whole Christmas season, celebrating a bastard boy born to a teenage mom in a manger, whose birth caused animals to talk and kings to bow down. And from time out of mind, this had been the season of giving, when those with hoarded wealth had to offer up food and warmth in the depth of winter.

His Majesty's Honour of Pontefract had its Christmas miracle, thanks to Lady Robyn and some unwittingly generous Italian bankers. She had robbed from the rich—King Henry, offshore bankers, and herself—to give to the Yorkshire poor, who desperately needed it. What would they think if they knew their outlaw lady was an "I do" away from being their duchess, too? Something worth drinking to. But right now she owed the Venetians more money than she could ever hope to repay, and when they found out, her Italian would not sound nearly so charming. More rents were due in the new year, on Lady Day, but who knew what things would be like then.

Women came up to thank her personally, begging m'lady's forgiveness, saying, "We feared that Lady Pontefract would be some curt-spoken southerner, wanting her exact due, even if it came out of your children's mouths."

Celebration carried over to Saint Adam's Day on Friday, a fast day, one of the ember days after the feast of Saint Lucy, when people avoided not just meat, but also "white meats" like eggs and cheese. But they still had salt fish and beer to go with their daily bread, and Saint Adam's Day had carnal connotations, being dedicated to the man who discovered sin. Jo told of secret sects of Adamites who rejected marriage and held naked assembles called "paradises"—all very heretical and illegal, but nonetheless fun. Or so Robyn assumed, never having been to one. She had her own personal heresy to attend to, since tonight was Witches Night and she desperately needed to seek out Edward, and warn him about the army gathering around her.

Withdrawing to her luxuriously private bedroom, she prepared for a rare Witches Night alone—much to Deirdre's disappointment. But this was no lesson in spellcraft; it was a determined attempt to stretch her powers, and she could not hope to drag a novice along. Casting her private circle on the bedroom floor, she closed her eyes, chanting lightly in time to her heart, sinking slowly into herself. Her way to Edward lay through her heart, and she centered herself on him, recalling his touch, his feel, his laugh, his smell, and how she hungered to see him. Free of Duchess Wydville's scrutiny, she could at last call out to her love. Instead of trying to hide her longing, she let herself sink into it, fully feeling her yearning for Edward, reaching out to him, wanting to know he was well, wanting him with her.

Darkness enveloped her, the cold bleak darkness of winter, the darkness of the grave, with only the warmth of her Witches Night candle washing over her, reminding her of spring to come. She let herself go, merging with the darkness, calling out to Edward. In return she heard the same rhythmic breathing in the dark as on Saint Lucy's Eve.

Only this time not in a musty tent. This time she felt the warm dry scent of a manor bedroom in winter. Following the breathing to a big canopy bed sitting in the corner of the room, Robyn drew back the silk curtains. Edward was there. She could tell by his scent and his breathing, and by the sureness of the spell. Edward, and Edward alone—thank goodness. This would be the absolute worst moment to discover he had found some Welsh serving lass delighted to keep her handsome Saxon lord warm on long winter nights.

Wanting more than a kiss this time, she lifted the coverlet and slid in between silk sheets, entering a warm dark world of strong male odors, always so strange and exciting. Having just given away almost everything she owned, Lady Robyn richly deserved a reward, and the best she could imagine was being held by Edward while he listened to her troubles, telling her things would be all right and making tender love to her—not necessarily in that order. Feeling with her hand, she found the solid body weighting down the feather bed, and for a long moment she looked at her love, her witch's imagination filling out what could not really be seen in a dark room on a moonless night.

She could barely believe they were back in bed together, her own private "paradise" on this Saint Adam's Night—magical and more.

Guided by the spell, she followed Edward's breathing to his lips, kissing him lightly, delighted by the thrill of contact across such a great gulf.

Edward stirred warmly at her touch, bare arms emerging from beneath the thick feather quilt, reaching out and seizing her, sleepily pulling her closer, letting her feel the full length of his splendidly nude body. Aroused in sleep, his leg slid over her hip, pushing up her black witch's shift and spreading her legs with his knee—all without breaking the kiss. Mouths and bodies seemed to come together like magic, fitting easily into each other, despite sleep, distance, and dead of winter.

Lady Robyn relaxed into the kiss, eyes closed in the dark, sinking into Edward's embrace, reaching down to direct his arousal to where it would do the most good. Things felt wonderfully dreamlike as she opened her hips to accommodate him, fearing neither fleas nor pregnancy. Practice makes perfect, and she guided his awakening erection to just the right place, slipping him easily into her. There was a moment of pleasant friction then . . .

She woke up, back in her palatial apartments at Pontefract, sitting on her bedroom floor facing a burnt-out candle, still smelling Edward's sweat and excitement. Damn. How unfair—just a titch longer, and she would have been a really wicked witch. Outside in the darkness, the lauds bell tolled in the church tower. Some Saint Adam's Night. Her watch read 3:42:02. Lauds was late—a sleepy monk had let the water-clock freeze.

Sunday, 21 December 1460, Feast of Saint Thomas the Apostle, Pontefract Castle

What an incredible Witches Flight! By far my most amazing ever (not counting the first one, of course). Gives me hope of someday being able to control this whole business, and travel not just miles, but centuries. I still have not broken the time barrier. I cannot even stretch it much, or I would never have settled for coitus interruptus.

Deirdre demanded details over breakfast toast and tea, and I gave encouraging if vague replies. Pleasant as that private "paradise" was, I have not been able to warn Edward. And more lords continue to join Somerset and Devon, including Holland, Percy, Latimer, Roos, and Greystroke—Tarzan himself has come out to oppose the Act of Accord. Even more oddly, Lord Neville was there, as well, a cousin to Edward's closest allies, as is Lord Latimer, showing just how little support York has among the northern nobility.

I wish I could just saddle up Lily and go looking for Edward, to warn him of the danger—but Somerset was right about armed men on the roads. There has already been a clash at Worksop on the edge of Sherwood, with Yorkist riders coming up from the south. Somerset's troops claimed to have killed scores of Yorkists, but they still had to give ground, falling back on Pontefract. Magic has become my best hope of warning Edward.

And this is the season for sorcery. Holy days lie ahead. From now on, almost every day is a saint's day, with special Masses for Christmas, the Feast of Stephen, Childermas, and for days dedicated to two different Saint Thomases—what locals call the halcyon days, when the kingfisher nests, a time of peace and fair weather surrounding Christmas. Yorkshire could certainly use a healthy dose of both.

Tuesday, 23 December 1460, Pontefract Castle

Today makes eight months in the Middle Ages. Unthinkable. Nine months ago, none of this existed for me, and I was in West L.A., toying with the notion of taking a surprise trip to England. Some surprise. Now I am sitting in a Yorkshire castle, furiously sewing on Christmas presents for noblemen and serving girls. I am making a silver-and-blue wool scarf for Somerset, since it is hard to shop for the duke who has everything—and Somerset deserves something for protecting me. Even if a scarf is not what he wants, it will still keep him warm.

Somerset remains my main protection from FitzHolland, which I need more than ever, having finally met Duke Henry Holland, FitzHolland's half brother. Next to him, FitzHolland seems almost normal. Descended from a family infamous for murder, insanity, and sadism, Duke Holland looks as dangerous as expected. He was once a prisoner here in Pontefract, charged with mayhem and treason—but alas, they let him out. Edward's sister Anne is flat-out married to the man. Talk about unholy matrimony.

I miss my own betrothed. Somehow I have to get to Edward. Tomorrow night, Christmas Eve, is Mother's night, and I will pray to Mary for guidance and support, for the night after Christmas will be Witches Night again, and I hope to get more than a kiss and tickle—maybe even a chance to talk.

Edward's father is said to be at Sandal Castle, near Wakefield, not more than nine miles away. If so, I wish him a very merry Christmas, as well—but do not expect to get a scarf. There is only so much I can sew.

Peace was the best possible Christmas present, and by Christmas Day, the truce had taken hold, set to last until the Feast of Epiphany on the sixth of January. Pontefract castle was decked with evergreen boughs, and the pine scented halls rang with hymns and carols, while lords and commons alike were entertained by fiddlers, jugglers, contortionists, stilt-walkers, talking animals, and an acrobatic dancer named Maud Makejoy. Some of the carols were easy to recognize, like the "Angel's Hymn," the one that goes

> Angels we have heard on high,
> Sweetly singing o'er the plains,
> And the mountains in reply,
> Echoing their joyous strains . . .

Also *"Adeste Fideles,"* but most of the carols were in Latin, with different words. Still, it is fun to sing out, *"Glo-ree-ah in excelsis Deo,"* for the first time knowing what it meant. To vary the repertoire, Robyn taught Deirdre and the serving women the carol sung to the tune of "Greensleeves":

> What child is this, who laid to rest,
> On Mary's lap is sleeping . . .

That and "Silent Night" cinched Robyn's reputation as a songwriter. Too bad she could not remember more carols, because the women were all eager to sing, and enjoyed doing it in English. And Duke Somerset liked his scarf, or at least pretended he did. Somerset could be politely deceptive when the need arose. He had yet to mention Joan Hill and his child, who were passing Christmas at home, without the good duke. Robyn offered a toast to Joy, Somerset's bastard sister, whose birthday was Christmas. Joy's half-brother drank with enthusiasm, unbothered by bastards in the family. Even his own.

Friday after was the Feast of Stephen, Boxing Day, though no one called it that yet. But the spirit of Boxing Day was alive and well, as locals besieged the castle, dressed in fools' costumes, singing bawdy carols, and demanding gifts from their betters. This was Christmas at its most leveling, and Robyn knew a carol to go with it, the one that begins

> Good King Wenceslas looked out
> On the feast of Stephen,
> When the snow lay round about,
> Deep and crisp and even.

and ends with the admonition

> Therefore, Christian men, be sure,
> Wealth or rank possessing,
> Ye who now will bless the poor,
> Shall yourselves find blessing.

Worthy thoughts for the Christian noblemen feasting at Pontefract, preparing for war during the season of peace. Saint Stephen's Night was Witches Night, as well, the last one of the year, hopefully her last one at Pontefract.

Her digital watch woke her at the witching hour, and she cast her private circle, lighting a tall black candle with her plastic lighter. Slipping the lighter into the pocket of her black silk shift, Robyn closed her eyes and started chanting to herself, calling on all the power she could, striving to break through to Edward.

Which she did, finding first the warm dry scent of his manor bedroom, followed by the sound of his breathing. Shutters were closed, and the dark room was utterly still, the quiet broken only by his soft rhythmic intake and exhale. Slipping over to Edward's bed, Robyn silently drew back the heavy Tripoli silk curtain. And found him awake.

His hand closed on her wrist, pulling her down toward the dark bed. Another arm slid up her side and curled over her shoulder, drawing her over to him. His mouth found hers, and they kissed, a long intimate melding that seemed to go on for minutes. When their lips parted, he whispered, "I have been waiting for you."

"You have?" she asked, surprised at how swiftly he had accepted her unannounced arrival.

"A week ago, I dreamed of kissing you," Edward explained, punctuating the statement with another delighted kiss—then adding, "And I wanted more, much more, but you vanished too quickly. I have been waiting ever since for this dream to return."

"This is no dream," she told him, realizing that Edward did not think she was here at all.

"What do you mean?" Edward laughed happily, enjoying himself immensely, pushing her black shift up past her hips. "This is my most pleasurable dream by far."

"Does this feel like a dream?" She leaned over and softly bit his firm round shoulder, not hard enough to hurt, just hard enough to be convincing.

"No, this feels like heaven." Pushing her shift up to her shoulders, he leaned in to kiss the hollow between her breasts.

"Maybe," she admitted as his lips and tongue slid over her naked skin. Certainly not the Christian Heaven, nor some heathen paradise either, where a pious young warrior-prince like Edward would rate at least forty flawless virgins. Feeling through the folds of her pushed-up shift, she found the plastic lighter and flicked it on. Soft yellow light flooded the canopied bed, falling on his handsome smiling face.

Delight turned to astonished surprise as Edward saw it was her, in the flesh and in his bed, lit by one of her futuristic gadgets. He asked, "How did you get here?"

Amused by his surprise, she told him, "I am not really here."

"Not here?" He reached out and traced the curve of her breast with his finger, sending a pleasant tingling down her belly and into her thighs. "You seem very real. How can that be?"

"Witchcraft," she admitted. "But do not ask me how I do it." She doubted she could explain it, even if she were allowed to.

"Another woman's secret?" Edward ran his hands down her half-naked body, admiring her solidity. Fingers from far off felt excitingly real on her bare flesh.

She nodded. "And really no more miraculous than making babies." Witches Flight was easier and safer than pregnancy, just not so common.

Edward laughed, "At least you let us in on that. So where are you, then?"

"Pontefract Castle." Leaning over, Robyn parted the blue silk curtains and found an oil lamp on the bedside table. She lit it and set down the lighter. Looking around the bedroom, she saw a richly furnished apartment with hand-carved paneling, a rose marble statue of the Virgin, and silver trim on the furniture. She asked, "And where is here?"

"Shrewsbury," Edward replied, keeping his hand on her breast, as if his warm touch could somehow keep her there. "What in heaven are you doing at Pontefract?"

From the way he said it, she could tell he only half believed her, despite the barred door and bolted windows. She hardly believed it herself, lying beside him in this huge feather bed, happy, warm, and comfortable. But she was in Pontefract, and Witches Night would last only so long. "I went north with Somerset, hoping you would intercept him, but he moved too quickly." That much Edward knew, or must have guessed. "I would have turned back when we got to Nottingham, but I had to go on. . . ."

Edward looked worried. "Why would you do that?"

She did not have time to tell him about seeing Mary of Cock Lane in Sherwood, or the path of flowery footprints leading north. And besides, that was a Witches Night secret. Instead she said, "I had to see the Honour of Pontefract."

Edward's smile returned. "So now that you have seen 'Pomfret,' what have you to say?"

"Things are terrible here," she told him. "Winter has people by the throat, and rain has ruined the crops. Tenants are eating their seed grain and slaughtering their breeding stock, living on bread crusts and boiled grass while Somerset and Devon feast on crab pâté and Christmas goose."

Edward said he was sorry to hear things were so bad in the Yorkshire, and she could tell he meant it—even though he was lying snug and happy in his silver-studded feather bed. "But that is not the worst of it," she warned, "there are more bad news on top of that."

Edward stared at her across the bed linen. "What could be worse than living on bread crusts and boiled grass?"

What indeed? The specter of starving children had already made her give up her royal revenues, but bad as these things were, she knew they were going to get worse. "Somerset and Queen Margaret are raising a huge army here at Pontefract. Thousands of northerners,

Percys, Nevilles, and a whole host of minor lords, plus border riders and Scots spearmen—"

"Nevilles?" That was clearly unwelcome news.

"Yes, Lord Neville, and Lord Latimer, as well. They are forcing tenants to join them, burning manors and looting the homes of those who resist, piling destruction on top of devastation."

Edward sighed, reaching up and running his fingers down her cheek. "I wish you were not there, but here."

She turned and kissed his fingertips, saying, "But I am here." For the moment.

"Really here, in body and in spirit. So long as you are at Pontefract you are in great danger." And it pained him to know he could not protect her. "I thought you would be here when I came west, and was sorely worried when you were not. Father has gone north to deal with Somerset and Devon. . . ."

She nodded solemnly, saying, "Word is that he is safe at Sandal Castle."

"That is most happy to hear. I am raising more men here in the Marches, and when I do, I will be coming north to join him." Edward's grip on her tightened. "But do not wait for me to come north. Please, my love, come south at once. Or if you cannot come south, seek safety with my father at Sandal until I arrive."

She smiled at his heartfelt concern, saying, "I will head south as soon as I can. There is a Christmas truce, and the road through Sherwood should be somewhat safe."

"Safer than your staying at Pontefract." Though she had said nothing about FitzHolland or Duchess Wydville, and her delicate relations with Somerset, Edward clearly sensed the danger she was in. "If you cannot come south at once, send me the ring and I will come for you."

"Do not worry." She leaned over and kissed him. "Nothing will keep me from you."

"But I want you here now, with me." He gripped her shoulders, bringing their bodies fully together, his chest pressed against her breasts, his thighs thrust against hers. Not willing to wait for her to get here in the flesh, Edward wanted her now, Witches Night or no, and would not waste a moment more. He had waited a week for this "dream," and mixing sex with magic seemed to turn Edward on—not very remarkable, considering the male mind. But surprisingly contagious. She felt thrilled as eager hands thrust her down into the bed, feeling him against the full length of her body, lifted up by love even as he pressed her into the feather mattress.

And then Lady Robyn woke up, back in her Pontefract bedroom, staring at a burnt-out candle. Double damn. Why could she not get it to last just a little while longer? Obviously something about sex made her lose control. Duh, what could that be? Ever hear the one about the dyslexic witch who could not spell and screw at the same time? Looking about, Robyn realized she had lost her lighter, leaving it on Edward's nightstand in Shrewsbury. At least when Edward saw it, he would know she had not been a dream.

Saturday, 27 December 1460, Holy Innocents' Eve, Pontefract Castle

Now that I know Edward is waiting in Shrewsbury, there is nothing to keep me from going to him. There is a truce in place, however shaky, no more fighting until the new year—1460 has seen more than enough, with battles at Sandwich, Newnham Bridge, Northampton, and now Worksop, not to mention the miserable siege of the Tower. Any more fighting will have to wait for 1461.

Though you could hardly tell it from the way they act around here. Somerset, Clifford, Sir John Grey, and all the other gay young blades are extra gallant these days, as if they expected action, rather than a round of New Year's partying. Somerset laughs it off, saying, "A knight must always be ready to die." Mayhap, but he seems like a man who expects to see blood spilled soon—maybe even his own—giving him a sort of whimsical gravity you do not normally see. Especially in Somerset. Part of Edward's attraction is he always faces life that way, never needing death threats just to be seriously charming.

So now is the time to fly south and into his arms. For once the weather is fair, and the land briefly at peace, and tomorrow is Holy Innocents' Day, Childermas, dedicated to the children Herod murdered trying to kill the baby Jesus, a sort of April Fools' Day in December—perfect for setting out to find your love. . . .

Telling Deirdre to pack, Robyn got out the last of her silver groats and started cutting them up—some even had crosses on the back, so they could be cut into four neat pie-wedge pennies. Literally making change, the medieval way of stretching your money. When she was done, she went off to see Duke Somerset and sweet-talk him into giving her safe passage south.

And she found the good duke in light conversation with Lords Neville and Latimer. Somerset was delighted to see her, only making her wait while he dismissed Warwick's cousins, then happily giving her a private audience in his keep apartments. He was far less delighted to hear her request, asking, "Whyever would you want to leave?"

This was hardly the moment to bare her soul to Somerset, admitting she just had to fly to the arms of his enemy. Instead she tried to stall him with the obvious, saying, "Your Good Grace, I now have nothing to keep me here."

She had nothing whatever, besides a borrowed bed and a wardrobe full of fancy gowns that she now must think of selling, plus a few cut-up groats, several fine horses, and a pair of servants who would soon be seeking new employment. Which did not stop young Somerset from stepping closer, taking her hands in his, and saying, "I would that were not true. Stay with us but a few more days," he implored, "then I will give you good reason to stay longer."

His fingers felt warm and comforting, and it was nice to know that no matter how destitute, she still had something noblemen desired. Raising that eternal question—how far did she have to go just to get away? Robyn tried desperately to change the subject, saying she must head south soon, "while the Christmas truce still holds."

"Truce?" Somerset sounded like he was not familiar with the term.

"Yes, between now and the Feast of Epiphany." The twelve days of Christmas were ticking away. "I must be on the road south before fighting begins again."

Somerset laughed, leaning forward and kissing her. "Worry not. Fighting will soon be over for good, at least in the Honour of Pontefract, and well before Epiphany." Somerset's bold, careless style said he was going into harm's way, without waiting for the truce to end. "The next few days hold danger, and I would see you safe here at Pontefract, not wandering south into trouble."

To show he meant it, Somerset kissed her again. Thanking His Grace, she managed to disentangle herself from the amorous young nobleman, without getting Duke Somerset's permission to leave. Nor was she likely to get it. She was lucky just to get out of his Grace's chambers. Despite the morrow being Sunday, and Holy Innocents' Day, as well, Somerset talked like fighting could resume anytime. Another sign these halcyon days would not last.

Sheepishly, she had to return and tell Matt and Deirdre that they were not leaving right away. Both her servants listened dutifully; then Matt asked, "Does m'lady want to leave on the morrow? For if she does, it may easily be done."

Deirdre agreed eagerly. "If m'lady wishes, we may all be well away by break of day on the morrow."

Robyn stared at her servants, who did not seem the least deterred by Duke Somerset's orders, asking, "How so?"

"Tomorrow is Childermas," Matt Davye explained, "when almost anything may be arranged by the stable boys, especially for my Lady Pontefract."

"Really?" What made her so special to the stable boys? She had done nothing for them, except for a tip now and then, in thanks for tending to her horses.

"Yes, indeed," Matt assured her. "M'lady is most rightly loved here in the Honour of Pontefract, by everyone from turnspits to stable hands. They may be uncouth northerners, but families from here to Ferrybridge owe their livings to you, and even Yorkshire knows how to show gratitude. Folks hereabouts will cheerfully overlook the orders of a southern duke, since until Lady Stafford came along, they thought all southerners cared only about collecting rents and taxes." Being a Devon man himself, Matt found that amusing.

"Will there be danger?" She did not want to see others risking their lives just so she could rejoin Edward.

"Very much so, m'lady." Matt did not seem in the least deterred. "Living in wartime is always dangerous, but there is dire peril in staying here, as well. Word in the stables says that fighting is just days away. Horses are being exercised and reshod, and weapons sharpened. Duke Somerset is merely waiting for Sir Andrew Trollope to arrive with reinforcements." Trollope was the professional soldier who betrayed Duke York at Ludford, sending Edward's family into prison and exile.

"Women are busy sewing Neville badges onto jackets and surcoats," Deirdre added significantly, "the Saint Andrew's cross and the white ragged staff." Which meant Somerset wanted some of his men to go into battle posing as Nevilles, the same trick FitzHolland used at Greenwich.

"FitzHolland has neither forgotten nor forgiven," Matt reminded her earnestly. "He is merely waiting for Duke Somerset to turn his attention elsewhere before he strikes. If the Duke rides off to war, m'lady loses her protector, and staying here will be no safer."

Plainly she had to get away. And to do it successfully, she must put herself in the hands of her servants. "But if we are sneaking off without permission, we cannot head straight south the way we came, through Sherwood and Nottingham," Robyn told her coconspirators. "Not with Somerset's riders patrolling the roads."

Matt Davye agreed. "We would not get so far as Worksop."

There were two ways to get to Shrewsbury from Pontefract; either take Watling Street south, the way they had come, which is what Somerset and FitzHolland would be watching for. "Or we could head west, straight into Yorkist territory, where Duke Somerset's writ does not run."

Matt nodded solemnly. "Wakefield is scant miles to the west, and south of it is Sandal Castle, the duke of York's last stronghold in Yorkshire. But will m'lady be safe there?"

Not likely, but she faced risks either way. West or south? York or Lancaster? With the north so deeply divided, she had to choose one or the other; there was no neutral ground. Her heart was still with York, and heading west was the fastest, surest way of finding Edward—while going straight south was impossible, with both Somerset and FitzHolland watching the roads as far as Sherwood. So it had to be west past Sandal. "There is a truce," she reminded her horse master. Curiously, the truce covered her only in Yorkist territory, since Somerset had already decided to break it. "Until the Feast of Epiphany."

"Let us pray it lasts so long," Matt replied piously.

After morning Mass, Deirdre hustled her back to her oak-paneled suite, where Robyn put on men's hose and a boy's jacket, hiding her short hair in a cap and smearing mud on her face. Deirdre, in turn, put on Robyn's blue-white riding gown, happily playing the Saxon lady—then they went to join Matt in the middle bailey.

Out in the baileys, Holy Innocents' Day was going full tilt as children dressed like monks and nuns paraded through the castle, blessing everyone they met, singing rowdy songs, and handing out honey-cake sacrament. Childermas was given over to children, and the prettiest virgin in Pontefract was mounted on an ass, being led about the baileys with a baby in her arms, symbolizing the flight into Egypt. No one noticed a maid in a lady's gown, attended by her mistress in drag, or if they did, it passed as part of the show. At the gatehouse, Deirdre and Matt mounted Ainlee and Lily; then a mob of laughing, jeering stable hands led them and the sumpter horses out the bailey gate, where drunken guards waved them through. Matt attracted the most attention, wearing a fanciful outfit, made from one of her silk blouses worn under a breastplate, a multicolored cape, harlequin leggings, and an improvised gold-fringed turban.

Slouching along with the cap pulled down over her dirty face, Lady Robyn strolled out the gate amid the capering stable hands. She heard children behind her parodying the holy Mass, singing childish Latin as they led the girl on the ass about the bailey, drawing loud shouts of "Hee-haw" from the troops. Then the gate closed behind her, and she was free, for the moment, escaping into winter.

Bones of snow lay on the farmland outside, long white stripes of slush left by the rain in deep-plowed fields. Crows picking at muck and offal spread on the frozen fields cawed loudly as her party passed. Taking a page's place at the head of the sumpter horses, she followed her "lord and lady" into the west, listening to Deirdre sing a Hollywood carol her mistress had taught her:

> Virgin Mary had a boy,
>   Doo-dah, doo-dah,
> Folks all say the dad's a goy,
>   Oh! doo-dah day . . .

About a mile out of Ackton, they stopped at a farm for breakfast, and laughing children poured out, greeting her servants with squeals of delight, inviting them in, happily calling them "m'lord" and "m'lady." Yorkshire cottages make London town houses seem like castles; this one smelled of dung and woodsmoke, and was constructed from arched tree trunks stuck in the ground to support a thatched roof and wattle-and-daub walls, which were blackened with soot, since the hearth had no chimney. Holy Innocents' Day frivolity was in full swing. The mother wearing her clothes inside out was cooking Childermas honey cakes on the hearth. Their father sat scrunched in a cradle, his legs sticking out on each side, wearing a bonnet and his wife's apron, sucking on a clay beer pot.

"Come, m'lord! Come, m'lady," cried the joyous children. "Enjoy our beer and cakes." They had been whipped awake at dawn by their parents, "To remind us how the Holy Innocents suffered." After that the children were in charge, gleeful for once to boss their elders around. Watery beer and a meatless feast showed that even honey cakes were a gross extravagance for this family, but for one day in deepest winter children got whatever they wanted. Thank goodness. Wishing these children were running the country, Robyn sat nibbling on a honey cake, not wanting to take a morsel from these people's mouths. After feeding and watering the horses, Matt paid with cut-up pennies, and they mounted to go. Children saw them off, hanging on her stirrups and loading her with honey cakes, then calling out after her in atrocious Yorkshire accents, "Far-tha-well! Far-tha-well! Lady Robyn."

It took more than men's clothes and a coat of mud to fool those kids—hopefully their elders were not so observant. Matt laughed at her concern, saying, "There is not a cottager in the Honour of Ponte-fract that would tell tales on Lady Robyn, not to some southern duke with a French accent. If m'lady wants to be a dirty-faced boy on Holy Innocents' Day, everyone hereabouts would swear it so."

That was the last bit of good news. Beyond Ackton she saw burnt farmsteads and ruined manors—a sure sign they had reached Yorkist territory. Hereabouts families celebrated Childermas around pathetic little fires, huddled in the ruin of their homes, cold, starved, and thoroughly scared. Hollow-eyed hungry children were a vivid contrast to the happy singing youngsters putting on a raucous show at Pontefract—a reminder of what gracious young Somerset had planned for anyone foolish enough to pay rent to the wrong lord. She gave away her honey cakes, and the bread she had hoarded for the road south, until she had nothing left to give.

Farther on, she saw foragers wearing the duke of York's falcon and fetterlock digging through the ruins of barns and sheds, searching for buried food. Shouts in Cockney accents showed the men were Londoners, a pleasant shock after months of exile, almost like coming home. She had not realized how much Londoners had become "her people." None of them knew her, not with men's clothes and mud on her face, but they insisted on taking "Lord" Matt and his red-haired lady to their captain.

Lady Robyn rode along with her servants, hiding behind her dirty face and boy's jacket, wondering what to do next. With scant silver and no food, her newfound sense of freedom felt hollow. Shrewsbury was ninety-odd miles away—two days if she pushed herself, three if she spared the horses. With Edward waiting, she would surely make it, even on a flat purse and empty stomach. What worried her more were these Londoners and the Yorkist tenants they had come to protect. Somerset meant to strike in the next day or two at most, yet she saw bowmen wandering about in small bands, looking for food—trusting in the Christmas truce. Much as she hoped to make a clean Holy Innocents' Day getaway, these men deserved some warning.

South of Wakefield, the Yorkist foragers led them through a wooded park, and on the far side she saw Sandal Castle standing on a hill surrounded by cleared ground. The huge fairy-tale fortress looked like a medieval book illustration come to life, ringed by walls and flanking towers that enclosed a complex of baileys and castle buildings, topped by tall round towers studded with cross-shaped firing slits. Ornamental trees lined the road leading to the great gatehouse. To make Sandal even more secure, the towered walls were augmented with trenches and redoubts of newly turned earth, studded with iron cannons. Sweating over these cannons was someone Robyn recognized at once, Master John Harrow, a London mercer who had fought under Salisbury during the siege of the Tower. He wore a sallet with the visor tipped back, and a red metal-studded brigandine, decorated with the Neville's white ragged staff.

This dry-goods dealer turned master gunner demanded to know Matt and Deirdre's business, and of course they had no ready answer. Robyn weighed options, wondering how the Christmas truce applied to her. Treason is the main charge against her, but the truce explicitly excluded arrests or detentions by either side. Or any molesting of women. With luck she could enter Sandal, deliver her warning, and then be on her way. Leaning forward in the saddle, she called out, "Master Harrow, how happy to see you again."

Master Harrow looked hard at her, asking, "Who might you be?"

She smiled, happy her makeshift disguise worked so well. "Lady Robyn Stafford. We met at Baynards Castle."

"Lady Stafford?" Harrow tried to recognize Edward of March's wayward lady beneath the dirt and stable hand's outfit—even on Holy Innocents' Day, she hardly looked the part. "How did you get here?"

"A terribly long tale," she told him—one she could hardly believe herself. "But right now I have a vital message to deliver to His Grace, the duke of York."

Harrow laughed and looked askance. "I hardly thought you were on talking terms with His Grace."

"His Grace will wish to hear what I say," she assured him. "I have just come from the royal castle at Pontefract, where Duke Somerset is preparing an attack."

Still skeptical, Harrow promised to send word to the good duke. While they waited, Robyn retired to a church just outside the walls, to wash, pray, and change into a riding gown. Here, too, children were in charge, wearing vestments and happy smiles, glad to entertain a mud-faced lady and her maid on Holy Innocents' Day. In among her things was her paperback history of the period, which would tell her just what perils Sandal faced. Once again, she was tempted to open it and read ahead. But how far ahead? Robyn was always afraid of reading something she did not want to know, and which she could not prevent. What if she found casual reference to Edward's death? Or his marrying someone else? Robyn had promised herself she would not open the book unless she had absolutely no choice. Things were not that bad—yet.

When she emerged, wearing Stafford red and gold, she found Earl Rutland waiting at the redoubt, splendidly attired in a blue-and-silver jacket, matching hose, and high leather boots. With him was Sir Thomas Neville, whom Collin had knocked butt-first into the Smithfield mud at the Saint Anne's Day tourney, half a year ago. Curtsying low before the boy earl, she waited for Rutland to give her leave to rise, saying, "It is most good to see Your Grace again."

Glad to see her, as well, the teenage earl of England's smallest county bid her rise and mount, then follow him. She entered Sandal Castle ahead of her overdressed servants, riding through a great projecting gatehouse, protected by a big barbican tower. Riding by her side, Rutland told her, "My brother Edward has missed you terribly."

"And I have missed him, too," she admitted, without saying she had seen Rutland's busy brother two days before in Shrewsbury Castle; she had trouble enough being believed without mentioning Witches Flights and virtual lovemaking. Instead she tried to picture Rutland as a stand-in for Edward as king—the boy was smart and caring, and certainly not full of himself. He lacked Edward's forcefulness, but maybe in a king that was not so bad.

"Edward will be most glad to hear you are safe," Rutland added, happily anticipating bringing the two illicit lovers together again, reveling in his role as go-between.

"I will be most glad to be safe." Despite the tall walls and towers, and thousands of armed men lounging about, Robyn felt she was riding into deathly peril. Truce or not, she was taking a terrible risk just by entering Sandal Castle—so the sooner she delivered her warning, and turned southwest toward Shrewsbury, the safer she would feel.

Lady Robyn did not get to see the good duke until well after vespers—which meant she could not leave Sandal until the morning—but that was better than being summarily clapped in irons. Duke Richard always made it a point never to take her needs or feelings into account. He interviewed her in a velvet-draped presence chamber, in the company of Rutland and several retainers, but not the Earl of Salisbury. Too bad. Robyn had hoped to tell her story to the senior Neville, as well, since if Duke Richard did not believe her, Salisbury might.

Duke Richard sat stern and tight-lipped in a tall, high-backed chair upholstered in royal blue atop a two-step dais, the only speck of furniture in the room—being shorter than she, he had to compensate somehow. Keeping almost regal state, he wore a dark wine-colored gown trimmed with ermine, and his short bowl-cut hair did not even come down to his ears, looking like a small furry cap worn underneath his duke's coronet. That and his absurdly pointed shoes, made Robyn feel like she was kneeling before the Gnome King in his hall of stone. She waited for him to give her leave to rise, which the good duke did not do, obviously liking the look of her on her knees. Instead he told her, "Tell us why you have come here."

Still kneeling, she launched into her story—abridged version—telling him about Somerset's army, which was easily double the size of

York's, and backed by Scots spearmen and border riders. "And I fear Somerset means to break the Christmas truce and attack, probably in the next few days."

York scoffed at her womanly fears, asking, "What makes you think Duke Somerset means to play us false?"

"Female intuition," Robyn replied, "mostly the way he came on to me."

"Came onto you?" His Grace sounded unfamiliar with the term, though the men standing on either side smirked, clearly getting her meaning.

"He made amorous advances like a man who is headed into battle," she explained. "And my horse master says they are shoeing horses and sharpening weapons, while seamstresses are sewing the Neville ragged staff onto jackets." Duke Richard had not seen the ruse FitzHolland used at Greenwich to try to take King Henry, since it happened while York was in Ireland and she and Edward were king-sitting.

For a long moment Duke York smiled down at her, plainly unimpressed by all she had to say, but glad to see her in her place. Finally he told her, "You are a most foolish godless young girl, with a natural bent toward trouble, always sowing dissension, first within our family, and now between us and our Neville cousins. Even dabbling in the dark arts in an attempt to get your way."

She started to protest, but His Grace silenced her curtly. "Enough! We do not fear your women's weapons. Nor the queen's schemes. Nor even young Duke Somerset's border riders and Scots spearmen. And worry not, Lord Neville is raising men under our commission— not Somerset's—the first of them will be joining us anon."

So you say. Her heart sank to see Duke York was not going to be dissuaded by hints from stable hands and seamstresses, or by Somerset's attempts to seduce his son's whore. She had no hope but to beat a hasty retreat, heading for Shrewsbury to give her warning to Edward—who would know what to do with it.

"Let our enemies break the holy truce if they dare," York declared smugly, glad to fight with God on his side. "If Somerset does, we will beat him with man's weapons—bills and bows, not silver needles and wax dolls."

She said nothing, kneeling patiently on the carpet, enduring Duke Richard's puffed-up vanity which had already ruined countless lives, including her's. So much for trying to talk sense to her future father-in-law—having given Duke Richard his timely warning, all she wanted now was leave to go. She could at least tell Edward she tried.

But she did not even get that. York looked to his second son, saying, "Earl Rutland, pray keep this deluded young woman safe, but do not let her leave the castle, for she still has grave charges to face."

"But Your Grace," she begged, "there is a Christmas truce, and I cannot be kept here against my will. All I have done is bring Your Worship fair warning of your enemy's plots."

Duke Richard smiled down at her from his high seat, determined to make her humiliation complete—to thoroughly punish her for attempting to save him. "You are charged with heresy and witchcraft, and the enemies of God enjoy no Christmas truce."

PART 3

The Paper Crown

The noble Duke of York,
He had ten thousand men,
He marched them up a hill,
And he marched them down again,
And when you're up, you're up,
And when you're down, you're down,
And when you're only halfway up,
You're neither up nor down.
            —Mother Goose

10

⊶ Wakefield ⊷

Monday, 29 December 1460, Feast of Saint Thomas of Canterbury, Sandal Castle, Yorkshire

What an idiot, thinking I could ever trust Edward's folks. Duke Richard of York has hated me from almost the moment we met—just because his oldest son loves me too much. And I foolishly thought that by being honest and loving I could somehow win him over, or at least give him fair warning. Now I have done neither, and am trapped here in Sandal. What a total fool! Somerset had no intention of honoring the truce, why should I think York would? And why do I keep supposing chivalry applies to me? Seeing Harrow and Rutland again, and hearing those Cockney accents lulled me into feeling I was home free, and anything was possible. Now I know better.

Four more days until Witches Night; then I can fly to Edward. When my love finds out what is happening, he will be here in a flash. Or so I hope . . .

*A*t least *Rutland* made a wonderful jailer—kind, considerate, and full of hope, telling her Edward would be coming north soon to set things right. He put her and Deirdre up in his own suite, giving her the pick of his rooms—a big bedchamber draped in red velvet, a smaller dressing room with a bathtub, and a private tapestried robe with a gold canopy enclosing the *chaise percée*, very fancy—especially compared with her windowless cell in the Tower, which only had a slop bucket and a rack. That did not stop her from trying to talk Earl Rutland into letting her go, saying Edward would come all the faster if she went to Shrewsbury and fetched him. Rutland refused, embarrassed but obstinate, claiming, "We all must trust in my father."

"Your father is like to get us all killed," she warned, starting to feel like Cassandra during the siege of Troy, doomed to know the truth but to have no one believe her, begging them to burn that wooden horse instead of bringing it in. She even had her hidden paperback that could tell her everyone's fate—for all the good that did. Thanks to the spell that brought her here, she now understood Greek as easily as Gaelic, and knew that *Cassandra* meant "entangler of men." And she had certainly entangled pretty young Rutland, who wanted desperately to please her without giving in. Too bad, because his older brother would have known just how to deal with her.

"Do not say such things," Earl Rutland begged. "We are in an impregnable keep, filled with thousands of bowmen and men-at-arms. How can we possibly be overthrown?"

"Duke Richard will find a way," she assured him, confident that since Richard of York had made a mess of everything so far—from Parliament to her betrothal—he was bound to scuttle the defense of Sandal Castle.

"Women are naturally fearful," Rutland protested, "knowing nothing of battle."

She sighed in exasperation, guessing young Edmund of Rutland knew very little of women, and even less about battle. "You forget, I was the one in King Henry's camp at Northampton, where I saw Duke Buckingham refuse your brother's attempts to make peace, putting his faith in thousands of men-at-arms in an entrenched camp studded with cannons. Half an hour later Duke Buckingham was dead."

With nothing to say to that, Rutland withdrew. She tried taking her case to Earl Salisbury, who listened in kind, fatherly fashion—not hating her like Duke Richard or dismissing her the way his own son, Warwick, did. She had served in the Salisbury household, and they had marched together from Sandwich to London in those heady summer days when all of southern England rallied to their cause. And Salisbury had fought to free her when she was a prisoner in the Tower, for which Robyn was always thankful. But the doughty old Neville earl was used to taking orders from Duke Richard, and he refused to believe that his cousin Lord Neville was actively plotting against them. "That is merely a ruse to keep Percy and Somerset at bay. I have Lord Neville's sworn promise that the troops he is raising are for us."

She tartly reminded him that Lord Neville had made the very same promise to Duke Somerset. "What makes Your Grace think that Somerset is the one Lord Neville will betray?"

"Lord Neville's men have already started to join us," Salisbury replied, "four hundred have arrived so far, and more are expected on the morrow."

Beware of Nevilles bearing arms, she thought, but did not say it, since Salisbury was the titular head of the Neville clan. Having never lost a battle, bluff, honest Earl Salisbury sounded justifiably over-confident. He had beaten a royal army twice the size of his at Blore Heath, putting an end to Queen Margaret's enthusiasm for viewing battles firsthand. Why should this fight be any worse? Salisbury promised to see if the charges against her might be reduced, for the service she had rendered them, but that was all he could do.

Curtsying low, she swore, "I shall happily do the same for Your Grace, if ever the need arises." Then she retired to her upholstered prison to sulk, tired of making a pest of herself. Two more days left in 1460. Two more until the first Witches Night of 1461. Four days and she could call on Edward. Four days would not kill her, hope-fully. She could hardly complain about the palatial accommodations, and Rutland was right, the place was untakeable, ringed with trenches and defended by cannons from the Tower. Duke Richard yearned to be king, and he had done amazingly well in Dublin; surely he could hold this place for the twelve days of Christmas. Before Advent was up, Edward should arrive, partridge and pear tree in hand.

She found the Feast of Saint Thomas remarkably meager, oat bread, salt cod, and a horrid blood pudding served with thin ale and sour wine. The lords at the high table shared some gamey swan that she would not have tasted on a dare. With most of the duke's manors looted, his stewards had been unable to stock the castle for York's arrival, much less the ten thousand Christmas guests who came with him—hence all the foragers. Nor was the meager meal sweetened by seeing Lord Neville's men sitting down to eat with them, some of whom Robyn recognized from Pontefract. Enemies were already in-side their "impregnable" keep, and they had not even needed a Tro-jan horse. After sharing some freeze-dried spiced apples with Deirdre, she retired early.

Sobered to see Lord Neville's villains making themselves at home in Sandal, Robyn got out her paperback history, with King Henry's picture staring back at her from the cover—a flattering portrait that still did not make him look the least like a king. She had not so much as cracked the book since she bought it—too fearful of what she might read. But now she had to find out just how much time she really had. Disaster hung over this keep, making each day precious. She needed four days to contact Edward. Two at least, if she just meant to get away.

Saying a prayer, she gingerly opened the book to the index, looking for Sandal Castle, hoping not to find it—which meant nothing noteworthy would come of her worries. No such luck. There were several entries, including a big fat one, several ominous pages in the middle of the book. Without looking at the text, she found the pages, then scanned them lightly for a date, finding the words "Christmas of 1460." Bugger. Something really bad was about to happen, and soon.

And there was nothing she could do about it, except maybe save herself. And those dependent on her. Covering most of the page with her hand, she read about the week after Christmas. There it was, ". . . the battle of Wakefield, 30 December 1460." Holy Mary! That was tomorrow! What a disaster—good thing she finally opened the book. Saying another prayer, she read further.

"Killed in action . . ." The book listed a great many Yorkist dead, headed by Richard, duke of York. Seeing his name there made her feel queasy. Robyn had plenty of reason to hate Duke Richard, but he was still Edward's father, and would have been hers, as well. And by this time tomorrow he would be dead. Making Edward the duke of York, heir apparent to the throne. She had not even dared look at Edward's entry in the index, but it was bound to be a big long one. And there was no entry for her; she had already checked. Robyn could think of all kinds of reasons for this, none of them good.

Salisbury's name was not on the list, nor was that of Edmund of Rutland, but it was plain from all the Yorkist names who lost the battle of Wakefield. When she got to the names of Lord Harington and Sir Thomas Neville she closed the book, having read more than enough. Hecate help them all. Sandal was going to fall, and she had to get ready.

She called to Deirdre, speaking Gaelic so her maid would know this was serious, saying, "This castle is doomed."

Deirdre nodded enthusiastically. "They say no herons nested in the castle park for all this year." Nothing was sure to Deirdre unless the birds foretold it.

"No." Robyn shook her head. "I mean Sandal will fall tomorrow.

There is going to be a great battle, and the duke of York will be killed, but not Edmund of Rutland or Earl Salisbury." She did not have the heart to go over the whole list of dead with Deirdre.

"Truly?" Deirdre gave her lady a long questioning look. The maid knew nothing of Robyn's book, and considered reading a bigger mystery than necromancy.

"Truly," Lady Robyn confirmed, "and we must imitate the herons and flee south. We need blankets, warm coats, boiled water, food for the road, and all our valuables." By now Deirdre knew just what to grab; food and water were what they needed most, along with modern conveniences like lighters and medicine, plus warm clothes since they were again escaping into winter. "And have Matt see that the horses are saddled and ready at first light."

Her maid whirled away to obey. Too bad it took absolute catastrophe to get the girl moving.

At dawn, a royal herald appeared before the trenches, reading a long list of insults from Queen Margaret, taunting York for cowardice and "being braved by a mere woman." Watching from a tower top, Robyn thought the last a bit unfair, since Margaret was not out on the frozen fields laying siege to Sandal—but was far from the fight herself, enjoying Yule with the queen of the Scots. Somerset was the man behind this insult.

Rutland stood beside her, saying, "They did that the last two days, as well." No wonder his touchy Highness-to-be took it so personally when she told him that Margaret's army was double the size of his. Women were thwarting Duke Richard at every hand, opposing his war, sleeping with his son, and slighting his courage. To make the insult even plainer, troops poured out of the woods between Sandal and the river Calder, bearing Queen Margaret's daisy flower, alongside Somerset's portcullis and chains, driving York's foragers before them. Here it comes, thought Robyn, standing on the tower top, watching disaster unfold in slow motion. She had skipped over the details of the battle—which the modern writer admitted were based on sketchy secondhand accounts—to get straight to the casualty list. Young Rutland looked aghast, saying, "This never happened before."

So much for the Christmas truce. Gripping the cold stone embrasure with bare hands, she saw dawnlight gleam on the sharp blades of pikes and bills below. Scary as this was, it hardly had the look of a real attack. Somerset had not even put his full force behind it—no cavalry, no cannons, just a thin line of bowmen backed by armored infantry. Nothing she would personally want to face, but from the safety of her tower top it did not look like enough men to seize the trenches, much less carry the castle. Why break a truce just to throw a few hundred men at York's trenches, wasting them in a doomed attack? What did Somerset hope to accomplish? It seemed so petty and pointless, but a lot of war came off that way.

Cannons opened fire from the redoubts, skipping stone balls across the frozen ground at Somerset's advancing troops, playing a ghastly game of bowls with men for pins. Matt came up to whisper to her, "Be ready, m'lady. Horses are being saddled for a sortie, and the gates are going to open."

She told him to alert Deirdre, then be ready by their own horses— if they were to escape, it had to be during the confusion of battle. Matt bowed, kissed her hand, and disappeared down the tower stairs. Sir Robert Aspsall, Rutland's tutor appeared, telling the young earl, "Your royal father is riding out."

"Riding out?" Rutland looked startled and scared, showing more sense than his doomed father.

"Yes, Your Grace," Sir Robert replied solemnly, glad to be giving grave tidings, preening for history. Sir Robert Aspsall was a pinch-nosed academic, more suited for grooming future princes than charging into battle. And a bootlicker, as well, always calling Duke Richard "His Highness" or "the king." He told his pupil, "Sir Davy Hall bade them stay, but His Highness would not hear it, asking, why should he dread a scolding woman, whose weapons are tongue and nails? Why should people see a woman make him a dastard, when no man has proved him a coward?"

"Where is Salisbury?" Robyn asked, hoping the Neville had shown some sense and they could get safely away with him.

"Earl Salisbury is riding out with His Highness," sniffed Sir Robert Aspsall, who disapproved of questions from footloose ladies.

So much for Salisbury. She could see it was now every woman for herself. All York had to do was sit tight in his castle until Edward arrived, but instead, he was charging blindly into a trap. Robyn had never actually seen a land battle before, having spent Northampton in King Henry's tent, but from safely atop the tower, it was not nearly so gruesome as she expected. Bowmen firing from the trenches and redoubts kept Somerset's men at a distance, though stone cannon balls still bounced through the stalled line, knocking men over here and there. But new men stepped up to take the places of the fallen, trusting in their luck and armor. Medievals took war surprisingly seriously, lavishing time and ingenuity on defense, trying their best to limit casualties.

Most medievals. Robyn saw the gatehouse portcullis rise and the drawbridge come down, and men-at-arms in blue and silver came charging out past the great barbican tower, horses snorting and armor flashing, with the falcon-and-fetterlock banner flying overhead. Here came Duke Richard, the man who would be king, aiming to swat aside that insolent line of infantry and their insolent daisy flower banners.

Without meaning to, Robyn began to mumble to herself, "Yea, though I walk through the valley of the shadow of death, I will fear no evil: for thou art with me . . ."

Sir Robert glared over at her, asking, "What are you saying?"

She thought for a moment, trying to remember; then she told him, "twenty-third Psalm, King James version," as best she recalled.

"King James of what?" Sir Robert demanded. "Scotland?"

"If you say so." She stared in anguish at the mayhem below.

"Then why is it in English?" Sir Robert asked suspiciously.

"Sounds better, I suppose." For an earl's tutor, the man acted incredibly dense. She watched Duke Richard's armored cavalry charge past the trenches, brave the rain of arrows, and crash into the bowmen, scattering archers who had no way to stop half a ton of armored horse and rider. Bursting through the bowmen, Duke Richard's knights slammed into the armored infantry behind them with a horrid screeching crash Robyn could hear from atop the tower, a ghastly amalgam of clashing armor, shattering lances, and screaming horses. There were not enough pikes to keep the horsemen off, and Duke Richard cleaved through the wavering line, nearly cutting it in half before footmen swinging six-foot bills brought the horsemen to a halt.

"Thy rod and thy staff they comfort me," she intoned, twining her fingers in front of her, praying for men on both sides. "Thou preparest a table before me in the presence of mine enemies . . ."

Rutland gave a cheer as armored infantry charged out the gatehouse in York's wake, hitting Somerset's line while it was still grappling with the cavalry. Somerset's men were thrown back from the trenches, retreating toward the woods and river; but it was a fighting retreat, forced back step by step, rather than breaking and fleeing. Robyn went back to her prayer, knowing the fighting had reached a crisis. "Thou anointest my head with oil; my cup runneth over. . . ."

Just when it seemed Somerset's line would be driven straight back into the Calder, the rest of the Lancastrian army burst suddenly out of the trees at either hand. Infantry in Clifford colors came up to support Somerset's faltering line, while Wiltshire's armored footmen emerged from the woods on one side and cavalry came charging out of the other, catching the outnumbered Yorkists in an armored vise. Duke Richard and his troops were trapped like a stag in a buckstall, hemmed in on three sides and unable to back out.

Now was the time to flee. Robyn hastily crossed herself, saying, "Surely goodness and mercy shall follow me all the days of my life: and I will dwell in the house of the Lord for ever. Amen."

Then she dashed down the tower stairs, tears in her eyes, taking steps two at a time. Seconds were incredibly precious, with Lord Neville's men already within the castle. Robyn remembered Edward's description of the sack of Ludlow by King Henry's army, where women were "vengefully defouled" or just plain raped. Edward had a horror of such things, making sure his troops did not molest the locals, and he was perfectly willing to hang his own men if they got out of hand. Queen Margaret's ragtag troops, filled out with border ruffians and Scots mercenaries enlisted for loot, were bound to be less picky.

She had on a man's hose and shirt under her jacket and red-gold riding gown, partly for warmth, and partly because she might end up having to shuck her dress and run if pursuit got too close. Her most precious and perilous possession—Edward's white rose ring—went into a hidden pocket in her padded jacket, alongside her paperback history of the period. Both were highly incriminating, and could not easily be replaced. Collecting Deirdre, she made for the stables, where Matt met them with the grim tidings that, "Lord Neville's men have seized the main gatehouse."

Which meant that Duke York's men were cut off from the castle, and Somerset's minions could enter whenever they pleased. "But we can still escape through the kitchen postern." Matt pointed toward a small recessed bailey gate, used by the kitchen staff.

Nodding, Robyn divided the last of her silver with Matt and Deirdre. "Once outside, anything can happen," she told them. "We should try to stay together—but do not be ashamed to run if you must." She was especially worried for Matt, not wanting to see him killed trying to protect her.

As she handed out the last little bits of silver, Rutland arrived with Sir Robert Aspsall in tow. The young earl was ashen-faced, horrified by how swiftly disaster had fallen, saying, "My father is cut off outside, and sorely outnumbered. While enemies have entered the castle."

Robyn did a quick curtsy to the teenage earl, saying, "Your Grace, pray come with us, for there is grave danger if you stay." She thought of Somerset's promises to root out all of York's seed. Duke Richard was done for, but Rutland did not have to die—in fact, the book in her pocket did not list him among the battle dead. If they hurried, they could all escape together.

Sir Robert protested that it was unseemingly for a king's son to sneak out a privy postern in sorted company. The buffoon still called York "king," though by now Duke Richard was most likely dead already, fated never to wear the crown he sought. She told the officious tutor, "Stay if you like, I was speaking to Earl Edmund, hoping he would accompany us."

Earl Edmund of Rutland looked around the bailey, which suddenly seemed very deserted, then readily agreed, telling Sir Robert to fetch their horses. Reluctantly the royal tutor obeyed, still acting like flight for their lives was somehow beneath them, that fear was a thing for ordinary folks.

Feeling very ordinary and afraid, Robyn was tempted to order Matt to saddle up the most likely looking mount and help Rutland aboard, leaving Sir Robert to his prejudices—but the prickly tutor managed to turn up two spirited stallions, wearing the duke of York's livery. Exasperated by the fellow's stupidity, Robyn ordered the duke's colors stripped off. Rutland was wearing a wine-purple furred doublet and gold cloak that fairly screamed royalty, but that could not be helped. Mounting up, they headed for the postern, where startled guards flung open the gate at Rutland's orders.

Outside the walls, Robyn entered a stark, eerie landscape, riding past empty trenches and redoubts sprinkled with deserted cannons. At first, the only soldiers she saw were fleeing Yorkists unable to enter the castle, ripping off their colors and throwing aside their weapons, taking to the woods or seeking sanctuary in the church where she had changed her clothing. Abandoned cutlery littered the frosty ground; bills, halberds, and big two-handed swords. Among them were incriminating Yorkist surcoats—medieval military buffs would have had a field day. Without warning, a knot of men-at-arms came riding up wearing blue and gold, UCLA colors, swinging axes from the saddle, knocking men off their feet.

Shocked, Robyn wondered, Why are they doing that? It seemed so incredibly unnecessarily cruel, inflicting terrible wounds on total strangers who had been doing nothing to deserve it. Then she realized these were the enemy, Lord Roos's riders, and they would do the same to Matt and Rutland if she let them. Turning in the saddle, she shouted to her companions, "Into the woods at once."

Spurring their horses, they all dashed for the trees. As she passed the church, Robyn looked back toward Sandal, seeing no sign of the thousands who had ridden out behind Duke York, just scattered bodies, fleeing footmen, and Lord Roos's happy riders, laughing and swinging their axes. An incredibly surreal scene, even for 1460. Then the first of the woods flashed past her, and she could not see the scene for the trees.

Crashing through the bracken, she looked back to see how Deirdre was doing, but there was no sign of her, or of Matt Davye, so she stopped to let them catch up. Rutland reined in beside her, terrified by what he had seen, shouting, "Should we not be heading south?"

She shook her head. "That is where they will most likely be looking for fugitives. Half your father's army will be heading south. We should try to get to Wakefield, where someone may be willing to shelter you." Wakefield was a Yorkist town, and the best place to hide was among people, not trees. If she got Rutland out of his royal purple doublet, no one would mistake him for an earl, or even a man-at-arms.

She looked about again; no Deirdre, no Matt. Where were they? Maybe somewhere ahead, between the woods and Wakefield. Hearing thrashing in the undergrowth behind her, her heart leaped, and she turned, praying to see her servants. Branches parted, and Sir Robert Aspsall burst out of the braken, his big floppy hat askew, breathing hard and loudly demanding to know, "Where is the prince? Where is Earl Rutland?"

"Right here," Robyn replied, exasperated by the fellow's absolute stupidity, calling out Rutland's name when Somerset's riders might easily be scouring the woods for York's son—too bad Aspsall was not on the list of dead. Afraid someone worse would show, she shouted out, "Let's go," steering Rutland in the direction of Wakefield. When they broke out of the woods, she looked frantically about. Still no Deirdre. What to do?

Here the river Calder curved east to cut them off, and men were fleeing in front of them, headed for the bridge that led to Wakefield. It was that or turn downstream toward the heath and woods between Wakefield and Pontefract. Neither option was perfect, but this might be their best chance to put the river between them and Somerset's army—then they could head north or west into the hills. And Wakefield itself was a large wool town, which might offer any number of hiding places. Rutland looked wide-eyed at her, asking, "Shall we cross?"

She nodded, not sure what was best, only knowing that they could not sit there, debating on horseback. Sir Robert started to suggest something, but by now both she and Rutland were past paying attention to him. The arching stone bridge had a chapel dedicated to Saint Mary in the middle, and Robyn said a silent prayer as she rode past. Inside the town, she saw armed men ahead, and her heart fell—they did not look like fugitives.

Reining in behind the nearest cottage, which sat at the Park Street end of Kirkgate, she suggested Rutland seek shelter inside. "I will hide the horses. Then when these men pass, we can ride on." A thin scheme, but it was that or ride back across the Calder, straight into pursuit.

Too frightened to speak, Rutland dismounted and disappeared into the cottage, followed by Sir Robert. She hustled the horses into a small shed behind the cottage, which was just big enough to hold them, but had no door. Deciding it would have to do, she barred the entrance with a pole, then slipped back through the bare frozen garden and into the rear of the cottage. There was no Rutland inside, and no Sir Robert, just a frightened gray-haired old woman in a shabby black dress. Robyn asked the gaping woman, "What happened to the two gentlemen who entered here?"

"They took them," replied the crone, pointing at her front door, which was latched and barred.

"Who took them?" Robyn asked, but the woman was too scared to speak. Lifting her skirt, Robyn spun about and went back out the rear of the house, then around to the street. Horrified, she saw that men in Somerset's livery had Rutland and Sir Robert cornered in front of the house. And riding up the street toward them in full armor was Lord Clifford.

Of all men, it had to be Clifford, thirsting to avenge his father, practically that last person she could to appeal to—only FitzHolland would have been worse. Before she could think what to say, Sir Robert stupidly called out, "Spare him, your lordship, for he is a king's son, and much good may come to you!"

Clifford swung out of the saddle, looking hard at Rutland and drawing a dagger, saying, "Whose son is this?"

Seeing the dagger, Sir Robert realized his mistake, and for once had nothing to say. Frightened senseless, Rutland turned about and began to beat on the old woman's door, but it was barred. Clifford grabbed the boy from behind with a mailed hand, jerking him back out into the street, where Rutland fell to his knees, hands clasped, silently begging for mercy. Clifford sneered at the the boy's pathetic appeal. "By God's blood, thy father slew mine! So will I slay thee, and all thy kin."

So saying, Clifford stabbed Rutland straight in the chest. Robyn could almost feel the knife go in, gasping as Clifford stabbed the helpless boy again and again, until Rutland collapsed in a heap at the lord's armored feet.

Sickened, she sank down herself, hiding her head in her hands, realizing Rutland's name was not listed among the battle dead because he was murdered afterward. If she had read further, the book probably would have told her all about this—but Robyn no longer cared what happened next. Having lost Deirdre and Matt, and having led Rutland to his killers, she sat sobbing into her hands, her chest aching with loss. Let Clifford come and kill her, too, for there was nothing she could do to stop him. Rutland had been the sweetest gentlest noble she had ever met, who had never hurt a mouse, but strove to be her protector nonetheless, giving her his best rooms and kind attention. Seeing him butchered as he begged for mercy was too much to stand. What an atrocious ungodly act. She cried not just for Rutland, but for Edward, as well, who had lost a father and brother in the same day. This was going to kill him, not physically—Edward was far too strong for that—but spiritually. And there was nothing she could do to shelter him from the shock.

"M'lady, is there naught that I can do for you?" asked a man in broad Northumberland.

Wiping tears from her face, she looked up and saw a bowman in a russet steel-studded brigandine wearing the Percy crescent and a dented pot helm. She shook her head, unable to speak; there was nothing anyone could to for her, except maybe Edward, who was so awfully far away.

"M'lady ought not to be sitting here alone," the bowman explained patiently. "There has been a battle hereabouts, and men are not at their best."

She nodded. That was for sure. Looking about, she saw that aside from this helpful bowman, she was alone in the dead frosty garden, nor was there anyone in the street, which was stained with Rutland's blood. Clifford was gone, as was Rutland's body, and ridiculous Sir Robert—it was too much to hope that Clifford had killed him, too. "Let me help you to safety," the bowman suggested. "You should not be here alone."

"I have some horses," she told him, nodding toward the open shed, where Lily was penned, along with Rutland's and Sir Robert's mounts.

"Not anymore," replied the bowman, "that shed is empty."

She glanced over and saw that the bar on the door was gone, and so were the horses. While she was crying over Rutland, someone had made off with Lily. Yet another loss, in a way even more personal. Lily had carried her here from Calais and had raced with her down Cheapside on Saint Anne's Day—now Lily, too, was gone. Robyn remembered that cold morning in Calais, when she first saw Lily at the kitchen gate, presented by a page in Edward's livery; her new big white mare had seemed so miraculous, standing there, blowing white clouds of steam in the cold morning. She started to weep again.

"M'lady cannot sit here weeping," the bowman explained. "You must have people nearby; please let me take you to them."

She looked up at the bowman, who was young and blond, and smiling at her, a farm boy in armor with a bow bigger than he was—in the third millennium, he might have been a pizza boy, or a surfer, instead of a friendly killer for the Percys. "There is a chapel to Mary on the bridge. You can take me there. I need to pray."

"As do we all," replied the philosophical young bowman, "as do we all." At the chapel door she kissed him good-bye, and he went merrily off, pleased with the reward for his good deed.

She had fled Sandal Castle fearing rape for her and Deirdre, and hoping to save Rutland, instead she ended up losing Deirdre, leading Rutland to Clifford, and kissing the enemy. Robyn went in to pray, falling down on her knees and pouring her heart out to Mary, begging over and again for forgiveness and guidance. But all she got was flashbacks of Rutland pleading for his life, and Lord Clifford's gloating sneer, then the knife going in.

Finally she gave up and looked about, seeing a chapel full of women and children, plus a few armed fugitives, sheltering from the war outside. What next? Crossing herself, she got up and went out on the bridge, and saw that the war had subsided—the only fugitives left were those praying inside. Armed townsmen stood guard on the north end of the bridge, keeping looters out of Wakefield. Law and order was slowly returning to this little bit of England. Time to take advantage of that. Somehow she had to get to Edward in Shrewsbury, but the war would be heading that way, as well. Not a pleasant prospect when she had no food, no horses, and nothing but a few cut-up coins in her purse. And she could hardly count on every blond bowman she met being such a sweetheart. Robyn remembered what the helpful bowman said, about her having "people" hereabouts— just to the east was the Honour of Pontefract, and someone there should be willing to help her.

So she said her good-byes to Saint Mary and slipped off the Sandal end of the bridge, taking the rutted wagon track east toward Pontefract. Villagers were busy robbing Yorkist dead, paying scant attention to a strange-looking lady walking along in a riding dress, and she struck off over the frozen heath alone. Crows had flocked in from miles around, picking at the bodies stripped by peasants. She thought about Duke Richard, riding out as confident as Custer at the Little Bighorn. Now the man who would be king was dead, dragging Lord knew how many others down with him, including his own son Edmund of Rutland. And friends and relations from Sir Thomas Neville to Master Harrow. Starved dogs from looted villages came to scatter the crows and sniff at the dead. What a colossal waste.

Depression dragged at her feet. Robyn had not eaten since dawn, and felt like she had been riding and running ever since. Her food and water were tied to Lily's saddle—wherever Lily might be—and she was unlikely to find anything to eat in this picked-over landscape. She finally broke down and drank cold bracing water straight from a stream, but it did little for her hunger or fatigue. A few miles farther on, she faced total collapse, unable to take another step, with miles more to go. Finding a soft grassy hole in the cold hard ground, she went to sleep. Her stay in the Middle Ages had come full circle. This was how it started: alone and afoot, penniless and homeless in a hostile landscape. In between she had been a pampered lady, beloved of a mighty lord and a friend of King Henry, for all the difference that made.

Crows woke her. She was deep asleep, when she felt something pulling on her hair. Then came a sharp pain stabbing at her eyelid. Reaching up, her hand hit a feathered body that cawed angrily at her, pecking her finger. Her eyes flicked open, and she found herself covered with big black crows, which were flapping and squawking.

Batting at them, she leaped up, shouting, "Shoo, shoo, leave me alone." Retreating out of reach, the crows cawed raucously at her, both indignant and amused. After feeding on corpses all day, they had expected her to stay dead.

She picked up frozen clods and threw them at the birds, driving them off. Looking about, she saw a huge black wolf worrying a half-naked body, just like the wolf she had seen running with Mary of Sherwood. She dropped her clod, not planning to disturb his feast. Whoever he was feeding on had fine white skin, colorful silk tights, and one good boot. Snarling a warning, the giant wolf hauled the bloody body away into brush, hoping to feed in private. Crows went hopping and flapping after him.

Colder and hungrier than ever, she staggered past barren fields and burnt barns, finally coming to an untouched farmstead belonging to a Pontefract manor. Dogs came snarling out to greet her, followed by wary farm folk armed with axes—these being unsettled times. Recognizing her at once, the family ushered her into an earthen house with rough-cut log rafters, plying her with watery beer and piling tainted food on her plate, glad to feed and comfort their bedraggled Lady Pomfret. She thanked them, pleading for boiled water in place of beer, and to put her pease porridge back on the hearth to simmer some more. Which they happily did, blowing on the fire to bring the porridge to a boil, filling the little hobbit home with wood smoke.

Enthroned in the only chair, she closed her eyes, feeling the warmth of the fire, smelling simmering stew and fresh dung, listening to the happy voices around her. Only thin wattle screens separated them from the animals, since cold, waterlogged fields and hungry, marauding soldiers were forcing everyone to winter with their beasts. Even in the depths of this hard wet winter, when folks had little enough to eat, this family was overjoyed to cater to her ladyship's picky twenty-first-century tastes. In a single morning, she had seen the worst and best of the Middle Ages.

Sipping hot thick porridge and thin wheat tea, Robyn relaxed for the first time since Queen Margaret's herald appeared before the trenches of Sandal, challenging Duke Richard to prove his manhood. Ironically, these people had heard of the battle at Wakefield, and they counted it a great victory. To them, all southerners were strangers, and therefore suspect. If local lords like Clifford and Roos opposed them, that was good enough for these folks, who thought Londoners spoke funny and had strange ways. They much preferred gentlefolk, "Like you, m'lady, who speak good Yorkshire, and listen to our needs."

She did not have the heart to tell them that she came from a place far stranger than London, merely thanking them for their hospitality and letting her full stomach lull her to sleep. This time she was woken by children pulling on her gown and saying, "M'lady, m'lady, there are riders in the yard."

"What kind of riders?" she asked warily, reaching for her crock of boiled water, wanting it with her if she had to run again. Though by the sound of things, it was already too late.

"They are wearing blue and gold, m'lady," the oldest announced. "Maybe Lord Roos's men." The others eagerly nodded their heads.

She went outside to see, finding it was nearly dusk, but she could still make out the white double water-bag badge of Roos's riders. Peering down from the saddle, while holding their lances erect, they recognized her, too. Their captain told her, "My Lady Stafford, Duke Somerset has been seeking you all the way to Sandal."

"Why Sandal? When I am here with my people." She nodded toward the assembled family, who were hoping these dozen armored horsemen did not mean trouble.

Lord Roos's captain tipped his steel sallet, saying, "Wherever m'lady has been, His Grace desires your presence at Pontefract."

They had several led horses—none of which was Lily—so she ended up riding a strange mount back to Pontefract, where she got a strange room to go with it, a private bedroom in the keep, where Somerset could keep close watch on her. She lay there in yet another borrowed bed, dearly missing Deirdre. Much as she might complain about sharing bedrooms with her maid, she had come to rely on Deirdre always being there, her ever-constant confidante and coconspirator, the only one besides Edward who knew all her secrets. Or most of them, anyway.

Now she was back in Pontefract, without Deirdre, without Matt, without even Lily. And most of all, without Edward. Three more days, and it would be Witches Night—then she could see Edward and tell him where she was and what had happened. Unless she got to him before then, which did not seem likely. She could not leave without Somerset's permission, not on a horse she half trusted. Heroines in novels hopped on some stolen steed and rode a strange mount through the night into their love's arms. Miss Rodeo Montana liked to know more about a horse before she put all her hopes on it. Especially when the road south would soon be swarming with armed riders.

There was always the prospect of just giving Somerset what he wanted. He was young, handsome, rich, and on the winning side. Any woman with half a brain would have given in long ago. Joan Hill was probably doing smashing back in Devon, peacefully raising her baby in a nice house by the sea, happily awaiting her lordship's return. Not lying in a bug-ridden borrowed bed, staring at the black ceiling wondering what the morrow would bring. One good heartfelt boink, and Somerset would be much more friendly. Enough giving in, and Somerset might part with a horse and a free pass home. First some coy resistance to whet His Grace's appetite—while wheedling what she needed out of him—then—wham—give the good duke a twenty-first-century good time he would never forget. Hollywood was way ahead of the Middle Ages when it came to that sort of stuff, light-years ahead, as Edward had been delighted to discover. Somerset would be happily surprised at what had not been invented yet.

But she did not want to sleep with Somerset, especially now. She had seen up close what Somerset stood for. Sacked farmsteads and burnt manors. Rutland's murder. Children wanting food, and women afraid for their safety. Somerset wanted war, the bigger the better, and would burn and kill until he got it—because only war could get him what he wanted: the power to do as he willed. Edward was a warrior, one of the best, but he much preferred partying and making love, and he was smart enough to fight for popular causes, like peace and sane government. Given a free choice, the people of England clearly preferred Edward. And so did she.

While she lay pondering her prospects, she heard a commotion in the courtyard, riders entering the inner bailey. Going to her window, she saw torches below. Someone important was arriving, a prisoner, by the look of it. Since she was not technically a prisoner herself, she went down to see. Slipping down to the gallery overlooking the main hall, she saw Earl Salisbury, the head of the Neville clan, being led in by torchlight, damaged but not dead. His Grace looked haggard and frightened, as he had every right to be. Salisbury's day had plainly been worse than hers. Robyn retired to her room with one more thing to worry about. Salisbury had always been good to her, so if he was still alive in the morning, she must plead with Somerset for the old Neville's life.

Next morning after Mass she got her chance. Somerset immediately granted a private audience, pleased to have her coming to him at last. Robyn knew she could have avoided the whole interview just by looking up Salisbury's fate in her book—but she did not want the book to start running her life, telling her what to say, and when. Her plea to Duke Somerset was a personal statement, made for herself, and for Somerset, as much as for Salisbury. Lords and ladies made statements with their persons, in battle or in bedroom. She had made Edward promise to spare Somerset. Now she needed Somerset to do the same for Salisbury, even if it took some gentle nudging.

Luckily Lady Robyn had her whole abandoned wardrobe to pick from, and she chose a sumptuous green gown trimmed with cloth-of-silver, its low neckline offset by a high white butterfly headress—Somerset would not know what hit him. Too bad she did not have the cleavage to totally carry it off, since medievals had a lot to learn about underwire bras and women's support garments in general. England's national supply of spandex was the tiny amount she had brought with her.

Somerset did not look so bad himself, happy and handsome as

ever, standing by the window seat in what had been "her" wood-paneled bedroom, with the walk-in fireplace, warm carpets, and outsize bed, backed by Garden of Eden hangings. She smelled the apples in the pantry. He wore a spendid white gown with angel-wing sleeves over gold hose, with his portcullis badge done in cloth-of-gold on his chest, neatly setting off his glittering brown eyes and dark bowl-cut hair.

She knelt in supplication, showing off the neckline, and Duke Somerset took his time telling her to rise. Somerset was plainly on top of the world, having crushed Duke Richard, capturing Earl Salisbury and Sandal Castle, winning all of northern England for Queen Margaret. Pretty women kneeling before him was one of the victor's perks, and Somerset meant to savor the moment. Lancastrians were no longer losers. Duke Somerset had personally put an end to a deplorable losing streak, his side having lost every pitched battle so far—Saint Albans, Blore Heath, and Northampton—making their cause synonymous with defeat, while adding to the long list of noble dead needing to be avenged. Wakefield had erased all that. Smiling triumphantly, Somerset told her, "Rise, Lady Stafford. I vowed I would be well done by Epiphany."

And in a mood to celebrate. Rising to her feet, she apologized for not believing him, promising, "Had I known, Your Grace, I would never have been so foolish."

Somerset easily forgave her, being in a supremely magnanimous mood, stepping closer and taking her hands. Firm fingers pulled her to him as he asked, "Is that why you came? To say you are sorry for running away on Holy Innocents' Day?"

He was making her desertion sound like a prank, giving her a chance to play the silly girl, coming back to the winning side. She shook her head saying, "No, Your Grace. I came to plead for Earl Salisbury's life."

Somerset looked distinctly disappointed, saying, "I had hoped you came here for me, not Salisbury. To compliment my great victory."

"My lord has won a most magnificent victory," she gave Somerset that, though he had to break a Christmas truce to do it. "Please, do not stain your triumph by making war on helpless prisoners."

"I do not intend to stain my victory," Somerset replied, "but to cap it." Saying that, he leaned forward and kissed her—not one of

those polite English hello and good-bye kisses they usually ex-
changed, but a forceful French kiss, that she had to return for Salisbury's sake.

Sensing acquiescence, Somerset tightened his grip, putting one
hand at the small of her back and the other at the base of her spine,
pressing breasts and groins together. Stirring a strange impersonal
desire inside Robyn—in spite of everything that had happened, or
perhaps because of it. She did not want Somerset the way she wanted
Edward, but half the young women in the north country were
swooning to be where she stood, and Lady Robyn was not immune.
Somerset had his qualities, brisk and brutal though they were; and
after being through what she had, any woman not thrilled to be held
by a stalwart young nobleman who would gladly see her safe and
happy was dead from the waist down. Nonetheless, she broke the
kiss, regaining her mouth for a moment, saying, "Please, Your Grace,
I came to plead for a man's life."

"Then my lady has found the fairest way?" Somerset told her, not
dragging her to the bed, but not letting go of her either. The good
duke had what he wanted in his arms, and he was not about to give
her up. His hand on her spine slid down toward her rear, while his
other arm came up to her shoulder, fingers playing with the low
neckline, feeling for flesh in the folds of the gown. "Duke Holland's
bastard brother claims you have been getting what you want from
Edward of March." Somerset knew just who to threaten her with.
"By witchcraft, or so Master FitzHolland vows. Why not use that
same witchcraft on me?"

Especially when these noble lords made such tempting targets.
Here was yet another royal duke begging to be bewitched in bed—
no wonder Duchess Wydville went straight from penniless foreigner
to duchess of Bedford, confidante to the queen. Ignoring the fingers
tracing her neckline, she told him, "All I beg for from Your Grace
is mercy."

"That is all?" Somerset asked, smiling wickedly. How evil was he
willing to be? He had her in his castle bedroom, surrounded by his
soldiers, with a man's life to hold over her. "You will not use your
spellcraft, even to save a man's life?"

"Please do not ask me to," she begged. It was one thing to lie in
her borrowed bed last night thinking of the royal time she could

show this regal duke—but quite another to actually do it. "It would bring shame to both of us."

"Admirable restraint," Somerset told her, still not letting go, "especially for a lady with your reputation. Though one could say there is a higher virtue in giving up your honor, for the life of another."

"And even greater virtue in not making the demand," she reminded him. "There must be something else I could do for you."

Somerset thought for a long moment, like there was nothing to compare to her, then suggested slyly, "There is always silver."

"Silver?" She had given her last bits of silver to that family that fed her. The only silver she had left was the thread in her gown and Edward's ring in a hidden pocket.

"My father's murder left me with little," Somerset explained, "and fighting a war is amazingly expensive, even for the winners. This victorious army clamors to be paid for its valor, while eating like heroes in the meantime. For suitable ransom, I will gladly set Earl Salisbury free."

"Really?" she could barely believe it was so easy. Easy for her, at least—excessive charity having left her with nothing to contribute— but the Nevilles certainly had the resources to ransom their clan leader.

"Yes," Somerset laughed at her surprise, "Salisbury may buy his freedom—but he must beg."

"Beg?" She looked at him quizzically.

"On his noble knees." Somerset clearly relished the image of the senior Neville groveling for his life. "Though, I would rather have you."

Some compliment, since she had never considered herself worth an earl's ransom—but Somerset did. He kissed her again, and this time Robyn's response was happy and heartfelt, overjoyed that Salisbury did not have to die. She could kiss Duke Somerset back with a clean heart, knowing he had come through for her when she needed him.

Big mistake. This time Somerset did drag her to the bed, emboldened by her response. Robyn found herself flat on her back, with Somerset on top of her, pressing her into the coverlet and kissing her harder than ever. Despite his strength and enthusiasm, she managed to break off the kiss, saying, "Please, please, no."

Somerset smiled down on her, asking, "Why not, silly girl? Salisbury is safe; this would just be between you and me."

Before she could answer, he kissed her again, pinning both of her arms above her head so he could have a hand free. Only able to shake her head, she fought off Somerset's kiss. No matter how grateful she felt for Salisbury's life and freedom, she could not make love with the man who trapped and killed Edward's father—not on the day after the battle. "Please, my lord," she insisted. "You must let me go."

"Must I?" Somerset cocked an eyebrow, still hardly believing she was saying no. What sane woman would not submit to her rich, handsome conqueror? His free hand had gotten down inside her gown, only to be stopped by the novelty of spandex panties. For a wordless moment they stared at each other—the young victorious royal duke and the woman who would not give him what he wanted. Fingers solved the problem of spandex, silently exploring the flesh beneath, tips brushing her pubic hairs. When he got no response, Somerset sighed heavily, saying, "I suppose I must. I shall not stoop to robbing what Edward of March gets freely."

Releasing her arms, he stood and let her get up. Medieval men were not saints in the least, and in the flush of victory, they would murder the helpless or rape the serving women, counting it a day well done. Robyn had read books of "courtly love" that cheerfully advised the aspiring knight that if a "low" woman caught his eye, he should "flatter and make much of her" to get her alone, then do what he willed. But Lady Robyn had a title to protect her, given to her by Mad King Henry. Attacking lordless ladies was a horrific breach of chivalry, which young Duke Somerset held far above the law. Laws were for peasants and peddlers, while nobles were judged by their deeds, settling their differences with a sword. Chivalry kept that lordly force from being used against the nobility itself—though Somerset had her in his castle, ringed by his troops, with all of north England in his grasp. It was just too much of a comedown to force her.

King Henry's constant attempts to protect Lady Robyn's virtue had paid off. Somerset would not tarnish his victory by immediately assaulting a lady under his "protection," no matter how richly she might deserve it. Straightening her green wrinkled gown, Robyn curtsied, then backed out of the room—another good-bye kiss being out of the question.

She went straight to Salisbury's room in the keep, telling the guards she had a vital message from Duke Somerset, and the guards were in too good a mood to question a pretty face, bowing m'lady through. Robyn found the old earl looking shaken and bewildered, a startling change from the confident noble who dismissed her fears at Sandal a couple of days before. Hearing Somerset's offer gave Salisbury new hope, and he called her, "An angel out of heaven, my Lady Stafford, a most beautiful and welcome angel."

Certainly a step up from witch and whore. She urged Salisbury to make the most of Somerset's offer, which would free both of them to head south. "Edward is in Shrewsbury," she told him, "just two days away, if we but hurry."

Earl Salisbury needed little urging, and when word came that Duke Somerset would see him, the earl hurried off to humble himself and offer up whatever ransom His Grace deemed fitting. Robyn waited in Salisbury's quarters, which were nicer and better stocked than her little room, preparing for the trip, washing, boiling water, scavenging blankets, filling a bread bag, and getting a good breakfast of lentils, toast, tea, and herring. As she worked, she missed having Deirdre to help, hoping her maid was safe, and with Matt. Witches Night was less than three days away—but by then she could just as easily be with Edward in Shrewsbury. If she were, Robyn vowed to dedicate the night to searching for Deirdre, assuming Matt and Deirdre had not already made it to safety.

Salisbury returned in better spirits, having Somerset's promise that he could go free, so long as he used his freedom to raise his ransom, and gave his parole not to fight again. "I am glad to be done with fighting," Salisbury confessed. "Do you know my son Thomas was killed?"

She said she hadn't heard it, and she was sorry. Like Somerset, Sir Thomas Neville was always spoiling for a fight; now the two of them had gotten their battle—and Duke Somerset had won.

"And Lord Harington, my son-in-law, is slain too. I did not see them die," Salisbury explained sadly, "but Trollope's men told me after they took me. I asked Somerset if it was true, offering ransom—hoping Trollope's knaves had lied to torment me. But Somerset said it was so, and sounded genuinely sorry."

Most likely missing the added ransom, Robyn thought, but she did not say so. Somerset must be desperate for money, given Queen Margaret's wretched record when it came to paying the men who fought and died for her. "What about Duke Richard?" she asked, knowing Edward would want to hear how his father had died, and she might easily have the sad task of telling him.

Salisbury shook his head, saying, "Duke Richard died well, fighting hard and refusing to submit or beg quarter, though the ground and numbers were against him." That, Robyn could easily believe—if Duke Richard had fought half as well as he had died, none of them would be in this fix. York was the one who threw away the advantage of a splendidly defended castle and ready reinforcements to fight in the open and outnumbered.

"Finally they pulled him from his mount and killed him. What happened afterwards is the greater tragedy," Somerset added solemnly. "Trollope's men say they propped his body atop a molehill, taunting it, putting a paper crown on him, and calling him King Richard. When they were done defaming him, they cut off his head, promising to put it on a spike atop Micklegate Bar, so everyone entering York can see it."

Robyn shuddered to think how Edward would feel when he heard. After Northampton, Edward and Warwick buried the enemy dead with all honors, before King Henry and his bishops—but Somerset's people had long ago given up on winning respect, meaning to rule through fear in the name of a mad king.

All the more reason to get packing and go, so she urged Salisbury to take swift advantage of Somerset's offer before anything blew the deal. Horses awaited them at the bailey gates just as Somerset promised, the same gates she escaped through on Holy Innocents' Day, only this time Lily was not there to greet her. Instead she got a bay gelding with black points, one of those slow, patient Yorkshire packhorses, and a big brick-red Brabant stallion was waiting for the earl. Three strong, compact Dales ponies were there to carry their packs. Salisbury was expecting an escort from Somerset, saying to her as he helped her mount, "Here they are coming now."

Looking around in the saddle, she saw a crowd of bowmen approaching, wearing steel sallets, quilted metal-studded jackets, and King Henry's crowned white swan badge. At their head was Gilbert FitzHolland, wearing a red-and-black brigandine and holding a longhafted ax in his right hand. Robyn stiffened with fear, clutching the bar in front of her saddle. Earl Salisbury looked surprised, saying, "Have you come for us?"

"Yes, indeed, Your Grace," FitzHolland replied, signaling to the bowmen, who grabbed Salisbury despite his protests. The earl's aged face went white with shock as men pinned his noble arms behind him, ignoring his protests. Then FitzHolland turned to her, saying, "Greetings, Lady Stafford. You will come with us, too."

Armed men took her reins and led her toward the bailey gate. She glanced back at Salisbury, who was being dragged along behind her horse. Shock had worn off, replaced by abject fear on his face. Armored bowmen marched them straight out the castle gate, by which time Salisbury was loudly demanding to see Duke Somerset, saying, "His Grace has given me safe passage, and swears I will not be harmed. Duke Somerset will be wroth if he hears I am mistreated."

FitzHolland, the former king's sergeant-at-law, nodded thoughtfully, ax in hand, saying, "I will see your demands are conveyed to His Grace."

Outside the castle gate an even larger mob was waiting, soldiers, camp followers, gentlefolk, and interested locals, who jeered the captive Neville. Robyn recognized Elizabeth Grey, née Wydville, waiting on horseback with her husband, Sir John Grey of Groby. As bowmen forced the protesting Earl Salisbury down onto his knees, the blond stately Wydville daughter urged her horse forward, a dapple gray Arab mare with a high black tail. Reining in beside Robyn, Lady Elizabeth leaned forward and asked significantly, "Do you wish our protection?"

"Protection?" Robyn stared at the cool blond witch, hardly believing what was happening. Looking about for someone else to appeal to, the only face she recognized was Black Dick Nixon, smiling at her from among Sir Grey's retainers, clearly glad to see her again, but unlikely to sympathize with some southern earl. She turned back to Lady Elizabeth, saying, "We already have Duke Somerset's safe conduct."

Lady Elizabeth gave her that thin, knowing Wydville smile. "In but a moment you will see what that safe conduct is worth. Unless perchance you sealed it in bed?"

Robyn said nothing, sitting on someone else's horse, with little besides Edward's ring in her pocket. Duke Somerset had made what he wanted plain, and she had not given in to him—leaving her with scant grounds to complain. Her free pass south was worth what it cost her.

"I thought not." Lady Elizabeth's thin smile widened; she wore her father's colors, a white gown decorated with big bold red Wydville squares, with the pattern repeated on her headdress. "Does Lady Diana desire our protection?"

Hearing herself called by her coven name, Robyn remembered all that was at stake. Besides being a duke's bastard and former prosecutor, FitzHolland was a witch hunter—which made her and the Wydvilles allies of sorts, for the moment, anyway. In theory, at least. Besides, better a woman than FitzHolland. "Yes." She nodded. "I would like your protection."

"Good." Lady Elizabeth straightened in her saddle, saying to her husband, "She accepts our protection."

Sir John Grey passed the message on to FitzHolland, who did not seem at all perturbed, merely saying, "First she must give me the ring."

Lady Elizabeth turned back to her, saying, "You must give him the ring."

"What ring?" Robyn was honestly surprised by the request, having forgotten all about the ring in her hidden pocket.

"The silver one with the white rose on it," FitzHolland replied promptly, as if the ex-sergeant-at-law could see right into her pocket.

"Give it to him," Sir Grey advised, "otherwise we cannot help you. Then he shall have both you and the ring."

Some choice. FitzHolland had the ring either way, but she could at least stay out of his hands. Robyn felt far better taking her chances with Lady Elizabeth, since the worst the Wydvilles would do was kill her. Reaching into her hidden pocket, she produced her betrothal ring and handed it to FitzHolland. He took it with his left hand, still holding the ax in his right, saying, "Many thanks, Lady Stafford. When I have finished here, there will be time for you."

Sir Grey of Groby reached over and pulled on her reins, guiding the bay packhorse away from the gate. Twisting in her saddle, she tried to see what was happening behind her. FitzHolland strolled, ax in hand, over to where Earl Salisbury waited on his knees; then the crowd closed around them, cutting off her view. "Someone must warn Duke Somerset," she insisted. "Earl Salisbury has his safe conduct."

"Attend to your mount," Lady Elizabeth told her tartly. "And be thankful you are not with him." Looking back, Robyn saw the ax rise over the heads of the crowd. She quickly looked away, but she still heard the crowd cheer the blow.

Horrified, she heard a second cheer, louder than the first—it takes some experience to do it in one. All Robyn could say was, "He had a safe conduct."

Duchess Wydville's daughter shrugged, saying, "Better by far than burning," reminding Robyn of the fate FitzHolland had in mind for her—both of them, actually, since serene blond Elizabeth was as much a witch as she, maybe more. Lady Elizabeth Grey had led her and Beth Lambert to Hecate's ironstone altar, then danced naked at their initiation. The daughter of the witch-duchess reminded her, "Mind what Joan of Arc said, 'Better seven beheadings than a single burning.' "

Robyn had no reply to that—still barely believing Salisbury was dead. Along with Rutland. And York. And Thomas Neville. She desperately hoped Deirdre and Matt were alive. She had not seen them since they went crashing into the woods south of Wakefield yesterday morning, which now seemed like centuries ago. Lady Robyn did not wake from her sad daze until they were at Wentbridge, where folks cheered her and brought out their sick children. Some were just starved; others had hurts she could not cure, but each got attention and a parting kiss. When she had done what good she could, she asked Duchess Wydville's daughter, "Where are we going?"

Lady Elizabeth laughed lightly. "Does it very much matter?"

Until now, Robyn had been so shaken, she had not even thought to ask, but seeing these people brought her back to hard reality. "Yes, it does."

"Conisbrough," Lady Elizabeth Grey replied primly, riding fashionably sidesaddle.

Conisbrough was an especially grim keep that she had seen on the way north, not far from Tickhill. She asked, "What is at Conisbrough?"

Again the thin mysterious smile, beneath sly heavy-lidded eyes. "You shall see."

She probably would, though Robyn doubted she would like it. As they continued south past the swollen Skell and Robin Hood's Well, more people came out to cheer their lady—not asking for cures or handouts, but coming to show support, seeming to know that things were not right. As hundreds lined the roads, Robyn realized that had she asked, they probably would have come to her rescue, since this was Robin Hood country, and each cottage had its bow. Not wanting to see more killing, she waved to them instead, and men doffed their hats to stand bareheaded in the snow as she passed. Behind her, cheers lapsed into sullen silence as her tenants watched southerners lead their Lady Pomfret away—an old story in Yorkshire, since whatever the north had worth taking always ending up going south.

Leaving her Honour of Pontefract behind, they struck out over rolling country dotted with bare trees, each mile bringing Edward and Shrewsbury that much closer. Wonderful. It was only current company that worried her. Going south ahead of the main army, Sir John Grey had his own mounted retainers, plus some Percy and Roos riders. Black Dick Nixon smiled at her whenever he got the chance, prompting Lady Elizabeth to ask, "Do you know that Percy horseman?"

"I saw him in sanctuary in London," Robyn admitted, "at the church of Saint Martin-le-Grand."

Lady Elizabeth studied the brigand smugly, saying, "He seems to have eyes for you."

"Mayhap it is you he is looking at," Robyn suggested. Elizabeth Grey was an eyeful, with her silver-gold Wydville hair, and roses-and-cream complexion, well set off by her white and crimson gown and headdress.

Lady Elizabeth laughed lightly, saying, "But I am a married woman, remember?" As if that mattered to a brigand like Black Dick Nixon, weaned on milk from his neighbor's cows. Then she asked, "Who gave you that beautiful silver ring—the one with the white rose?"

"A friend," she replied, not liking to think that FitzHolland had Edward's ring, wondering what use a witch hunter would make of it. One more thing she must warn Edward about. In two days it would be Witches Night.

"Was that friend Earl Edward of March?" Lady Elizabeth asked coyly, knowing full well it was.

"Mayhap," she replied, not wanting to fall into obvious lies. She was immensely grateful to Lady Elizabeth for saving her from FitzHolland, but that did not make her trust the Wydvilles in the least—since they were the ones who set Sir John Fogge on her in the first place, getting her accused of heresy and treason.

"What is young Edward of March like?" Lady Elizabeth asked softly, showing serious interest this time; the blond witch might tease her about Black Dick Nixon, but a lot of women wanted to hear tales about Edward.

"Like a knight-errant," Robyn replied, happy to sing Edward's praises to this bothersome blond witch, "brave, bold, and gallant, forgiving to his enemies, and a gentle protector of women." Qualities she hoped the Wydvilles would emulate.

Lady Elizabeth looked slyly over at her, adding, "And now he is duke of York." Not offically, perhaps, but King Henry would soon make it so, since Edward was now the male head of the House of York. "Is he as stalwart a knight at night?"

"You are a married woman, remember?" Robyn replied tartly.

Lady Elizabeth laughed again. "Someday, my dear, you may be married yourself—if you are so lucky. When that happens, you will find you are still a woman." Robyn certainly hoped so. Lady Elizabeth had been married six years or more, and had two small boys, exactly the time in life when a lot of wives started looking around. Too bad divorce was so difficult these days. Lady Elizabeth had only adultery to look forward to, or widowhood.

Conisbrough looked as grim as she remembered, and incredibly old, its towered curtain wall standing atop a built-up mound and enclosing a grim gray buttressed keep, ninety feet tall with walls fifteen feet thick, looking down on fields and woods below. Dismounting in the bailey, Robyn followed Lady Elizabeth up a long flight of steps between the keep's south buttresses to a second-floor entrance, level with the wall-walk. Ushered up a curved staircase, she found herself in the lord's chamber, with a private latrine, fireplace, and washbasin, all built into the thick stone wall. Cold, dank, and utterly cheerless. Lady Elizabeth and her husband got the bedroom above, sandwiching her between them and the guards below. This is where she would spend the last night of 1460. Totally fitting.

Wednesday, 31 December 1460, Conisbrough, Yorkshire

Good-bye to 1460, a year I never expected to say hello to, but I now know all too well. One hell of a year, full of ghastly surprises, like war, witch hunters, and thrush-tongue pie. Thought at least it would go in peace, but 1460 had one last surprise left.

Alas, 1461 looks like more of the same. Bitter cold in this old stone keep. And what is this trek south about? Sparring with Lady Elizabeth was entertaining, but gave no hint of what to expect. Where are we headed? And why? So far, no one will say. If this was yet another lame attempt to recruit me to the dark side, the Wydvilles get an A for effort, or effrontery. Either way, I must play along. For the moment, at least.

According to my watch, it is 12:00:01. Happy New Year. I wish I had Edward to kiss. Two more days until Witches Night.

New Year's Day dawned cold and clear, with the smell of snow in the air. And they set out, still headed south, skirting the west edge of Sherwood, following the border between Derbyshire and Nottinghamshire, past a long string of small country villages with funny names like Bolsover and Long Duckmanton. To the east lay Sherwood, and to the west wooded hills rose up the high moor and peak country, affording plenty of hiding places if she decided to bolt; but every mile brought her closer to Edward in Shrewsbury, lightening her heart. She could hardly have made such good time if she were free and on her own. Despite dire expectations, 1461 looked better and better all the time—an excellent beginning, anyway, though she was the only one who noticed. To everyone else, today was merely the first of January, since their New Year's did not come until Easter.

And tomorrow would be Witches Night, the first one of the new year. Perfect for finding Edward. She said a prayer to Diana, who watched over divides, under her Christian name of Mary, the virgin huntress of the greenwood who searched for lost souls.

Where the lower reaches of Sherwood and the Peak country came together, they came on Codnor Castle, a Grey stronghold covering the southern end of the gap between forest and peak. They were greeted at the gate by Lord Henry Grey of Codnor, who wore the black ostrich feather badge of the Prince of Wales, as well as his own livery. Lord Codnor had clearly been expecting them, and he happily gave them a tour of his keep and crude laboratory. His lordship was an amateur alchemist, striving to change lead into gold. "Though so far I have been barely able to make brass," Codnor confessed.

But not for lack of trying. He showed off his furnaces, stills, and chemicals, vials marked with Arabic terms, which Lord Codnor was shocked to find Robyn could easily translate, words like *alkali* and *naphtha* and *alcohol*. She even gave offhand descriptions of their properties and possible uses. Amazed and pleased to find a woman so familiar with alchemy, Lord Codnor told her, "Most females think alchemists are foul creatures, smelling like goats from their elixirs, or frauds who hide gold in their wands and sleeves, then make it miraculously appear."

Lady Robyn admitted she had heard as much, and Lord Condor hastened to correct her, saying, "Actually, alchemy is like a virgin whore, having many lovers, but giving herself to none of them, turning wise men into fools, rich men into paupers, and philosophers into talkative simpletons who know nothing, but profess to know all."

Robyn could well believe it, looking over his chem-lab-cum-moonshine-cookery, crammed with sealed beakers and bins of powders. Such men's magic was legally protected, and Lord Codnor showed her a permit for his work given him by the witch-hating King Henry, issued with the pious hope that Codnor's work would "cure disease, lengthen men's lives, heal wounds, and find antidotes to poisons." Only at the end of the document did His Highness add that Codnor's work might also enrich the kingdom by "turning base metals into gold." King Henry had small use for gold, except to give it away.

As Codnor happily showed her about, she slipped one of the small stoppered flasks marked AQUA VITAE into a secret pocket, never knowing when "water of life" would come in handy. She asked Lord Codnor if by chance he had any coffee.

"Koffey?" His lordship looked puzzled but intrigued.

She tried the Latin term. "*Coffea arabica.*"

Excited to have someone who spoke his language, Lord Codnor showed her a bin of green beans marked, QAHWE, saying, "I tried boiling some of these and drinking the water like I was told, but all I got was a most bitter brew."

She laughed. "You have to roast and grind them first."

"Roast and grind?" Lord Codnor looked around for ink and parchment to start writing this down.

"Yes," she explained, "roast the beans until they are dark brown, being careful not to burn them. Then grind them into a fine powder, add boiling water to the powder, filter out the wet grounds, and presto change-o, you have got coffee."

Lord Codnor went straight to work, and soon the warm rich aroma of roasting coffee filled the keep. And when he was done, he rewarded her with a bag of fresh ground coffee to go with her stolen "water of life." 1461 was looking better and better all the time. Teach Lord Codnor how to steam milk, and they could all have breakfast lattés.

But all her New Year's cheer came crashing down that night at suppertime when Lord Codnor invited her to sit with him at the high table before a big meal of spiced boar's meat, with the beast's glaring tusked head for a centerpiece. Sitting at the head of the table, with her daughter and son-in-law, was Duchess Wydville, wearing a gold gown and tiara, fresh from spending Christmas in Scotland with Queen Margaret and Queen Mary.

Seeing Her Grace happily presiding over the feast made Robyn realize what this trip south was about. She had been brought here to this magical castle to be a pawn in the Wydville's game, most likely to trap or harm Edward, who was now titular head of the House of York. Trying to reach out to Edward tomorrow night would be hopeless with Duchess Wydville here. Lady Elizabeth she could have dodged or dealt with, but not Mom. Any contact with Edward was a danger to both him and her, so long as Duchess Wydville was here.

Despite repeated Wydville attempts to cheer her, Robyn could only pick at her minced boar meat. Then she retired to her room, which had a door barred on the outside—but at least it was hers for the moment.

There she prayed to Diana, whose day this was, the goddess of birth and death, of beginnings and endings. As New Year's Day drew to a close, she begged Diana to somehow, some way send her aid and guidance—for she feared to face the Wydvilles alone. She had been pinning all her hopes on contacting Edward tomorrow. Now she saw she had to escape first. Shrewsbury was just sixty-odd miles to the east, a long day's ride if she could get past that locked door.

As she finished up her prayers, she heard the bar on the door scrape back. She was about to have a midnight visitor. Would it be Duchess Wydville come to gloat? Or Lady Elizabeth trying to talk some sweet sense to her? Or mayhap Lord Codnor, coming to share some late-night alchemy tips with his pretty prisoner? She actually hoped it was him. Lord Grey of Codnor could be her best bet, and the Wydville's weak link. Being a man, he was not in on all their witchy secrets, and he was clearly smitten with her. If she could somehow parlay that into a free pass out of his castle, she stood a decent chance of getting to Edward.

She heard a knock on the door. Making herself as presentable as she could, she asked through the door who was there. No answer. Which most likely meant it was a man with something to hide. Better that than Duchess Wydville. She lifted the inside latch and peered though the crack.

By the light of an oil lamp, she saw Black Dick Nixon staring back at her through the crack. His bearded felon's face broke into a big gap-toothed grin. "Ah, m'lady Stafford, I was hoping to see you here. And wondering if you would maybe like to take a midnight ride with me?"

11

⊹⟾ Sherwood ⟸⊹

Like any competent stock thief, Nixon had it all planned out; stable hands lay in a drunken stupor, giving them their pick of the horses. She chose the bay gelding she came in on, a strong patient animal, easy to handle and already used to her. Even when running away, it was nice to have something familiar beneath her. Any doubts about going were dismissed by the horse Black Dick Nixon brought out—a big red-roan Brabant stallion with black points. Thinking it a sin to leave Wydville employ on the same horse he entered on, Nixon was stealing a mount fit for a count, that had, in fact, briefly belonged to an earl. Robyn recognized the strong lines and the rich brick coat. This was the horse that had been readied for Salisbury, but which he never mounted. And now the stallion was here in the Codnor Castle stables, wearing Duke Holland's colors. Holland's lions and fleurs-de-lis were also on the bridle hanging by the stall.

Someone in Duke Holland's service had left Pontefract shortly after she did, riding the dead earl's horse, and probably carrying something. Maybe a message, but most likely a ring, her silver ring with the white rose. She whispered to Nixon, "Whose horse are you stealing?"

Nixon smiled as he put his own saddle on the stallion's thick red back, saying, "I believe he carried Duke Holland's bastard brother here, but yew might as well say he belonged to the Earl of Salisbury."

So FitzHolland himself had brought the ring to Duchess Wydville—one more reason to be gone as quick as she could. Robyn had wondered why FitzHolland was so set on having the ring, thinking he was just being cruel, or hoped to use it as evidence against her. Well, now she knew why. Witch hunter and witch-priestess had struck some unholy bargain, and Lady Elizabeth Grey and Gilbert FitzHolland had played good cop, bad cop with her at Pontefract, proving Medievals knew something of modern police methods, after all. Lady Elizabeth offered her Wydville "protection" to get her co-operation, while FitzHolland flourished his headman's ax and seized her ring, then took it to the Wydvilles.

If Duchess Wydville meant to draw Edward to this magic castle on Witches Night, the witch-priestess would want the ring. And her. That playacting at Pontefract separated her from the ring and brought her here voluntarily, to where Edward was within reach—before he could even know of his father's defeat. If they could seize or kill Edward, the male head of the House of York would be eleven-year-old George. And only Warwick would be left to oppose the queen.

Robyn shuddered to think what FitzHolland would be getting in return. And she had thought the worst the Wydvilles would do was kill her. How horribly naive. Nothing could be done about the ring—which might already be on its way to Edward—but she could get herself well away from Codnor. All the way to Shrewsbury, if she was so lucky.

Stepping over the sleeping stable hands, they guided their stolen horses to the stable gate, a small bailey postern covered by a short stretch of inner wall. The wooden gate was locked, but Nixon had the key, and the hinges were freshly greased, so it swung open without a squeak. Guided by a big bright moon filtering through the clouds, they crept silently away from the castle, leading their pilfered steeds over shining patches of snow. No one seemed to notice their stealthy departure, castles being built to keep enemies out, not to lock visitors in.

Once safely away, they stopped to confer by a small stream running down toward the Erewash. So far neither had said where they were going. Presumably Black Dick Nixon had personal reasons for sneaking out of Codnor in the dead of night, but he was no more eager to share them with her than she was anxious to tell Nixon her secrets. Plus Robyn assumed that whatever Nixon told her would most likely be a lie, so why trade truths about herself for some poorly spun tale? But now they must strike some bargain or go their private ways. "I am headed west," she told the bandit, leaving no doubt about *her* direction. "Come with me, and I will see you well rewarded."

"West to where?" asked the crafty thief, alert for anything that might be to his advantage.

"To the Welsh Marches." Nixon did not need to know more than that.

"So m'lady misses her young earl o' March?" He shook his head in mock sympathy, then asked, "How well rewarded?"

She was penniless at the moment, but Edward would pay amply for her safe return. "More silver than you could ever imagine."

Black Dick Nixon grinned in the moonlight, "I am a man of boundless imagination."

She could well believe it. "Then imagine what you could do with a hundred silver marks." Most English families never saw that much in a year.

"Make it pounds, and I will gladly show m'lady the way to Shrewsbury."

"Done." The bandit was asking a knight's ransom, but she did not doubt Edward would pay it. Love is like that. Edward would do almost anything to get her back—which was what the Wydvilles were counting on. Her, too.

"Then let us away, m'lady." Nixon courteously helped her mount, without even stealing a feel, showing there was some honor among horse thieves. "West of here there is an old Roman road, Ryknild

Street, that will take us to the road running west out of Derby."

Swinging south to avoid Ripley, they struck the Roman road and headed south, making good progress until the stone road started to break up beneath them, turning into a rutted trail. Nixon said it was time to turn west for Shrewsbury, so they dismounted and set out across country, walking ahead of the horses. By now the bright moon had gone behind clouds, and she fished a flashlight out of her hand-sewn leather purse, the only light she had left. When she flicked it on, Nixon looked shocked. "Gwad, m'lady, what sort of wand is that?"

"A good sort," she assured him. "It will show us where we are going."

Nixon shook his head soberly. "M'lady is really and truly a witch."

"But a white one," she protested, "who means no harm to any-one."

"So I hope." Nixon's sly smile returned, and they went back to thrashing through dark thickets and stumbling across icy streams. Despite her flashlight, Robyn was soon thoroughly lost and turned about in the cavernous darkness. Every so often Nixon would ask her to turn off the beam, saying it was distracting him. Then he would stand and let his eyes adjust to cloudy moonlight before set-ting out again. Then the beam itself began to fade as the batteries ran low, and all her spare batteries were in Lily's saddlebags, wherever Lily was.

Numbed from the cold and thoroughly exhausted, Robyn was ready to give up and wait for first light when they stumbled on a fresh stretch of Roman road running right across their path. "Here she is," Nixon proudly announced, "and these stones will take us straight into Staffordshire, avoiding Derby and Tutbury on the Dove."

If you say so. Robyn studied the line of ancient Roman stones by the fading light of her flashlight. They disappeared straight into dark-ness in both directions. She pictured the line extending across the English landscape, stretching from here to Staffordshire. They had been headed south, so if they took the road to the left, it should lead them west towards Shrewsbury and the Marches. Thank goodness, no more thrashing about in the dark. Turning off her light, she struggled back aboard her mount, making herself as comfortable as she could, half-asleep and letting Nixon lead.

Leaning forward against the saddle bar with her cloak tight about her, she let the *clop-clop* of shod hooves on old stones lull her into and out of sleep, while black frigid miles went by, each one taking her closer to Edward. Several times Nixon led her off the road, to skirt darkened towns along the way. Dogs barked, but no one came out into the night to look for them. Slowly the sky above grew lighter, and the dark stones beneath her got clearer, though no less frozen. How much farther? Plenty, she bet. Cold, hungry, and tired, Robyn guessed she still had a full day of riding ahead. By now she should be nearing Staffordshire, the "home" she had never actually visited. Buoyed by that happy thought, she dozed off again.

False dawn finally broke overhead, only it came in the wrong place. Lifting her sleepy head she looked about and saw that dawn was coming up over the trees to her right, not straight behind her, the way it should have been. Growing up on a Montana ranch made her used to tracking the sun, and she was fifteen before she even owned a watch. What did that mean? Robyn racked her tired brain for a reason. If she were headed west, sunrise ought to be behind her in the east, or at least over her right shoulder—but she could clearly see the brightest part of the sky without even turning her head.

So she was not headed west—in fact as best her fatigued brain could figure, she was headed almost due north. She looked down at the stone road, realizing this was not the road west, this was Ryknild Street, and they were going back the way they'd come. She reined in, meaning to tell Nixon that they had made a horrid error. But as soon as she saw the gap-toothed smile on Black Dick's face, she knew there was no mistake; he had turned her around in the dark and put them on the road north, back toward Pontefract and Yorkshire. "You bastard—" She shook herself awake. "—what do you think you are doing?"

Nixon swung easily out of the saddle, saying, "I am taking you home, m'lady."

"Home?" She had thought for a moment that he must be taking her to FitzHolland, though that hardly made sense, since her nemesis must be back in Codnor, blissfully asleep. "Home to where?"

"To Tynedale, m'lady." He strolled back to where she sat, a

braided rope in hand. Before Robyn could stop him, he seized her wrists, tying them tightly together. She tried to resist, but she was terminally tired, and found Nixon far too strong. Lashing her hands to the saddle bar, he tested the knot, grunted in satisfaction, then took her reins, and remounted.

"Why are you doing this?" Robyn demanded, confused, angry, and scared. Up to a minute or so ago, everything had been going her way—now she was headed in a totally different direction, and had been for half the night. Unknowingly going north, instead of toward Edward. And now Nixon had unaccountably turned against her. "Why have you betrayed me?"

"Because I like you, m'lady." Nixon set out again, leading her mount up Ryknild Street, grinning over his shoulder at her. "I like you greatly."

Why did men think that excused any sort of mistreatment? I like you, so I'll do as I like. She twisted her hands, trying desperately to free them, but the frigid wet knots were far too tight. "You have a remarkable way of showing it."

"I am sorry about the rope, yer ladyship," Black Dick apologized sincerely. " 'Tis merely to make you come along. Honestly, there was no other way."

That was for sure. Nothing but brute force could get her headed north again. She relaxed, slumping back into the saddle, exhausted and amazed by this calamitous turn of events. "What do you mean to do with me?"

"I told you, m'lady, I am taking you to Tynedale. It is a terribly pretty place," Black Dick Nixon explained. "Home to Armstrongs, Elliots, Nixons, Turnbulls, Halls, and Hendersons. And of course, yer Kerrs and Crosers. All yer best riding families. You will like it well."

She snorted, hearing some of the most notorious names in the north country among her new neighbors. "I very much doubt that."

"Give it a chance," Nixon suggested, "the land there is lovely, and folks are warm and friendly. Not at all like southerners, who are a cold, grasping lot, always meaning to profit off you. Look how sorely they mistreated you."

"What do you mean?" She had certainly been mistreated, but no more so than now, being dragged north again because some new man had taken a shine to her. Already her fingers felt numb from the frigid ropes.

Nixon ticked off her troubles. "Duke Holland's people hate you, for no good reason that I can see—for you are a fine friendly lass, especially for a titled lady. And Somerset would not save you from them, though it was perfectly in his power, showing how little sense it takes to be a royal duke these days. And those Wydvilles you were with, what a crew! They wanted you only for what they can get out of you, and would discard Yer Ladyship as soon as it suited them—you may count on that. Bad cess to all their Frenchified good breeding." He looked merrily back at his prize, asking, "What man of feeling could stand to see someone so naturally kind and lovely being so thoroughly ill used?"

Certainly not Black Dick Nixon. Appreciating the sentiments, if not the tactics, she asked, "Why not just take me to Edward. That is where I want to go."

"Young Edward of March would only ill-use you, too," Nixon assured her. "For he is far too full of himself."

"No, no," she protested, defending her absent love. "Edward loves me very much."

"Then he is a most foolish boy," Nixon observed, "who should have come for you long before now."

Hard to argue there. Robyn lapsed into silence, listening to the cold hollow clop of her horse's hooves carrying her farther and farther away from Edward.

"My lord of March may be a good and generous gentlemen," Nixon informed her, "but all these grand nobles are too full of themselves to truly care for you. Matters of great principle and high estate are their true loves. Here is His Lordship's lady, borne away by a common brigand, a stock thief from the Tyndale, and my lord of March is much too busy to save her."

Robyn stared off into bleak empty forest, seeing her breath fog in the freezing air. Nixon had an answer for everything, making theft a necessity and kidnapping a compliment. "M'lady, it takes a thief to tell quality," the bandit explained, "to know what is truly worth risking yer neck for. And you are a lass to make even the most right-thinking felon face hanging with a grin."

Dawn broke above the trees, a bloodred smear spreading slowly along the horizon, heralding the second day of 1461, which year no longer looked near so handsome as it had on New Year's Day. Seeing another town ahead, Nixon turned off the road toward the dawn, picking his way through the frozen fields past bare copses of trees, heading for the western fringe of Sherwood, somewhere between Mansfield and Bolsover—as best Robyn could guess. Closing her eyes, she went back to sleep in the saddle.

When she awoke they were fording a stream, surrounded by tall trees. On the far side, a forest trail led deeper into the woods. Here Nixon called a halt, dismounting and cutting her hands free, helping her down, but not untying her wrists. While she sat numb and tired against a tree, he made camp, seeing to the horses, and starting a small fire using twigs, dead wood, and tinder from his saddlebag. He gave her the bottle of boiled water from her own saddlebag and untied her wrists, working the circulation back into her frozen hands. In theory she might have brained him with the bottle and gotten away—but only in theory. She simply did not have the strength and determination to take on an accomplished armed ruffian in mail and leather.

Passing a leather strap around her waist, Nixon knotted it tightly with a rope, then tied the rope to himself and to a tree, lying down by the fire and inviting her to, "Make yerself comfortable, m'lady. We should get ourselves some sleep, for we have a hard day of riding ahead, and it were better if you were well rested."

How thoughtful. For a vicious bandit and ready-handed killer, Black Dick Nixon was amazingly considerate and insightful. Just like Gilbert FitzHolland, he was criminally obsessed with her, and could not stand to see her running free, but FitzHolland's solution was to torment her and then put her to death as horribly as possible. Nixon was a simpler and more direct fellow—in London she had refused his offer to come to Tynedale and be his mate, so he had bided his time; then at the right moment he threw a rope around her, as if she were a sleek-looking mare who had caught his fancy. He had not beaten her or raped her, though that would no doubt come later if she kept refusing him. Border bandit gallantry went only so far.

When she heard him start to snore, she searched around for something to cut the rope with, but Nixon had made sure that the fire and all the edged weapons were out of her reach. The frozen knots on the wet braided rope were tight as slippery steel, and she eventually gave up digging at them with her nails. She would have days ahead to plan her getaway, and tonight was Witches Night. Curling up next to her big warm kidnapper, she went gratefully back to sleep.

He was up when she awoke, cheerfully cooking oat cakes on a small flat griddle while using his pot helm to boil water for her. "Good morrow, m'lady." Nixon brought her an oat cake and a cup of steaming water, saying, "You are even more beautiful by daylight."

She thanked him primly, keeping her heavy cloak tight about her, feeling like an absolute mess in her wet, stained riding dress and wool hose—but it was nice to hear a compliment, even from her kidnapper and rapist-to-be. Searching through her purse, Robyn found her brush and went to work on her hair, while Black Dick Nixon beamed at her like a man in love, happy to have her no matter how shabby she looked. That she did not want him was just a minor irritant, one that bothered Nixon not at all. Men are so easily pleased when they are getting what they want.

Putting away the brush, she got out one of her mocha packets, her second to last—but it represented her best chance of giving Black Dick the slip. Tearing the foil open, she poured half the contents into Nixon's cup, stirring it in with a twig, and taking a sip. Caffeine went straight to her brain, brightening up the dull winter day. Welcome to 1461. Coffee made the new year look that much better.

Nixon watched as she drank, intrigued by the aroma, asking, "What witches' brew is that?"

She smiled to hear the same question Edward had asked her on Saint Anne's Day, half a year ago. "I will show you." She got out the flask of aqua vitae she had lifted from Lord Codnor, pouring a good jolt into the cup. From the smell, it had to be over a hundred proof, triple distilled. Great. Get Nixon totally swacked, and escaping would be that much simpler. "Here—this makes it even better."

Nixon looked dubiously at the flask, asking, "Would m'lady try to poison me?"

She laughed, thinking of herself as *la belle dame sans merci*. "Probably," she told him, "but not with this. This is the water of life."

She took a sip to prove its safety and then handed him the cup. Nixon sipped suspiciously, then broke into a big bearded smile, saying, "This brew is most amazingly delicious." Even big black-visaged bandits were suckers for sweet drinks. "And it warms you wonderfully from within."

"We good witches know our stuff," she replied smugly, topping off the cup with fresh alcohol. "Here, have some more."

Nixon did so, cheerfully downing the whole cup; then he stood whistling through the gap in his teeth while she fixed him another. She handed him the steaming cup, saying, "I was not lying about the hundred-pound reward."

"I did not think you were lying, m'lady." Taking half the cup in a single gulp, he wiped his beard with the back of his hand. "If I mistrusted you in the least, I would not be swigging your potions, now, would I?"

"Then why are you doing this—" She nodded to indicate the strap around her waist. "—when you could make a hundred pounds in silver by taking me to the Marches?" Where she very much wanted to go.

He grinned at her over the cup, saying, "M'lady is worth far more than a hundred pounds."

"What about two hundred?" she asked hopefully, topping off his cup again.

"Money is not everything, m'lady," Nixon replied airily. "Gold is cold and heartless, and silver alone will never make you happy. You are the finest thing I have found in all the southland. You are pretty and generous, with a keen head on your shoulders, and all kinds of magic powers." He reached out and stroked her cheek. "Why, I could not buy yer like for a thousand pounds."

Unable to argue with that, she took his empty cup, pouring him a straight double shot of "water of life." But Black Dick Nixon did not seem to care, or even note the difference, happily cutting her free from the tree, but not from him. Giving her a boozy kiss, he helped her mount, and they started off again over frozen forest paths. Lady Robyn and the bandit headed deeper into Sherwood, she in her stained gown, Black Dick with his huge sword across his back, drunkenly singing bloodstained border ballads:

> Last night I dreamed a dreary dream,
> And I ken the day's thy ain.
> My wound is deep, I am fain to sleep,

Take thou the vanward of me,
  And hide me by the bracken bush
  Grows on yon lilye-lee . . .

Throughout the sodden serenade, she kept peering ahead past the gaunt trees, hoping someone would come along and rescue her, though Robyn had no idea who. The sheriff of Nottingham would hardly be out scouring the forest for scofflaws absconding with wayward ladies—but she could always hope. Her horse at least gave her no trouble, being Yorkshire born and bred and just as happy to be headed home.

Late in the afternoon they met a foot peddler with a great heavy pack on his back, a poor fellow who was fairly horrified to find himself facing an armed and mounted ruffian with one victim already in tow. The hapless peddler had only a knife in his belt to pit against Nixon's sword, spear, buckler, and brace of daggers, one in his belt and one in his boot. "Good day," Nixon called out, full of drunk bonhomie. "Where are you headed with that fat pack?"

"To Ripley," the frightened merchant replied, staring past Nixon at her. "To the Saturday market."

Knowing this would not be her rescuer, she smiled at the scared peddler, trying to set him at ease, totally ignoring the strap around her waist and the leash tucked into Black Dick's belt. Any appeal for aid would most likely get the poor peddler skewered. Seeing the looks passing between them, Nixon reached back and tugged on the rope, drawing her to his side, saying to the peddler, "You, too, must sometimes find your woman hard to handle."

"I do not have a woman," the man on foot admitted, trying to plead ignorance, pretending there was nothing so unusual about a lady on a leash.

"What do yew have?" asked Nixon, eyeing the peddler's pack.

"Yarn for weaving," replied the peddler warily, "also needles, scissors, and whetstones to sharpen with."

Nixon was not impressed by the sewing supplies. "Any knives?"

"None but the one in my belt, which has a broken point," admitted the peddler. "For I have naught to defend."

Black Dick Nixon shook his head at the impoverished peddler, who hauled wool yarn and women's trash through the snow for small profit—though it probably saved the poor fellow's life. Kicking his horse into motion, Nixon waved good-bye with his near-empty cup. "Here is hoping you find yerself a woman."

Setting off down the forest trial, dragging Robyn behind him, Nixon returned to his drunken serenade:

> Thou shalt not yield to lord nor loon,
>   Nor yet shalt thou to me,
> But yield thee to the bracken bush
>   Grows on yon lilye-lee.

Lady and outlaw rode deeper into Sherwood, as a light sprinkle of snow sifted down. No matter how drunk she got him, Black Dick Nixon did not seem to be dropping his guard. At least he was taking her farther and farther away from Duchess Wydville. But would mere distance be enough? Duchess Wydville had her ring, and this was Witches Night. Could the duchess use that to trick Edward, the way the witch-priestess had tricked her with that wax statue? For all she knew, Duchess Wydville could dress up Lady Elizabeth to look just like her. Somehow she had to warn Edward, which meant getting away from Nixon, since she could not imagine doing a successful ritual with this boozy bandit breathing down her neck.

Dusk brought more snow, which came down in big flat flakes, and Black Dick called a halt, declaring, "This looks to be a hellish night, and we may as well camp here."

Dismounting, she did as she was told, and helped him unpack in the shelter of some trees—all the while looking for a chance to flee. When they were done, Black Dick unwound the rope from his waist, wrapped it tightly around one of the trees, and then tied the free end to a sapling well out of her reach. Satisfied that she could not escape, Nixon told her, "Amuse yerself as best you may, m'lady. I will gather wood and see to the horses."

"Wait," she called out, producing the flask. "Have a spot more to keep you warm."

Enticed back by the liquor, Black Dick held out his cup. She poured her captor a stiff jolt of grain alcohol, then sat down in the snow, putting the stopper back on the flask. Nixon took a swig from his cup, then headed merrily off to his task, whistling between his teeth. As he did, she reached out and stealthily slid the dagger out of his right boot. Numb inside and out, Black Dick never noticed.

Saying a short prayer of thanksgiving, she gave Nixon enough time to get well away, but not enough time to notice the missing knife. Then she cut the rope tying her to the tree, picked up her purse and a pair of blankets, and slipped off into the gathering gloom. Robyn wished she had her horse, as well, but drunk or sober, Nixon was far too good a horse thief for that—he might lose sight of his "lady love" but not a strong bay gelding. Since Nixon was too big to fight, escaping on foot would have to do, so she set off running, with her cloak wrapped around her shoulders and the blankets clutched to her breast.

Snow flew in her face as she ran, bigger flakes than before, seeming to silently appear out of the darkness above. Flat, white, feathery flakes coming straight out of the cold dark air made it almost impossible to see. Soon she was blundering into trees, stumbling over exposed roots, and slipping on the slick icy ground. Searching her purse, she found the flashlight and flicked it on. Flakes of snow fell through the dim beam, shining briefly and then vanishing into blackness. At least she could see the trees before she slammed into them. Lady Robyn set out again, following the fading beam deeper into the forest, hearing nothing but the soft crunch of her footfalls.

Cold cut through the folds between her gown and cloak, where her body was not covered by the blankets, and snow wet the wool hose above her boots, stinging her calves. How utterly foolish, staggering off alone into the freezing dark, without a horse or any hope of shelter. When the flashlight went out, she would not even be able to find her way. Still she forged ahead through the falling flakes, determined to reach out to Edward and give him his warning as soon as she could.

Suddenly there was a loud commotion behind her, a crashing and bellowing coming closer. Stopping to listen, she could hear Black Dick Nixon cursing and calling out her name, his shouts combined with the thud and crash of mounted pursuit. Nixon was coming after her on Earl Salisbury's big brick-red charger, guided by the waning flashlight beam. Unable to outrun him, she flicked off the flashlight, plunging herself into total darkness. No longer able to see, she crouched down in the snow, pulling the blankets around her.

Hunkered down in the snow, Robyn could hear Nixon coming closer, no longer calling out, but casting about in the darkness, hoping to stumble over her. She held her breath as the sound of movement and breaking branches slowly caught up with her. Nixon got so close she heard his labored breathing almost on top of her. Her own heart thumped so loud she feared it might give her away.

But it did not; instead, the thrashing sounds started to fade as Nixon's noisy mounted search moved off to her right. She listened intently as the sounds vanished into the soft falling snow. She was alone.

Silence descended. She was able to breathe again. Amazing. For the first time in days Robyn was totally alone, free to do as she willed—so long as it did not include moving about. But right now what Robyn most wanted was to pray, and she poured her heart out, begging Hecate and Mary to keep Edward safe. She could not cast a circle in the snowy darkness, but this was Witches Night, in the same magical forest where she had seen Mary of Cock Lane leaving flowery footprints. That had to count for something.

She pleaded with the powers above to keep Edward safe from whatever the Wydvilles had planned. She had meant to have a proper ritual, to seek Edward out and warn him, but Black Dick Nixon had made that impossible, so this would have to do. Cold and alone, with nowhere to go, she asked nothing for herself, so long as Edward was safe. Please, Holy Mary, listen to me in this hour of peril, hear my love, and accept my sacrifice. She finished with a simple prayer to Mary, Mistress of the Greenwood, who bore her child in winter:

> White are the hilltops, cold the streams,
> Leaves are fallen, birds have fled.
> > Mary, bless me in my body,
> > Mary, bless me in my soul,
> > Mary, bless me in my life,
> > Mary, bless me in my love.

Having done her best, she sat huddled under her cloak and blankets, beneath a slowly thickening layer of snow, breathing softly. Stinging cold came through wet gaps in the fabric, and shivers shook her weary body. How long could she survive like this? Not terribly long on such a horrid night. She had no hope of starting a fire or of finding shelter in the frigid darkness. All Robyn could do was curl up and go to sleep, hoping to awake when the storm ended—though the chances of that seemed awfully slim. Starved, weak, and frozen, she had no resources to draw on. Close her eyes now, and it would likely be for good—nor would she ever even know if her sacrifice succeeded. Edward might already be in Wydville hands.

What a silly fool, striking out on her own into the depths of winter with no real plan and little hope, thinking prayer could somehow set things right. Tears rolled down her cheek, to freeze on her collar. How incredibly stupid. Had she stayed with Black Dick Nixon, she would surely be warm right now, both inside and out, lying in a lean-to beside a crackling fire, sipping aqua vitae and getting to know each other. But it was too late to take advantage of Tynedale hospitality. She had made her choice, and must suffer the consequences.

Or maybe not. She heard a huge thump of falling snow, followed by the muffled snap of branches. Nixon was coming back. Unbelievable. How had the fellow found her, blundering drunk and blind through the snowy night? Border stock thieves must have some incredible sixth sense when it came to straying quarry. Straining her ears, she heard a solid *clump-clump* in the snow coming straight toward her, followed by the heavy snort of a horse. Sitting as still as she could, Robyn waited to see if he would pass her by again, wondering why she did not just give in. That would be the smart choice. Death before dishonor was for dummies.

Clumping came to a stop, and she heard a saddle creak as the horseman dismounted. Heavy male breathing came from just above her. Shivering with cold and dread, Robyn clutched Black Dick's sharp steel dagger in her right hand, not sure what she would do with it. Why keep fighting when she was already lost? After all, it made far more sense to give it up and have a warm snuggle with the heathen bandit than try to battle it out in the snow. It was not like Nixon meant to kill her—far from it, since by his savage lights Black Dick was bent on saving her from herself, by breathing life back into her and then showing her ladyship a thumping good time.

"Found you at last, my love!" exclaimed a happy familiar voice muffled by the falling snow. Strong triumphant arms lifted her up; then beardless lips pressed against her cold, shivering mouth. Sobbing with relief, she recognized the voice and lips, fervently kissing him back—it was Edward.

12

⊶ Nine Ladies Dancing ⊷

What a difference Edward made. Moments ago, her case had been hopeless, faced with freezing to death or spending the night with Black Dick Nixon—death with dignity, or putting out for her kidnapper, never her two favorite choices. Now anything was possible. Holding tight to his big warm body while snow fell around her, Robyn whispered, "How is this possible? How did you ever find me?"

Edward laughed, holding her tighter, pulling his cloak around them both. "You must tell me. You are the witch, *vraiment*? You called to me."

"I did?" She had meant to warn him and keep him safe, not bring him here to Sherwood—if he was here. She could barely believe this really was Edward and not some extremely solid hallucination brought on by fear, fatigue, and desire. "When? How?"

"You sent me your ring," Edward explained, "showing that you needed me."

She certainly had not done that. Shaking her head, she told him, "No, I did not. I lost the ring." Actually FitzHolland had taken it from her, just before he killed Salisbury.

"Nonsense. Of course you sent it," he insisted. "How could you have lost the ring when I have it with me in my wallet? Come, you are senseless from the cold. We must warm you up."

There was no arguing with that, and she nodded weakly, resting her head against his chest while more snow piled up around their legs. Edward called Caesar over; in the snow and darkness she had mistaken the big black Friesian for Nixon's brick-red Brabant. With Edward holding her close and Caesar pressed against her back, she felt suddenly sheltered from the storm, though she still could not feel her feet. Kissing her numb lips again, Edward hoisted her up onto Caesar sidesaddle, wrapping her shivering fingers around the saddle bar.

Snow and cold hit her again, slapping her in the face and freezing her fingers to the saddle. She managed to free one hand and find the flashlight, handing it down to Edward. Her hands were too numb to work it, but by now Edward was used to such bits of modern magic, able to operate a flashlight or childproof lighter. He could even program her digital watch, delighting at how the shining numbers leaped about on command—though his newfound skill had few practical applications for a fledgling duke.

Switching on the dim light, Edward led his warhorse into the blinding snow, searching for shelter from the storm. Robyn could hardly imagine where they would find it. Snow was piling up everywhere, covering the thickets and burying any fuel they might use for a fire. And her overused flashlight batteries were fading fast; soon there would be nothing but cold and blackness. Holding tight to the saddle bar, she prayed silently to Mary, begging for guidance.

Dimming even more, the flashlight beam dwindled into a feeble glow, and Edward switched it off. For a long moment they stood shrouded in the darkness while Robyn wondered what to do next. By now Black Dick Nixon was probably in his cozy camp, dining on King Henry's deer—too bad they could not just go and evict him.

As her eyes adjusted to the darkness, she saw a glimmer of light ahead. At first she thought it was mere imagination, but as she strained her eyes, the glow grew stronger, and she called to Edward, "Do you see that light?"

"What light?" Edward asked, just a few feet in front of her, but totally invisible.

"Straight ahead." Her heart lifted, hoping it was a campfire or the open window of a warm hovel, though both seemed incredibly unlikely. Whatever it was, it offered light and maybe warmth, unless it was a hopeful hallucination. Kicking Caesar with her frozen feet, she nudged the warhorse toward the glow.

"It does not seem far off." Edward saw the light, too, leading his pitch-black charger forward through the snow.

Like a Witches Night candle flame, the glow grew and expanded, becoming a circle of light among the trees. As the circle widened, Robyn realized she could see into it, as though it were an open window partly obscured by the falling snow—but instead of looking into some forester's hovel, she saw sunlight and greenery. Passing strange, even for some Witches Night hallucination.

As they approached the circle of light, the snowfall lessened, melting in midair, turning into sleet, then becoming a light warm drizzle of rain, then vanishing completely. The snow on the ground started melting, as well revealing bright green grass beneath Caesar's black feet. Unused to such miracles, Edward slowed to a stop, awed by this emerging vision of spring. Leaning forward, she put her hand on his shoulder, saying, "Do not worry; all will be well."

"What is it?" he whispered, staring into the widening tunnel of light bordered by green boughs and snowless limbs, with a strip of blue sky showing overhead. Warm, green, earthy smells welled up from the sunlit forest floor. Running down the middle of the green space was a line of footprints, formed by bright spring wildflowers: lilacs, primroses, violets, and buttercups. This was the first time she had ever seen Edward hesitate or show the least fear at forging ahead.

She squeezed his shoulder, whispering, "Do not worry. All will be well—it is merely magic." And good magic, at that.

"It seems like a whole new world." Edward sounded unsure, not knowing if they should enter it. Until now, his experiences with magic had been simple and useful, like her miraculous watch, and her ability to understand anything that was said. Easy and convenient, but not especially world-shattering. This was something utterly unexpected, and unexplainable.

"Now you know how I felt, when first I came here." When she first entered Medieval England, she had gone straight from fall to spring, and it had not seemed nearly this inviting. "Let us go," she suggested, feeling the warmth in her face, while her rear was still freezing. "Follow the footprints."

Edward led her cautiously forward, through the shining gateway into spring and down the flowery path, leaving night and winter behind. Snow melted off their bodies, the white flakes turning to sparkling drops in Caesar's long, dark mane. Each step took them farther into bright spring day, warming the air and filling Robyn with strength and hope. Feeling returned to her frozen fingers, and she tried to flex her toes, praying they were still there. Edward luxuriated in the warm sunshine filtering down through the greenery, asking, "How can winter night become a day in spring?"

Good question, and Lady Robyn had no ready answer, aside from the obvious, "Magic." No breezy lecture on the seasonal shift in the tilt of the prime meridian could explain this little bit of spring. All

Lady Robyn could say was, "Nothing is beyond the power of Holy Mary."

"Holy Mary?" He looked up at her, puzzled but hoping to hear more. Like a lot of medievals, Edward had a very practical view of religion. He went to Mass and said his prayers, leaving everything else up to the Church. Witchcraft interested him because of its many marvelous uses—not because of any metaphysical issues spellcraft raised.

Robyn barely understood it all herself, but she explained it as best she could. Everything turned on her decision six months ago to dally on her way to the Saint Anne's Day tournament, going the long way around Saint Paul's, up Cheapside and out Newgate, instead of going straight out Ludgate to Smithfield. Something about the turn away set this all in motion, since after that everything seemed predetermined, or at least out of her hands. She saved Mary of Cock Lane because she could not stand to see an innocent girl burned alive. Then, five weeks ago, on her first trip through Sherwood, she asked Mary's guidance, and was answered by seeing the girl again, and the flowery path heading north. "Which I had to follow, or I would not have seen the devastation in the Honour of Pontefract, and I would not have known to give up my rents and revenues."

"You gave up your revenues?" Edward looked shocked, this being the first he had heard of her ridiculous generosity.

"I had to," she explained, "those people were suffering mightily."

"Just like you had to save Mary of Cock Lane?" Edward shook his head. "I spent much time getting Mad King Henry to give you those revenes, making His Highness think it was his idea."

"For which I will always be grateful." She leaned down from the saddle and kissed him long and lovingly, enjoying the feeling even more now that her lips were not numb. "Had you and Henry not granted me those revenues, I could never have given them away."

He shook his head again, this time with a smile, saying, "Sometimes you are as mad as Henry."

She smiled back, showing her dimples, "But twice as pretty, I ween."

"Ten times would be nearer the mark." Edward's expression turned serious, and he asked, "So was that poor girl we saw in Saint Martin's Holy Mary herself?"

"Mary is in all of us," she reminded him. "And not just in Christians, either. Mary is the All Mother, the Great Goddess that is not just our Mother, and God's Mother, but the virgin girl and the death crone, as well. She is Diana and Hecate, and the Venus that our distant ancestors venerated." Before coming to the Middle Ages, none of this had mattered to her, and now it was literally life and death.

"Some men would call that heresy," Edward reminded her. He might be free and easy about his own religion, but he lived in a country where it was illegal to be a witch, or a Muslim, or a Jew. If the powers that be knew about Buddhists and Hindus, they would be illegal, too.

"Some men would," she admitted, "which is why I am telling this only to you." These were, in fact, women's secrets, but love made her willing to bend the rules a little, for this man at least. And Mary must approve, since Edward had not exactly been struck blind. Blameless nuns lived and died without ever seeing such miraculous proof of Mary's power.

Edward nodded, saying, "I think I understand you, or at least I hope I do. But why Holy Mary is doing all this remains very much a mystery."

"As it is to me," she confessed. "All I really know is that we should thank her." And she did, having Edward help her out of the saddle and onto her shaky knees, where they gave thanks to Mary, kneeling side by side, their cold, wet clothes steaming in the warm sunlight. Like children happy that spring had come, they poured out their hearts in prayer.

Afterwards, Edward helped her remount, and they set out in silence, following the path of flowers, still not knowing exactly where they were going. Royal deer came daintily out to feed, and spring birds seemed to materialize out of warmth and sunlight. Robins hopped ahead on the path. Cuckoos called lewdly at them from the trees, and Robyn heard a woodpecker knocking somewhere ahead. Despite the beautiful surroundings, Robyn had difficult things to say, and she started by asking, "How did you get here?"

"Caesar brought me," Edward replied, proudly patting the stallion's strong black flank, "all the way from Shrewsbury."

She, too, stroked the black charger beneath her, trying to imagine where Lily was now—the proud property of some thieving Scot, no doubt. She wondered what the fellow made out of the contents of her saddlebag. "I mean how did you know to come to me? How ever did you find me in the middle of that snowstorm?"

"Snowstorm?" Edward looked innocently up at her. "What snowstorm does my lady mean? This day seems most passing fair."

They both laughed, giddy to be alive and warm, and together in the midst of such an unimaginably bad winter. Edward reached into the tooled-leather wallet hanging from his belt and produced the white-rose ring, saying, "You sent this to me, or at least it appeared on my bed table two days ago."

She shook her head. "I did not send it. FitzHolland took it from me at Pontefract. He must have given it to Duchess Wydville, who sent it on to you, hoping to draw you here." Which it did, though not in the way Duchess Wydville wanted.

Slipping it back on her finger, he told her, "Whoever sent it, I knew it came from you, and that you needed me. The rest was remarkably easy, more so than I ever imagined. From your midnight visit, I knew you had been at Pontefract, so I headed north as quick as I could. The only real decision came when I rode into Sherwood as it started to snow. I should have taken shelter with some forester, but instead I was drawn into the storm to look for you. Absolutely senseless, but I could not get the notion out of my head, remembering that first night when I found you on the *Fortuna*. So I started searching through the snow, giving Caesar his lead, unless I felt pulled in a particular direction. Finally I heard you calling me, not in my ears but in my heart, and I followed the calls to you."

Witchcraft, for sure, but no more miraculous than the rest of this Witches Night, which had now become a bright spring day. She reached down and took his hand, saying, "I wanted to come to you, and would have if I could. I called to you to warn you, to tell you the Wydvilles had the ring, and would use it to trick and trap you."

"And instead of warning me away, your calls brought me to you." Edward was starting to grasp that spellcraft was not an exact science, relying heavily on irony and misdirection for its best effects.

Dipping down, the green tunnel crossed a brook where the king's deer had gathered to drink. On the far side, the flowery path led into a narrow limestone gorge carved by a stream running down the center. This was where the magic stopped, because at the far end of the ravine snow was falling. Caves lined both sides of the gorge, some low down near the stream, others high up on the cliff face. Edward picked one close to the stream and big enough to shelter in. Helping her down, he went to water Caesar and gather wood for a fire.

She sat in the cave watching the magical May day fade, the shadows lengthening and turning back into night, the snow starting to come down in white swirls, filling the canyon, even blowing into the cave. As the day faded, she got out the flashlight and found its feeble light had returned. Maybe another miracle, maybe rest had recharged the batteries. She saw the cave was littered with bones, big ones, reindeer and rhino horns, even the upper half of a skull with thick brow ridges, that had to be a Neanderthal. She had hunted fossils at home in Wyoming, but never with such success. Amazing. It made her wonder if she was still in medieval England. How long had it been since rhinos and mammoths lived here? Had they somehow walked back to the Paleolithic? Hardly likely, but at this point anything was possible. Near the entrance she found the broken remains of rough stone axes and some fine leaf-shaped flint points shoved in a corner, another sign folks had lived here.

Leaning back against the rough cave wall, she tried to draw strength from all the generations that had lived here, a human home older than Stonehenge, older than Atlantis, one that made Old London town seem brand-spanking-new. She thought of thousands of children growing up in the cave, cutting their teeth on juicy mammoth bones and searching for treasures among the hyena teeth. Closing her eyes, she thanked Mary for saving her and bringing her to this shelter. And for giving her something to believe in.

Until coming to the Middle Ages, she had lived a casual life with little to care for beyond having a palatial apartment and a cool job working for creeps—while being ready to throw it all over in a moment if the right guy came along. Now, amazingly, she had the right guy, even if he was in the wrong century. And with Edward had come a connection to the cosmos, to eternal mysteries, and to people from London to Pontefract, to folks yet unborn and others long dead. Thank you, Holy Mary, for showing me the right, and for giving me the strength to change. She would have thanked Mary for bringing Edward to her, as well, but the Wydvilles had done that, the Wydvilles and her silver ring. Witchcraft has a way of coming back at you, especially when used for selfish ends.

That was the easy stuff; the worst still lay ahead. Now that she was safe and sheltered, Robyn dreaded having to tell Edward what she had seen at Wakefield. Did he know his father was dead? And his brother, too? Not to mention Salisbury and the others. If not, she had to tell him, not the sort of job she ever wanted. Hecate help her, this was going to be terribly hard, harder by far than freezing to death, which merely felt like falling asleep. She prayed to Maid Mary of Sherwood, not for herself, but for Edward, who faced such terrible tidings. And for Deirdre and Matt Davye, wherever they may be, hoping they were safe and headed south. Along with Lily.

Edward returned with firewood, bringing wine, food, and a bundle of clothes from his saddle pack. By now it was fully night outside, and snow dusted his blue-and-gold doublet, but the wood and tinder were dry. He lit a fire at the cave entrance, using her lighter, the one she left on his bed table last Witches Night, blowing heartily on the bits of tinder, then patiently feeding twigs into the fire until the bigger pieces caught. Satisfied, he sat back, grinning broadly. "Does my lady wish to eat first, or should I free you from those wet clothes? I did not bring a fresh gown, but I do have a dry jacket and undershirt."

She shivered, relishing the thought of being both warm and dry, and held by Edward. Taking her silence as consent, he pulled off her boots and drenched stockings, using a silk scarf to dry her feet, at the same time rubbing life back into them with his big warm hands, one foot at a time, first the toes, then the arch and instep, followed by her ankles and calves. When tingling feeling had returned to her legs, he started unlacing her damp bodice, slipping it off her shoulders, taking time to daub up drops of melted snow with his scarf. Stopping every so often to kiss the dry spots.

His hands on her body felt incredibly reassuring. She might be huddled in a snowbound cave, half-frozen, hounded by Wydvilles, with her handsome revenues gone and her Honour of Pontefract in enemy hands, facing a mountain of bad debt, and some serious charges if she was lucky enough to ever get back to London alive— yet Edward's strong touch literally made it all better. She did not doubt Edward would get her safely south again, if only to have her next to him in a warm feather bed. Edward would move earth and sky for that.

Helping her stand on newly steady legs, he slid off her gown, draping it by the fire to dry. Her silk shift was still wearable, though horribly stained and sweaty, so he helped her into his wool hose and livery jacket, then wrapped a dry cloak over her shoulders. Pleased to see her warm and dry, as well as wearing his colors, Edward inquired, "Now what does my lady wish to eat?" He laid out the food he had brought—bread, sausage, dried fruit, almonds, and boiled eggs. "Shall I crack you a nut or break open an egg?"

"Start with the wine," she suggested. "I have hard things to say."

Looking suddenly worried, Edward poured wine into his horn traveling cup, gently handing it to her. "Here, this will warm you from the inside."

Taking a sip, she found the wine strong, bracing, and tasting of cloves, not the fruity sweet wine of summer or the vinegary dregs served at Sandal, but a spiced and fortified claret meant to see you through a hard winter. Firelight flickered on the cave walls as the spiced wine spread through her body, giving her courage for what had to come next. Wishing she were not the one who had to say this, she asked, "Do you know your father is dead?"

He nodded grimly, all his happy exuberance gone in an instant—the first instance she ever saw Edward looking truly hurt and angry. With his royal upbringing and astounding string of successes, this was probably the first time Edward ever faced such staggering losses. The ease and swiftness with which Edward always won had made him magnanimous and forgiving, but now his voice sounded unbelievably hard and cold, making her fear for Somerset. "I know. I heard about what happened on the way north. Nottingham is ringing with the news."

"And yet you kept coming north?" She was amazed he had come for her alone, following his heart through snow and storm, even though he knew his victorious enemies would soon be headed south, hoping to complete the sweep by killing him and Warwick. Love and spellcraft were stronger than common sense, or even self-preservation.

Edward's hand came up, gently tracing the line of her cheek down to her chin, though his voice stayed hard and grim. "I have lost my father. I did not wish to lose you, too."

Tears welled up as she thought of how she tried to tell Edward's arrogant officious father of the danger—only to see the proud idiot ride stubbornly to his doom with banners waving gaily. Her vain attempt to warn Duke Richard had cost her dearly, losing her Deirdre, Matt, and Lily, along with almost everything she had not already given away. Dropping her head, she whispered miserably, "I tried so hard to warn him."

Edward pulled her chin up and kissed her on the lips, not tenderly this time, but forcefully and firmly, taking total possession of her mouth. They might be huddled together in a snowed-in cave, hunted by his foes, but he still meant to have things his way. When he was done, he told her, "Yes, I am sure you did warn him. Just as you warned him in London, and on Saint Crispin's Day, but he did not listen. He was too blinded by his desire to be king. So blinded, it killed him."

And not just him. "Your brother died, also," she whispered. "I was there when it happened, and it was horrible." Tears poured down her cheeks as she remembered how Rutland had begged for his life, and how gleeful Clifford had been, stabbing a helpless boy who had done no one any harm.

Edward put his arm around her shoulder, pulling her closer, saying, "Yes, I knew that, too. That Edmund was dead, not that you were there. In Nottingham they said Lord Clifford killed him."

"It was Clifford," she assured him tearfully—no error there. "And it was terrible."

"Enough, enough." Edward brushed aside her tears, trying to soothe the sorrow beneath. "Say no more. A time will come when all will be set right." From the way he said it, she knew Edward would not be near as forgiving next time. His foes had broken a Christmas truce to kill his father and murder his brother. Edward's proverbial forgiveness could no longer be counted on—nor did she have any good arguments for mercy—not with half his family massacred. Her only hope was that he would still spare Somerset, who was not implicated in the worst of it—so far as she knew.

"Come, you need food," Edward told her. "Wine will only keep you warm, but food will fill you." Determined to change the subject, Edward meant to put off thoughts of revenge until he could turn them into action. He peeled her a couple of eggs, to go with wine and winter sausage, which normally she would not have touched, but right now she was ravenous. Robyn shoved the sausage in her mouth, savoring the hunks of fat and onion mixed with the meat. Cracking nuts with his knife hilt, Edward cheerfully declared the cave to be a regular robber's den. "Robin Hood himself could have hidden here. We should search the far recesses for loot, or dragon bones."

Wiping tears away with her sleeve, she showed off the treasures she had found—flint tools, hyena's teeth, the broken Neanderthal skull, and a crude rhino head carved on a piece of bone. He picked up the Neanderthal skull and asked, "Who is this ogre?"

"Possibly a relative." Though she doubted it. A lot of medievals looked like Neanderthals, short, squat, and bulky, with thick dark brows and feral faces—but not Edward, with his golden-boy good looks. Black Dick Nixon made a better caveman. "They were cousins to humans, mammoth hunters who lived here during the Ice Age."

"Was that before or after the Flood?" Anything beyond Moses was bound to be murky to a medieval.

"Long before my time, anyway." She would leave reconciling bones and the Bible to others. The inerrant word of God, the King James Bible, was not even written yet, and medievals were still making do with those early Latin, Greek, and Hebrew editions. But these bones were way older than any Bible, older than paper or the pyramids, older than Greek, Hebrew, or any written word. Here people had lived, loved, and fed themselves, dreaming their dreams, raising their children, and singing their songs, praying for happy days, fine health, and a good hunt. "Neanderthals were supposed to be strong hunters who made stone tools and buried their dead, but did not grow crops or make war—probably why they died off, making way for grain-growing warriors. Turning up a skull like that shows these caves were living spaces and sacred places for tens of thousands of years."

"And wolves' dens, as well, from the look of it." He turned over a gnawed and splintered bone.

"Or hyenas." As Miss Rodeo Montana, she had worked with a wolf-recovery project, and had never seen one crunch through bone like that. Wolves had big slicing canines, while hyenas were scavengers with massive premolars designed to break up tough uneaten parts of a kill.

"Hyenas?" Edward sounded like he had never heard of them.

"Doglike African scavengers," she told him, between bites out of her second sausage, this one flavored with thyme. While she chewed, she showed him one of the huge premolars, which were big even for a hyena.

"And they ate these hairy unicorns?" He studied the carved rhino head.

"When they could." She nodded at the heaps of bones poking out of the cave mud. "Ancient England must have been a pretty exciting place."

"And you make it even more so," he told her, putting down the rhino head and kissing her again; then he packed away the remaining food and added more wood to the fire, making the flames leap higher, sizzling snowflakes in midair. Using the blankets for a bed, Edward wrapped the cloaks around both of them, hugging her to him, his large firm hands gently massaging her, bringing feeling back to her tired happy body.

Bundled up against his warm strong form, with his hands rubbing life back into her, she felt secure at last, immensely so, convinced this ancient cave could be a new beginning for both of them. Lying together amid these old bones, they had little left but each other. She had lost everything—her money, her servants, her standing in London, her horse, and her Honour of Pontefract—clearly she had nowhere to go but up. Edward was not exactly penniless, but he had lost his father and brother, so aside from Proud Cis, they were orphans. And he was starting a whole new life, as duke of York and heir apparent to the throne—should they get safely to Shrewsbury, they could start that new life together.

Desire stirred inside her, a tense longing to feel in the flesh what she had merely tasted last Witches Night. Clearly Edward wanted that, too, as she felt his body tense and move against her. His hands slid inside her jacket and down her back, pushing up her shift and feeling for her buttocks, rubbing skin against skin. She had been stiff and cold, but now she felt warm and ready for almost anything, so long as Edward took his time.

Which he did, kissing her lips, licking her ear, and nuzzling her neck, while fingers fumbled in the dark, opening her jacket front, then pushing up her shift. Without loosening the cloak and letting in the cold, his hand went round to the bare hollow of her back, drawing them closer together, pressing breasts to chest, and hips to groin, fitting her body to his. As he pulled down her wool hose, she felt him growing bigger and firmer against her, pressing hard on the soft inner curve of her thigh. Nothing was going to stop them this Witches Night.

Relaxing into Edward's grip, she opened her legs, letting his stiff erection fill the wet hollow between her thighs. Sweaty friction gave way to long, sure strokes, building momentum, prolonging her hungry ache of pleasure. His mouth found hers, and suddenly they were kissing, locked at the lips and the hips, totally joined as the tempo increased, and he drove deeper into her with each stroke.

At long last she had him, and he had her—who knew it would be in a robber's cave in Sherwood? Mary of the Greenwood might have, but certainly not Lady Robyn. Only hours ago she had given herself up for lost, expecting to be frozen by now. Or in bed with a border bandit.

Her lord had managed to shed everything but his open shirt without breaking stride, and she hugged his bare heaving chest, reveling in how heavenly he felt surging inside her. No longer worried she would be suddenly transported somewhere else, Robyn gave in to the darkness and the magic, feeling a total joyous abandon take hold, lifting her up and sending her soaring. Waves of delight rolled over her, a dark orgiastic ocean rising up to shatter on a distant shore, then slowly subsiding, leaving her spent with pleasure. Edward continued to rock rhythmically within her, kissing and nuzzling, keeping her safe and warm as she drifted off to sleep. What a magical Witches Night. Her only fear was that Edward would disappear at dawn.

That night she dreamed strong, vivid dreams, but the only one she remembered was the last. It began with Rutland, alive and upbeat, inviting her to dance with, "Nine ladies of good standing and solid repute." Despite knowing he was dead, Robyn readily agreed, glad to see Rutland again even in a dream, enjoying the boy's wry wit and ready courtesy. Rutland showed the same sly enthusiasm he had at the base of Louse Hill, when he led her to Edward. This time he took her up another grassy hill, to a plateau top sprinkled with wind-blown snow, a stretch of high heath bordered on the north and east by even higher hills. And there, just as he claimed, on this ninth day of Christmas, nine ladies danced in dawn light on the winter heath.

Most of the ladies wore Wydville red and white, frothy silver gowns with crimson trim topped by white silk headdresses trailing scarlet streamers. She recognized Duchess Wydville and her five oldest daughters, Anne, Margaret, Mary, Jacquetta, and Lady Elizabeth. With them danced Jo and Bryn, but not Joy or Deirdre, who were merely novice witches and not ladies in the least. Leading the dance was Mary of Cock Lane, still in her doeskin, Our Lady of the Hunt, the virgin huntress with the power to draw animals down from the hills. Despite her wild demeanor, Mary led her ladies through a stately dance of interlocking circles, closing in and opening up, turning one within the other, while the ladies danced in silence, welcoming in the sunrise, accompanied by their swishing skirts. Holding high their joined hands when they came together, they let them lightly fall as they turned away—just as if they were in a king's hall at a state banquet instead of on a deserted stretch of half-frozen heath. All that was missing was the music and the men.

Seeing a gap open up, Lady Robyn joined the dance, magically hearing the music in her head and somehow knowing every step, leaving Rutland to stand and watch. She spun about, paired first with beautiful Bryn, then with Lady Elizabeth, and finally with Mary herself, who looked young and wild in her tanned doeskin. As she danced with Mary, the others fell back, twirling about them in a circle, while Robyn and Mary spun together in the middle. Leaning closer and rising to her bare toes, Mary kissed her on the lips, whispering, "You did well, Lady Robyn, you did well. Here is your reward."

With that, Mary stepped back into the circle of women, and the ladies all turned instantly to stone. Robyn found herself alone on the winter heath, surrounded by a ring of low-standing stones worn down by the weight of untold ages. Rutland had also turned to stone, becoming a block of millstone grit a few yards away. Uncanny and then some, even for a Witches Night dream.

Standing there, studying the stones, she heard a horse snort and whinny. Looking up, she saw Lily trotting slowly toward her, as pale as the snow in Sherwood, head held high, white mane whipped by the wind. Lily trotted between the stones, coming right up to her and whinnying softly, happy to have found her mistress. Robyn reached up and patted her lovely dream mare's ivory neck, sorry she did not have a lump of sugar, or even a carrot. Lily had no saddle or bridle, so Robyn seized a hunk of mane and pulled herself easily onto her mare's white back, feeling whole and free, with a new day dawning around them.

Then she woke up and found herself lying alone on the cave floor wrapped in cloaks and blankets, with the fire out and Edward gone.

Cold dawn light filtered through the cave entrance onto the piles of old bones. Half a Neanderthal's skull eyed her from atop the shadowy pile. Hecate help her, how much had she lost? Lily, for sure. Rutland, as well. But not Edward, too? Nor Caesar either—that hardly seemed fair. Was she going to have to walk to Shrewsbury on her own? Dodging Black Dick Nixon, Codnor Castle, and Heaven knew what else on the way. She shuddered at the thought of trudging alone over the frozen road south, always looking over her shoulder for pursuit.

"Awake at last?" a voice asked. "You never used to sleep this late in London."

Turning back toward the entrance, she saw Edward framed against the snowy landscape, still wearing his blue-gold doublet and carrying more wood and tinder. Smiling with relief, she told him, "Good morrow, my lord. Glad to see you did not disappear."

"Disappear?" Putting down the wood, Edward knelt beside the blackened fire pit to carefully arrange the tinder. "Why should I disappear?"

No good reason that she could see. How good it was to have him here, to know that she would be warm and safe. Whatever else had happened to her while she was in the Middle Ages, she had never suffered a speck of harm while she was with Edward. "Like I disappeared from your tent on Saint Lucy's Eve," she reminded him, "after just a kiss. And then from your room in Shrewsbury, twice."

"Once in my dream, and once on Saint Stephen's Night." His face lit up at the thought of how they parted, and he set aside the tinder, reminded of unfinished tasks. He slid his hand beneath the cloak, feeling for her, and he admitted, "At first I thought you were but a welcome dream, prompted by my heart's longing."

Flattering to think she was the stuff that dreams are made from. His fingers slipped between her jacket and shift, finding flesh, and she shrieked, fending off his freezing touch, saying, "Cold, too cold. Start your fire."

Laughing, Edward withdrew his hand and went back to piling precious dry twigs about the tinder. Then he lit it with her lighter, feeding in the driest bits of wood. "Until last night," he told her, "I never really believed you."

"Believed me?" Burrowed within her cloak and blankets, she admired her hayseed earl's woodsy technique. Both of them had been brought up in the country, just five hundred years apart. "About what?"

Leaning close he blew life into the fire, his breath sending flames flaring through the wood. "About your witch's secrets."

"How else did you think I got here?" She had been the world's biggest skeptic, before magic landed her in the Middle Ages. Reaching out into the cold, she found her coffee and metal cup, saying, "Boil me some water, and I will show you how to brew my morning wake-up potion."

Satisfied with the fire, he filled her cup with water, then propped it where it would boil. Sitting back down next to her, he smiled and rubbed his hands together, saying, "You might merely have been a very good liar, or some daft Staffordshire lass with a marvelous imagination."

She had a most marvelous imagination—only it was not what got her here, not directly at least. Though none of this could ever have happened to a dull person. "Yet you still would have made me your countess?"

He sat back on his heels, smiling at her as he warmed his hands. "Daft or sober, lost lass or wicked witch, you were what I wanted." Men in love are marvelously immune to your faults. And now he could have what he wanted. Ghastly as it was, his dad's death put him at the top of the feudal heap, the Yorkist heir apparent, anointed by Parliament, holding London and King Henry—not to mention such far-off places as Dublin and Calais. Edward could have whatever he wanted, lands and riches, the kingship—even her. So long as his hands were warm.

"What about my magic watch? My electronic journal?" She might be more mad lass than wicked witch, but she had proof of her marvelous advent in the Middle Ages.

"They are indeed amazing," Edward admitted. "But they might be purely mechanical, marvelously contrived by some far-off artisans, according to foreign methods—but not really magic."

How true. Her watch might just be a fancy timepiece, destined to become a weird wristband when the battery ran out, which might happen any time. All her spare batteries were in Lily's saddlebag. Edward held up her clear plastic lighter, declaring, "Your magic fire sticks are merely flint, steel, and fluid, one can see right into them and watch them work. When the burning oil is gone, will they magically refill?"

"Only if we pray extra hard," she hazarded, smiling at his seriousness. Though Edward had never heard of the scientific method, he always cut to the core of a question, even when he could not foresee the consequences of his words.

Setting the lighter down next to her head, he told her, "When this appeared by my bed in the morning, followed a week later by the ring, I began to believe. Yet until last night, I had seen nothing unimaginable."

"Me, too," she whispered, leaning over and giving him a kiss of gratitude on the back of his hand. Last night she had gone from alone and freezing in the snow to warm happy rapture, and she owed it all to him—plus a bit to Duchess Wydville for sending him the ring.

Edward preened at the compliment, then protested, "Even love cannot turn winter into spring."

She arched an inquiring eyebrow, asking, "Wanna bet?"

Instantly guessing her meaning, he slipped under the cloak, filling the cold void behind her with his big body. Warmed by the fire, his hand reached around and slid inside her jacket, massaging her breasts through the sweaty silk shift, then sliding down farther, raising tingles as he went, until his fingers found flesh. She clamped her thighs hard together, catching his hand between her legs, and asking him, "There, my lord, is that not much warmer? Practically springlike?"

"Much warmer, my lady," he agreed, his sure fingers finding just the right spot to massage. Waves of aching pleasure spread outward through her thighs as she clamped down harder on his hand, moving her hips against his groin. Keeping one hand between her thighs, his fingers eagerly at work, Edward reached around with the other, slowly tracing the line of her lips, then turning her head toward him. Her tongue met his finger, licking the round salty tip. Then their mouths met, and they were kissing, as well, a deep luxurious kiss that promised long, loving days ahead. No more of this miles-apart nonsense.

When their lips parted, she told him, "There, if that does not bring the spring, then what else could?"

"Kissing brings the spring?" This bit of third-millennium science was new to Edward.

"Of course." She herself had never seen it before, but it was so obviously true. "Turning toward the sun may make the world warmer, but it is love that brings out birds and flowers, and the green buds of spring. What do you think the frogs sing about?"

"Frogs sing of kissing?" His fingers continued their massage, keeping her hips in motion, rubbing her rear against his stiff morning erection. One delight of being with a enthusiastic teenager was how he was always eager for her.

"Have you not heard them on spring nights?" she asked coyly. "Croaking for some girl-frog to come and turn them into a prince?" To show the principle in action, Robyn gave her prince another long, deep kiss, brimming with promise.

Edward smiled when their lips separated. "My Lady Pontefract makes her points most vividly."

Even in a robber's cave in Sherwood. Shutting her eyes, she told him, "Love brings the spring, year in and year out, millennium after millennium, awakening seeds in the earth, driving green shoots out of the ground, filling the air with nectar and birdsong. Is that not more of a miracle than one warm night at midwinter?"

Enjoying this hands-on biology lesson, Edward whispered, "You are a very wise woman, even for a witch. And a most beautiful lady, to boot."

And she gave herself to him, body and soul, which was what her lord wanted. To show his gratitude, Edward made her coffee afterward, opening her last instant mocha packet, pouring it into the boiling water, and stirring it with a twig—proudly mixing his first magic potion. He reached around her to do it, keeping her close, making her feel like she had an extra pair of brawny arms that reached out of the blankets and into the cold, tending the fire and fixing coffee, eagerly obeying her instructions. Another nifty bit of women's magic. Did other cavewomen get such service? Probably not from a belted earl—but she hoped so, since it made waking up on a snowy morning an absolute delight.

When the coffee was done, they shared it, going over the day ahead. Edward, as always, meant to move quickly, claiming, "We must go over the hills straight to Shrewsbury. I gave out that I was going hunting, not saying for what. When word of Wakefield arrives and I cannot be found, there will be panic."

Comfy as the cave had become, she agreed. Somerset's riders would already be back scouting the fringes of Sherwood, and the Wydvilles would be out searching for her and Edward, as well as Black Dick Nixon and his beautiful stolen Brabant stallion. Which meant they could not just ride down Ryknild Street straight to Derby without alerting Edward's armed enemies, who now held pretty much everything north of Nottingham. Their best bet was to take to the hills, crossing the southern fringe of the Peak country, where the people were few and hospitable. The far slopes of these hills were within an easy day's ride of Shrewsbury.

Or so Edward assured her, saddling up Caesar and helping Lady Robyn into her bedraggled riding gown, now dry from the fire. "When I heard that Father was dead, I sent my squire back to Hastings, saying I was headed for Sherwood and hoping to come back through Staffordshire—Hastings will know what that means." He could not help smirking, transparently pleased to have her back in his bed, something dear cousin Hastings had not managed. "So if we can just get across the Dove, we could be with loving friends."

Accepting his smugness as a compliment, she dressed and seated herself behind him, wearing his jacket over her gown, and a cloak atop that, tolerably warm and smelling of wood smoke. Sipping the last of the coffee, she braced herself to rejoin the medieval world— with another wild Witches Night under her belt, the first of 1461. No more summertime miracles in cozy caves. Back to battles, bedbugs, and outrageous banquets. Roast starlings in sweet ginger sauce, or just a plate of eels to go with your morning eggs. Thank goodness the place had maid service. She finished off the coffee, saying a prayer for Deirdre and Matt, and for Lily, whom she saw last night in a dream.

Leaving Sherwood behind, they swung south and west through Whaley Wood, avoiding Bolsover and Chesterfield, riding over frozen fields south of Scarcliffe, headed straight for heath and moor that connected with the Peak country to the west. They saw almost no one, aside from a few cold souls searching for wood beneath the snow, bent-over wretches with sticks lashed to their backs, who straightened up to stare. Edward wore his breast plate and half-armor, with his sword, mace, and sallet helm hanging from his saddle. Seeing a knight come riding out of Sherwood with a lady on his crupper was a surprise even in medieval Derbyshire.

Crossing a rough stretch of Ryknild Street where what was left of the old Roman road lay buried in snow, she saw nothing but a double line of horse tracks headed south, left by a pair of riders, or a man with a packhorse. No one had come north since last night's snow, a good sign. Codnor Castle was just a few miles to the south, but no Wydvilles had come up Ryknild Street to cut them off from the western hills, putting them well ahead of any possible pursuit. Anyone hunting for them had to come from Codnor, since no one coming down from the north could know she and Edward were on the run.

Almost no one. At the edge of the woods they met the rider with a packhorse—it was Black Dick Nixon, looking a bit bleary and hungover from yesterday's introduction to grain alcohol, but still wearing a happy grin beneath his pot helm. Nixon had on a dented breastplate and held the big hand-and-a-half bastard sword he usually kept slung across his back. Behind the border bandit was Robyn's bay packhorse, with one of King Henry's deer hung over the saddle. He called cheerfully to her, "M'lady Stafford, how wonderful to see you. We must have lost each other in the night."

"Master Nixon, what an amazing surprise." And how delightful to talk to the bandit with Edward's big armored body between them. "How did you know where to find me?"

"Nothing could be simpler, m'lady." Nixon reveled in his own ingenuity. "I knew yew would not succumb to the snow, not on a Witches Night. So, I asked myself if I was headed from Sherwood to the Marches, where would I cross Ryknild Street? Assuming I hoped to avoid Codnor and was shy about meeting a sheriff. This lonely stretch naturally presented itself, only I had supposed yer ladyship would be alone."

"You know who I am?" Edward asked evenly, his hand on his sword hilt.

Black Dick made a nodding bow without letting go of his sword. "Indeed I do, Yer Lordship. Or rather, Yer Grace," Nixon corrected himself, "seeing you are now duke of York. Something I am glad to have had no hand in. It was Trollope's men who killed yer father, and fitted his body with a paper crown. An evil deed if you ask me. And it was Lord Clifford who killed yer brother, most foully so they say—though I was not there myself. . . ."

"I was there," Robyn admitted, "it was Lord Clifford who killed him."

"So in neither case can there be any blood feud between us," Nixon concluded happily, still keeping his bared blade between them.

Edward nodded, saying, "I have no blood feud with you, nor with any Nixon that I know of." His hand stayed on his sword, though he made no move to draw it.

"If only the whole world could say that," Nixon sighed wistfully, "creation would be all the merrier. So if we must fight, it will be over this woman, and that would be a terrible waste."

"How so?" Edward sounded amused by the bandit. "She seems well worth fighting over to me."

"Only because she loves you," Nixon pointed out politely. "If she loved me, I would fight for her too. She is pretty, brave, and proud, and a white witch as well, though appallingly lacking in foresight. I would gladly risk my life for her—if she were my lady. But I will not risk it for another man's."

Smart policy for a thoughtful kidnapper, especially when faced with an unbeaten young knight who had height and reach on him. Nixons had not gotten their reputation by raising stupid children. Robyn rose up, calling over Edward's steel shoulder, "Many thanks for bringing my horse."

"Your horse?" Nixon acted like he had not heard correctly. "What might m'lady mean?"

"Behind you"—she pointed at the bay—"beneath that poached deer."

"This deer was never poached," Nixon protested, deftly switching the subject, trying to hide one crime with another. "I found him like this. . . ."

"I know, I know," Robyn dismissed his excuses. "You found this buck fainted dead away beside the road, knocked senseless by a runaway beer wagon, and you are taking him home to revive him with tender regard and warm broth. Godspeed to your good efforts, but you must do it without my horse."

Black Dick saw she had him. What competent horse thief would fight a knight for a packhorse, when they were letting him make off with an earl's Brabant charger? Business sense alone suggested he should take the immensely valuable warhorse and be gone before its owners arrived. Nixon seemed to see the bay for the first time, saying, "But, of course. You looked so natural riding pillion with that young lord, I never remembered you on so sorry a hobby as this."

"Well, now that you have, I would have him back." She and Edward would travel twice as fast on two horses. Having that extra mount could easily be the difference between escape and recapture.

Seeing he had no choice, Nixon made a show of dismounting and slinging the dead deer across the Brabant's rump, which the warhorse did not like. Then he led the packhorse over to her, bowing and offering up the reins to her, saying, "Here he is, m'lady, as good as when yer ladyship left him. With no charge for feed or stabling. Make that a gift from me to you."

Taking the reins, she graciously thanked him for looking after her horse, politely ignoring the deer blood on the saddle. Black Dick bowed and kissed her hand, and on his little finger was the gold ring she had given him to watch over Mary, at the sanctuary of Saint Martin-le-Grand. But it turned out that Mary had been watching over both of them. Then Black Dick Nixon rode out of her life yet again, still headed north. This time at least, she was a horse richer for having met him. Seeing him go, she prayed he would not stop until he got to Tynedale, wishing all the men Queen Margaret had brought south would turn about and head home. And if each took a little of the southland with him, they might all go home as happy as Black Dick Nixon—but she doubted it would be that easy.

Nothing was going to be easy from now on. Now there was only one frail life between Edward and the crown, the weak and unstable King Henry, who despite heredity and common sense still occupied the throne. And if Henry died, there was no Rutland to possibly take the crown. Henry's other heir was the infant prince of Wales, being raised by Queen Margaret—and the only good thing said about His young Highness was that he could not be king for ten years or more. She put her arms back around Edward's armored waist, knowing she was hugging the obvious choice. Wise, gallant, and forgiving, Edward had all the qualities most folks wanted in a king. Or a man, for that matter.

Going straight west into Peak country to avoid Codnor, they rode up the Amber to the wooded tops looking down on the valley of the

Derwent, locked in peaceful winter beneath a sprinkling of snow. Descending to the Derwent, they crossed at a slick frozen ford and then climbed the heights on the far side, coming on a wide stretch of high heath, where wind had blown away the lighter snow leaving a few deep patches on the dead grass.

Spread across the heath south of Stanton-in-the-Peaks were ring cairns, ancient burials, and low stone circles scattered about in no apparent pattern. Or at least none that Robyn could see as she rode past. Then at the high end of the heath she came on a circle of nine low standing stones set on the inner edge of a slight embankment. Robyn reined in, instantly recognizing the stone ring from her dream.

"They are called the Nine Ladies," Edward told her. "Ladies who danced so long and so solemnly on this high heath that they became a part of it." He pointed at the millstone block where Rutland had stood, adding, "Hereabouts they call that block the King Stone."

And she had hoped Rutland might one day be king in Edward's stead—now everything was just what she had seen in her dream. This had happened to her once before, at Hunsbury, an ancient ring-fort near Hardingstone, where she had been initiated into Duchess Wydville's coven. She had seen the place on Witches Night, and then come on the real thing without warning, on her way to Northampton. Hunsbury turned out to be a gate between the past and future, which had let her revisit third-millennium London. This place could be just as important to her.

But how? She hesitated, unsure what to do next, telling Edward, "I need to stop here and pray." And mayhap ask directions.

"Why?" Edward seemed surprised. "Do you know any of these Nine Ladies?"

"Perhaps." At Baynards Castle he himself had danced with Jo and Bryn, and several of Duchess Wydville's daughters, but Witches Night dreams were women's secrets, especially when they included coven members. Dismounting, she tried to put all such thoughts out of her mind. She had to decide here and now how much she trusted her magic. Witches Nights dreams could not be easily dismissed. She had dreamed about this place for a purpose, putting herself there, along with Lily and the nine ladies. But what purpose? And whose? So far, Witches Flights and waking dreams had led her to miraculous powers, and to no end of trouble. Was her latest dream an invitation, or a warning? And if an invitation, from whom? Wydvilles had been there in force. Even if Duchess Wydville had not sent the dream, the witch-priestess might easily be alerted by it.

Robyn had to put her trust in Mary, who had led the dance in her doeskin. Maid Mary of Sherwood had been in her dream, as sure as when she had seen her running with the wolf and deer. Robyn doubted Duchess Wydville would dare fake that, even if the witch-priestess could. Some things were too holy to mock. Witchcraft worked with natural causes and reactions, with love, hate, fear, and hope, and all spells worked best when they were invited in. On Halloween she had reached out to the shade of Duke Somerset, but this time she had merely given thanks and prayed for guidance. And her answer was to dream of here. How could she just ride idly by?

Naturally Edward did not see it that way, being all for going on, wanting to be back in Shrewsbury by dusk on the morrow. "I must be able to calm the public when news of the defeat spreads. Better to have people hear the truth from you than rely on rumor made worse by retelling."

He was talking sense, they were but twenty miles from Sherwood, and the day was not near done. If they pushed on, they could be almost clear of the Peak country by dusk. But magic did not have to make sense, and if she was going to sacrifice her feelings to the political situation in Shrewsbury, she might as well give in and be queen. "You chose the route, and this is where we have arrived. We have been brought here for a purpose, and must see it through."

"Must we?" Edward did not look convinced. "Our purpose is to pass through this Peak country and cross the Dove into Staffordshire, where friends eagerly await us. Keep going, and we shall sleep safe in Staffordshire tonight, how is that for an omen?" Robyn Stafford had been all over England and Wales, including such exotic parts as Ireland and Calais, but she had never been to her supposed birthplace of Staffordshire. "Linger here, and it will mean a long day tomorrow; up at dawn and still getting to Shrewsbury in the dark."

She leaned across and kissed him, saying, "You make it sound so inviting. Dawn it is, then." In her dream Lily had been here at dawn.

Edward had meant that as an argument against her, not an offer, but was too gallant to take it back. He had promised his lady to stay at Stanton-in-the-Peaks and to see her to Shrewsbury on the morrow, and he was medieval enough to think that was all that mattered. She kissed him again in gratitude, saying, "If you want me, you must take my witchy parts, as well."

"I would have it no other way," he protested, surveying the stone rings and lone cairns scattered about them. "What I saw in Sherwood was most amazing, miraculous beyond anything I ever imagined. I used to think that I had to do everything, or it would not be done right. I chafed at my father for failing to act, or acting too rashly when he did, thinking that if he would only listen to me, all would be well. Now I see there are things happening that are larger than I, and we are like actors in one of your real-life plays, inventing our lines as we barge about, thinking we are in control. Whenever I have gone with the good, I have won easily and well. My father opposed events and died needlessly—even a fool would see the lesson there."

"What lesson is that?" She was honestly not sure what Edward thought of all this, of being made heir to Henry, then losing his father and Rutland in such a pointless fashion.

"Why, that England wants peace and good governing." He looked surprised that she had to ask. "Just as you are always saying. England will look kindly on any lord who offers justice, and resent any lord that withholds it, no matter how noble. My father put himself above the peace of the kindom, and found no one would rally to him."

She reached across and took his hand, saying, "Except for those that did truly love him, and his cause." She thought of Salisbury and Master Harrow, and young blades like Sir Thomas Neville. "Many came most willingly to fight for him."

He squeezed her hand, adding, "As did witches trying to warn him."

She had not dwelled on Duke Richard's pigheadedness, but Edward was smart enough to picture the scene. They found lodging at a widow's croft, sleeping in a smoky loft away from the fire, but happily above the vermin. Their rushes were fresh and dry, and the woman's stew was clean if tasteless. Edward scored points with the hostess by producing a bag of salt, which the woman ate by the pinch. He introduced himself as the earl of Ulster, a title that had now come to him, totally charming the lonely widow and swearing her to secrecy, thrilling her with his trust. If they were found out here, it would have to be by magic.

To test the magical waters, Robyn went out alone at dusk, leaving Edward to entertain their hostess. She went to the Nine Ladies to pray, staying until she saw three stars overhead, trying to get a feel for the place. All she felt was cold creeping out of the ground and into her calves and knees. Witchcraft was not all streaking around from winter to summer, and it included a lot of silent prayer in cramped positions, pondering past mistakes and future prospects.

When she got back to the farmstead, the widow was waiting for her with a sooty light, saying her knight was already up in the narrow loft. Giving her a wry smile, the widow whispered, "Girl, you beware of this boy, and do not give in to him unless he will marry you."

"Worry not." Robyn smiled at the widow's concern, saying, "He will marry me." Problem was that Edward wanted to make her queen, as well.

"So you say," the widow snorted, "I have watched dozens of winsome girls like you running off with handsome young squires, earls, and the like—always to the girl's ruin. Leaving her begging to feed her bastard, when she would have been far happier having an honest dairyman or woodcutter, working himself to death just to please his pretty wife."

This well-intended widow already had her pregnant and married off to a tradesman, so Robyn tried to set her at ease, saying, "Do not worry much over me, I am a lady with some resources of my own." And the debts to go with them.

"Tosh? You a lady?" Her hostess laughed at the thought. "Your speech is pure Peak country, and I bet you were born no farther south than Staffordshire." For once, Lady Robyn Stafford found herself hard-pressed to argue.

"You are no more a lady than that handsome young rascal in armor is really earl of Ulster." But the old widow led her to the loft ladder anyway, conniving in their secret sin. "Next you will be telling me you know the duke of York."

13

⊷⇒ Bridge on the Dove ⇐⊶

Up at dawn, she meant to delay Edward's return to Shrewsbury as little as possible, trying to gather her clothes and slide silently out of bed. Right away she discovered Edward did not mind being delayed, so long as it was done by her in a warm snug loft. Politics, family, military necessity, and his most pressing need to get to the Marches were all forgotten when he had her in a real rope bed, not some hole in the snow. How do you stop a blazing boy juggernaut? Not with armored pikemen and batteries of cannons. One winsome woman in her nightgown can easily succeed where ten thousand lances had no chance. Robyn did not even have to be all that winsome, since Edward awoke fully ready, determined to test the strength of the loft supports.

"Steady, my lord," she whispered, "I think this loft was made for sleeping."

"That is so," he admitted, "but it will serve. Here, get on top of me." But the loft supports were saved by the sound of a horse outside—fast, eager hoofbeats followed by a familiar snort and whinny. Much to her lord's disappointment, Robyn pulled on her wool tights and threw a cloak over her shift, insisting on seeing what horse had arrived. Edward helped her down the rickety ladder, then came himself with sword in hand, in case the horse meant trouble. Shooing aside geese and chickens, she stepped out of the croft and onto icy ground, wishing she had waited to pull on her boots.

Lily was there, whiter than the windblown patches of snow, snorting and stamping amid the low stone monuments, just like in her dream. Robyn called to her mare, and Lily came trotting over, pleased to see her mistress, who had been lost since last week's fracas at Wakefield. Lily had no saddle, no trappings, not even a bridle—but the mare was plainly anxious to have things return to normal, trotting up to her mistress and stopping, eagerly nodding her head. Happy to have found her owner once again, Lily hoped there was a reward in it.

And just like in her dream, Robyn seized a hunk of mane and pulled herself onto the mare bareback. Unlike her warm, hazy Witches Night dream she had a real excited animal beneath her, and a frigid wind whipping between her wool cloak and thin shift. Her bare feet dug into Lily's white sides for warmth.

"Where did she come from?" Edward asked, looking very romantic, standing half-naked on the heath, sword in hand, like a young heathen warrior from the sagas. When in reality he was a most Christian prince, a royal duke, and heir to the throne, if you accepted the Act of Accord.

Which Robyn still did not; Edward might have her body but not her vote—though like most folks, Lady Robyn of Pontefract did not have a vote. Politics for her was all peril and spellcraft. She rose in her seat, calling out to him, "I do not know. I lost her at Wakefield, five or so days ago."

Wakefield was some forty miles away, over the hills to the north. How had Lily known to come here? Maybe her mare had a dream, as well. Mary was Our Lady of the Beasts, prayed to since Paleolithic times for her power over animals, able to call them to people in need. Whatever wondrous story lay behind the mare's miraculous appearance, Lily would never tell. Some things always remained a mystery.

However this had happened, it was a dream come true, not in some hazy unexpected sense, but an explicit granting of a heartfelt wish clearly foretold in her sleep. An offhand bit of magic, as welcome as it was mysterious. Robyn had been working so hard to get her waking life in order that she had given scant attention to her dreams, which were now becoming so solid and real. More than just the return of her horse, this was a reminder that her growing powers were a psychic whole, not divided into logical categories like waking and dreaming, wishing and seeing, past and future, or even human and animal. Lily plainly meant to find her as much as she needed to find her mare. Guiding Lily with her knees over to where the Nine Ladies stood frozen in their dance, she gave thanks on horseback for the dream and its fulfillment.

Being up and half-dressed, Edward remembered his haste to get back to Shrewsbury, no doubt already alarmed by his absence. With Shrewsbury a long day's ride away, they could perhaps prevent another sleepless night for his friends. Edward helped her dismount, and instead of dragging her back up to the loft, he turned her over to the widow, while he saw to the horses.

Sorry to see her go, the widow helped her dress, treasuring the feel of her silk chemise and designer underwear, and the soft linen that went beneath her riding gown—but the life of a wayward lady did not tempt the poor upright cottager in the least. "If yon young knight mistreats you, the way they always do, you are welcome back anytime. Never let it be said I turned a lass away, however daft and hapless."

"And if you ever need loan money, or help with the rent, apply to Lady Robyn Stafford of Pontefract." Hopefully she would have some to lend. Giving the widow a kiss good-bye, she mounted the bay with Edward's help, since Lily still had no saddle or bridle, and she did not trust the bay to stay with them—the poor beast had changed ownership several times this week, and was just getting used to being back with her.

Fast as Edward was getting ready, they did not get clean away. From atop the packhorse, Robyn saw two riders coming south out of the hills past Stanton-in-the-Peaks. She could tell by the way they were casting about, that they were searching for something, most likely Lily. She warned her knight, "Company coming."

Edward mounted immediately, loosening the heavy mace that hung on his saddle, slipping the leather loop on the handle over his wrist. He had on his chain mail, and Mortimer blue and gold, and at a distance might easily pass for one of Roos or Somerset's riders. She wore Stafford colors, as did the newcomers. As they drew closer, she recognized more than their colors, "It is my wayward household."

Deirdre and Matt Davye rode up and reined in, excitedly talking together in different tongues. Overjoyed to be back in her service, they explained how they had fled eastward from the woods below Wakefield, finding shelter in a farm near Pontefract. "People there were happy to hide anyone wearing your colors," Matt explained. "We stayed there two days, until we heard you had been seen headed south through Wentbridge."

"Accompanied by Wydvilles," Deirdre added significantly.

"We took the road south looking for you, through Wentbridge and Skelbrooke, all the way to the edge of Sherwood. Past Tickhill we lost word of you, and were going mainly by guess," her horse master admitted, "with scant sign of success."

"But we did find Lily," Deirdre declared happily.

"That was below Skelbrooke," Matt told her. "Your mare was in a string of horses being led south by some of Lord Clifford's Yorkshire riders. Saddles and trappings were still on most of them, loaded with loot from Wakefield, arms, armor, and dead men's boots. Clifford's crew are lewd, uncouth fellows, even for northerners."

"Was Lord Clifford with them?" asked Edward casually. Robyn could tell he ached to lay hold of Clifford—not that she much blamed him. Luckily, the man she must plead for was Somerset, who had at least tried to spare Salisbury.

"No, we saw nothing of Lord Clifford," Matt confessed, adding, "they were not his lordship's personal men-at-arms, but merely mounted ruffians wearing steel bonnets and Clifford livery—turning their lordship's public quarrel into private profit, then boasting about their cleverness in bad Yorkshire."

"Matt stole Lily from them." Her red-haired maid sounded thrilled by Matt's unsuspected talent for thievery.

" 'Twas not much of a theft," Matt modestly objected. "As soon as Lily saw Ainlee, she wanted to come away with us. I just had to loose her hobble when the northerners were drunk and distracted. But they doubtless counted it theft, so we took to the Peak country, keeping off the roads, heading south during the day and staying in crofts at night. Last night we lodged with a shepherd family north of Stanton, sleeping warm and snug among the sheep."

"And this morning Lily got straight away," Deirdre talked like the mare had planned it carefully, "untying her hobble rope with her teeth, but waiting until we were up before kicking off the hobble and heading south. We have been chasing her since sunup. Lily would let us almost catch up, then bolt over the next hill as soon as we got out her bridle."

Lily plainly knew where she was going, even if the hapless humans chasing her did not. Robyn reached over and patted her smart, miraculous mare, who had barely left her side since first arriving, asking, "You have her bridle? What about her saddle and packs?"

"Her saddle we left with the shepherds," Matt nodded to the north. "But I have the bags she carried. Clifford's men took only the silver, leaving everything else untouched."

"There was no silver left to take." She laughed at anyone's chance of making a living off robbing her. Looking into the packs, she saw they had barely been opened. Someone had rummaged through them for valuables, spilling tampax, blush powder, and antibiotic pills, but not seeming to have taken anything. "And none of this other stuff much appealed to them."

Matt shrugged. "If you cannot spend it or drink it, Lord Clifford's riders would not want it." Thank goodness for that, because she sorely needed her things, tiny necessities like cold pills and flashlight batteries that made the Middle Ages more livable.

Before leaving, Robyn rode over to say a private good-bye to the Nine Ladies. Dismounting beside the low circle of stones, she thanked Mary for returning Deirdre, Matt, and Lily to her, bringing her tiny household back together. She was leaving the north, having lost nothing but the Honour of Pontefract, which had hardly been hers to begin with. Praying to Mary to make her strong, and able to stand whatever lay ahead, she wondered how many women had knelt here throughout the ages, with these same wishes in their hearts. Thousands at least, links in a great chain of life. Crossing herself before the pagan monument, she rose and remounted, rejoining her servants and her betrothed.

Riding south and west, making straight for Shrewsbury, they reached a bit of high wooded ground near Cratcliff Rocks, where a natural gap in the long snow-dusted escarpment was backed by an impressive limestone pile, called Robin Hood's Stride. Beyond the gap lay the line of the Dove, and the Staffordshire border, the southern exit to Peak country. At the top of the gap they stopped beneath gaunt trees to look back, and Matt spotted riders on their trail, coming from the direction of the Nine Ladies and Stanton-in-the-Peaks. Edward asked, "What are their colors?"

Matt rose in his saddle, straining his eyes, then saying, "White and red."

"Wydvilles," Edward concluded, glancing at Robyn for confirmation. My lord of March had so many enemies, it was lucky they came color-coded.

She nodded in agreement, not even needing to see their coat of arms. Who else but the Wydvilles would know to search for them at the Nine Ladies? Duchess Wydville did not send her that Witches Night dream of the Nine Ladies, but clearly the duchess knew about it. After all, Duchess Wydville and her blond daughters had danced in the dream on sacred ground, a sure sign that they had been touched by the vision. To so much as name the duchess on Witches Night was to invite her in.

"We must beat them to the Dove," Edward decided. "Hastings is expecting me to return through Staffordshire, so we can hope for help once we get there."

They set out at a gallop, cutting through fields and pounding down woodland trails, making for the line of the Dove, a little over five miles away. It was a fast, frightening five miles that Robyn covered in record time, still aboard her northern bay, constantly having to urge the stodgy gelding to go faster; slow patience would not do today. Lily ran easily along beside her, carrying nothing and enjoying the chase. Edward led the retreat, with Deirdre in tow, while Matt Davye brought up the rear, ready to render assistance if a horse should fail or fall.

Crossing the remains of a Roman road, they climbed the last ridgeline overlooking the valley of the Dove. From the crest, Robyn could see a dozen or so riders gaining on them, who were indeed wearing Wydville red and white. They must have had fresher mounts because they got visibly closer while she watched, and she could see Grey of Codnor with them, the friendly lord alchemist, now heading a knot of armed riders wearing his livery. Guilt welled up inside her; had she not insisted on staying the night at the Nine Ladies, Edward would have gotten clean away. Whatever happened would all be on her—yet again.

Descending into the valley of the Dove, they made straight for the river, splashing down a muddy road that hopefully led to a bridge. Here the Dove wound through high heath and green-brown moorland dotted with bare trees before plunging down into steep, thickly wooded Dove Dale. Once across the river, they had hope of finding friends and shelter; but first they must find a bridge over the Dove, which was swollen with rain and snowmelt, turning the peaceful little river into a broad rushing barrier. And the Wydvilles were less than a mile behind them, closing swiftly.

But when they got to the bridge, there were more armored riders in front of them, a half-dozen wearing Wydville colors, and twice that many showing among the trees on the Staffordshire side. Her heart sank, seeing even more armed men ahead. What was the point of all this running, except to tire their horses? Horrified by what she had dragged them all into, she called to Edward. "Should we try for a ford upstream?"

"No," Edward shouted back, reining in and pointing at the riders across the river. "See those men over in Staffordshire, wearing murrey and blue—they are Hastings's people."

Sure enough, the men beneath the trees on the far side were wearing purple and blue, though at this distance she had trouble telling the shade of purple—it might indeed be murrey. Either way, they were not Wydvilles. Looking closer, she saw the Wydvilles were facing the river, keeping the men on the Staffordshire side from crossing. The narrow stone bridge could have been easily blocked by one man, much less six.

Strapping on his back-and-breast, and donning his sallet, Edward prepared to force a crossing. Matt had a sallet, as well, and wore chain mail, which left her and Deirdre woefully underdressed, in their gold-and-scarlet riding gowns. Neither had a decent headdress, much less a helmet. Matt offered up his metal-studded brigandine jacket, a sweet gesture considering the circumstances.

Robyn just told him to put her saddle on Lily. She and Deirdre would have to rely on their gowns for protection, hoping no man would fire on them. Like cruel vengeful Lord Clifford said, they were the prize of battle, not the foe. Besides, there was only one brigandine, so she and Deirdre could not exactly share it. Matt obeyed and buckled on the brigandine.

Edward unlooped the mace from his saddle, handing it to Matt, and saying, "Let me lead. You make sure the women are safe and close behind us."

"Yes, Your Lordship," Matt replied, hefting the heavy mace. "You knock them over, and I will see they stay down."

"Excellent." Edward sounded pleased with Matt's tactics, swinging easily back into the saddle despite his plate armor. "We will show them why horsemen must never try to hold ground."

Mounting Lily for the second time that morning, Robyn leaned over and gave Edward a long kiss—which once again might be their last—saying when they finished, "Try not to kill anyone."

"Why, of course, my lady." Edward brimmed with confidence, further emboldened by her kiss. "It is much too fine a morning to mar with bloodshed." Then he drew his sword, and they set off through the trees at a charge.

Keeping a sharp watch into Staffordshire, the Wydvilles did not see them until they were breaking from the trees. Still, they neatly divided their forces, sending three men-at-arms to face Edward and Matt, while leaving three to hold the bridge. As the three men in half-armor trotted forward, they spread into a line and lowered their lances, not much alarmed to be facing a man-at-arms, a squire, and two ladies.

Edward and Caesar tore into them like a steel twister, taking the middle man for their target. Deftly turning aside the man's lance point with his sword, Edward slammed straight into the surprised fellow, giving him a ringing blow in the helmet that sent the shocked rider reeling from the saddle. Edward's follow-through nicked the next man's horse on the unprotected rump, sending the startled animal and helpless rider galloping off down the road. Turning Caesar swiftly about, he took the third knight by surprise, delivering a stunning backhand blow before the fellow could even get his lance turned around. Edward's next blow sent him flying from the saddle.

In seconds, Edward had disposed of three armored riders, who were now either stretched on the ground or routed. Before the Wydvilles at the bridge could credit what had happened, Edward was among them, slashing and parrying. Matt was right behind him, just like he said, flailing away at anyone who tried to get up. Robyn and her maid dodged between the downed men and riderless horses, making for the bridge at flank speed.

Brushing one man aside and unsaddling another, Edward caught the last Wydville, the one actually holding the bridge against Hastings's men, before the fellow could turn around. Hitting him like a lightning bolt from behind, Edward sent the white-and-scarlet knight heels over helmet into the Dove. All the bridge's defenders were either flat on their armored backs, floundering in the muddy river, or fleeing for the hills. Cheers came from the far bank as Edward backed Caesar off the narrow bridge, letting the ladies pass.

Her handmaid in tow and a frightened horse in Wydville livery fleeing ahead of her, Lady Robyn Stafford of Pontefract rode peacefully over the Dove bridge, to resounding applause from the armed men drawn up to receive her. Behind her came Matt Davye, who managed to guide her tired bay packhorse across ahead of him. Last of all came Edward, sword in hand, slowly bringing up the rear, in case the stunned Wydvilles attempted a countercharge. Looking at her watch, Robyn saw that the mayhem had lasted less than a minute and a half—leaving them the rest of a rare sunny morning to enjoy themselves.

Hastings's men greeted her with *hurrah*s and cries of, "Well ridden, Your Ladyship." As if she had ridden through the Wydvilles on her own, instead of relying on Edward's cool head and brawny sword arm.

By the time Lord Grey of Codnor arrived at the far end of the bridge, it did not take an alchemist to see that Duchess Wydville's plan had fizzled. Edward was across, having completed that most difficult of military exercises, a river crossing against superior forces while encumbered by women and baggage. Lord Grey was left with the unappealing task of trying to force the bridge against an eager and victorious enemy, who was at that moment calling out, "Come cowards, do not be shy. Chasing women is easy, see how you do with men."

Grey of Codnor had not come all this way to be laughed at, and he turned his horse around. Wydvilles picked themselves off the ground and followed in his wake, to more catcalls from across the river. "What? Running so soon? Afraid of wetting yourselves? Stay, we will meet you halfway."

Seeing the danger had passed, Edward doffed his sallet and dismounted, then helped her down. His grinning face glistened on a cold day, but otherwise he showed no sign of having just bested a half-dozen armed men in mounted combat. Happy to have her in his arms, he set her lightly on the ground without letting go, saying, "Welcome home, my lady."

"Home?" She stood there secure in his grip, but still shaky on her feet, barely believing both of them had gotten through that sudden burst of mayhem absolutely unhurt. That hardly meant she was home. She had never been to the valley of the Dove, in this or any millennium. Home for her was still Montana, or maybe L.A. London was the closest thing here and now.

"In Staffordshire." He nodded at the quiet little valley, which even in the grip of a horrible winter looked pretty enough for camping grounds and RV parks—and probably had them in the third millennium. This was where she had claimed to come from, without ever actually seeing it, a lie so old it sounded natural. "Never having been here, you are truly home at long last."

And so she was, Lady Robyn Stafford of Staffordshire, safe in the home she never knew. Reveling in their escape, she held him tighter, while young men around them stood and grinned. Anything more would have to wait until they had less of an audience. Squire Hastings himself was not there, but his felonious younger brother Thomas was eagerly waiting to report to Edward. And since Edward would manifestly not let go of her, bold Master Hastings had to report to both of them, doing a hasty bow. "My lord, half of Shrewsbury is out searching for you."

"And how lucky that you should have found me." Edward never considered himself lost, but clearly did not want young Hastings to lose the credit due him.

Thomas modestly touched his cap, saying, "Brother William said Your Lordship was coming west from Sherwood, and told me off to cover the bridges over the Dove, while he took the Trent, and Ralph the Churnet."

"But you found the right bridge," Edward pointed out, "and there must be several at least."

Thomas nodded eagerly. "Six, my lord, that I have seen myself, counting fords and stepping stones—but it was passing easy to find the right one."

"How so?" Robyn asked; having young Hastings here seemed like yet another miracle.

"Why, my lady, Wydvilles would not let us cross here." He nodded toward the men-at-arms on the Derbyshire side picking themselves up and heading home. "We assumed they had a reason."

"Excellent assumption." Edward commended his logic. "Now ready your men to ride, for we must be in Shrewsbury by nightfall."

Another day of riding ahead. Too bad, because the place was pretty, and this was the first secure peaceful moment she had with Edward in months—though it was hardly private. Men bustled about, fixing food and saddling horses, laughing and joking, happily reliving the morning's swift bloodless bit of combat. She was still sitting in a daze, wondering what to do with herself when her knight brought her a plate of eggs and onions, cooked on a flat griddle over an open fire. Edward of March, the new duke of York, who had done almost all the fighting that day, made it his first order of business to see she had one of her favorite breakfasts, profoundly apologizing for the lack of toast, but vowing his men were boiling water to make her witches' brew. Some service. He smiled as he laid down the plate and a shining clean steel spoon, saying, "From now on, my lady will want for nothing."

She thanked him, hoping it was true. It was certainly about time. Technically, she was still a fugitive from justice, charged with heinous crimes, but so was Edward when she met him, along with Hastings and his brothers. All her worries about the law were washed away by the blood at Wakefield. Though no one said it aloud, the deaths of Duke Richard and Earl Salisbury all but eliminated the older generation—aside from poor Mad Henry, who was no match for anyone. From now on, the fate of the nation would be in the hands of a new generation, including Warwick and Somerset, and headed by the handsome teenager serving her scrambled eggs. He told her, "When we get to Shrewsbury, we shall have things exactly as we please."

"With plenty of time to be together?" Mortally tired of all this hard riding and perilous politicking, Robyn was ready for some partying and dancing, and long winter evenings listening to the lute.

"From now on, we never need be apart," he assured her, watching the last of the Wydvilles desert the far bank of the Dove. "And we shall do just what we want to do."

She nodded solemnly. No more hiding behind Parliament and Duke Richard. Marriage, the succession, and the fate of England— all in their hands, and on their heads. Good enough. Lady Robyn of Pontefract would not wish it any other way. "Only what we want to do."

"Of course, Somerset will be coming south," Edward admitted, "so I must raise an army to defend London." Of course. There were still such mundane considerations. Matters of state, an armed rebellion, and a miserable winter. But this was the Middle Ages; there was always a wet spring to worry about, or a homicidal French queen leading an army of Scots maniacs. Medievals made do, and so could she.

"But not right now," she told him, enjoying the warm taste of the eggs and onions seasoned with a pinch of pepper from the exotic

Indies. She had seen Somerset's army, which was easily as disorganized by victory as the Yorkists were by defeat. Look at all the looting, unauthorized executions, and casual kidnappings—it would be some time before the loose assembly of border riders, bickering lords, and unwilling recruits could be gotten back together and headed south. "Right now, Good Duke Somerset is enjoying his fine suite of rooms at Pontefract—which used to be mine. And probably planning to head north and meet with Queen Margaret, who last I heard was in Scotland."

Edward nodded, not shocked to find the enemy in total disarray, reeling from the effects of a rare and unexpected victory. He asked, "How are you so happily informed as to Somerset's plans?"

"We witches have our ways." Who knew she had such a talent for espionage? Spying was not something she ever meant to excel at—all she wanted was to be an actress.

"When they do come south, we will have the crown and people behind us," Edward prophesied. "Queen Margaret and Somerset can only hope to be beaten."

Amen to that. "And what about King Henry?" she asked. "When we get to Shrewsbury, will Henry still be king?" The temptation must be there in Edward to make the sweep complete, to toss out the last and least competent member of the older generation, and start doing things right for a change.

Edward laughed at her concern, saying, "We both have every reason to wish Henry well. You because you do not want to be queen, and I because Henry is my king." Edward said it lightly, but with real feeling. Henry was his king, and not by accident of birth, or by God's grace, or through fear of horrible punishment, the way Henry was king to every other Englishman. To Edward alone, Henry was his king of choice. Edward was accepted as heir apparent by almost all the country, and he had Henry in hand. If Edward had Henry set aside, or killed, then his only competition would be an infant that few wanted to see on the throne. Henry wore the crown because Edward wanted him to be king, which made Edward the only free man in England, the only one whose vote really mattered.

Edward took her hand, saying softly and earnestly, "You and I share a miracle, a secret miracle of love, hope, and spring. What we saw and did on that night in Sherwood means more to me than all

the thrones on earth. Or all the sermons from all the pulpits. Whatever happens from this day forth, that shared miracle binds us forever."

Amen. She smiled at her young lord, who was more eager to be
serving her breakfast in bed than to be king of England. For the first
time since Halloween they were safe and together, and free to make
their own fate. And tonight they would sleep in Shrewsbury, the
capital of the Welsh Marches, ancient seat of the Princes of Powys—
but first a day of riding through Staffordshire, the home she was just
now getting to know. Too bad they were surrounded by pesky retainers. What should have been a long, lazy ride—with just Matt
and Deirdre for company—had become another armed parade. It
was back to being cheered wherever she went, but so long as they
sang her to bed at night, she could hardly complain. When Hastings's
men brought the boiled water, she got out Lord Codnor's *Coffea
arabica* and showed her sweet and cunning royal lover how to brew
fresh-ground coffee.

14

⟨⟨⟩⟩ The Devil's Chair ⟨⟨⟩⟩

Tuesday, 6 January 1461, Twelfth Night, Shrewsbury Castle, Shropshire

Shrewsbury is a town in mourning for Duke Richard and the dead at Wakefield, so Twelfth Night is not the final Fools' Season debauch I was told to expect, with masques, plays, and amazon tourneys, where women fight at barriers on foot in half-armor against men, and among themselves. We had to settle for drinking and backgammon, so am I beating the doublets off Edward, Hastings, the unlucky Lord Audley, and a young Welsh gentleman named John Donne. Literally. I emptied their purses, and they had to leave their jackets as pledges for their debts—hopefully that will just tempt them to play again. At this rate, I could pay back the Venetians—two years from next Michaelmas.

Games are the one thing modern folk are clearly better at. Medievals are like kids, too concerned with having fun to try and brainstorm every move. I beat Edward regularly at chess, and no one will play cards with me, except for kisses. But they keep thinking they can beat me at backgammon. "Even a witch cannot make the dice roll what she wills. . . ."

Wanna bet?

Y*our roll." Edward* offered up his dice, beautiful hand-carved ivories with gold dots. Stopping her typing, Lady Robyn took her turn. Her lord was down to his shirt and hose, having already pledged his doublet, cap, and boots—in private, these games often turned into strip backgammon. Tonight she was wearing funeral black, except for Lord Audley's shining doublet draped over her shoulders, a prize that perfectly matched her colors, being crimson velvet covered with bright gold butterflies.

Saying a prayer to Fortune, Robyn threw an eight, double fours, boxcars. Thank you, Lady Luck. Men around her groaned, and there were more drunken accusations of witchcraft. Hastings complained, "How can she hex your own dice?"

"Luck is a lady," she reminded Master Hastings as she swiftly moved her stones two at a time and then doubled the bets. "How could she not be on my side?"

Deirdre laughed, leading the ladies present in polite applause. Audley had brought Cybelle, his pretty, dark-haired French mistress, and Hastings had both a younger sister and a girlfriend with him, while Welsh knights had brought their wives. Edward grinned at her across the backgammon table—their first meeting in the Middle Ages having been aboard Baron Wydville's *Fortuna*, off the coast of Eire. Lady Luck was their private goddess, or how else could they ever have gotten together?

Such easy talk of witchcraft showed how much had changed. All charges against her were dropped, and here in Shrewsbury, she was Lord Edward's lady, the new Lady of the Marches, and next countess of March—not to mention duchess of York. Already she outranked every man in the room, except for Edward and Audley. As such, she could do very little wrong.

"This doubling makes it damned difficult," Hastings complained, boldly matching her bet.

"And expensive," Audley added, eyeing his glittering pawned jacket.

"That is what makes it a game," she explained. Who needed witchcraft? She alone realized that each move must set you up for the next roll—all they cared about is rolling a big score. Or doubles. Even Edward preferred bold swift movement to crafty plotting—witness his approach to politics. It helped that she was the only one half-sober.

"All that adding hurts the head," Hastings insisted, sipping wine spiked with anise.

"Just beat me, then," she suggested demurely, playing the helpless female. "I shall gladly figure my debt and do my poor best to pay what I can." Which brought hoots of laughter, since everyone knew Robyn had given her revenues away and dared not lose when playing with lords and earls. Returning the dice to Edward, she went back to typing in her diary:

Here in Shrewsbury Castle, I am lady of the house, no longer afraid to hear the word *witch* or say what I feel. Justice is in our hands—for good or ill, and cannot be used against me. I set the fashions, and Edward tops the social pyramid—literally no one but King Henry outranks us. Plus, we have the love of the commons. So if Edward's lady is a witch, then witchcraft is in fashion, like doubling bets at backgammon, or having mint tea at breakfast instead of starting the day straight off with beer.

Civilization has finally come to this little corner of the Marches, complete with weekday baths, teatimes, love poetry, and simple justice. Not everyone likes it—many are aghast at its loose ways and outlandish notions, but they are going to have to live with them. It no longer matters what FitzHolland, or Lady Frogbottom thinks, for I am the new Lady of the Marches, whose lord rules by right of the "rusty sword" wielded by his Mortimer forebearers. On top of that, I speak Welsh like a native, and have the unbeaten Sir Collingwood Grey for my personal champion. It would take an armed Tudor uprising to unseat me. . . .

And this was not going to be your grandmother's stuffy old English aristocracy. Closing her electronic notebook, Lady Robyn surveyed the crowd around the backgammon table, seeing hardly a noble face among them, just ne'er-do-well younger sons, Welsh bandit knights, ambitious squires like Master Hastings, and the footloose young women who followed them, from a pretty amoral French poetess to a Welsh-Irish witch-to-be. Not a great noble among them, unless you counted Edward.

Highest to lowest, most of these people had proved their personal commitment to Edward and his cause, from Lord Audley, who broke with queen and family to change sides, to Deirdre, who helped deliver the king at Northampton. These were the people who shared Edward's secrets, went on his private missions, brightened his parties, carried his messages, and fought his battles. After Wakefield, no one else counted. The older generation of Yorkist leaders had died there en masse—some would say committed suicide. Either way, their passing was something to be mourned, not emulated. Let Duke Somerset keep doggedly making the last generation's mistakes.

Edward's mistakes were confined to the backgammon board, where he redoubled the bet and ended up losing eight times his wager. He had already lost his boots and doublet, and Robyn was wearing his black velvet cap. Looking sheepishly over at her, the Lord of the Marches asked, "Would my lady take my promise to pay?"

"No promises," cried Audley's French girlfriend. "My lord only hopes to save his shirt."

"His shirt, his shirt," shouted the tipsy crowd, with some of Edward's men traitorously joining in.

"His hose," suggested Deirdre, who had seen her lord without both. "Then you will see something really marvelous."

"Marvelously useful, you mean." Being French, Audley's poetess strumpet freely mocked the English heir.

Edward raised his hand in surrender, something else few of them had ever seen. Without a word, a smart young page in murrey and blue came to his master's aid, bearing a carved wooden box decorated with enamel hearts and doves. Motioning for the page to set down the pretty box, Edward begged, "My Lady, let me at least reclaim my cap."

"Oh, do it," one serving girl suggested in mock horror, "so my lord may have it to wear when he loses his hose."

"That will take a bigger cap," Deirdre declared confidently.

Lady Robyn waved her laughing women to silence, doffing the black velvet cap and holding it out to Edward. "Here is your pledge, my lord. Where is my prize?"

Edward took back the velvet cap and adjusted it carefully at his accustomed jaunty angle, drawing another laugh since he was still standing barefoot in his undershirt and royal purple hose. Robyn could never imagine King Henry, or even Somerset, being so relaxed with his people—one more reason why Edward was winning. With a flourish, Edward opened the box, saying, "I swore to give this to you before the twelve days of Christmas were up."

Lined with red velvet, the box held a round gold circlet studded with six rubies, a lady's coronet done in her colors, not as grand as a duchess would wear—but well beyond the means of Lady Pontefract. Women around her gasped in awe, and all Robyn could manage was, "My lord, it is magnificent."

"Nothing compared with who will wear it," Edward told her, taking it out of the box and holding it up in the torchlight. Their betrothal was an open secret, certainly not news to anyone in the room—though the public announcement and wedding date were delayed out of respect for the dead. But Edward was a boy of deeds rather than words, and when she appeared at his side wearing this coronet made for a countess, his plans would be clear to everyone.

Solemnly, he set the gold circlet on her head with the same elaborate care as he had placed his cap—her drunk love was determined to do it right. He did, drawing cheers from the assembled women, while his knights and commanders looked on with sly smiles, amused by their lord's human side. Edward wanted the wife of his heart, not the politically correct choice. Great nobles would surely take it amiss, having a "lady" of so little standing outranking all their wives— Warwick, for one, would be livid—but Edward's people had learned to expect nothing less from him.

Gold felt cold and heavy circling her brows, and Lady Robyn could tell at once why folks took Shakespeare's "hollow crown" so seriously. Nicely matching the jacket she had won, this weighty gold circle would not just announce her engagement, but it would also set her apart from nearly everyone she knew here and now. Or in the future, for that matter. She was not just marrying a man, but a people and a cause, as well, giving up any claim to a private life. No matter who was king, Edward would be ruling England for the foreseeable future, and she would be at his side. So be it.

Edward sealed the act with a kiss, drawing cheers even from the men. After all, Edward might have saddled them with some foreign princess who spoke down to them in French, and expected to be served. Instead Edward picked a "lady" who had been with them on the march from Sandwich and risked her life at Northampton. If camp followers were good enough for his men, they were good enough for him—which said something about Edward's leadership.

Thrilled and excited, she did not have the heart to ask for his forfeit hose, not until they were abed.

Wednesday, 7 January 1461, Saint Distaff's Day, Shrewsbury Castle, Shropshire

Wore my coronet in public for the first time this morning, appearing with Edward at Saint Mary's for a special Mass to mourn the dead at Wakefield, many of whose names were not known until I arrived. Today was when Somerset's "truce" was supposed to end. Aside from the coronet, I wore deepest black, but that only made the gold stand out as I walked with Edward in the silent procession and prayed at his side. All my prayers were heartfelt, for I was plenty nervous. Word must have spread, because there were more people filling the crooked little streets when we got out, and staring from upper-story windows, getting a good look at the next countess of March. Since it was a memorial Mass, no one shouted their feelings, but word is sure to spread—Lord Edward is marrying his lady.

In private, we have set the date, the first Monday after the month of mourning ends, February 2, Groundhog Day. Edward does not want to waste a minute when we could be in wedded bliss. Hereabouts, Groundhog Day is called Candlemas, with a special Mass for Mary, celebrated by filling the dark castle with burning candles—sounds like a lucky day, indeed, so long as I have his promise not to make me queen. England is going to have dueling witch-duchesses, which should be quite enough.

There is no Saint Distaff on the Church calendar. This is another of those delightful folk "holidays" that supplement the official holy days. Having no mass entertainment, medievals must make their own. Not that Saint Distaff's is much of a holiday, since it marks the end of the Christmas season and a return to normal work, which for women is dominated by the distaff, since everyone hereabout wears homespun. But medieval women take an ironic view of the holidays; after all, no one gave us a "Christmas break." Lady Robyn spent the Yuletide cooking, sewing, and cleaning up between bouts of running, hiding, and dodging the law. Some vacation. So the young unmarried women make a holiday out of their "return" to work by washing the men.

Swear to Hecate. We heated water in the castle cauldrons and filled tubs in the bathhouse, then washed as many of the young men and stable boys as we could catch, including a line of volunteers headed by Edward. Good hygiene does not have to hurt. There was a deal of ribbing and giggling, and terrible "disstaff" jokes, but otherwise just good clean fun. Heaven knows the whole castle could use a thorough scrubbing, so why not make a game out of washing the hardest parts to get at? You can certainly smell the difference. . . .

Public reaction came on Friday, when Edward set out to visit the family castle at Ludlow, a day or two south of Shrewsbury. Edward, Hastings, and Lord Audley went ahead, gathering troops to face Somerset's impending invasion, agreeing to meet the ladies at Acton

Burnell, a fortified manor some miles out of town. With the luxury of a late start, Deirdre took forever packing, as did "Lady" Cybelle, Lord Audley's poetess mistress, the pretty black-haired French girl who lived by selling her verses and sleeping with rich young men. Audley had met her in Calais, and Cybelle had helped convince her lord to come over to the rebels; in fact, she had landed with them at Sandwich and marched to London composing verses to inspire Edward's little army. "Calais is nice enough," Cybelle explained, "but it gets to be such a prison. I wanted to see someplace new, even if it was England."

Already packed, Lady Robyn helped the poetess primp, stitching together the tight waist of Cybelle's formfitting gown, sewing her securely into the dress. Here is where spandex would come in handy. "So does Shrewsbury meet your expectations?"

"Only too well," Cybelle admitted with a sigh. Having high hopes for her literary career, Cybelle had named herself after a Greek goddess, rejecting her mother's more prosaic Isabella. Her father was variously given as a gypsy prince, a defrocked priest, or a royal duke. Somewhat surprisingly, Lady Cybelle had two children of her own, "lovely little dears living with their pious grandmother, a widowed nun—I see them when I can and send money." Her poetry had gone straight over the heads of the rebel troops, being artful rhymes in court French, but drew cheers from Kentish bowmen and London militia nonetheless, since Cybelle inspired men with her mere presence. Perfect for dressing up Edward's recruiting drive, Cybelle was coming south to Ludlow though her lord stayed in Shrewsbury.

Cybelle came out the castle gate fashionably sidesaddle in a blue-white silk gown, colored like a swatch of summer sky, trimmed with silver fleurs-de-lis, and topped by a white-silk winged headdress. Silly and self-centered, Cybelle was yet another sign they were winning. Talented, footloose young women could not afford to attach themselves to losing causes. For an escort, they had Matt and Hastings's young brothers.

But it was Lady Robyn people cheered, still wearing funeral black broken only by her coronet. As soon as she and Deirdre rode out in their mourning cloaks, citizens of Shrewsbury doffed their hats and happily greeted the new Lady of the Marches. Which touched her greatly, even more than hearing it from Londoners. She had done a lot for London, but to Shrewsbury she was just Lady Pomfret from somewhere in Yorkshire, though she spoke pure Shropshire. Already Shrewsbury liked the look of her, proud of Edward's unspoken choice.

Weirdly moving. She had marched half the length of England with Duke Somerset and never saw him given such easy affection. Folks doffed their hats and *hurrah*ed the good duke, but except for those who wore his livery, no one had pretended to love him. Nor did Somerset pretend to love them.

Sometimes Robyn thought they were winning because they totally upstaged their opponents, throwing the coolest parties and having the best boyfriends. That was surely part of it, but there was a lot more to being popular, as Robyn kept discovering. Medievals were not stupid, and they knew who cared for them, and who cared less— even in 1461. More so, maybe, since Somerset did not have slick media types posing him with sick kids, telling him to smile and sound concerned. Half a year ago, on Saint Anne's Day, she had turned to go riding through London instead of taking the easy way straight out Ludgate to the lists, the first step on the journey that had taken her to Pontefract and beyond. She took that turn toward London because the grand excitement of young nobles slamming into each other seemed an empty show; what drew her into the city were real people with their everyday triumphs and mundane tragedies. She made that choice, and Mary raised the stakes, saying this could not be idle slumming by some lady bored with castle life. Robyn must be willing to risk everything—life, freedom, comfort, privilege, even her smug sense of "reality"—to stand up for the rights of others, in the face of law, religion, and brute force. Otherwise, her concern for the "people" was as hollow as Somerset's, or Mad King Henry's.

So far, Robyn felt she had stood the test—but only just barely. And she had done nothing for Shrewsbury; these folks loved Edward because he plainly loved them, and assumed it was the same with her. Some compliment.

Robyn knew all this could be swept away at any time—leaving her as destitute as on that snowy night in Sherwood. Medievals doted on the temporariness of life, and she saw why, having been lifted up by the wheel of fortune, then cast down again—a couple of times, at least, going from prison cell to eating off the king's plate, to hiding in caves and hovels. And it could happen again. Right now she was riding high on the wheel, but someday Edward might really have to decide whether he wanted her or the kingship. So long as they had King Henry, that day would not come right away. And Henry had ten good years left in him, maybe more. Properly cared for, Henry could last twenty, even thirty years, a good, durable, unambitious but well-liked head of state—and in that time anything could happen. She and Edward might have a tall, stalwart son, aching to be king. Or there was small, serious Richard, Edward's youngest brother, who showed so much promise. In twenty years, Richard would be old enough to be king. But that was a long way off, which was all the more reason to enjoy things as they were.

Acton Burnell turned out to be more picturesque than useful, an abandoned fortified manor sinking into decay. Any Brunells had long since vanished; but Robyn found Edward and the others waiting for them under some trees. Showing off the ruin, Edward guessed, "This has not been lived in since my grandfather's time."

Hastings agreed. "Still, it might make an advance post, covering the roads south toward Ludlow and London."

Edward vowed to keep the crumbling manse in mind. Robyn saw such decay as a hopeful sign, showing the wild Welsh Marches were pretty peaceful these days, and fortified manors were becoming things of the past, even in 1461. Greystone was an exception, since Robyn had seen it five hundred years in the future, bigger than ever and inhabited by a future Sir Collingwood Grey, with similar incarnations of Jo and Joy living nearby. But the Greys were immortal witches, reborn again and again throughout the centuries—not all families had their special needs. Welsh armies no longer came pouring out of Powys to steal cattle, sack villages, and blackmail the cities. When war came, it was private war between noble families—something not lost on the locals. Appeals to justice and patriotism counted for less than family ties and the hope of advancement, and Edward could not resist doing some recruiting in person among his own tenants, taking it as a chance to hear what folks were saying. Riding south along the line of the Roman road through Leebotwood and Stretton, he lobbied local knights to join his cause, and he talked to veteran bowmen who might sign up because it was a hard winter, and because all Edward's troops were paid.

Enthusiastic crowds gathered to cheer their lord and his lady, and Cybelle read her poems to great applause—but few grabbed up their bows and pot helms. Being poor did not mean people had nothing to do. Most folks had farms to work, since the astonishingly small population and primitive hand-farming made land fairly plentiful—forcing lords to offer terms, or their tenants would look elsewhere. Right now the land was sleeping, but there was pruning to be done, and Plow Monday was not far off. After that would come the lambing. Which made Edward glad for every man he got, saying, "Better one man fully with us than a dozen whose hearts are in digging and hedging."

Having seen some of Somerset's halfhearted troops, Robyn agreed. "And the homesick eat as much as heroes, more sometimes. A lot of Somerset's people will be coming south just for loot." What sane Scot really cared who sat on the English throne?

"So long as they loot only London, not many in the Marches will mind." Edward smiled at his tenants' good sense.

Robyn did not like to think of war coming to London or the Marches. They stopped at vespers, staying in a farmstead of Edward's at the head of a beautiful valley between the rounded whaleback of Long Mynd and the stark ragged Stiperstones. Set in high moorland, the place was a small hall smelling of sheep, but people were pleased to entertain their young lord. Land was poor on these high moors, and largely in the hands of small owners, so the manor's main profit came from lead mines worked here since Roman times. She and Edward got the best lodging, the master bedroom above the main hall, which was splendid for privacy but a poor place for Witches Night. "Do not mind me," Edward told her. "Come cast your circle here; I'll most likely be asleep."

Fat chance. Edward was getting enough education in witchcraft as is. Fortunately, the night looked to be cold but clear, with a waning moon, and west of the farmstead were the Stiperstones, witchy peaks where the southern heaths met northern moors—perfect for making magic. And a place that Jo would surely know. She had to make contact with Jo, telling her what had happened up north, and a familiar location would make it that much easier. Moreover, it would draw Jo to them, which was better, since Deirdre had never done the Witches Flight. Nothing special was needed tonight—just straight, simple contact in a place that Jo would know. But any spell had its risk. She gave her love a long kiss good-bye, promising, "I will be back well before the witching hour."

"I will be waiting," Edward told her, not liking to see her going off without him at night, even on his own lands—but knowing he could not dissuade her. "Give my best to Mary."

"Men may pray, too," she reminded him, slipping on her cloak. Looking forward to lying warm and snug beside her lord, she blew Edward one last kiss and left.

Setting out at dusk, she and Deirdre wore black gowns, furred gloves, and heavy dark cloaks over their witch's shifts, for the night was bitterly cold. Robyn could not resist wearing her gold coronet, as well, so Jo could see at once how much had changed—if she could find Jo on this broken heath in the black of night. Backed by the last of the light, the jagged line of the Stiperstones reared above her, topped by a horned outcropping called the Devil's Chair, a place of weird mists and dark magic. Perfect for her purposes. Using her flashlight to pick her way over rising ground sprinkled with snow, Robyn watched for the gaping pits left by lead miners, wishing she were indoors, not stumbling through the cold—but there was no privacy at the crowded farmstead, and Sherwood had taught her that you could not do spellcraft at your convenience.

She did not even have privacy on the high dark heath, since Deirdre immediately spotted a cloaked figure following in their tracks. Robyn doused her flashlight and waited in the dark, letting her eyes adjust to moonlight, wondering who in the world could be after them in this bleak, deserted place. Slowly, the cloaked figure slunk nearer, seeming to hesitate at times, then lunged forward alarmingly.

Lady Robyn braced herself, clutching her flashlight, which was far too small to be a weapon. She should have brought her saxe knife or borrowed Edward's mace, but who knew you needed to be armed for a lonely night walk on the moors. As the mysterious cloaked figure got closer, Robyn saw it was a woman, staggering and stumbling, cursing the darkness—in rhymed French couplets. Lady Cybelle.

"Turn your wand back on," the wayward poetess called out. "I cannot see."

"What are you doing here?" Lady Robyn demanded curtly.

"Tripping and cursing," Cybelle called back. "What became of that light?"

"Why are you following us?" Robyn let her flounder, keeping the light off. They were attracting enough attention already.

"You may not leave me alone with the men." Cybelle made an

unconvincing attempt to sound helpless. What aspiring court poetess could not handle an earl's hall full of drunken young knights and squires? That sort of gig was what made reputations. Seeing her protests were failing, Cybelle went over to the attack, saying, "Come, I know you are going to make witchcraft."

"What makes you think that?" Now it was Robyn's turn to pretend ridiculous innocence.

"Is it not obvious?" Cybelle complained. "*Mon Dieu,* slinking off all in black, in dead of night, headed for some hellish spot on the heath—all you lack is a cat to sacrifice. . . ."

"And you still want to go with us?" asked Robyn in exasperation—this is what came of running such a loose household.

"Why else would I name myself Cybelle?" asked the poetess.

Good point. Winsome Alice betrayed them at Baynards Castle, but Cybelle was someone different—the poetess had been with them since Calais and had no ties to the Wydvilles, or to anyone else in England, aside from her liaison with Lord Audley. Cybelle was not here for anyone but herself.

So what to do with her? Sending Cybelle back was hardly an option, and even if it worked, it was bound to produce bad feeling. Cybelle was certainly a bundle of raw talent—better to bring her in than have her on the outside making mischief. "Come then." Robyn flicked on the flashlight. "Follow in silence. Three of us makes a coven."

"Ooh," Cybelle marveled at the flashlight beam. "*Mon Dieu,* but you are a witch. When do I get mine?"

Robyn shushed her and set out again, feeling like she was holding a light saber. Cybelle further restricted what could happen tonight. Looking up at the clear winter constellations, Lady Robyn tried to draw strength from the familiar stars, the same ones she saw growing up in Montana—though they had new names for them here. She had never done a ritual by starlight and a waning moon before, but no candle would stay lit in the freezing night wind, and she could not see using a flashlight. Finding a flat spot that felt good, Robyn doused the light and said a prayer, then cast her circle, her gold coronet feeling cold and heavy on her head.

She used the first keening chants that Jo had taught her, starting Cybelle out easy, while strengthening the link to Jo. Sinking into the chant, she reached out to Jo, who right now should be sleeping, or starting a similar ritual way off in the Cotswolds. Jo, join with me, she prayed, for I have not seen you since last November in Coventry.

And she heard Jo calling back to her, vague distant cries that seemed to come from the bottom of the sea. Robyn redoubled her efforts, reaching out harder to Jo, trying to bring them together by sheer strength of will.

Fog descended. Wind and cold vanished, replaced by wet clammy whiteness, lighter and markedly warmer, tinged with the pearl gray of morning, though it was nearer to midnight. Passing strange, but Jo called to her out of the warm mist, clearer and stronger, so loud she felt Deirdre and Cybelle had to hear her too. But the rest of her little coven was lost in the fog, dutifully observing a holy silence.

Jo's calls came closer, sounding more real each moment. Staring hard at the source of the sound, Robyn saw a shape moving in the slowly lightening mist, which was weird, since without moon and stars, the night should be pitch black. But the moving shape resolved itself into a black-haired woman wearing a long dark coat. It was Jo, looking incredibly solid and real.

Just as abruptly Jo vanished, heading off downhill still calling Robyn's name in the fog. Clearly Jo had not seen her. Robyn reached out to Deirdre and Cybelle, to signal them to rise, but all she found was empty mist. Damn, she felt around but found no one. She had lost her coven in the fog. Figures. But it could not be helped, and she did not want to lose Jo, as well—not after going to all this trouble.

Saying a silent prayer, she rose and headed downhill, groping through the fog, following Jo's calls. Her flashlight was in her hand, but she barely needed it in the weirdly luminous mist. Gray ground lay at her feet, but she could not see more than a couple of yards ahead. Jo's calls faded into the wet air, becoming so soft, Robyn could no longer tell their direction. Then the cries vanished completely, leaving her totally alone, blundering through the night and fog.

What an absolutely absurd Witches Night. Robyn stopped to adjust her coronet and get her bearings. She had thought she had been totally in tune to the cosmos, but ended up lost in the fog. Heading off downhill, the way Jo had been going, Lady Robyn got her next shock when the mist abruptly lifted.

She was in daylight, not bright day, but definitely early morning, with the rising sun just burning through the mist. And there was an odd but familiar tang in the air, one she could not quite identify. Worried, she glanced at her watch. 11:09:01 P.M. Not yet midnight— batteries must have finally gone out. But dawn was coming far too early, leaving a long stretch of Witches Night unaccounted for, which seriously scared her. Worse was likely on the way.

"Can I help you?" asked a friendly female voice behind her.

Turning, she hoped to see Jo, but was instead confronted by a solid white-haired woman wearing a man's coat over a wool sweater and print dress, holding a metal pail in her hand. All Lady Robyn could manage was a weak, "Mayhap."

"We do not normally have young lasses wandering out of the Stiperstones wearing a black gown and gold crown," the old woman explained cheerfully, her accent sounding way thicker than it should have. And what was some Shropshire peasant doing wearing a print dress over what looked like orthopedic shoes? This jolly, smiling apparition asked, "Are you American?"

"Yes." How did the woman know? Something was amazingly wrong about all this. "But I am Lady Pomfret, staying at Lord Edward's farmstead."

"Lady Pomfret? Lord Edward's farm?" Shaking her head, the old woman claimed never to have heard of the place. "These are the Stiperstones, and over there is the road to Bog. But here's someone who may help. . . ."

"Robyn!" From over her right shoulder came a familiar voice, asking, "Is that really you?"

She turned to see Jo, who was still wearing the same long black coat as in the mist. Relieved, Robyn threw her arms around her friend, happy to have someone familiar to hold on to. "Hecate help me, it is so good to see you."

"You, too," Jo agreed, grinning happily and hugging her back— but looking vaguely different, wearing heavy dark bangs not at all popular in the Middle Ages. Robyn realized that Lady Grey had on a worn black coat with a faux-fur collar, and neat, smart designer earrings half hidden by her straight black hair, which smelled of peach shampoo. This was not Lady Grey of Greystone; this was Jo Grey, her third-millennium reincarnation, family outcast and unwed mom living on handouts with her daughter, Joy.

Cold reality washed over Robyn like an ice bath; she was no longer in the Middle Ages, not even close. This was the twenty-first century. Somehow, someway, she was back in her home time. What an unbelievable catastrophe! She asked Jo shakily, "What day is this?"

Jo answered with the full date, adding cheerfully, "You have been gone a week."

This was the Friday after she left the third millennium. Looking around, she saw trees in bright fall colors. It was October again, and the snow had vanished from the ground. Edward was gone, too—sweet, loving Edward, along with Deirdre, Matt Davye, and all the rest of the Middle Ages, lost in a huge five-hundred-year abyss. Tears stung her eyes. How was such a ghastly turn of events even possible?

"Weird old Widow Wydville insisted I would find you here," Jo explained cheerfully.

"Widow Wydville?" That was the third-millennium incarnation of Duchess Wydville, a local eccentric and seeress who lived in an ancient cottage near Dursley. Robyn had met her briefly on her last fateful stay in modern England.

"Yes, that dotty old witch." Jo shook her head in amazed admiration. "Who would have thought it? But the Widow Weirdville knew right where you would be. Uncanny even for a sorceress."

Small surprise, really. Duchess Wydville had clearly sent her here. When she gave Her Grace the slip at Codnor and got away across the Dove, Duchess Wydville must have decided Lady Robyn was useless for laying hands on Edward—so the witch-priestess sent her "home." Using Robyn's desire to contact Jo against her, Duchess Wydville had somehow substituted this Jo for the medieval one, deftly landing Robyn in another age—stranded in her "proper" century with scant hope of ever rejoining the people she loved.

"Come," Jo told her. "Joy is dying to see you." Drained by this latest disaster, Robyn let her friend lead her down the hill to where Jo's car was parked alongside the road to Bog. Jo drove a big battleship-gray Bentley with bad shocks, built sometime in the last century, nicknamed *Bouncing Bettie* or *QE2* and reputed to have been through the blitz—a Grey family heirloom on wheels. Another sure sign she had left the 1400s far behind.

Waiting in the car was Joy, looking just like the Joy she left in

1461, happy to see her favorite American friend, calling out gleefully, "You are here, just like Widow Weirdville said. Where have you been? Where did you get that crown?"

From the heir to the throne. Robyn did not say it, knowing how absurd it would sound. Jo opened the passenger door and helped her in, making sure the medieval gown did not catch on anything, telling her daughter to make room, "And do not pester Robyn with questions."

"But this is most amazing," Joy protested. Today was a schoolday, but the witch-child got liberal amounts of "home schooling" in spellcraft and pagan rituals. Putting her arms around Robyn, the black-haired girl pleaded, "Oh, please, will you say where you have been?"

"I was in the Middle Ages." But not anymore. Robyn stared at the silver wyvern badge on the glove box, which she had last seen on Sir Collin's shield.

"Amazing, a week in the Middle Ages!" Joy was beside herself, forgetting that time ran differently in the past. "What was it like?"

"It was not a week. . . ." Robyn looked at her watch, which still read, FRI 1-9-61.

"Well, six days . . . ," Joy admitted, being prone to exaggeration.

"I was there eight months," she whispered, adding up the time in her head. "Eight months, two weeks, and three days. And until a few minutes ago, I thought I would be spending the rest of my life there."

Even Joy had nothing to say to that. Jo slid in behind the wheel and looked over at her, keys in hand. "So what do we do now?"

"I want to go back," Robyn told her.

"But it's too soon for you to go back to America!" Joy complained.

Jo tried to compromise, sliding the keys into the ignition and saying, "I am sure Hollywood can wait, for a day or two, at least."

"Not to Hollywood." Robyn shook her head. "To 1461."

"Oh, my—that will be harder." Jo stared at her, hand still on the ignition key.

"But not impossible," Robyn told her. "That is one thing the Middle Ages teaches you: Nothing's impossible."

Jo nodded, approving the medieval sentiment, and then asked, "Will you at least be staying the weekend?"

Apparently. Having no place to go and nothing but the clothes on her back, her silver white-rose ring, and the gold coronet on her head, Robyn replied weakly, "If you will have me."

Joy squealed with delight, shouting, "We will! We will!"

"Then it is unanimous." Jo smiled, turning the key and kicking the gray supercharged Bentley into gear, setting off down the road. Robyn stared at the twin Marchall headlight beams boring through the last bits of fog, and she felt trapped by the big steel automobile and all the glass and asphalt around her, trapped in her "own" time. Having won Edward and tamed the Middle Ages, she thought it an utter waste to be in the present, despite the many modern conveniences. Love and soul meant more to her than hot running showers and ninety-seven channels with nothing on. Last Halloween night, she had prayed to be here—now she was horrified to have her prayer answered, wanting only to go back to the past. Beware what you wish for, especially when you are a witch.

She could not shake the feeling that this metal machine was taking her ever farther away from Edward as they rolled through sleeping villages with names like the Bog, Pennerley, and Snailbeach, headed for A488 into Shrewsbury. Actually, Edward did not exist anymore, and he could not get farther away than that. Edward was dead, along with Deirdre and Matt, and everyone else she had come to care about. She had been beaten by an older, smarter, and more powerful witch, separated from the man she loved, and who loved her.

But not forever. Somehow, someway, she vowed to get back to Edward. She and Edward were soul mates, despite being separated by centuries at birth, and their love could reach across the ages. Love and magic could make this all come out right, she told herself, if she just learned the right spells. Staring through the windshield at the awakening English countryside, she said a silent prayer to Mary as they merged with the morning traffic headed into Shrewsbury, which had now spread out to cover the south bank of the Severn with concrete and asphalt. Her own world seemed strangely hostile, with its many things and its myriad signs advertising still more things— all available for a price, in money she did not have. Too bad she left her VISA card in the Middle Ages, along with her backgammon winnings. All she had with her was her gold coronet and silver rose ring. But she told herself not to despair. After all, Lady Robyn had been in worse places than this, way worse.